TRUE
WOLF

PAIGE
TYLER

sourcebooks
casablanca

Published by Sourcebooks Casablanca, an imprint of Sourcebooks
P.O. Box 4410, Naperville, Illinois 60567-4410
(630) 961-3900
sourcebooks.com

Printed and bound in Canada.
MBP 10 9 8 7 6 5 4 3 2 1

Also by Paige Tyler

STAT: Special Threat Assessment Team

Wolf Under Fire

Undercover Wolf

SWAT: Special Wolf Alpha Team

Hungry Like the Wolf

Wolf Trouble

In the Company of Wolves

To Love a Wolf

Wolf Unleashed

Wolf Hunt

Wolf Hunger

Wolf Rising

Wolf Instinct

Wolf Rebel

Wolf Untamed

Rogue Wolf

X-Ops

Her Perfect Mate

Her Lone Wolf

Her Secret Agent (novella)

Her Wild Hero

Her Fierce Warrior

Her Rogue Alpha

Her True Match

Her Dark Half

X-Ops Exposed

CHAPTER 1

Turkey

"IS IT JUST MY IMAGINATION OR DO THESE GUYS SEEM A LITTLE tense to you?" Caleb Lynch murmured as he and the other members of his Special Threat Assessment Team followed their heavily armed escort of American soldiers into the ammunition storage area along the backside of Incirlik Air Base.

Forrest Albright and his girlfriend, Misty Swanson, the two team members nearest to him, threw glances at the collection of American and Turkish soldiers lined up on either side of the nearest section of concertina-topped security fencing.

"I think tense might be an understatement," Misty said, looking back at Caleb. In the glow coming from the various lights positioned around the base, her long, purple hair was practically iridescent. "Given how tightly they're gripping their weapons, I'm worried one of them might end up taking a shot at *us* sooner or later."

Caleb grunted. Misty wasn't wrong. As a werewolf, it was impossible for him to miss the sounds of the soldiers' elevated heart rates as they stood guard. Something definitely had these guys on edge.

But what?

Considering he and the rest of the team had been flown straight from Washington, DC, to Turkey on a private jet that hauled ass told him something damn bad had happened here. But hey, that's what STAT did. They dealt with bad crap—particularly of a supernatural variety.

"Colonel Vinson, you planning to tell us why we're here?" Jake Huang, fellow werewolf and leader of their STAT team, asked the army officer dressed in tactical gear and toting a loaded Beretta 9 mm on his right thigh.

The stern-looking man simply held up one finger to momentarily silence any further questions as he led them past yet another security gate and into a dimly lit tunnel with a concrete floor that slanted distinctly downward. Some of their armed escort remained topside, but six of the men, wearing tactical gear similar to the colonel's, followed them down.

Caleb could tell from the way Jake's mouth tightened that his team leader was pissed the colonel hadn't answered him. Luckily, Jake was an alpha, which meant he was in complete control of his inner wolf, unless something big pushed him over the edge. Caleb, on the other hand, was an omega. While he was as big and strong as Jake, he didn't have any of that same control. He probably would have growled at the colonel already if the guy had ignored his question.

In another couple hundred feet, the floor leveled out, revealing a broad, curving tunnel that disappeared to the left and right. It was merely a guess, but Caleb figured they must be at least fifty feet underground now. Another brief walk along the curving tunnel that was easily wide enough for a pickup truck to drive through, and then they were at a set of huge steel doors mounted in the side of the tunnel wall.

Vinson stopped in front of the open doors, then turned to face them, and for the first time, Caleb had a chance to see how exhausted the thin, gray-haired man appeared. The lines around his mouth seemed more pronounced than they had outside, and his hazel eyes were grim.

"Sorry I couldn't respond to your question earlier," the colonel said, looking at Jake, "but I couldn't risk any of the Turkish nationals overhearing what I'm about to tell you. If they knew what happened in here, we'd have a full-scale international incident on our hands within the hour."

Vinson's gaze went from Jake to Caleb, then the rest of the team. He was openly curious as he took in Misty and Forrest, alpha werewolves Harley Grant and her soul mate, Sawyer Bishop, and Jestina Ridley—aka Jes—the most experienced agent on the team as well as Jake's soul mate. It was obvious from the expression on the colonel's face that he wanted to know what the hell STAT was and why he was talking to them and not someone higher up in the army or air force—or anyone in a military uniform, for that matter. It probably didn't help that Caleb and his teammates had flown in on an unmarked luxury jet that had been practically smoking from flying so fast to get here.

"This is weapon storage vault nine," Vinson said, motioning toward the steel doors behind him. "A little over eleven hours ago, the command post received an alarm from the intrusion detector system inside."

"What kind of alarm?" Sawyer asked, his British accent giving away the fact that his background was a little bit different than the rest of the team's.

The colonel seemed to take it in stride as he focused his attention on Sawyer. "The motion sensors were tripped. A security detail was on scene in less than two minutes, but they didn't see any signs of a break-in from the outside. They were still trying to figure out if anything was amiss when the command post received an alarm from vault ten, and then, thirty seconds later, a similar alarm from vault eight. Since the security detail didn't see anything out of place at any of those, either, they thought it must be a sensor failure. But when we got the same alert from two more weapon vaults, I gave the order to open the doors on one. That's when the situation went…sideways."

Vinson turned to lead the way into the vault. The *situation* he'd been referring to was obvious the moment Caleb walked into the dimly lit room along with everyone else. The vault was smaller than he anticipated, maybe thirty square feet. It reminded him of a

self-storage unit—the kind where people kept something really...
really...*really*...valuable.

Inside, the place was a mess. Pieces of metal were scattered
everywhere. Off to one side, more twisted metal had been slammed
against the walls so hard it had knocked out gigantic chunks of the
concrete. He knew absolutely nothing about the subject, but from
the shape of the metal, Caleb guessed that the pieces might be the
tail fins off some kind of bomb. In the very center of the room, the
concrete had been pulverized, like an explosive charge had gone
off there.

"I'm assuming the vault doesn't normally look this trashed?"
Caleb asked drily, his inner wolf finding it impossible not to poke
at the tense military officer. But in his defense, he'd had a problem
with authority figures for most of his life. It was a character issue
he planned to work on at some point. Right after learning how to
play the oboe.

Vinson shook his head, mouth tight. "No. This is the way it
looked when the security detail got here. That's when we realized
the weapons had been stolen."

"Nuclear weapons?" Jake asked, though it really didn't sound
like a question to Caleb. It figured Jake would know stuff like that.
The alpha werewolf had been a U.S. Navy SEAL at some point in
his life.

The colonel nodded. "These vaults are designed to hold up to
four B61 nuclear bombs, each with a variable yield of up to 340
kilotons." Letting out a sigh, he pointed toward another pile of
twisted metal in the corner. "During a crisis, the bombs are lifted
by that elevator to the aircraft shelter directly over our heads. The
waiting plane can be loaded and gone within minutes. All four of
the nukes in this vault are gone, along with sixteen other weapons
from the four adjacent vaults."

Caleb's head spun at the implications of the U.S. losing that
many nukes. He had no idea how big 340 kilotons might be, but

it definitely sounded bad. But while it was obviously a catastrophe, he wasn't sure exactly what any of this had to do with STAT. Missing nukes weren't necessarily their bag. Not unless those nukes had been taken by something supernatural.

"If the door was closed when the security detail arrived, how were the weapons stolen?" Jes asked.

The colonel pointed at the rubble in the center of the room. "Through there. Or at least, that's our best guess, since we can't come up with any other explanation."

Caleb moved closer to the pile of broken concrete along with the rest of his team and was stunned to see a hole about twice the size of a traditional city manhole cover beyond it. He leaned over the opening, his nose picking up a scent that worried him.

Blood.

As an omega werewolf, Caleb's nose wasn't all that useful at the best of times. Sure, he could pick up really strong scents, like gas or melted asphalt, but the only time he could distinguish most other smells was if he was extremely close to them—or if there was a whole lot of it there.

He got the feeling it was the latter in this case.

"How many bodies are down there?" Harley asked, staring down into the hole, her blond ponytail falling over her shoulder. Her alpha werewolf nose was way better than his but still not good enough to divine if there'd been one person bleeding a lot or a lot of people bleeding a little.

Vinson threw a surprised look at her. No doubt he wanted to know how she knew there were bodies down there at all, but apparently, someone higher up had told him not to ask questions.

"Twenty-five," he finally said in a somber voice. "Fifteen from the original security detail that went down there, ten from the backup team I sent in after we lost contact with the first group. The initial response team dropped down in the hole the second they realized the weapons had been stolen." He paused, like he was fighting for control over his emotions with everything he had in him. "They were probably in there for less than thirty seconds when the shooting started. The backup team arrived three minutes later. They didn't last much longer. No one else has been down there since."

Caleb leaned out a little further over the hole in the floor, wondering what they were going to find down there, when Misty asked the question that had been in the forefront of his mind since he realized there were dead bodies down there.

"Why haven't you sent anyone down there to get them out?" The words were soft, the sympathetic look in her violet gaze making Caleb think she knew how hard it must have been on the colonel to leave members of his unit down there like that. "How do you even know they're all dead?"

Vinson's face went pale, his eyes suddenly haunted. "Every member of both the primary and backup response teams were wearing sound-activated voice mics while the squad leaders had video cameras strapped to their helmets. The signals feed straight into the command post, where I was forced to stand there listening and watching as my soldiers died. Those people were like family to me, and there's nothing I'd like more than getting them the hell out of there. But after what I saw in those videos, listening to them scream in terror as they were slaughtered..." He shook his head. "I knew none of them had made it, and I knew I couldn't risk sending anyone else down there."

"What did you see in the video?" Caleb asked. "What killed your soldiers?"

"Unfortunately, I have no idea," the colonel said. "All I can say for sure is that the things were maybe three or four feet tall, vicious as hell, and so fast they left nothing but a blur on the screen. The moment headquarters got a look at the video, my commander told me to pull back and wait for the specialists to arrive."

Vinson's shrewd gaze drifted across all of them again, taking in their lack of tactical gear and rather limited weaponry, then shrugged. Once again, it was obvious the man wanted to know who the hell they were, but like before, he kept his questions to himself.

"Apparently, that's you people."

"Any reason to believe the things that stole the weapons and killed your soldiers are still down there?" Jake asked.

The colonel frowned. "After the fighting stopped, both squad leaders ended up facedown on the ground, so the cameras didn't give us anything after that. But the batteries on the mics stayed good for almost eight hours. Just before they went out, we picked up the sound of scratching and scraping. So something was down there moving around, at least up until three hours ago. There's no way to know if they're still there now."

At Vinson's nod, the armed men with him started handing out flashlights. The colonel lifted a brow when Caleb, Jake, Harley, and Sawyer all declined the offer. Seeing in the dark wasn't an issue for werewolves.

Caleb was a little surprised when Vinson and his soldiers moved to follow them. Apparently, so was Jake because his teammate held up a hand to stop them.

The army officer glared at Jake. "Those soldiers who died down there were my responsibility," he said before motioning at the six men with him. "And these have a combined twenty years of combat experience between them. They're the best I have. We're going down there with you, and you can't stop us."

That wasn't even a little bit true. Caleb and his fellow werewolves could have easily kept Vinson and his men from going with them, but Jake merely shrugged.

"Okay, I understand," he said. "As long as you realize that anything you see down there is going to be classified out the wazoo."

The colonel let out a snort. "We don't care about any of that. We only want to get down there so we can find our nukes and bring our people back above ground. And if we get a shot at the things that killed them, even better."

Jake nodded. "Okay. But watch where you point your weapons when we get down there. No matter what you see."

Vinson looked confused and opened his mouth to almost certainly ask what the hell Jake meant by that, but Jake didn't give him the chance. He nodded at Caleb.

"Take point" was all he said.

Caleb gave him a nod in return, then pulled his .45 Colt automatic from its holster and dropped into the darkness of the hole. Considering that they had no idea what any of them were jumping into the middle of, it made sense to have him go in first. As an omega werewolf, committing acts of extreme violence was kind of his thing. He was basically the STAT team's personal berserker.

His heavy boots thudded on rough stone at the bottom of the hole after a drop of maybe twenty feet. He was a little surprised to see that, while the ground was rough and jagged under him, it wasn't the usual mess left after an explosion.

Turning, he looked down the dark tunnel ahead of him. Unlike his nose, his eyes worked nearly as well as an alpha's, and he could see without much of a problem. The opening was roughly circular shaped, about five feet high, maybe a little wider than that. He shook his head, trying to envision how the hell whoever took those nukes had blasted—or dug—through solid rock without anyone on the surface realizing it. It must have taken weeks—even months—to do it.

The odor of blood was stronger down here, even though he couldn't see any sign of where it was coming from. He stood where he was, listening for a moment, but didn't hear any of the scratching and scraping the colonel mentioned. In fact, there didn't seem to be anything moving around down here at all.

"Looks clear," he murmured into his mic. "It's about a

twenty-foot drop to the floor of the tunnel. You're going to need ropes to get everyone down here. I'm moving ahead."

Before Jake could tell him not to, Caleb ducked and began walking forward. He wanted to clear as much of the tunnel as he could before it got crowded down here.

Caleb was tall, which made getting through the tunnel a pain in the ass, especially in those places where the ceiling was lower. In other spots, the passage through the solid rock narrowed to the point where it was nearly claustrophobic. But the creepiest part of the tunnel was the circular holes he found here and there along the walls. All of them were the same size—maybe fourteen or fifteen inches in diameter. Some were close to the floor, while others were up near the ceiling. He would have thought they were merely air vents if it wasn't for the blood he found running out of some of them.

He stared into one of the holes for a moment, swearing he could almost feel something staring back at him. But after long moments passed without anything jumping out at him, he gave up and kept walking. Even then, he couldn't shake the sense that something was watching him from the multitude of openings.

It was easy to lose sense of direction and distance down here, but Caleb guessed he'd only gone about forty or fifty feet before the tunnel widened a bit, and there was a passageway heading off to the right.

That was where he found the first body.

It was obviously one of the soldiers from the security detail—the army uniform and tactical gear were a dead giveaway. But, beyond knowing the body belonged to a male American soldier, it was damn near impossible to say anything else about it because the guy had been torn to shreds. There weren't more than a few places on the body where the skin was left intact. Everything else was just…a mess. Even the ceramic plates of the soldier's tactical vest had been sliced to pieces.

Caleb leaned in close, trying to get a lock on the thing that had done this. He had a hard time imagining what kind of creature could generate this kind of damage.

The soldier's short-barrel M4 carbine was lying on the floor of the tunnel behind him, the bolt locked back on an empty magazine. Caleb pictured the man running through the tunnel, firing wildly at whatever had been chasing him as he tried to get back to the hole in the floor of the weapons vault.

Obviously, he hadn't made it.

Caleb kept going for several hundred more feet, calling in his discoveries as he found three more side tunnels, almost certainly leading to the other vaults where the nukes had been stolen. He also found several other members of the security detail. Half a dozen of them were all packed in close together at one of the tunnel intersections, some lying shoulder to shoulder as if they'd died trying to protect each other to the very end. Every single weapon was empty, every body shredded. A glance farther up the tunnel revealed no other bodies within sight, just a lot of bloody smears on the ground, and Caleb found himself wondering where the rest of the corpses were. Had the battle drawn them so far away from their only escape route back in the weapons vault?

"Who the hell did this?" a choked voice said from behind him in the tunnel.

Caleb turned to see Colonel Vinson standing there with two soldiers, Jake and Forrest, directly behind them.

"I think it's more of a *what* than a *who*," Caleb said, "because whatever did this definitely wasn't human."

When the colonel angled his flashlight in Caleb's direction and saw the mangled remains of one of his soldiers, the older man went so pale that Caleb thought he might pass out. The two soldiers with him tightened their grips on their weapons, their hearts beating faster.

"With all the rounds these guys fired in here, you'd think we'd find a few bad guys among the bodies," Jake said. Squeezing past Vinson and his soldiers, he crouched down to sniff one of the corpses. "The fact that I can't even pick up a trace scent of their blood worries me."

"Either these things are too fast to hit," Forrest said from where he still stood behind the colonel, "or they're bulletproof."

"Now wait a minute," Vinson said harshly. "What the hell are you saying? They're bulletproof? You can't be serious."

Before Caleb—or anyone else—could say anything, a loud scraping sound echoed through the tunnel network around them. For a second, Caleb wasn't sure if it was coming from ahead or behind them. Factor in those smaller holes in the walls and the noise could have come from anywhere.

But when the sound echoed around them again, Caleb decided to simply take off and trusts his instincts.

In his earpiece, he heard Jake calling out orders over the radio, telling everyone to watch themselves. "We have no idea what's down here. These things could come at us from any direction. Keep an eye on those holes in the walls, too."

In front of Caleb, the tunnel suddenly widened at the same time the floor began to angle downward. As his feet moved faster and faster to keep up with his hurtling body, a strange scent of old dirt and oily musk struck his nose. It was like nothing he'd ever smelled before, and he couldn't even begin to guess what kind of creature it was.

As Caleb rounded a slight curve in the tunnel, he saw a shadow of movement ahead of him. Whatever it was, the thing was a hell of a lot smaller than he expected, and it was dragging something behind it that bounced and thudded across the rough floor like it was a child's toy.

It occurred to him then that whatever the creature was pulling along behind it was what had been making the scraping sound he'd heard earlier. It wasn't until he almost slipped on the fresh blood on the floor that he realized the bulky shape the thing was yanking across the ground was a dead soldier.

The creature abruptly stopped and snapped its head in Caleb's direction. In that moment, the vaguely shaped shadow coalesced into something more defined. It was maybe three feet tall, though it was hard to be sure with its hunched-over posture. At first, he thought he was looking at some kind of large baboon that had somehow found its way underground. Then the thing's massive shoulders, arms, and thighs caught his attention as well as the fact that the creature was almost completely hairless except for a few wisps along its chest and belly.

Nope, definitely not a baboon.

The thing charged at him in a blur of motion, completely silent except for the click-clack of four sets of long, curved claws against the stone.

Caleb immediately brought his .45 Colt up and squeezed the trigger, even as he felt his body begin to shift, the muscles of his back and shoulders thickening, claws and fangs extending for the impending battle. He fought to retain as much control as he could. A clear head and steady aim would help him more than his omega werewolf's out-of-control aggression, especially down here in a pitch-black tunnel full of his teammates and a bunch of soldiers who'd almost certainly never seen a supernatural creature in their lives.

But then two of his .45-caliber rounds bounced off the creature charging his way, the heavy bullets not even making its large, luminous eyes do more than blink. If that wasn't enough to push his already tenuous control further toward the edge of the cliff, the sight of three more of the fast-moving creatures rounding the corner definitely was.

The first creature closed the space between them in a heartbeat, ricocheting from floor to wall in a blur before launching straight at Caleb's chest. Another round in the thing's stomach did nothing to slow it, and then razor-sharp claws were ripping through the fore-arm Caleb lifted to protect his face. Pain seared through his arm, and he swore he could feel the creature's claws grating on bone even as its fang-filled jaws opened to bite him.

Caleb reacted out of pure instinct, clubbing the creature to the ground with the butt of his weapon before emptying the rest of the magazine of ammo into the thing at point-blank range. The results were less than impressive, and the muscular creature sprang right back on its feet, ready to throw itself at him once more.

Then Jake, Forrest, and the soldiers were at his side, gunfire filling the tunnel from side to side, the noise of them all firing at once so loud that Caleb's sensitive ears immediately shut down until everything was muted to a dull roar.

Unfortunately, the four creatures weren't fazed by the hail of gunfire, bouncing right up and coming at them again. Caleb started reloading, but at the sight of all those fangs and claws, he knew his handgun wouldn't do a damn thing to slow them down. His inner omega decided to take over, and he dropped his weapon to take them on in hand-to-hand combat instead.

He vaguely heard Jake shouting at him to stop, but he was too far gone by then. That's how it was to be an omega. When his inner wolf took over, he was essentially shoved into the back seat and granted a fuzzy view of what was happening around him but given little control over his actions. It was both terrifying and exhilarating all at once.

Caleb wasn't aware he'd closed the distance between himself and the creatures until he found one of his hands wrapped around a squirming muscular neck, his fist coming down over and over to pummel it until something gave. He felt the smaller bones in his hand cracking, a minor inconvenience of pain far away in the background, barely a nuisance.

He wasn't sure when he lost his grip on the thing's neck, but the next thing he knew, he was holding its leg instead and smashing the creature onto the rough stone floor again and again. Another one of the creatures leaped on his back, slashing and hacking at him, but he ignored the pain to continue trying to kill the one in his hands.

Shouting somewhere nearby distracted him for a moment, though he wasn't sure which of his teammates was warning that there were more creatures coming at them from behind, slipping out of those smaller holes in the walls he'd seen earlier. The intensity of gunfire increased, and some part of his mind knew his friends were in trouble.

The distraction allowed the creature in his hand to get away, its blood making it too hard to hold. Caleb's inner omega didn't care. He simply growled and reached up to grab the one still on his back. With a roar that echoed through the tunnels, Caleb got a grip on the thing's head and bashed it against the wall. When it stopped resisting and went still in his arms, he reached for the next closest one he could find—the one slashing at Colonel Vinson, who was doing everything he could to fend it off.

Everything was a blur, like it always was when his omega took over. He attacked, smashing, punching, clawing, even biting. He had no idea if he was killing the creatures. Something inside him suggested he wasn't, but he kept at it anyway. At some point, his other teammates arrived, his fellow werewolves fighting to protect those without any supernatural abilities. Math wasn't something he was capable of at the moment, but part of him knew there weren't as many soldiers fighting now as there should be.

When he found his hands empty of a target for his uncontrolled aggression, Caleb turned to see one of the creatures racing away down the tunnel. Like a predator chasing fleeing prey, his inner wolf forced him to follow. Jake and the others yelled at him to stop, but that wasn't really a possibility.

The creature ran—he chased.

Caleb had no idea how far he went, but the rational part of his mind—the part that was merely along for the ride—noticed that the floor of the tunnel had angled upward, heading for the surface. Was the creature trying to escape out of the tunnels? His inner omega growled in delight, knowing the thing would never get away on open ground.

He caught up with the creature as it disappeared into one of the smaller side holes, slowed somewhat by the object it was attempting to take into the hole with it. Caleb grabbed the bulky thing and dragged it back, only realizing it was the remains of one of the soldiers when he saw the camo material and shreds of tactical gear.

The creature fought him for the prize, its lips peeling back to show bloodstained fangs. That image, along with the ravaged body, jarred him enough to finally comprehend what he was seeing, even through the omega mist shrouding his mind.

The creatures were *eating* the soldier's bodies. It's why they'd come back so many hours after the initial attack. To recover the meal left behind.

Caleb wasn't sure how long he stood there, his hands clenching hard on the remains of the soldier, but at some point, the creature finally gave up and left. Then Forrest was there at his side, softly saying words that were probably meant to be calming. It wasn't necessary, though. His inner omega had finally let go and given up the control it had usurped from him.

After telling him that all of their people were okay, Forrest led him away from the body on the floor of the tunnel. Caleb assumed they were going back to the weapons vault, so he was a little surprised when they headed the other direction, ultimately ending up outside, in a tree-shrouded area that was well outside the air base perimeter. Breathing the fresh air went a long way to clearing his mind. He replayed the previous few minutes, hoping he hadn't hurt any of their own people. He didn't remember doing that, but then again, it wasn't like he'd know.

Jake, Jestina, Colonel Vinson, and one of his soldiers were

standing in a loose circle about ten or fifteen feet from where the tunnel opened up on the surface. There were all looking intently at the ground. All four looked up as Caleb and Forrest joined them, the colonel and his soldier staring at Caleb like they were waiting for him to attack. He couldn't blame them. They'd seen him lose control—anyone would be scared of him after that. There was also the blood on his arms and shirt from all the slashes he'd gotten from those creatures.

"They had a vehicle waiting for them," Jes said, studying the heavy tread impressions in the soft ground. "A large truck, based on the tire and axle width."

Caleb stood there trying to wrap his head around the idea that someone had apparently *hired* those vicious creatures to help steal a large number of nuclear weapons right out from under the control of the U.S. military—literally. The things had been so insanely aggressive, it was difficult to comprehend they could be trusted to handle a theft like that. Unless there had been humans working with them.

He wasn't sure which of those was more terrifying.

CHAPTER 2

CALEB LEANED BACK IN HIS CHAIR IN ONE OF THE MEETING rooms of the Akar International Hotel in Ankara, propping the sole of his boot on the edge of the table and sipping his coffee while flipping through the half-dozen English-language newspapers scattered across the conference table. He was waiting for the other members of the team to arrive for this morning's intel briefing, where the STAT analysts would hopefully have something to tell them concerning who'd stolen the nukes and where they might be.

The well-healed scars on his arms reminded him of those creatures he'd fought last night. They'd packed one hell of a punch, so the fact that he was still in one piece—albeit with a few extra seams—was something he could live with.

He normally didn't read newspapers—actually, he couldn't frigging stand the things—but he'd been curious to see if anything had slipped out about the missing nukes. Something this big should have gotten out by now. So far, though, a full twenty-four hours after climbing out of those damn tunnels, they'd yet to hear a single peep from the media.

Caleb wondered how that was possible, considering all the Turkish nationals who worked on the air base. Between the nighttime alarm, the number of dead and missing American soldiers, and the STAT team coming out covered in blood, it made sense one of them would have leaked something by now. One more thing Colonel Vinson apparently excelled at was keeping secrets.

They'd left the air base for the capital city of Ankara shortly after coming out of the tunnels, hanging around only long enough to review the video and audio files the command post had from the time of the theft. It had been difficult listening to the replay of the massacre, especially after everyone on the STAT team had lived through the same horrible experience. And knowing that many of those soldiers had been dragged away to be eaten was going to leave all of them with nightmares for years to come.

Caleb was flipping through the back pages of the last paper when he heard voices in the hallway outside the small meeting room. A moment later, the door opened, and his teammates walked in along with a new STAT agent named Genevieve Porter. Tall with long, blond hair, she had a huge binder in one arm and reading glasses perched on the end of her petite nose. She barely looked a day over twenty to Caleb, but she must have known her stuff if she'd been assigned to the team.

Forrest seemed surprised Caleb was already there waiting.

"I'd didn't expect to see you here," his dark-haired teammate said as he sat down on the other side of the table beside Misty. "I thought you hated these briefings."

"Couldn't sleep." Caleb shrugged. "Jet lag, you know?"

He saw Jake, Harley, and Sawyer glance at him out of the corners of their eyes, expressions clearly dubious. Probably because jet lag wasn't something werewolves ever had to deal with. But at least they didn't say anything. Because he didn't want anyone making a big deal out of it.

Truthfully, he hadn't slept well in weeks. He couldn't pin down exactly when the problem had started, but he knew it was around the time of their mission in France several weeks ago, when they'd stopped a terrorist named Yegor Shevchenko from scattering radioactive fallout over half of Europe. He hadn't said anything to his teammates, but part of him was worried he'd gotten poisoned or something during the raid on that nuclear power plant near Calais. One of the reactors in the place had come damn close to going into total meltdown, so there'd been a lot of radiation in the air. It hadn't seemed to bother Harley and Sawyer, who'd been right on top of the thing. But then again, they were both alphas, so maybe they were immune to that kind of thing while, as an omega, he wasn't. Considering all the ways in which he felt different from the alphas, he wouldn't be surprised. He'd definitely gotten the short end of the stick when it came to the werewolf stuff.

While Misty established a secure laptop connection with STAT headquarters, Genevieve helped Forrest set up the scramblers that would douse the room in high-frequency noise, making it impossible for anyone to electronically eavesdrop on their conversation. Unfortunately, a by-product of the scramblers was a constant whining sound that was irritating as hell for the werewolves, but that was just something they had to live with.

Five minutes later, they were talking to Nathan McKay, their boss back in DC. With his brown hair sporting a touch of gray at the temples, McKay looked exactly like Caleb pictured a federal agent would, down to the dark suit and wire-rimmed glasses. From the expression on the man's face, Caleb could already tell he had something interesting to say.

"We've been working hard to find those nukes but have, thus far, come up with very little," McKay said. "However, someone who may know something useful called me last night with information that could be vital to locating them. She's just arrived at your hotel and should be joining you any minute."

Jake frowned. "Who is it? And how do you know we can we trust her?"

McKay's mouth turned upward in a small smile. "Actually, it's someone you're all familiar with. As far as whether you can trust her, I think that's something you'll have to decide for yourselves."

Caleb opened his mouth to ask McKay what the hell he was talking about when the sound of footsteps in the hallway caught his attention. A second later, Tessa Reynolds, one of the senior agents on the STAT support team, opened the door.

"McKay said you'd want to talk to her ASAP, so I brought her straight here from the airport," Tessa said without preemption, stepping aside to let whoever was with her into the room.

Caleb almost choked on his coffee. Setting his cup on the table, he dropped his booted foot to the floor and stared, transfixed, as a tall, beautiful woman walked in, her dark, mesmerizing eyes scanning the people around the table until they landed on him. He thought, for a moment, his heart might seize up in his chest simply from the intensity in their chocolate-brown depths.

"Brielle," Jake said from the far end of the table, the surprise in his voice unmistakable. "Please don't take this the wrong way, but what the hell are you doing here?"

Her eyes stayed locked with Caleb's for a second longer than necessary before looking at Jake. "I heard a rumor that you were looking for some missing nuclear weapons and thought I'd help you find them."

Around the table, Caleb's teammates exchanged dubious looks. He supposed he couldn't blame them. Brielle Fontaine had worked for Yegor, the wacko who'd wanted to eradicate half of Europe. Using a supernatural ability that she refused to talk about, Brielle had tracked down other supernaturals to help Yegor carry out his crazy scheme. If that wasn't bad enough, she'd also used her unusual gift to help him find supernaturals he could sell to the highest bidder to raise money to carry out his plans. It went without saying that the people who'd been sold hadn't been treated well, and some of them were still missing.

In her defense, Brielle had been forced into helping Yegor. Her brother, Julian, was a dumbass of cosmic proportions and had gotten himself into serious trouble with the psychopath. Working for Yegor had been the only way to save her sibling. The stuff she'd done had been regrettable for sure, but in the end, she'd done it to save her brother. Caleb could definitely understand making bad choices. Hell, he was the frigging poster child for it.

"How could you possibly know anything about the weapons

stolen from Incirlik?" Forrest asked, doubt and distrust dripping off every word. "And more importantly, what would you want in exchange for the information you have? Because I think we all know you wouldn't be here if you weren't expecting something in return."

Caleb winced at how bluntly Forrest had put that. But honestly, the guy probably wasn't wrong. Brielle had helped them take down Yegor and his goons. She simply hadn't done it out of the goodness of her heart. STAT had wanted to lock her and her brother away and leverage her gifts to find other supernaturals to work for them. She used her knowledge of Yegor and his plans to negotiate her way out of the situation. Making deals when lives were on the line might be a bit cold-blooded, but Caleb could definitely understand making the best out of the cards you were dealt. It was how he'd gotten himself out of prison and into STAT.

Brielle ignored Forrest's question and moved over to take a seat in the chair directly across the table from Caleb. He thought she said something about how long and tiring the flight from Quebec had been, but he had to admit he wasn't paying that much attention. Instead, he was focused on what it was like having the gorgeous French woman this close to him again.

In the days just before the mission in Calais, Caleb had been sure there was something between him and Brielle. A spark. He'd caught her looking his way more than a few times, her expression openly intrigued. And she hadn't looked away when he'd gazed right back. The sexual chemistry had been palpable enough for even Caleb to pick up on it, and he'd been sure they would end up in bed sooner rather than later.

But then he'd come back after the mission was over to discover that Brielle and her brother had disappeared and that no one had a clue where they'd gone. He guessed Quebec was the answer to that mystery.

"To be honest, I didn't know the weapons had been stolen from

Incirlik," Brielle said, casually leaning back in her chair. "Though now that you mention it, that does make complete sense. And as far as what I want for helping you, I'm sure this won't be a shock to anyone, but Julian is in trouble again. I'll help you find your missing nukes if you help me find my missing brother."

There were a few snorts of disgust from around the table, but at the same time, Caleb knew that every one of his teammates understood exactly what Brielle was doing and probably would have done the same thing in a similar situation. Of course, he doubted that any of them had a family member who could get themselves in trouble with the regularity Julian seemed to manage. The guy was a screwup of major proportions.

"Why don't you tell us about your brother," Jake asked softly. "and we'll see what happens from there."

Brielle regarded Jake for a moment and then looked at everyone else around the table. Her gaze settled on Caleb again. Finally, after a few moments of hesitation, she seemed to come to some kind of decision.

"Julian called two nights ago," she said, then shrugged her slim shoulders. "Well, two and a half nights ago, with the time change between here and Quebec, I guess. Anyway, it was late. I'm not even sure why I answered the phone, other than the fact that I hadn't seen or heard from Julian in a few weeks."

"He moved to Quebec with you?" Caleb asked, his normally nonexistent social side suggesting he should probably at least act like he cared about her brother if he ever hoped she'd give him the time of day.

Brielle nodded. "Yeah. Not that he stayed there very long. About a week after we got there, he said something about meeting up with some new friends and never came back. When the phone rang in the middle of the night like that, I knew it was him."

"What did he say?" Jake prompted.

"'I'm in trouble again,'" Brielle said softly, her brow furrowing a little. "Those were the first words out of his mouth. Not *Bonjour* or *How have you been*? No, he only called to let me know he needed me to save his butt again. You wouldn't believe how much I wanted to hang up on him."

Caleb was tempted to ask why she hadn't but stopped himself. His teammates probably weren't interested in hearing about Brielle's problems. He was kind of shocked to realize that he *was*. Caring about other people—especially people he didn't know all that well—wasn't his thing. Before he could think too much about that epiphany, her lightly accented voice broke him out of his reveries.

"I knew it was bad because Julian was whispering, like he was afraid of someone hearing him," Brielle added. "He said he'd gotten a job he thought would pay him well only to discover he'd gotten in way over his head."

"Did he say who hired him?" Harley asked.

She shook her head, her silky bangs parting slightly to give him a peek at her perfect brows. Damn, he'd always been a sucker for long hair and bangs.

"No," she said. "I asked him, but he started rambling about people hiring him because of his drug contacts in Turkey and his ability to get large shipments in and out of the country. At first, I thought that's what he'd done—gotten involved in another drug operation there—but then he started to freak out about these people planning to hit an American base to steal some nukes. Julian wanted me to know he'd tried to back out, but that wasn't an option. I told him to get away from them, but he said it was too late for that. He said I was the only one who could help him."

Brielle seemed like she was on the verge of tears, and it was all Caleb could do not to each across the table and take her hand, try to offer some kind of support. Which baffled the crap out of him, since it had been a frigging lifetime since he'd cared about anyone enough to even consider doing something like that.

"There was more, right?" Sawyer pushed from his seat next to Harley. "He mentioned a name or something or where they were taking the weapons, maybe? I mean, at least tell us that he gave you some idea of what they were planning to do with the bloody things."

She shook her head again. "He might have been ready to tell me more, but then he said that someone was coming and that he couldn't let them catch him on the phone. The only thing he was able to say before hanging up was the word *Surinda*. Then we were disconnected. I tried to call and text him back a dozen times since then, but the number is no longer in service."

"Surinda?" Jake echoed with a frown. "Does that word mean anything to you? Maybe it's code for something?"

"I don't have any idea what it means," Brielle said. "I was hoping someone in your organization could figure it out."

Beside Forrest, Misty held up her phone. "Not to discourage anyone, but there are 113,000 hits for the word Surinda in Google alone, including a scientist on LinkedIn, a yoga retreat in Vermont, a massage salon in Australia, an obscure territory in central Siberia, and everything in between. And that's assuming I'm even spelling it right."

"Our analysts back here are running into the same problem," McKay announced over the speaker on the laptop. "Right now, we're focusing on people with that name who have some kind of criminal background. Our second priority is on places that would be suitable as a storage location—or a target—for the nukes. But as Misty said, that's still a lot of possibilities to work through."

"Isn't there anything we can do in the interim?" Caleb asked. "Some other lead we can run down? What about these creatures that dug those tunnels? Do we have anything on them yet?"

McKay nodded. "At Jes's suggestion, our medical examiners pulled the autopsy reports from the attack on her old CIA team and compared the wounds to those on the soldiers in the tunnels.

They agree that the creatures you fought down in those tunnels are the same kind that wiped out her former team. They also confirmed that the creatures dug the tunnels you fought in—with their claws."

Caleb frowned. Damn.

Jes had mentioned yesterday she was sure she'd seen those creatures before when she'd been in the CIA. Her whole team had been wiped out during a mission in Rome by a hairless creature with big claws. Obviously, those claws were good for tearing through a lot of things.

"However, we still don't have any idea what those creatures are or how they're related to the people who stole the nukes," McKay added. "We're putting all our resources into finding answers to both of those questions, but so far, we've got nothing."

Caleb had a hard time understanding how the hell the analysts back in DC, with all their computers and books, couldn't identify these diggers when they had Jes's description from the attack in Rome as well as the team's account and even photographs from the air base. How many creatures out there could dig through solid rock and rip apart heavily armed soldiers, then walk away with twenty nuclear weapons that weighed four or five hundred pounds apiece?

Then again, it hadn't been so long ago that STAT thought werewolves were a Hollywood legend, so maybe he should cut the analyst nerds a break. It wasn't like they could look this kind of stuff up on Wikipedia.

The briefing lasted another fifteen minutes, but as far as Caleb was concerned, it could have ended much earlier. Sometimes, he thought his teammates talked because they liked the sound of their own voices.

"So you'll help me find Julian?" Brielle asked, getting to her feet along with everyone else. "And help me get him out of whatever trouble he's gotten into?"

Caleb held his breath, not sure what his team would say to that. He knew what his own gut was hoping for, but he was also aware that the information she'd provided on her brother wasn't particularly helpful. Even if it was more than they'd had before.

"We'll help as much as we can," Jake promised, and Caleb was finally able to breathe again. Though why he cared so much was anyone's guess. "*If* you help us find the weapons in return. We know you have certain abilities you don't like to talk about, and we're going to need you to use them on our behalf—not just your brother's—whatever those abilities are."

Caleb almost snorted out loud. *Certain abilities.* That was a polite way of saying Brielle seemed to be able to do things that defied explanation—like slipping Yegor and her brother out the front gates of a Turkish prison without anyone noticing. Or going toe-to-toe with a three-hundred-pound supernatural beast without breaking a sweat.

Brielle nodded her head and made a soft sound that Jake must have accepted as agreement.

"One more thing," Jake said, giving her a hard look. "I know you came to us, but with our previous history, I'm sure you understand how difficult it is for us to trust you. So to make sure we don't have any problems, I'm going to need you to stick close to Caleb while you're with us. I want him to know where you are twenty-four seven."

Brielle went so rigid that Caleb could hear her muscles stiffening, but a moment later, the tension seemed to drain from her body.

"Fine," she said, glancing at Caleb coolly as she headed for the door. "I'll be at the front desk getting the key to my room."

Clearly, Brielle was less than thrilled at the idea of having a babysitter like him. Caleb almost reached out to catch her arm, needing her to know that none of this was his idea for some reason. But she was moving too fast, leaving behind nothing but the mesmerizing scent of honeysuckles. She must be wearing a hell of a lot of perfume if his crappy nose was picking it up. But it was nice all the same.

"Caleb, are you listening to me?" Jake demanded.

Caleb jerked his head around and took a startled step back. Crap, he'd been so out of it he hadn't even heard Jake move over to stand beside him.

"What?" he asked.

Jake gave him a strange look, like he was wondering what the hell was up with Caleb. Or maybe he was simply irritated because he thought Caleb wasn't listening to him. Which he supposed was technically true.

"I asked if you're okay keeping an eye on Brielle?" Jake said. "I need someone to watch her, but if you don't want to do it, I'll get someone else."

Caleb didn't say anything, not sure how he even felt about the job Jake had given him. But that was a lie. He knew exactly how he felt about spending time with Brielle.

"Yeah, no problem," he said, trying not to look too eager. "If someone has to take a hit for the team, it might as well be me."

CHAPTER 3

Croatia

"HAS ANYONE EVER MENTIONED THAT YOU CLEAN UP NICE?" Brielle murmured, glancing at Caleb as they followed the hostess through the crowded restaurant.

"No," Caleb said casually, one of his hands resting warmly on her lower back, completely oblivious to the attention he was getting from the other women seated at the tables in the fancy dining room.

Brielle couldn't blame them. With his shaggy, dark-blond hair that looked like it hadn't seen a brush in a week, Caleb was the closest thing she'd ever seen to masculine perfection. Throw in the way he carried himself, all animal grace and power, and he simply demanded attention. It didn't hurt that the expensive suit he wore fit him so perfectly. The dark material highlighted his wide shoulders, broad chest, and long, lean body like it had been tailored specifically for him.

All in all, he was scrumptious.

And even if the only reason for this *date* was because the STAT team needed somebody inside the restaurant close to the person they suspected of stealing the nuclear weapons, Brielle was still thrilled she was going out to dinner with him. Which, when she thought about it, was a rather sad commentary on her nonexistent love life.

Caleb pulled out her chair when they reached their table. As she sat, he carefully nudged the seat in for her, and she could feel the warmth of his breath on her cheek as he leaned down to put his mouth close to her ear.

"You look absolutely gorgeous yourself, by the way," he murmured, his deep, husky voice doing crazy things to her pulse. "That dress is breathtaking on you."

She glanced down to take in the black, off-the-shoulder gown that was easily the most expensive dress she'd ever worn. In addition to the slit up the side that showed off a lot of leg, the bodice did amazing things for her cleavage. From his position behind her, she had no doubt that Caleb was taking advantage of the view. And she enjoyed knowing he was looking. Which was absolutely crazy, since she was only here with Caleb as a means to get her brother back safely.

Right?

Wrong.

Or at least, partially wrong.

She'd felt an inexplicable attraction to the big, handsome werewolf from the moment she first laid eyes on him all those weeks ago. And the strange, almost mesmerizing sensation she felt around him had only grown the longer she'd been around him. That was the main reason she had turned tail and run as soon as the mission in Calais was over.

Since she was a little girl, Brielle had been able to *sense* people around her—some more than others. It hadn't taken long to figure out that the people she could sense were different...unusual... *supernatural*. That realization had scared the crap out of her, and she'd gone out of her way from that moment on to ignore her gift and any of the sensations that came with it. When she'd met Caleb and felt a connection like nothing she'd ever experienced before, she'd run as far away from him as fast as she could. She hadn't known what those tingling sensations up and down her spine meant whenever she was close to him, and she hadn't wanted to hang around long enough to find out.

Now, here she was, having dinner with him, and the electrical tingles were more powerful—not to mention more confusing— than even the first time.

"Have you ever been to Zagreb?" Caleb asked as he moved around the table and took his own seat, then picked up the menu their server had set in front of him.

Brielle saw him glance casually at the large table in the back corner of the restaurant, where their suspect, arms dealer Surinda Lestari, was supposed to be having dinner with his potential buyers tonight. But the table was completely empty at the moment, leaving Brielle to wonder if the information STAT had come up with might be wrong. She hoped not because that would mean they weren't any closer to finding Julian. She only prayed her brother was still okay.

"No, I've never been anywhere in Croatia." Brielle picked up her own menu but didn't open it right away. Instead, she took a moment to look around the beautiful restaurant with its high tray ceiling illuminated with soft pink lighting, delicate crystal chandeliers, and antique wood floor inset with large marble tiles. Semi-private booths hidden in alcoves were all around the perimeter of the main dining room, and there was even a small dance floor at the far end. Two older couples swayed to the soft music coming from the speakers in each corner. "Though if I'd known it was this beautiful here, I would have made it a point to visit," she added, turning her attention back to Caleb. "You?"

Caleb snorted. "Does it make me sound stupid if I admit I didn't even know Zagreb was in Croatia? Hell, if we're being honest, I would have a hard time even finding Croatia on a map, much less Zagreb."

Brielle didn't bother to hide her smile. In her experience, there weren't many men whose egos could handle admitting they didn't know something, especially in front of a woman. The fact that Caleb could do so without giving it a second thought was a trait she found very attractive.

"No, it definitely doesn't make you sound stupid," she told him. "Lyon, the place where I grew up in France, is probably only a thousand kilometers away from here, and I don't know much more about this place than you do."

Caleb regarded her thoughtfully, like he was trying to decide if she was lying about that or not, but before he could say anything, they were interrupted by their server. Caleb ordered a Jack and Coke while Brielle went with a glass of white wine.

The woman just left to get their drinks when Jake's voice came through the tiny earpieces Brielle and Caleb were wearing.

"Surinda Lestari and his entourage just arrived in the parking lot," he said.

"The bug I put under the table earlier is transmitting loud and clear," Misty added. "We should have no problem hearing everything they say."

Less than a minute later, the hostess led six men into the dining room and directly to the table in the back. Two of them moved to take up positions in the furthest corners of the room, probably so they could keep an eye on the main entrance, the kitchen, and the other diners, along with the table in the back, which meant they must be Surinda Lestari's bodyguards.

"Copy that," Caleb said into the microphone hidden in the lapel of his suit jacket. "We have eyes on him." Turning off his mic, he regarded the men for a moment, then looked at Brielle. "I'm not sure what I was expecting, but I thought a man ballsy enough to steal twenty nuclear weapons from the United States would look a little more…I don't know…badass?"

Brielle swept her eyes across the room, making it seem like she was taking in the beautiful decor as she got a closer look at the man STAT intelligence believed had stolen the nukes. While Lestari might not look as intimidating as Caleb, with his jet-black hair and dark eyes, the man didn't exactly seem like a pushover, either.

"Really?" she said, running a finger over the delicate flower pendant on the necklace she wore, turning off her own tiny microphone and turning her gaze on Caleb again. "He looks scary enough to me."

Caleb still didn't seem impressed, but he didn't say anything as he went back to reading the menu.

Brielle was trying to decide what to order when the server set their drinks on the table.

"Shall I tell you about our menu?" the petite woman asked.

Brielle nodded. "Please."

As she described each dish in detail, Brielle got the feeling that a fancy restaurant like this wasn't Caleb's kind of place. But he hid it well, smiling and nodding, saying all the right things at the appropriate moments. When the server was done, he looked at Brielle, asking what she'd like. Truthfully, this place was a bit fancy for her tastes as well, but when Caleb suggested the marinated pears in port wine with warm brioche and orange butter for the appetizer, followed by risotto with carrot juice and lamb fillet in a creamy rosemary sauce, then a tangerine mousse for dessert, she eagerly agreed. It might not be the kind of food she ate every day, but it did sound delicious.

"You do know you picked the most expensive things on the menu, right?" she asked as the server walked away.

"I figure if we have to eat in a fancy restaurant, we might as well see how the other half lives," Caleb said with a grin. "Though I'll probably have to go out to McDonald's after this for something a little more filling. You're welcome to join me if you want."

"Already asking me out on a second date before the first one is even over, are you?" she teased with a soft laugh. "I never say no to fries, so you're on."

Male voices rumbled through their earpieces as Lestari and the other men at his table discussed the menu. Brielle glanced at them and immediately realized that their lips weren't syncing up with the words she was hearing, and it took her a moment to remember what Misty had said about using a software program to translate from the Serbian language the men were speaking straight into English. According to Misty, the software could handle almost all of the languages and dialects common throughout Europe and Asia, which was very convenient, she had to admit.

She sipped her wine, listening to the men carefully, but after hearing nothing of interest, she turned down the volume on her earpiece. Across from her, Caleb did the same. Listening to the man babble on about food, wine, and traffic, it was hard to believe Lestari was one of the most cold-blooded and ruthless arms dealers in the world. According to the file STAT put together, Lestari had made his millions selling weapons and explosives throughout Indonesia and South Asia, particularly in India and Sri Lanka. While nuclear weapons seemed to be a big step up for Lestari, it was difficult to ignore the fact that one of his ships had slipped out of the port city near Incirlik barely an hour after the weapons had been stolen. The same port city her brother had used during his short-lived drug operation. That ship had sailed straight for the Adriatic Sea and the city of Rijeka, a little more than two hours from Zagreb. They'd moved fast, just in time for this dinner between Lestari and a group of men supposedly interested in staging a coup in Yemen.

Yes, it was a lot of circumstantial evidence, but taken together, Brielle could understand why STAT thought Lestari had the nukes. And once they had the weapons back, Jake promised to make sure Surinda Lestari told them everything he knew about her brother and where he was.

The fact that she hadn't heard from Julian in nearly a week terrified her, but she had to believe he was alive and well. She wouldn't be able to keep going if she let herself imagine anything else.

"So you and Julian grew up in Lyon?" Caleb asked, sipping his drink. "What was that like?"

She picked up her wineglass and took a sip. It was fruity and sweet and not dry at all, which was nice. "I wish I could say that it was charming, idyllic, and heartwarming, but that would be a lie. And something tells me that you'd prefer me to be honest."

Caleb was silent a moment, as if considering that. "I'd prefer if you didn't lie to me. The idea that you might bothers me for some reason."

Brielle filed that away for later. She was surprised to discover that she didn't want to have any secrets from Caleb. No matter how dangerous that might be.

"Our mother passed away when my brother and I were young," she murmured. "I was barely twelve at the time, and Julian had just turned seven. It was hard on us but even worse for our father. Maman was the glue that kept our little family together, and to say our father didn't handle it well would be an understatement."

Brielle bit her tongue in a vain attempt to distract herself from the pain that memories of her mother's death brought back. For some unexplainable reason, she found herself wanting to tell Caleb everything, even though she'd never confided to anyone about it before. She only hoped she didn't start crying in the middle of the restaurant. That would be too much.

"We didn't have any other family. Papa tried to take care of us as best he could. But without Maman, his heart wasn't in it."

She fell silent as the server placed their appetizers in front of them, then nibbled on the warm brioche topped with orange butter, losing herself in the bright citrus taste and using it as another excuse to distance herself from the emotions she'd never been able to process, even after all this time.

"My father started drinking—a lot," she finally said, picking up her spoon to scoop up a small piece of wine-poached pear. "As you can imagine, things went downhill from there. He was able to stop a few times for Julian and me, but the periods of sobriety never lasted long. I was fourteen when he lost his job for good. By that point, I was already doing all the cooking and cleaning, and I was paying the bills with whatever money he brought home. It wasn't much of a leap for me to get my first job. At that age, I couldn't do much legally, but we had a family friend who took pity on us and let me stock shelves in his store at night after it closed. The pay wasn't much, but between that and the expired canned goods he let me take home, it kept food on the table."

"What about Julian?" Caleb asked.

Brielle looked up, surprised to see that he'd already finished his appetizer and his drink. She'd been so lost in her story that she'd barely noticed.

"Julian didn't handle our mother's death any better than our father did." She nibbled on her brioche, then ate some more of the pear. The fruit was made even sweeter from the port and would have been a delectable dessert with a big dollop of whipped cream. "He disappeared into a shell for a long time, and when he finally came out, he wasn't the same. I was the one who had to make sure he ate, went to bed on time, got to school, and did his homework."

Caleb gave her a sympathetic look. "That must have been tough on you."

She shrugged. "It was. I missed Maman, too, but I was so focused on taking care of Julian that I didn't have time to process everything."

They both fell silent as the server showed up with small bowls of risotto with carrot juice. The dish was topped with burrata, which both resembled and tasted a lot like mozzarella, Brielle discovered, but with a creamier consistency.

Across from her, Caleb started to say something as he dipped his spoon in his risotto again, but then he paused, taking a moment to listen in on the translated conversation going on between Lestari and the other men at his table. Brielle was starting to think STAT had been wrong about this guy because they'd been eavesdropping for at least thirty minutes and had yet to hear a single word related to the stolen nuclear weapons.

"Did things ever get any better for you and Julian?" Caleb

finally asked, turning his attention back to her, gazing at her in a way that made her breath hitch a little. "After that, I mean."

She shook her head. "Our father passed a few days after my eighteenth birthday, and I went from raising Julian to being legally responsible for him. I'd just taken my qualification exams and been hoping to go to university, but there was no way I could do that, not when I had to provide for Julian. So I got two more jobs and committed myself to taking care of my brother, paying the rent and bills, and putting food on the table."

"I'm sorry," Caleb said quietly, reaching across the table to take her hand, his long fingers curling around her own. His skin was so warm and his touch so comforting that it took everything in her to remember this wasn't a real date. "It must have been hard raising your brother when you were pretty much still a kid yourself. Did he help out at all?"

"No. Honestly? Julian was a complete jerk." She would have laughed at how much of an understatement that was if there'd been anything even remotely funny about it. "He got arrested for the first time when he was thirteen—for shoplifting. Instead of scaring him into behaving himself, it made him even more impulsive. He never once considered the consequences of his actions because he was too busy looking for a quick score. He barely made it through his secondary education. He got involved with the wrong people and fired from every job he somehow managed to get. By the time he was twenty, he'd been labeled an incorrigible delinquent by the authorities and was involved in car theft, larceny, possession of an illegal substance, and the sale of alcohol without a license. I can't tell you how many times I had to bail him out of jail or arrange to get him a lawyer."

Caleb scowled and pushed his empty bowl aside. "If he was such a screwup, why keep going to his rescue?"

"Because he's the only family I have left." She glanced down and realized she'd finished her risotto, too, without even remembering eating it. "I'm never going to give up on him, no matter how many times he screws up. That's what family means. To me at least."

She expected a negative comment out of Caleb—or, at the very least, something snarky—but instead, he nodded, his handsome face thoughtful.

"I've never really had a connection to my family," he said after a moment. "Not like the one you have with your brother—good or bad. But I understand what it means to have someone in your life who leads you to make irrational decisions. That part I definitely have experience with."

Brielle opened her mouth to ask for details, but the server chose that exact moment to bring out their main course, and as they started eating, it seemed that the moment to ply him with questions had already slipped away. Instead, she found herself telling him stories of some of Julian's dumber exploits, starting with the time he'd tried to sell a truckload of stolen toothpaste and ending with his scheme to sell heroin in Turkey. That one had ended up with him being sentenced to twenty years in the worst prison on the planet.

"You never did tell us exactly how you got him out of there," Caleb said casually, glancing at her as he speared a piece of lamb.

"No, I didn't." She wasn't ready to get into that part of her personal life with Caleb, even if she was incredibly comfortable with him. "Perhaps another time."

Brielle expected at least a little push back, so she was pleasantly surprised when he nodded and took another bite of lamb. She did the same, chewing slowly. The meat was so tender that it practically melted in her mouth.

"So…Quebec? That's where you and Julian disappeared to after leaving Calais?" Caleb asked, steering the conversation back onto more comfortable ground. "They speak French there, right? Is that why you picked the place?"

Brielle ate some of the parsnip puree before answering. "It

certainly didn't hurt, but I speak several languages, so we could have moved somewhere else. We went there mostly because of their immigration laws. It's simple for a French citizen to move there and immediately get a job. I thought Julian and I could blend in easily. At least, until STAT forgot about us."

Caleb gazed at her again, and she was startled at how effortless it was to get lost in those warm brown eyes of his. For a dangerous, violent man, they were so soft and inviting. Then again, perhaps that made him even more dangerous, just in another way.

"I'm sorry STAT and McKay threatened you the way they did," he said. "Holding a lifetime prison sentence over you and your brother so they could use your abilities to find other supernaturals to recruit was a shitty thing to do."

While she agreed, Brielle shook her head. "It's not on you to apologize for what they wanted to do," she said and hoped he realized that she truly meant it. "I never thought it was you or the other members of your team who wanted me locked up in some secret American prison for the rest of my life. Besides, McKay already apologized a long time ago."

Caleb looked shocked. "He did? When?"

Strangely happy at the idea of catching him by surprise, Brielle almost laughed, but then stopped herself as she remembered what else had been happening around that time.

"It was while you and your teammates were moving on the nuclear power plant to stop Yegor," she said softly. "I was waiting in the operation center with everyone else when McKay pulled me aside and apologized, saying he'd never intended for things to happen the way they had. He gave me his private cell number and told me to call him if I ever changed my mind about working for STAT—or if I ever needed help. Which, as it turns out, I did."

Whatever Caleb was going to say was interrupted by two big men entering the dining room and heading straight for Lestari and his table. Thanks to her brother, Brielle had been around enough bad people to recognize them when she saw them. Tensing, she glanced at Lestari's bodyguards, expecting to see weapons coming out, but instead, they remained where they were as the two newcomers stopped in front of their boss.

Caleb keyed his microphone. "Jake, we have two new players in the game. And from the way Lestari is looking at them, something tells me that he's been waiting for them."

"We got them on video, and Misty and Genevieve are running facial recognition right now," Jake said. "I'm hoping Lestari will address them by name so we can identify them quicker. Until then, sit tight."

That hope went out the window the moment Lestari and the two men started talking and nothing but gobbledygook came through their earpieces.

"Crap," Misty said over the radio. "I'm not sure what language they're speaking, but it's nothing the software recognizes. So unless one of you guys happens to understand what they're saying, we're screwed."

Brielle set down her fork and pushed back her chair. "I'll be right back," she said to Caleb. "Meet me on the dance floor in two minutes."

Caleb frowned and started to get to his feet, but she waved him back down, praying he wouldn't do anything stupid.

She made her way toward the back corner of the restaurant, taking a circuitous route through the tables, then skirting the dance floor so that her path took her right past Lestari's table. As she stepped around the two newcomers, she pretended to stumble, grabbing on to one of the men's shoulders. He turned sharply in his chair to catch her, and she immediately took the hand he held out, steadying herself.

She murmured an apology in French even as she opened the connection between them. He smiled back at her, and a moment later, she was on her way to the restroom down the hallway near their table. The tingles settled into her skin before she even reached the ladies' room. Once inside, she counted to twenty, then left to go back to the dining room.

Caleb was already on his feet and heading her way, meeting her on the dance floor with a forced smile on his face. Brielle wondered if he was more upset at her unexplained actions or the fact that he had to dance with her.

For a big man, Caleb moved much more gracefully on the floor than she had expected. Though that was probably thanks to his inner werewolf. Regardless, the two older couples on the floor smiled at them broadly in that way elderly people did when the "kids" did something old-fashioned and romantic. If they only knew that Caleb could sprout fangs and claws at a moment's notice—not to mention rip their heads off if he was having a bad day—they probably wouldn't be smiling nearly as much.

Still, Brielle definitely wasn't complaining as Caleb led her through a dance step that suggested someone had actually *taught* him to dance at some point. She would have asked, but unfortunately, there were other priorities at the moment.

"What was that all about?" Caleb growled softly as they moved closer to Lestari's table.

Damn, she had to admit that growl thing he did was kind of sexy.

"Shh," she whispered. "I'm trying to listen to what Lestari is saying."

Caleb looked confused as hell but didn't say anything else as they kept dancing.

It was hard to hear Lestari and the other men over the music, even though it wasn't much more than background noise. Even so, she could only pick up every third or fourth word. It took a few moments for her to make sense of what she was listening to. It was always like that right after she first made contact with her target.

"They're talking about making a deal for the weapons right

now," she whispered, her gaze focused on Caleb but her ears tuned in to the conversation at the table a few feet away. "The two buyers have already wired partial payment to Lestari and will transfer the rest of the money after they see the weapons."

"Wait a minute," Caleb said, his eyes narrowing. "You understand what they're saying? Since when?"

"I told you I speak several languages," she said, not wanting to get into details at the moment.

What she'd just done was too complicated to explain quickly, and they didn't have time. Unfortunately, Caleb didn't appear to be buying her excuse. He opened his mouth to say something, but thankfully, Misty interrupted.

"What language are they speaking?"

"I think it's called Nuaulu," Brielle said hesitantly. She'd only picked up a vague concept of what the language was when she'd touched the man's hand.

"Wait. A. Minute," Misty said, pausing in between each word. "You're telling us you speak a language only spoken by a couple million people that live around the island of Seram in the middle-of-nowhere Indonesia?"

Brielle honestly had no way to answer that question simply. It didn't help that Caleb was staring at her like he knew she was lying about something. Fortunately, Lestari and the men with him chose that moment to stand and head for the exit of the restaurant.

"We can talk about this later," she said, tugging Caleb with her as she moved to follow. "Because they're heading to make the exchange right now. And the handoff is happening somewhere close to here."

Over the radio, Jake cursed, then ordered Harley and Sawyer to track Lestari and the others once the men were outside, while the rest of the team got ready for a raid.

"Be careful," Jake added. "We have no idea what we're walking into."

That concern didn't stop Caleb from looking at Brielle sideways after he paid the bill and they headed out the door. "I know something strange happened back there. As soon as we get those nukes back, we're going to talk about it."

CHAPTER 4

"They're in two vehicles heading south toward the train tracks," Harley announced over the radio as Caleb and Brielle reached the way-too-small rental car they'd driven to dinner. "On the main road, two blocks west of the restaurant."

"We need to hurry if we're going to catch up to them," Brielle said as he cranked the engine. When he made no move to put the car in gear, she added, "We *are* going after them, right?"

Caleb wanted to say no. He wanted to sit there outside the restaurant and demand that Brielle tell him what had happened in there and how she'd been able to understand what those men had been saying when he was damn sure she hadn't been able to speak their language before she tripped and almost fell into that guy's lap. It wasn't the fact that she had secrets that bothered him. Everyone had secrets. He had so many he needed to rent storage space to keep them all. But for some stupid reason, it stung like a hell that she was keeping these secrets from *him*. It felt...wrong.

But then Misty was on the radio, interrupting his thoughts, saying she'd identified the two men who'd met with Lestari as obscure revolutionaries out of Sri Lanka. Exactly the kind of people who might want to possess one or more of their missing nukes. That knowledge was enough to once again convince him that this conversation would have to wait until later.

"We're going after them," he said to Brielle, putting the car in gear. "But we stay in the background until the last moment. We can't risk tipping them off if they remember us from the restaurant."

That seemed to satisfy her.

They followed Harley's directions toward the railroad tracks. He remembered seeing them on the way to the restaurant, a little surprised to see an industrial-sized rail yard located so close to the upscale part of the city.

"They made a left on Koturaška," Harley said over the radio. "It's a small access road just over the tracks. We're falling back so they don't get suspicious. Forrest, you and Misty come up and take point."

Caleb tried to listen to the muted conversation between his teammates as he drove, but most of his attention was focused on the mesmerizing woman sitting in the seat beside him. In the tiny compact car, with the heat turned up, her scent was even more enticing than it had been in the restaurant. He kept telling himself it had to be her perfume, even though he'd never smelled a honeysuckle scent from a bottle that was so sweet and intoxicating.

During dinner, it had taken all his strength to maintain a semi-intelligent conversation with Brielle. It had gotten ten times worse on the dance floor, when she'd been in his arms. The urge to bury his nose in her long, silky hair and breathe in that delectable scent had been nearly overwhelming. He'd be lying if he said he wasn't a little shaken by the effect she had on him. He refused to allow himself to think too much about why his inner wolf was reacting so strangely, though. No way in hell was he letting his mind go in *that* direction.

"They just pulled into a dirt parking lot at the end of Koturaška," Forrest said over the radio. "Google Maps shows several buildings near it, including a cluster of warehouses. We've pulled onto a side road right near them."

Caleb and Brielle got there less than two minutes later to find the rest of the team crowded around the front of Jake's car in the darkness, looking at something on a laptop. When Caleb and Brielle joined them, he saw a real-time satellite image on the screen of the area around the dirt parking lot. The suspects' vehicles were parked directly in front of the warehouses, but it was a collection of railcars located on a side spur a few hundred feet away that everyone seemed to be focused on.

"There are at least half a dozen men guarding those cars," Sawyer said, motioning at the shadowy figures meandering around them. "They might be dressed to blend in with the rest of the yard workers, but they're definitely all carrying weapons."

Brielle leaned closer to get a better look at the screen, her face intent. "If the nukes are in one of those boxcars, that means my brother might be one of those men."

"We won't know for sure until we get a closer look," Jake said, glancing at her. "He could just as easily be inside the warehouse where they're making the deal."

Brielle straightened up, letting out a delicate snort. "Julian wouldn't be inside. He's too much of a screwup for something like that. The chances of him opening his trap and saying something stupid at the worst possible time is a given. If he's here, he's somewhere outside, where he's less likely to make a mistake."

The words might be harsh, but Caleb didn't miss the slight smile curving the corners of Brielle's mouth. He couldn't imagine having a connection to anyone in his family like she had with her brother.

Jake quickly and succinctly laid out the plan, splitting up the team with Caleb going into the warehouse with him, Jes, and Forrest while Harley, Sawyer, and Misty would deal with the guards near the railcars.

"Brielle, I'd like you to come into the warehouse with us in case we need you to translate anything they say," Jake added.

"No!" Caleb said.

The word came out in a snarl before he even had time to process why he was so violently against the idea. Everyone on the team turned to look at him in surprise, but it was Brielle's stunned expression that held his attention. He thought he saw a flash of pain in her eyes, though he couldn't understand why.

"It's too dangerous," he said in a softer voice, taking a breath and forcing himself to calm down. "She doesn't have any tactical training. She'd be nothing but a liability in there."

Brielle squared her shoulders and glared at him, her eyes shooting sparks his way. "You don't know anything about me or what I can and can't do. You have no say in deciding what's too dangerous for me. If Jake thinks it will help get my brother back safely, I'll go in there if I want. And you won't have a damn thing to say about it."

Caleb may have…possibly…sputtered a bit at that announcement. Given the fleeting smile that crossed Forrest's face, it was likely. But then Jake was giving rapid-fire orders, and everyone was scattering. Instincts that Caleb yearned to ignore had him heading for Brielle's side after tossing his suit jacket on the hood of the car, but a single scathing look from her sent him moving in a different direction. He did his best to make his about-face seem intentional, but once again, a smirk from Forrest told him that he likely failed.

It took a ridiculous amount of effort to force his mind to focus on the task at hand, since all his inner omega seemed interested in was protecting Brielle. He kept telling himself that Jake would keep a close eye on her, but that didn't help very much.

A series of tree-covered apartment buildings stood between them and the dirt parking lot near the warehouses. Caleb moved into the heavy shadows of the trees, using the cover they provided to work his way around to the right side of the warehouse complex. It was hard to believe the arms dealers were doing the exchange right here in the middle of such a respectable-looking place. He'd expected a darker, more menacing location. Then again, maybe that made this the *perfect* place.

The warehouses turned out to be nothing more than three cheap metal buildings shoved together. They'd obviously seen better days, and the aluminum roofing on the one closest to him was in seriously crappy shape. He stood outside, listening carefully for a few seconds, realizing that only the largest building in the middle was occupied. He glanced up to see a row of dimly lit windows on the second floor. That seemed to be the only entry point on this side.

Despite still wearing a suit and tie, Caleb quickly scrambled up the gutter of the decrepit building, careful not to rip the whole thing off the wall. Then he shimmied across the roof until he could peek through the windows he'd spotted from below. It was hard to see anything through the cloudy glass, but he saw enough to know the second floor of the building was more storage than anything else. He reached out to gently touch the window, grinning when the frame flexed slightly.

"I'm on the roof on the southern side of the warehouses," he whispered into his mic. "I'm gonna slip in through one of the windows."

"Copy that," Jake answered. "Be careful. Jes, Brielle, and I are coming in the north side, and Forrest is looking for a back door on the east side. Don't make a move until we know for sure where all the weapons are. That boxcar out there might only hold some of the nukes that were stolen."

Caleb hadn't considered that but realized it was a valid concern. This particular deal might only be for a portion of the weapons. Because really, what kind of terrorist needed twenty nukes?

He slowly eased the window frame loose, mindful not to make any noise. He was focused on what he was doing, but he could still hear a running commentary in his ear as the other members of his team moved into place around the warehouse and railcars. Brielle didn't say anything, but he told himself that she was fine. He had to trust that Jake and Jes would keep an eye on her. If he had time to think about it, he would have pondered the implications of how a woman he barely knew had crept inside his head like this.

The entire window popped out of the frame without a sound, and he carefully placed it on the roof beside him, then crawled through the opening. The moment he was inside, instinct made him jerk his head around. He wasn't sure if it had been a noise, a flash of movement, or simply a barely perceived scent, but something had him staring out into the darkness. He didn't see anything there, no matter how long or how hard he looked.

"Forrest, did you move around to the southeast side of the warehouse?" he said into his mic.

"Negative," Forrest replied. "I just slipped in through the back door. Did you see someone out there?"

Caleb stared out into the darkness behind the warehouse again, trying to understand what had caught his attention, but finally gave up. There wasn't anything there.

"Negative," he said softly. "Moving inside now."

Looking around, Caleb saw that he'd been right about the second floor. It was filled with boxes and other crap that looked like it hadn't been touched in a decade. He weaved his way through the mess, heading for the nearest railing so he could get a look at the lower level, praying all the dust up here wouldn't give him a sneezing fit.

The first floor was much neater than the loft where he was currently hiding, though it was difficult to tell what kind of business they conducted in the place. All he could make out were several worktables loaded with four heavy-duty wooden boxes. Each of them was about forty inches long, maybe half that wide and deep. You could definitely get a B61 warhead in a box that size, particularly if you stripped the nuclear package out of the bomb. He had to admit he was a little disappointed by the lack of *Warning— Nuclear Warhead on Board* stickers on the box. But he guessed that might be expecting too much.

"I have eyes on the targets," Caleb murmured softly into the radio. "Surinda Lestari is down there with the other men from the restaurant, including the Sri Lankan revolutionaries. There are another eight to ten men scattered around the perimeter of the warehouse that look like muscle for both sides of the deal."

"What about the weapons?" Jake asked.

"There are four wooden crates on the tables in the center of the warehouse," Caleb answered. "The size is right for the nukes, but no way to know for sure."

"I'm not picking up any radiation signatures yet," Misty said.

Caleb snorted. Only Misty would think to bring radiation detection equipment on a raid.

"We're close enough to hear them talking," Brielle said softly, and Caleb felt his gums tingle at the knowledge that she was inside the warehouse with all these armed men. "They're discussing the final payment being ready to transfer once they've inspected the weapons."

Down below, Lestari stepped closer to one of the boxes and popped the latches as the other men gathered around. A second later, Lestari flipped open the lid.

The moment Caleb got his first look at the weapon inside, he realized something was wrong. He wasn't exactly sure what a B61 warhead looked like because he hadn't paid all that much attention during the tech briefs, but he was pretty sure it wasn't this. The things in the box Lestari had just opened were barely six inches in diameter and pointy at one end, painted dark gray with two green stripes around the middle.

"Guys, I think we have a problem," Caleb said.

But before he could explain that the weapons Lestari was selling weren't the stolen nukes, Forrest's urgent voice came over the radio, interrupting him.

"Yeah, a big problem," Forrest said. "Four heavily armed men just slipped through the back door and are heading for the exchange. I think they're planning to make a move on Lestari and the others."

The words were barely out of Forrest's mouth when the four men in question stepped into the dim glow that filled the center of the warehouse, shouting instructions in what sounded like at least half a dozen different languages. English was the only one he understood.

"Drop your weapons and get on the floor!" one of the party crashers shouted, swinging a submachine gun to cover Lestari and the Sri Lankans.

Caleb barely had a second to wonder if Lestari and his people were going to comply before bedlam broke out as everyone on the first floor started shooting at once. As the first of the four newcomers hit the ground, Caleb decided that, nope, that had definitely not been a good idea. It wasn't until he heard shooting outside that he realized their whole plan had gone sideways.

He was more than ready to let the various players in this clusterfuck bleed each other dry before intervening. But then a three-round burst of automatic gunfire slammed into one of the weapon crates on the table. Okay, maybe letting these idiots wipe each other out might not be such a good idea.

Jake must have thought the same thing because he and Jes popped out of the shadows and began taking down the goons who'd arrived with Lestari. That would have been cool if Brielle hadn't popped out with them, still wearing that sexy dress and holding a damn weapon. She obviously meant to help but had completely missed the fact that she'd put herself squarely in between the two groups of combatants.

Brielle was in danger.

Caleb didn't pause to think—not that he ever did—but jumped to his feet and launched himself over the railing, cutting loose a wall-shaking roar as he dropped down into the anarchy below.

He ended up landing directly atop Surinda Lestari. There was a grunt, the sound of crunching as a few bones broke, then Caleb was up and moving toward the next threat. He didn't lose control this time—not completely, anyway. But that was only because he'd put himself between Brielle and everyone with a gun.

The sounds of gunfire faded away as the third man went down under his swinging claws and fists, and Caleb thought the fighting was over. But then, he caught movement out of the corner of his eye and saw someone point a weapon in Brielle's direction.

He definitely *did* lose it then.

Letting out a growl, he ran across the room toward the tall, dark-haired man he'd seen yelling at everyone to drop their weapons and get on the floor earlier. Eyes going wide, the guy swung his weapon away from Brielle and aimed it at Caleb instead.

Bullets tore through his shoulder—bullets that would have hit Brielle if he hadn't gotten in the asshole's face. Snarling, he grabbed the guy by the front of his shirt and slung him aside, bouncing him off a column. Then he strode toward the guy, determined to finish him.

"Caleb, no!" Jes shouted from somewhere that seemed extremely far away. "Don't kill him!"

He ignored his teammate, continuing toward his prey. But before he could reach his target, Jes jumped in front of him, putting her body between him and the man he intended to kill.

"I said you can't kill him," she said, actually having the nerve to put her hands on his chest and shoving at him in a feeble attempt to stop him. "Caleb, he's one of us. Stop, dammit!"

The message still wasn't making it through the fog of anger surrounding him or the omega hell-bent on destruction, and likely wouldn't have, until he felt a sharp sting across his face, only to realize that Jes had smacked him. Well, it wasn't the first time she had to do it to get his omega to back down.

"Snap out of it!" she said, looking up at him with an expression that made it obvious she wasn't gonna move out of his way until he showed her that he was back in control of his inner wolf and in a communicative mood.

Caleb took a deep breath, the act working his shoulders, the sting in the left one reminding him that the man in question had shot him. Despite that, he let his fangs and claws retract.

"Why did you stop me?" he demanded. "He tried to kill Brielle."

Jes frowned and took a step back, the tension leaving her body. "No, he didn't. He tried to kill you. And considering how scary you look when you go all omega, I can't say I blame him."

"That doesn't answer my question," Caleb said.

She sighed. "I couldn't let you kill him because he's CIA, and McKay frowns on us killing other federal agents."

The entire warehouse went quiet at that announcement. As one, Caleb's teammates turned to look at the man still sitting on the floor, rubbing at a jaw that was almost certainly going to bruise up soon.

"I suppose this is the part where I introduce myself," the man said, getting to his feet. "I'm Hudson Kerr. Like Jes said, I'm CIA." He glanced around, taking in Caleb and his teammates. "Something tells me you're with that new Special Threat Assessment Team. I'd heard rumors that you guys were a bunch of freaks. Guess they were right."

Caleb growled. "Something tells me I'm going to regret not killing you."

With that, he turned and walked out of the warehouse.

CHAPTER 5

"So...LET ME GET THIS STRAIGHT," HUDSON SAID SLOWLY, regarding Caleb intently for several long moments before looking at the rest of the STAT team seated in the back booth of the mostly empty McDonald's located half a dozen blocks from the train yard. "You're seriously telling me that werewolves exist? And that the people you work for at STAT know?"

Brielle bit her lip to keep from saying something she shouldn't. Like reminding him that he'd already seen Caleb in action and that he should know the answer to the first question at least. The raid at the warehouse and train yard had been more than two hours ago, but while most of the team was busy focusing on where to turn next in their hunt for the nuclear weapons, the CIA agent kept pulling the conversation back to Caleb and the things he and the other members of STAT had revealed to him.

Hudson was definitely having a hard time adjusting to this new world he'd suddenly found himself living in.

Beside Brielle, Caleb smirked as he slowly chewed a mouthful of fries. "I think I've already confirmed the part about werewolves existing. And as far as people at STAT knowing...well...where do you think the *Special* in Special Threat Assessment Team comes from?"

Across from her Hudson sat there with an expectant look on his face, blue eyes intent. Like he was waiting for Caleb to laugh and say, "Got you!" When Caleb simply went back to unwrapping another double cheeseburger, all Hudson could do was shake his head.

Brielle nibbled on her fries, listening as the STAT team—including Genevieve from the support team—talked over their options moving forward. It wasn't surprising to see the warmth and camaraderie between everyone. But what did surprise Brielle was the way the team kept including her in the conversation, like she was one of them. She'd been on her own for so long that it was almost enough to make her cry.

But regardless of how much they tried to include her, Brielle remained quiet for the most part, spending most of her time watching as the werewolves put away a stunning amount of food. Caleb had eaten six double cheeseburgers already and seemed to have no intention of slowing down.

Seeing Caleb eat with a gusto and enthusiasm that had definitely been lacking earlier with the small portions of fancy food at the restaurant brought a smile to Brielle's face and a rather pleasant warming sensation to her stomach. Her gaze was drawn to the left side of his chest. He'd put his suit jacket back on before they'd come in, but she knew there were bullet holes in the dress shirt underneath from where he had been shot because he'd stepped in front of a gun pointed in her direction.

It was going to take some time to unpack all the implications of that selfless act. She didn't know much about Caleb, but something told her that he'd protect his teammates with his life. So maybe she shouldn't be surprised he'd do the same for her.

Instead of continuing to bang her head against that particular wall right now, Brielle turned her attention to a much bigger issue. They hadn't found Julian. And while the STAT team was focused on finding the nukes, she was still stuck worrying about how she was going to find her brother.

After all the shooting had ended and the wounded members of Hudson's team had been taken to the hospital, they'd discovered that the crates in the warehouse, as well as those out in the boxcars, were filled with 140 mm rocket warheads containing sarin nerve gas. They were dangerous as hell, yes, but they weren't the nuclear weapons they'd been looking for. Julian wasn't in Zagreb and probably never had been.

It had been devastating to everyone to learn that Surinda Lestari never had the nukes and that the entire trip to Zagreb had been a complete waste of time. Now, they were back to square one, and no one seemed to know where to look for the weapons next. Worse, after Hudson had learned about the nuclear weapons, the CIA had quickly attempted to insert themselves into the recovery effort.

Brielle knew very little about the dividing lines between the CIA and STAT when it came to something like missing nukes, but from what she'd overheard, it sounded like the CIA had made a move to take over the operation. That would have been a catastrophe for Brielle. She was sure the CIA would never have considered helping her find Julian.

In the end, McKay had brokered some kind of deal with the CIA. Brielle had no idea what leverage McKay had at his disposal, but ultimately, the CIA agreed that they wouldn't interfere in the operation as long as one of their own—or, more precisely, Hudson—remained involved. The scary part of the whole thing was that none of them knew how much Hudson had revealed concerning STAT's use of supernatural agents. Had he told his bosses that Caleb was a werewolf? Would he spill more of their secrets if he learned them? There was no way of knowing, but Brielle definitely had no plans to trust the man with any of her own secrets, that was for sure.

"Okay, so Caleb's a werewolf." Hudson interrupted the conversation at the table again, apparently still fixated on the subject. "What about the rest of you? Are you all werewolves, too?"

Everyone looked at Jake, clearly waiting to see what he would say. There was a tension in the air that was impossible to miss, though. Brielle suspected that no one on the STAT team would be any more comfortable with Hudson—and the CIA—knowing their secrets than she was.

"I'll admit to being a werewolf, but I'll leave it up to the other members of the team to decide whether they trust you enough to share that kind of personal information," Jake said softly. "As I'm sure you can guess, having that kind of information out there is dangerous for people like us. If it falls into the wrong hands, we're dead—or worse."

Hudson didn't say anything for a while but merely chewed thoughtfully on his fries, those gears in his head continuing to turn. After a few moments, he nodded. "I get that. And for what it's worth, I didn't mention anything about Caleb's unique abilities when I talked to my bosses back at Langley."

That caught everyone by surprise, including Brielle. Were they wondering if Hudson was telling the truth? She hoped he was, for Caleb's sake.

"Well, thanks for that," Jake said, though whether he believed Hudson or not was anyone's guess. "And, in the interest of open and honest communication concerning what you're getting yourself into if you work with us, you need to know that werewolves aren't the only supernaturals around. There are a lot of other creatures out there in the world, including the ones that were involved in stealing those nukes."

Hudson sat there with a stunned look on his face as Jake described the things they'd run into in the tunnels below Incirlik and how they'd torn those soldiers—and Caleb to a certain degree—to shreds. This was the first time Brielle had heard the details about the underground fight with the creatures that had yet to be identified. Hearing how they'd hurt Caleb twisted her stomach into knots, and it was all she could do to sit there and listen to it.

They talked for another fifteen minutes, covering everything they had as far as leads on the locations of the nuclear weapons, especially the Surinda clue they'd gotten from her brother. By the end of the discussion, they weren't any closer to knowing where the nukes were than they'd been at the beginning, at least from Brielle's perspective.

"Okay, so where does all this leave us?" Caleb asked. He'd finished all his double cheeseburgers and was now nursing his milkshake. "We were wrong about Surinda being a person, and we still don't have any idea who stole the weapons or how those creatures that dug the tunnel figure into this whole thing. The only thing we've accomplished so far is to give whoever took those weapons one hell of a head start on us."

From where she sat beside Hudson, Genevieve sighed. "We go back to the drawing board, toss out all of our previous assumptions, and look at every piece of evidence from a fresh perspective. I know it feels like we're wasting time, but it's the only choice we have. Hopefully, this time, we'll find something that points us in the right direction."

"And hopefully before it's too late," Brielle said softly.

The longer it took to find her brother, the more the odds worked against her ever seeing Julian alive again. It tore her apart to think that, but the truth was, it had been nearly a week since he'd called her. For all they knew, he might already be dead.

As she got to her feet along with everyone else, eager to head back to the hotel for some sleep after a long, frustrating day, Brielle felt Caleb take her hand, his face earnest.

"We'll find your brother," he promised. "*Before* it's too late."

Brielle nodded, touched by his concern. As they walked toward the door, she had to wonder if werewolves could read minds. Because she'd really needed those words of encouragement right then. And when Caleb was the one saying them, she found herself believing them.

CHAPTER 6

Russia

"ARE WE SURE THIS IS SURINDA?" CALEB ASKED SOFTLY, HIS warm breath frosting the late-night air as he crouched in the fresh snow on the hill overlooking the small village below them. His enhanced hearing didn't pick up any sounds from the collection of simple wooden houses. "I mean, the place is a ghost town. How many people are supposed to live here, again?"

"Almost a hundred," Genevieve murmured from the other side of Brielle. "They're mostly Evenki reindeer herders, along with a few other indigenous groups. At least, that was the number at last count a couple years ago. Maybe they all moved away since then."

Beside Caleb, Jake let out a snort. "And left the lights on and the fireplaces lit in most of the houses?" he pointed out, motioning toward the smoke coming from chimneys in several of the nearer buildings. "I don't think they just up and moved away."

Caleb was tempted to point out that maybe everyone in this sleepy central Siberian village had simply gone to bed. To say this place was on the backside of nowhere was an understatement. On the way here, he'd seen an old man *riding* a reindeer. A frigging reindeer. He was pretty sure there weren't any Netflix shows in these parts to keep the people who lived here awake this close to midnight.

He didn't bother saying any of that, of course, because ultimately, he knew Jake was right. There was something else going on here. It wasn't even the silence shrouding the town that made him believe that. It was the eerie stillness surrounding the village. The lights might be on, but no one was home; he was sure of it.

It was entirely possible that everyone who lived in the place had been slaughtered.

"Do you smell any blood?" he asked, glancing at Jake.

Harley or Sawyer could have answered that question, but since they hadn't revealed they were werewolves to Hudson, Caleb sure wasn't going to out them by saying the wrong thing at the wrong time.

Jake lifted his face to the breeze and inhaled sharply several times before shaking his head. "No blood. But I'm also not picking up as many scents as I should if there are a hundred people living down in that village, either. Something is definitely off."

Caleb frowned down at the tranquil village below. "Okay, aside from the disturbing lack of people, is anyone seeing anything to make us think the nukes are actually down there somewhere?"

"Maybe," Forrest said.

Caleb glanced over to see Forrest looking through a set of night-vision binoculars, apparently fascinated with whatever he was seeing.

"Take a look at the east side of the village about two hundred meters to the right of the last cluster of homes and tell me that structure doesn't stick out like a sore thumb."

Caleb followed the direction of Forrest's gaze until he saw the tall chain-link fence surrounding a small building. But it wasn't the fence or the squat, windowless building that caught his attention. It wasn't even the dozen or so trucks, some of them with a definite military design to them, that were parked inside the enclosure. No, it was the large metal tower that rose at least fifty feet above that building. That was the *structure* Forrest was talking about.

"Is that a cell phone tower?" Hudson murmured as he peered through his set of night-vision binoculars. "Behind a high-security fence?"

Caleb had never really paid much attention to what cell phone towers looked like, but he got the feeling this one wasn't right. It looked too rugged. And those vertical cylinders running straight up through the center of the thing seemed more like smokestacks than anything a cell phone tower needed.

"A cell phone tower in the middle of a Siberian farming village? I don't think so," Jake said. "But we won't know until we get a closer look. Split up into your teams and move in. Misty, I want you going in first, in case there are surveillance cameras."

Decked out in a heavy gray parka to protect against the below-freezing temperatures, a big hood covering her long, purple hair, Misty nodded. From the corner of his eye, Caleb saw Hudson getting that curious look on his face again, like he seriously wanted to ask if Misty was one of those other supernaturals Jake had mentioned to him the other night, but the CIA agent held his tongue.

Caleb got to his feet, ready to lead Misty, Forrest, and Brielle down the hill and into the village. In her black parka with the faux-fur-trimmed hood pulled up, heavy snow boots, and ski gloves, Brielle looked even colder than Misty, and Caleb had to resist the urge to put his arms around her to warm her up. He'd tried to convince Jake to leave her behind with the support team, but his complaints had landed on deaf ears—again. For some reason, Jake thought Brielle might be helpful on this reconnaissance mission. Caleb didn't know how.

Growling under his breath, Caleb took his team around to the east side of the village, coming at the fenced-in enclosure from the direction of the tree line. Luckily, the moon was mostly full, so they didn't need flashlights or even night-vision goggles. The route would provide them good cover right up until the last twenty feet or so, but it also meant trudging through some deep snowdrifts. That didn't bother him much because werewolves didn't get cold, but it would probably suck for Brielle.

He almost snorted. When the hell had he started giving a crap about how comfortable Brielle was on this mission when he'd been telling anyone who'd listen earlier that she shouldn't be coming with them at all?

"We're almost in position on the west," Jake said over the radio. He, Jes, and Hudson had taken an easier route near the cluster of houses at the edge of the village. "We haven't come across anyone so far."

"Same here on the north side," Harley said, answering for Sawyer and Genevieve. "We've looked in a few homes along the way, and they're all empty."

Caleb exchanged glances with Brielle, Misty, and Forrest, but none of them knew what to make of that information any more than he did. Giving them a nod, he led them toward the chain-link fence, the only sound their boots crunching through the icy snow cover as their breath frosted the air around them.

He and the rest of the team had spent a few days sitting on their asses in Zagreb while the analysts from both STAT and the CIA worked to find the stolen nukes, waking up every morning wondering if it would be the day they'd see pictures of mushroom clouds on the TV.

The analysts had started from scratch, focusing their attention on every seaport within a day's travel of Incirlik, ultimately coming up with a list of nearly five hundred ships that had moved out of those ports around the time the nukes had been stolen. Then they'd tracked every ship on that list, using images from satellites and port cameras to see where they were headed and what they'd offloaded during their various stops.

Caleb hadn't envied what had to be a grueling task, but in the end, they'd stumbled across an image of someone resembling Julian standing on a dock in Odessa, Ukraine, watching as a large crate was loaded onto a truck. The picture was grainy, but Brielle had sworn up and down that it was her brother. The crate was the perfect size for a B61 warhead, though there was no way of knowing if there was only one crate on the truck or twenty. The vehicle had certainly been large enough to hold all of them.

That truck had gone straight to the international airport where it had driven into the back of a large cargo plane, then flown non-stop to a city in Siberia called Krasnoyarsk. STAT had lost visual on the truck at that point, but as it turned out, about a hundred miles to the northeast was a tiny village named Surinda. It was a coincidence that couldn't be ignored. Less than twenty-four hours later, Caleb and the rest of the team were stomping through the snow in an abandoned town, praying they hadn't made another mistake.

"I'm not seeing any security cameras," Misty said, scanning the small building and surrounding area with her night-vision binoculars. "No motion sensors, either."

Caleb frowned. It didn't make sense that a place with a weird-looking tower and a building with a fence around it didn't have cameras.

"Let's take a closer look," he said.

When they reached the gate along the east side of the perimeter fence, Caleb was even more surprised to see that there wasn't a chain or any other kind of locking mechanism on it. His teammates mirrored his concern.

"Is it just me or does this feel like a trap?" Misty muttered. "I mean, we don't even know how many people are in that building."

"It isn't just you," Caleb confirmed. "Watch yourselves."

As they moved across the fenced-in area toward the small building, Caleb realized that given the number of vehicles inside the fence line, they could be dealing with twenty or thirty people in there. While he wasn't necessarily concerned about those odds when it came to the team, he was worried Brielle could get hurt in the crossfire.

The thought was so terrifying he actually stumbled on the uneven, snowy ground. From the corner of his eye, he saw Forrest and Misty looking at him strangely, the latter mouthing the question, *You okay?* with a concerned expression.

Caleb nodded and pressed his ear against the heavy steel door, motioning for the others to remain silent as he listened for sounds of movement inside. While his nose wasn't worth much, if there were people inside the structure, he would be able to hear them, even if they weren't saying anything—a person couldn't hide their heartbeat.

"There's no one in there," he said, turning to see that Jake and the rest of his teammates had shown up.

If they were in Maine, Caleb would have thought they'd slipped into a Stephen King novel. But seeing as Siberia was about as far from Maine as they could get, probably not. Drawing his weapon, he gave the heavy door a solid shove, sending it flying back, ready to shoot the first person—or balloon-wielding clown—he saw.

The room was empty. Other than a few electrical boxes mounted here and there, the tiny space didn't have a damn thing in it.

Except for a set of closed elevator doors.

"An unmarked building in the middle of a deserted village in Siberia equipped with some kind of communication tower on top and an elevator inside," Jake murmured, glancing at Genevieve. "Do you think this is some kind of Russian military complex? That the warheads were brought here for exploitation?"

"A military complex?" Genevieve said with a grimace of doubt. "Without any military guards?"

They all stood there in the middle of the room for a few seconds, staring at each other.

"I guess we take the elevator?" Caleb finally said.

With a nod, Jake moved forward and poked the single unmarked button to the right of the polished silver elevator door. "I guess we don't have any other choice."

A moment later, the door slid open, and they all crowded inside. Like the outside, there was only a single button inside on the control panel, with no indication of a floor level or anything like that. When Harley pushed it without saying anything, Caleb couldn't help but think that this was a really bad idea.

The car began to drop in complete silence, the descent continuing much longer than Caleb thought it would…hundreds of feet at least. It was strange being in an elevator without the typical numbers to give an idea of how far they were going. Hell, at this point, he would even have appreciated some of that boring music to break up the growing tension.

In the silence, Caleb picked up the sound of a rapidly beating heart, and he looked at Brielle standing slightly ahead and to the right of him, fear and anxiety radiating off her in waves. Following instincts he didn't even try to understand, he took a small step toward her until his arm was pressed firmly against her back. She moved her head just enough to see him out of the corner of her eye but didn't say anything, even as she leaned a little into the contact.

The elevator abruptly stopped, and Caleb immediately turned his attention toward the door.

"Everyone be ready," Jake said as the door slid open.

Caleb refrained from pointing out that they were all stuffed inside an eight-foot-by-eight-foot steel box. If there was anything waiting for them, they were screwed. But when the door finally slid all the way back, the corridor outside the elevator was completely empty. That didn't make him feel much better. One look at the familiar walls and floor and Caleb had no doubt that every member of the team was thinking the same thing he was. That they'd all been in a tunnel exactly like this not that long ago beneath the air base in Turkey. Yes, this one might be significantly larger than the one they'd been in the first time, with lights mounted every ten feet or so, but it had definitely been carved by the same creatures.

But at least that confirmed they were in the right place. With tunnels like these, the nukes had to be somewhere in here.

"Watch yourself," Jake warned as they started moving down

the tunnel. "I don't smell them right now, but those creatures obviously dug this tunnel. And as we learned the hard way, they can come out of nowhere."

Caleb quickly moved out to take point, instincts making him turn to look back and find Brielle, wanting to know where she was at all times. If he had his way, she'd be back on that damn elevator right this second. But it was too late for that now.

Behind him, he heard Hudson ask about the creatures Jake mentioned, but he didn't have time to worry about what the CIA agent knew or didn't know. If they ran into those things, the man would figure it out fast enough.

The tunnel network proved to be much larger and more complex than the one in Incirlik with full-size side tunnels branching off every fifty to a hundred feet. Harley and Sawyer moved up beside him, and he let their noses lead the way.

Caleb pointed out the first camera they passed. "If there's anyone in here, they're going to see us coming. Not a damn thing we can do about it."

"There are people in here for sure," Sawyer said. "In fact, there have been people moving through these tunnels very recently. A lot of them."

When they reached another large intersection, Sawyer pointed them down the one with the freshest scent tracks. The path took them through multiple twists and turns, and Caleb wondered why someone would build a complex like this in the middle of frigging nowhere. Worse, how many of those damn creatures would it have taken to dig a place like this?

"About a dozen people up ahead," Harley murmured, bringing her weapon up a little higher. "Coming this way fast."

The words were barely out of her mouth before a group of heavily armed men in dark tactical gear came running around the corner ahead of them. Caleb immediately started shooting, as did Harley and Sawyer.

Bullets skipped off the floor and walls, ricocheting everywhere. Even if Caleb knew he could survive any gunshot wound that wasn't through the head or heart, he still couldn't help flinching when a bullet zipped by and slammed into the stone wall nearby, peppering him with fragments. He might be an omega, but that didn't mean he was stupid. Getting shot hurt like a son of a bitch.

With no side tunnels nearby to slip into for cover, there was nothing he and his teammates could do but stand there in the middle of the main passageway and exchange gunfire with the men trying to kill them. Jake moved up beside Caleb, Harley, and Sawyer, their combined bodies shielding their more vulnerable teammates behind them.

The knowledge that Brielle was back there somewhere in danger was enough to almost make Caleb fall back to get closer to her. But he didn't because he knew she was safer behind him.

Then he heard a burst of automatic gunfire from back there. Caleb spun around to see more of the dark-garbed men running at them from that direction, heading straight for Brielle. In the warren of seemingly endless tunnels, some of the shooters had managed to slip around them.

Jake had given Brielle a small handgun, but he doubted it'd be much protection against their attackers. She'd be killed in seconds.

But then Brielle was running, her hand brushing Forrest's for a fraction of a second before she threw herself forward into a roll across the rough floor. Instead of doing it to get to safety, she threw herself at the closest bad guy, diving under the hail of bullets he sent her way.

What the hell does she think she's doing?

Caleb wasn't sure when he'd started running, but he realized he was charging toward Brielle faster than he'd ever moved before, his fangs and claws coming out without thought. But he was still ten or fifteen feet away when she jumped to her feet, closing the distance to the bad guy in front of her before the man could adjust his aim and hit her.

Brielle's left arm came up and knocked the man's assault rifle aside at the same time that her right fist snapped forward, slamming into the guy's throat. Once…twice…and a third time. Then she was ripping the weapon from the man's hand as he collapsed to the floor. Without hesitating, she twisted and pulled the trigger, spraying the passageway behind her. And even more amazing than that? She was actually hitting the bad guys.

What the hell?

Caleb stumbled to a halt as the last of the bad guys dropped unmoving to the floor. A quick glance back at his other teammates assured him they were all okay. The shooting was over, and there was no one left to fight.

Well…crap.

His inner omega must have figured out the implications of the sudden silence before Caleb did because his claws and fangs were already retracting. He turned back to Brielle, his instincts demanding he check to make sure she was okay. But before he could even take a step—much less ask her outright—she was already moving, heading toward Jake and the others. As she moved, she reached down and pulled a spare magazine from the body of one of the dark-garbed shooters, reloading her Russian-made assault rifle with a speed and efficiency that was as stunning as it was unexpected.

Again…what the hell?

Brielle continued past Caleb, barely throwing him a glance from the corner of her eye. Genevieve and Misty followed, leaving Forrest and Hudson to bring up the rear. The CIA agent gave him a confused look, confirming that he'd just seen what Caleb had and couldn't understand it, either.

Thirty seconds and two twisting turns in the main passageway later, they discovered what those men in black had been fighting so hard to keep them away from when they found three main tunnels all coming together in what could only be called a control room of sorts. At least, with all the tables, computers, monitors, and walls of blinking electronic equipment, that was the best way Caleb could describe it.

Caleb moved down the line of computers and monitors, trying to understand what he was looking at. Some of it was obvious, like the blurry video views of men and women running through tunnels similar to the ones he and his teammates had just been in. Many of them were dressed in the same dark tactical gear as the bad guys they'd taken down. But there were just as many wearing lab coats. A few were even wearing hard hats.

He had no idea who the people were, but one thing was obvious—they were getting away. Even as he watched, a whole load of them crammed into an elevator while the rest disappeared through a doorway that likely led to a stairwell. The part that concerned him the most, though, was that the elevator on the screen didn't look like the one they'd ridden down on.

"Should we try and stop them?" he asked, glancing over his shoulder at Jake.

"No," Jake said. "There are so many scent trails running all over this place, it would take hours to figure out which ones to follow. They'll be long gone before we ever get close."

"Guys," Hudson called out from where he stood in front of a bank of monitors a half a dozen feet away. "You really need to see this. I think we might be in trouble."

Caleb and everyone else except for Misty and Genevieve headed Hudson's way, leaving them to tap and poke at several of the nearer keyboards doing whatever computer geeks did at a time like this.

The moment he reached Hudson's side, Caleb immediately recognized what had him so concerned. The screen the CIA agent was staring at showed a cylindrical, gray object sitting horizontally on some kind of metal fixture with what looked like a thousand wires and cables running in and around the thing. The object was sitting in the middle of a big intersection of at least six tunnels surrounded by even more wires and cables of every shape and size.

"That's one of the stolen nukes," Jake said.

Caleb was stunned to hear Jake's heart beat faster. That worried Caleb more than he would ever admit. Jake was one cool cat. Caleb had never heard his heartbeat jump like that, not even in the middle of a violent firefight.

"What the hell are we looking at here, Misty?" Jake called out, glancing at her. "Please don't tell me they've rigged that thing to blow."

Misty didn't say anything for a several long moments as she continued to tap away at the keyboard. When she finally looked up, Caleb knew from the expression on her face that it was bad before she said a word.

"Okay, I won't tell you," she said.

Reaching out, she spun one of the computer screens around to face them. There were a series of numbers displayed there, and it didn't take a computer geek to figure out what they were for or what they meant. Caleb's stomach dropped. It was a countdown timer. And they had less than twenty minutes left before it reached all zeroes. He had a pretty good idea what happened then.

"I don't know why they're doing it," Misty said. "Maybe they want to see how powerful the nukes are. But that thing is going to blow—soon."

"Any chance of us finding it and stopping it from going off?" Hudson asked without a shred of hope in his voice.

And Caleb thought that *he* was cynical.

Misty looked over at Genevieve for a second before shaking her head. "I wouldn't even know which way to go to find it. We have no idea how big this tunnel complex might be. The nuke could be around the next corner or half a mile away. Hell, it could be right underneath us for all I know."

"Can you do your thing and get into the computer to stop the countdown?" Jes asked, her eyes widening as she saw the number click down under eighteen.

"We're going to find out," Misty said, reaching out to touch the computer in front of her.

"Wait!" Jake shouted, stepping forward with a hand out. "You can go in there, but you have two minutes to try and do your thing. That's it. Then you need to get out so we can escape before that thing blows. Understood?"

Misty nodded. A split second later, her eyes turned cloudy white and her face took on that signature *nobody's home* expression.

"What the hell just happened?" Hudson said, staring at Misty like she had two heads—and flippers.

Jake glanced at the countdown timer before looking at Hudson. "She's a technopath. She can merge her consciousness with any electronic system, slipping inside and communicating with it, for lack of a better word."

Hudson's mouth was hanging open a little as he glanced around the room, like he was once again waiting for someone to say, "Got you!" But obviously, that didn't happen.

Two minutes rolled off the countdown timer faster than Caleb could have ever dreamed possible. And then the counter was streaking toward fourteen minutes.

"Um…guys," Hudson said slowly. "Two minutes is up, and Misty isn't out of the computer yet. Should we…I don't know… give her a nudge or something?"

"It doesn't work that way," Forrest answered, moving closer to the woman he was in love with. It might not be a werewolf soulmate thing, but Caleb knew they had it bad for each other. "Once Misty is in a computer, she doesn't have any connection with her body. She won't feel anything if we try and get her attention that way."

"Well, we have to do something," Hudson said, glancing at the diminishing counter with a worried look. "The elevator ride alone will take us two or three minutes. Can't we just pull her away from the computer and snap her out of it?"

"Maybe you weren't listening to me before." Forrest's hand moved to rest on the weapon holstered at his side, like he'd shoot the CIA agent if the guy so much as took a step toward Misty. "That would trap her mind in the computer, and we'd never get her out."

No one said anything, not even Hudson. Instead, they all stood there staring at the counter, watching the time run out.

"Everyone out," Jake said suddenly. "Head for the elevator now. I'll stay here and grab Misty the second she comes out. I'll be right behind you."

Caleb appreciated the heroic offer, but it went over about as well as he expected, earning several amused snorts and even more firm "No ways!" and "Like hells!" Jes especially looked like she wanted to smack her mate. And it was obvious Forrest wasn't going anywhere without Misty.

Jake scowled. "If we all stay and that nuke goes off, it's over."

Before anyone could argue, Brielle sat in the chair beside Misty, slamming one hand on the side of the computer and the other on Misty's. Then Brielle's eyes went cloudy white, and her body went totally still, her face as expressionless as Misty's. To say Caleb was as stunned as everyone else in the room was an understatement.

"What did she just do?" Hudson asked, his eyes wide.

"She went into the computer to get Misty," Caleb said.

Grabbing a chair of his own, he flopped down in it. If he was going to go out in a brilliant flash of light, he might as well be comfortable.

CHAPTER 7

"Oh crap, Brielle. What the hell have you gotten yourself into now?"

Brielle carefully opened her eyes and slowly looked around, her head spinning as she tried to make sense of what she was seeing. One thing was for sure. She wasn't in the control room anymore.

Everything around her was in darkness, lit only by pulsing lines of white and blue neon that seemed to stretch away in every direction as far as her eyes could see. For a moment, she thought she was in another tunnel full of boxes, pipes, and cables. Then realization hit her, and she began to tremble.

She was inside the computer she'd just touched.

She moved to put her hands on her hips to keep from hyperventilating, only to quickly discover that losing her breath probably wasn't going to be an issue since her body apparently hadn't come with her on this trip.

She couldn't put into words how mind-numbingly terrifying it was to look down and see nothing but a vaporous collection of light where her body should be and arcs of crackling energy in place of where her arms, legs, and fingers should be.

Touching Misty and following her into the computer might end up being the biggest mistake of her life. But standing there waiting with everyone else as the countdown timer had clicked closer and closer to zero wasn't an option any more than leaving Misty behind to die in a nuclear blast. So she'd done the only thing she could do. Touched Misty's hand so she could bring her out of her trance—or whatever she was in.

Brielle hadn't been sure what she'd expected. Suffice to say, it wasn't this.

Knowing she had no time to waste if she was going to find Misty and get the both of them out of this place in time, Brielle forced herself to calm down and focus, trying to let her gift take control and guide her.

That's the way it had always worked with her supernatural ability from the very first time it had manifested itself when she was a kid. She'd never understood how touching a person could let her use their skills and knowledge, be it understanding a foreign language or firing a weapon she'd never even seen before. She touched them and simply knew what to do.

She only hoped it worked that way this time.

"Find Misty," she murmured, holding her nonexistent breath until she saw a little wisp of neon appear ahead of her, trailing off into the distance like a trail of breadcrumbs. She didn't know what the lights were or where they might lead her, but she moved to follow them anyway.

Brielle hadn't given any thought to how she could walk in her present form, seeing as she didn't really have legs to speak of. But before she even had a chance to worry, the bizarre alien landscape was zipping by beneath her, the little balls of light disappearing with an inaudible pop as she passed them. She seemed to be moving fast, into and out of little boxes that a corner of her mind recognized as microchips, processors, and network server components. But for all her speed, she didn't feel any wind. In this place—in this form—she guessed that concept didn't exist.

Many of the things she moved past and through probably would have made sense to the part of her that had access to Misty's gifts, but at the moment, she was too focused on finding Caleb's teammate to pay much attention to the landscape.

Brielle almost missed Misty in her rush to move fast, mostly because the young woman's amorphous shape was almost lost in the tangle of circuit board traces and wires she was lying among. Brielle wasn't even sure what it was that convinced her that the dimly glowing figure was Misty.

She just knew.

Brielle moved closer, alarmed at the scurrying…things… roving over Misty's form. They were glowing wisps similar to the balls she had followed but darker in color, almost menacing. *Intruder protection software*, that little voice told her as she jumped down and began to smack at the blobs, the arcs of energy that made up her fingers flicking them away as fast as she could. Even as she worked, she swore she could see the light coming from within Misty dimming even more. The fact that the things trying to kill Misty were kind of like bugs was enough to make Brielle's not-really-there body shudder. She *hated* bugs.

Once all the gnawing creatures were gone, it was impossible to miss the damage they'd left behind. There were little tears in Misty's virtual form. Like the things had been eating her. Brielle shivered all over again.

She'd hoped Misty would wake up—or at least moan or something—but she didn't so much as move.

Praying Misty was still alive, Brielle leaned closer, mentally picturing herself scooping Misty into her arms. It didn't quite go the way she'd planned. She melded with Misty more than picked her up. But the important thing was that Misty was off the ground… or circuit board…or…whatever. That was the only thing that mattered.

Brielle turned and started running again. Or whatever you'd called an amorous shape zipping through a digital world at light speed. Regardless, she moved fast, letting her instincts guide her, hoping she got the two of them out of this computer hellhole quickly. Brielle had no idea how long she'd been in there and really had no desire to finally pop out only to discover the countdown timer had reached zero.

One second, she was zipping and praying, and the next it felt like she was being shoved through a spaghetti strainer. Light flooded her eyes, overwhelming her senses until everything began to darken again. Then there were strong arms wrapping around her and a warm, deep voice calling her name.

Her eyes fluttered open to find Caleb leaning over her, his beautiful eyes filled with concern. "Caleb?" she whispered, the sight of him almost taking her breath away.

"Brielle is back with us," he called out, lifting his head to look at someone off to the side, out of her line of vision. "What about Misty?"

"She's a little out of it, but she's okay," Forrest answered. "Let's move!"

Brielle fully intended to stand up, ready to run out of there as fast as she could, but Caleb didn't give her the chance. Instead, he scooped her into his arms, cradled her against his chest, and took off running. This time she could feel the rush of the wind at the speed of their movement, along with the flex and twist of his arm and chest muscles as she cuddled against him. He was so damn warm underneath his winter jacket that she couldn't resist the urge to press her face against him and revel in the sensation.

Beside them, Forrest was carrying a barely conscious Misty. By the time they reached the elevator, Forrest, Jes, Genevieve, and Hudson were gasping for air while Caleb and the other werewolves might have been out for a stroll down the street.

The tension in the air was palpable as they waited for the elevator to arrive. Brielle almost had a panic attack right there in Caleb's arms as she had a terrifying thought: What if the elevator wasn't working now? What if the bad guys had disabled it?

But then the door slid silently open, and she sagged with relief. As soon as everyone was inside, Harley pushed the button multiple times, as if that would help make the thing go faster. Caleb could have put her down at any point, but he didn't, and Brielle didn't complain. She felt safer this way.

"How much time do we have?" she asked, wincing a little as her voice broke the silence that filled the elevator.

"Less than five minutes," Sawyer said, not even bothering to look her way. Instead, he stood there staring straight ahead like everyone else, waiting for the damn elevator to get to ground level and the door to open.

Crap.

"Is that enough time for us to get to safety?" she asked.

Even if Caleb and the other werewolves could somehow carry all of them at once—which they couldn't—Brielle couldn't see how they'd make it to the vehicles they'd left just outside the edge of the village.

"We have to hope the warhead is far enough underground that the blast wave and fireball don't wipe us out once we're on the surface," Genevieve said.

Double crap.

When the elevator doors finally opened, they all took off running, moving as fast as they could.

"Four minutes!" Sawyer called out as they burst outside.

Fresh snow was coming down, and more than one member of the STAT team slipped a little as they raced across the fenced-in area.

"Everyone in the back of the big truck!" Caleb shouted, pointing toward the dark-green military-looking vehicle with the uncovered cargo section.

While the ride in the back would be freezing, Brielle realized it was the only vehicle large enough to hold the whole team.

Everyone piled in the back as fast as they could while Caleb carried her around to the driver's side door. Opening it with one hand, he pretty much tossed her inside. She bounced on the canvas-covered bench seat and slid all the way over to the far door.

Brielle barely had a chance to right herself before Caleb was ripping wires out from under the truck's dashboard. He snapped some in half, stripping the ends bare with his teeth. She was about to ask if he knew what he was doing, but then the truck's big engine rumbled to life. And he shouted out the window for everyone to hold on tight.

The partially open gate went down under the truck's heavy front bumper and then the engine was roaring as Caleb pushed the vehicle to insane speeds on the snow-covered road.

"You might want to slow down before you kill us," Brielle said, grabbing hold of the side of the bench seat and desperately searching for a seat belt that didn't exist.

Caleb pushed the gas pedal down to the floor, the rear of the vehicle swerving violently to the right before straightening out and zooming down the rut-filled road through the center of the village. "Okay, I'll slow down"—he glanced at her—"when you tell me you're fine being toasted by a nuclear blast."

Brielle didn't have a comeback for that one, so she stared out the windshield—which she could barely see through, even with the wipers going, because the snow was coming down so heavily—and held on for dear life.

"Two minutes!" Sawyer called from the back of the truck.

They made it through the village, past the last farmhouse where they'd left their own vehicles, and started up the winding road leading out of the valley. Although *road* may have been something of an exaggeration. *Trail* was probably more accurate. Regardless, Caleb drove as fast as he could, the back wheels of the big truck spinning like crazy and kicking up long plumes of snow and ice. Every few seconds, they'd lose traction completely, the vehicle sliding toward the deep ditch along the side of the path. Brielle held her breath every time it happened. If they got stuck, it was over.

"Less than a minute!" Sawyer shouted. "You're going to need to drive faster! We have to get out of the valley and over the top of the ridgeline or we won't stand a chance!"

Caleb cursed but didn't respond, too focused on keeping the truck centered on the slippery road. Brielle could tell from how hard he was gripping the wheel that he was as worried as everyone else.

"You're going to get us out of here. I know it," she told him, putting every ounce of faith and trust into those simple words.

They must have worked because Caleb took a deep breath of the freezing cold air, dropped the truck down to a lower gear, and forced it up the mountain even faster than before.

They were a hundred meters shy of the ridgeline crest when the ground rumbled under them. Eyes wide, Brielle chanced a quick look in the side mirror. Her heart froze when she saw a ten-foot-high wave of earth and snow chasing them up the valley slope.

"Faster, Caleb!" she said.

But it was too late. A second later, the back end of the big truck lifted up, and they were shoved forward like a ball batted by a child. Inertia slammed her back in the seat, and then Caleb was wrapping a big, strong arm around her, dragging her close to him and holding her tight.

The rear of the truck continued to rise, and they began to tip. Brielle feared for everyone in the back, praying they wouldn't all end up crushed and broken. But Caleb fought the steering wheel, somehow maintaining control and keeping the front of the vehicle on the road.

The impact as the truck slammed back down shook every bone in her body, and Brielle felt her teeth clack together. They bounced several times as the vehicle slid in a slow sideways drift before finally slamming into a snowbank with a thud.

As they came to a full stop, the truck facing down the hill into what was left of the village, a blaze of white light filled the night sky, dazzling her sight. For one terrified moment, Brielle thought it was the nuclear fireball forming and that they were all seconds from death. But then the blaze of light coalesced into a beam of pure energy shooting straight toward the heavens, so intense it was hard to look at, its origin at the remains of the little building and the tower that still stood there.

One moment the beam of light was there, and the next it was gone, leaving a ghost image behind in her eyes like she'd stared at the sun for too long.

"What the hell just happened?" Harley asked numbly from behind them, and Brielle turned to look out the cracked back window to see that everyone had miraculously managed to stay in the bed of the truck. They seemed pretty beat up, but they were all alive. "What was that bright light?"

Nobody had an answer to that, including Brielle. They all merely looked at each other—when they weren't staring at the leveled remains of the village down in the valley. The place hadn't been much, but now it was completely gone.

"Right now, I'm a little bit more concerned with whether we're going to die from radiation poisoning," Forrest murmured, Misty awake and cradled carefully in his arms as he leaned against the rear tailgate. "We were less than a mile away when that nuke went off."

"I'm pretty sure all the radiation was contained underground," Genevieve said, still looking back at the village. "The fireball never broke the surface, so I think we're okay."

"Think?" Jake asked, his voice flat.

All Genevieve could do was shrug, which wasn't exactly the most comforting gesture in the world.

"Caleb, get us the hell out of here," Jake growled. "We don't have a clue what the hell just happened, but I'd feel a lot better trying to figure it out somewhere farther away."

Caleb grunted, shoving the truck back into first gear, then wrapping his arm back around Brielle's shoulders and pulling her close to his side again.

CHAPTER 8

Ukraine

"AND WHAT THE HELL WOULD YOU HAVE DONE DIFFERENTLY?"
Jake demanded, leaning forward in his chair to glare at the people
on the other end of the video camera on the conference table.
"Your team wouldn't have gotten to Surinda any faster than we
did, they wouldn't have been able to stop the nuke from going off,
and they damn sure wouldn't have survived the shootout and the
nuclear blast without casualties. At least my team accomplished
that. *And* got out with intel on what they were doing under that
village."

The guy on one of the monitors—some jackass from the
CIA—immediately shouted something back in reply, but before
Caleb could figure out what it was, the rest of the people on the
other screens joined in, everyone fighting to make themselves
heard.

Caleb leaned back in his chair next to Brielle, glad they weren't
yelling at him. He definitely didn't envy Jake being the team/pack
leader. Tuning them out, Caleb turned his attention to the Odessa
city map he'd pulled up on his cell phone. Hopefully, he could find
a place to get something to eat after the briefing was over. He was
frigging starving.

They'd flown straight back from Siberia to Ukraine, then
come directly from the plane to this CIA safe house in Odessa.
The briefing had already been in progress back in DC when Misty
and Forrest set up the computer, with tempers flaring and people
yelling. They hadn't even gotten a chance to grab a cup of coffee
before entering the fray.

Jake had told the CIA everything that had happened—leaving out the supernatural parts, of course—then Hudson had added a few details. At least the guy was nice enough to not out any of them. Not that it mattered. Things had gone downhill from there, regardless.

Caleb found a pub on the map that looked fairly close. A quick search on his cell phone told him that the place offered pizza and beer, which sounded about perfect to him. He leaned over and covertly showed the map and phone to Brielle, who quickly nodded her head. He almost laughed when her stomach growled. She was as hungry as he was.

He and Brielle hadn't had a chance to talk since the stuff that had happened in the tunnels, but he noticed she had stuck close to his side the whole way back to Odessa. She'd even fallen asleep with her head on his shoulder on the plane. To say it had felt nice would be an understatement.

When she pulled back and focused her attention on Jake and everything else going on at the table, Caleb put away his phone and took the opportunity to glance around the big room. This was, without a doubt, the largest classified video teleconference he'd ever been part of. Besides McKay and the normal analysts from STAT and Hudson's homies from the CIA, they were also graced with the presence of a gaggle of suits from the National Security Agency. He supposed it made sense that the NSA had gotten invited to this little goat rope, considering everyone assumed that at least some of the missing nukes would end up being used against the U.S. at some point. Still, he couldn't imagine how having yet another spy organization involved was going to make this mission any easier to deal with.

But as crazy as it was to have all the alphabet soup organizations on the call, it was the nerd herd from the Lawrence Livermore National Labs in California that really took the cake. Seriously, one of those guys was wearing an actual pocket protector. Apparently, they'd been called in to figure out what the whole beam of light thing was that they'd seen. Because it wasn't like anyone else had a clue.

"Enough!" McKay finally said, his voice easily overriding those from the CIA and NSA, but only because he'd turned off their microphones. They were still yelling, but no one on this side could hear them any longer. It was kinda hilarious. Juvenile, yes, but hilarious nonetheless.

"I'm well aware that both of your agencies have voiced your concerns repeatedly about STAT having jurisdiction over this particular situation," McKay said firmly, his expression hard as he stared straight at the camera. "I'm also well aware that the reason you're complaining so much now is because your gripes have gotten you nowhere. So I'll cut to the chase and make this simple. You were invited to this call to help. If you don't wish to help, I'll disconnect you from the call, and STAT will continue dealing with this situation on our own."

Caleb almost chuckled as McKay's words hit home, and the suits from both the CIA and NSA sat back in their respective chairs like they'd been slapped. The message was clear. *Get on board or we'll take our ball and play the game without you.* Considering he was a suit, Caleb had to admit McKay wasn't half-bad. Sometimes, he could even be sort of badass.

"Now, what do we have on that beam of light our team reported seeing?" McKay asked once the microphone connection had been reestablished with the CIA and NSA, moving the topic of conversation away from who could have done the Siberian mission better and onto something more important. "Any theories on what it was?"

"More than a theory," the nerdy guy from Lawrence Livermore with the pocket protector announced, sitting up taller in his chair. "What your team saw in Siberia was a fully functional nuclear-pumped laser being fired."

The briefing room took on that silence where you could hear that proverbial pin drop…at least until Caleb snorted.

"Nuclear laser? Are you serious?" he asked. "Sounds like something from a sci-fi movie. Or James Bond."

"Very serious," Pocket Protector announced, adjusting his glasses, his face solemn. "Lawrence Livermore has worked on the concept off and on since the seventies. We've never done much beyond proving the theory with a series of small-scale tests, but at one point, the technology was going to be the cornerstone of Reagan's Strategic Defense Initiative, with nuclear lasers being used to take down hundreds of inbound intercontinental ballistic missiles—or ICBMs, at a time—destroying them before they ever reached the lower atmosphere."

Well, damn.

"And you think what we saw in Siberia was a test of this nuclear laser system?" Jake asked. "Someone using a B61 warhead to push the concept to the next level?"

"With the setup you described? There's no doubt." Pocket Protector turned his gaze on Jake. "They used the twists and turns of the tunnels to strip out most of the blast and thermal energy while capturing the gamma, X-ray, and neutron energy. But whoever pulled this off did more than push the concept to the next level. They've advanced it beyond anything we've even considered. It's decades beyond current technological capabilities."

Caleb leaned forward, resting his forearms on the table. "This is all very interesting in a Bill-Nye-the-Science-Guy kind of way," he said drily. "But why do we care that somebody used a nuke to shoot a laser beam into space?"

"Because they didn't simply shoot the laser into space," one of the suits from the CIA said.

The man tapped a few keys on a keyboard just out of view. A few seconds later, a collage of pictures showed up on their side, the large monitor making the images pop off the screen. The photos had obviously been taken from far away, then enlarged to allow whoever was looking at them to see the details. Caleb wasn't sure what he was even looking at. In one photo, the thing kinda resembled burnt, twisted metal sitting in shallow water. Other photos showed pieces of debris along a smoldering hillside.

"As I was saying," the CIA guy added, "that laser beam wasn't shot randomly into space. It was aimed directly at a satellite positioned above Siberia in low earth orbit. That satellite, in turn, bounced the beam off several others until it was split into two separate beams and redirected back to earth. The pictures you're seeing now are the results of those beams hitting their targets."

From the expressions on their faces, this was obviously news to everyone on the call. Caleb heard murmurs of concern from not only the NSA and Lawrence Livermore's contingent but McKay and his STAT teammates, too.

"The pictures on the left were taken at the Sangnam-ni Missile Base located in North Korea, about 250 kilometers north of the DMZ," the CIA agent added. "What you're looking at are the remains of a Hwasong-10 intermediate-range ballistic missile. The radiation signature we picked up from the site confirms the missile was equipped with a nuclear warhead."

Complete silence reigned now, unless Caleb counted the sounds of elevated heart rates as some of his teammates realized the implications of what the man said. Caleb's heart was beating a little faster, too. Someone had used this laser thing to blow up a North Korean weapon. Wars had been started for less.

"The pictures on the right were taken near the Yulin Naval Base on Hainan Island, China," the CIA guy continued. "The twisted metal just visible above the water is all that's left of one of their Jin-class nuclear-powered ballistic missile submarines. It was destroyed at nearly the exact same time the missile in North Korea was hit. That type of submarine can carry multiple nuclear-capable sub-launched ballistic missiles. We don't know how many were on this particular sub, but the entire base has been evacuated, which suggests that the contamination release wasn't trivial."

"Holy hell," Forrest murmured.

Caleb silently agreed. This was beyond bad. World War III may have already started for all they knew.

"North Korea remains completely silent, not even acknowledging the event occurred, while China is downplaying the severity of the situation, claiming it's a minor issue with the sub's reactor core," another CIA agent said, her voice grim. "But behind the scenes, tensions are high. Russia is trying to claim they had nothing to do with it, but everyone knows the laser beam originated in Siberia. The lid's staying on the boiling pot at the moment, but barely."

Caleb zoned out again as everyone started arguing about whether Russia really was to blame for this. The nerd herd at Lawrence Livermore refused to believe anyone in Russia had the technical know-how, while the NSA thought it was a rogue movement within the Russian government behind the attacks willing to start a war to gain what they were after. The CIA insisted the Russians were scurrying around in a panic, trying to figure out who was framing them for this mess. That only led to more arguments and debates between the three agencies.

It was enough to give Caleb a headache, trying to keep track of all the different moving pieces and the possibilities.

Caleb's stomach was about to crawl out to find some food on its own by the time the briefing was finished. The end results of all the talking and complaining were that STAT would continue to lead the operation in the field while the CIA and NSA continued to provide intel support, with everyone's attention focused on finding the other nineteen missing nukes—not only where they might be located but also who had the technical know-how to build a nuclear-powered laser as strong as the one fired in Siberia.

"Can we go eat now?" Caleb asked the second the last person dropped off the video teleconference. "I'm so hungry I'll even pay."

Most of the team seemed on board with the idea, especially when Caleb mentioned there was a pub that served pizza within walking distance of the safe house. But then Misty said she wanted to start looking for clues on who'd built the facility in Surinda, mentioning she'd seen something while inside the computer there that might help point her in the right direction. Forrest immediately said he'd stay with her.

Genevieve begged off next, saying she was going to start researching the satellite system that had been used to route the laser beam from Siberia to the two target areas. "It shouldn't be that hard to figure out who owns those satellites. Knowing that should lead us to the people behind this whole thing."

Jake and Jes decided to stay behind to help her, leaving Caleb, Brielle, Harley, Sawyer, and Hudson. Caleb was kinda surprised Brielle wanted to come with them. While she'd looked eager to grab dinner earlier, he could tell that she had a lot of other stuff on her mind at the moment.

"Hey," he said, pulling her off a little to the side as the others started getting their coats on and taking orders for what everyone staying behind wanted to eat. "I understand if you want to stay back here and work on trying to find a new lead on Julian. I'll even go through all the intel reports with you again and see if we can figure out where your brother went after that last photo we have of him here in Odessa."

Brielle gazed up at him with those beautiful dark eyes of hers for a long moment. He tried to read her expression and decipher what she might be thinking based on how she was looking at him, hoping she understood how much he wanted to help her. When she finally smiled, it did absolutely stupid things to his insides.

"Thanks for the offer, but I think I'd rather get out of here and focus on something other than my brother for a while," she said.

"Works for me." He grabbed her coat, holding it up for her so she could slip it on. "If it's a distraction you're looking for, you're in luck. It's one of the few things I'm good at."

They were halfway out the door, moving fast to catch up with the others, when he heard her murmur something that sounded like *I'm sure there's something else you're good at.* But since he wasn't sure what she'd meant, he decided to let it go, even as his inner werewolf challenged him to show Brielle exactly how right she was.

CHAPTER 9

BRIELLE PULLED HER COAT A CLOSED AS THEY WALKED TOWARD the pub Caleb had found on the map. She assumed being close to the water had something to do with how cool it was out, but after being in the frigid temperatures of Siberia, the brisk evening air in Odessa felt downright balmy.

As they walked, she couldn't help but notice the way Caleb stayed close to her side. It wasn't obvious at first, but when two guys passed a little too near her and he actually bared his teeth a little at them, it was hard to miss.

His behavior didn't surprise her. Ever since she'd come to in those tunnels under Surinda, he'd been acting protective, carrying her when she could have run, putting his arm around her and holding her close so she could fall asleep on his shoulder during the flight to Odessa. Even his offer to stay and help her go through old intel reports in the hopes of finding her brother had come from a place of concern. He knew she was worried about Julian and had gone out of his way to try and make her feel better.

Brielle had to admit, she found herself liking the attention more than she'd ever would have thought. She'd spent her whole life taking care of her brother, and it had left her little time for romance or anything even close to it. That a man like Caleb would look at her like she was the most precious thing on earth was more than nice. Even if she knew it couldn't turn into anything. Why would a guy as amazing as he was ever want to get involved with her? When she wasn't bailing her brother out of whatever problem he'd gotten himself into, she was trying to figure out how to have a normal life.

The pub Caleb led them into was nothing like what Brielle had imagined. The walk through the charming streets of Odessa had already shown her that the city was a lot more modern than she'd expected, with beautiful buildings and sidewalks illuminated by ornate streetlamps. But still, walking into the pub and seeing the long, polished bar that stretched the length of the interior along with a stage set up on one side and bright, exposed-bulb signs decorating the walls was surprising. This pub would have fit right in back home in Lyon.

Thankfully, it was the middle of the week and relatively late at night on top of that, so the place was almost empty. No band was playing on the small stage, and only a few people sat at the bar, chatting softly as they drank their beers.

Like she'd told Caleb, forgetting about her brother for a while was the entire reason she'd agreed to come out with him tonight in the first place. She needed somewhere she could hang out and unwind for a little while. If that included something delicious to eat and maybe a drink or two, even better. She wanted to do anything but think about the fact that they hadn't found Julian yet. This looked like the perfect place to do that.

The blond waitress who met them at the door pegged Caleb and his teammates for Americans right away, welcoming them to the city, adding that they got a lot of tourists there.

"Are you here for food or just some drinks?" she asked.

When Caleb said they were there for dinner, the woman took them to one of the larger tables in the back of the pub, though her eyes widened at the amount of food they ordered.

"Ten large pizzas for the five of you?" she asked. "And five more for takeout?"

Brielle almost laughed at the expression on the woman's face. She'd been with Caleb and his team for a few days, so she'd already seen how much they ate, and she was still amazed at how much food he and the other werewolves could eat at one time.

After the waitress gave the order to the kitchen, she brought beer for Caleb and the other guys as well as wine for her and Harley. The moment she walked away, the conversation immediately centered on the briefing from earlier.

"Do you really think someone is trying to start a war?" Sawyer asked, looking around the table at the rest of them. "I mean, what else could whoever is responsible for this expect after taking out a North Korean missile and a Chinese submarine?"

Brielle didn't know much about geopolitics, but it wasn't that difficult to figure out that firing a huge laser at two extremely aggressive militaristic neighbors was a great way to start a war, which made her wonder why Russia would do it. Was anyone that suicidal?

They were still talking about who might be behind it and the ramifications when their pizzas showed up. Brielle was surprised when Caleb, Harley, and Hudson admitted their own country could be behind it as much as anyone else's, essentially "stealing" their own nukes and making it look like someone else had done it. That seemed crazy to Brielle. Sawyer, on the other hand, insisted that the UK would never do anything so despicable, which made Harley laugh so hard she nearly choked on her food.

The conversation lightened considerably after that, and Brielle found herself laughing along with everyone else. She couldn't remember when she'd had this much fun. Friends were yet another thing she'd been forced to do without in her screwed-up version of a life.

"Can I ask you something, Brielle?" Hudson asked in between bites of cheese pizza, interrupting Sawyer's bizarre rant about the difference between British and American bacon.

She nodded and sipped her wine.

"How were you able to slip inside the computer to get Misty out?" he asked. "I have to admit that I barely understand how Misty was able to go in there herself, but from what Forrest told me, her technopath talent is unique. It's kind of incredible that you just happen to be able to do the same thing."

Brielle set down her glass, not sure how to explain it. "Um…"

Beside her, Caleb glowered at Hudson across the table. "Jake made it clear you'd have to wait until everyone else on the team trusted you enough to tell you their secrets."

To his credit, Hudson returned Caleb's look with a glare of his own. "I didn't realize Brielle was on the team. When did that happen?"

"The moment she saved Misty and the rest of us down in those tunnels," Caleb snarled, and Brielle was shocked to see his eyes glowing ever so slightly blue. "So you need to back off. Now."

Brielle reached out to gently place her hand on Caleb's arm where it rested on the table between them. "Calm down," she said, glancing around the pub to make sure no one had picked up on the sudden tension at their table. "I don't mind that Hudson asked. For better or worse, I knew everything would come out the second I decided to use my ability to help Misty. I might as well tell you now, since there's no reason to keep trying to hide it."

Caleb gazed at her for a moment, then looked at Hudson, blue flaring brightly in his eyes for a split second before they returned to their normal color. "If you spread a word of what she tells you to anyone, I will frigging end you. Got it?"

Brielle squeezed Caleb's forearm, giving him a smile when he glanced at her. "Caleb, it's okay. I'm good."

She held his gaze until the tension in his body relaxed a bit. Not completely, of course, because she got the impression he was never completely chill. She'd realized that within minutes of first meeting him weeks ago. He'd always be a live wire, a dangerous man poised to cause damage.

When Brielle was sure Caleb was as in control as he was likely ever going to be, she turned and looked at Hudson to see him sitting there waiting as patiently as Harley and Sawyer for her answer.

"Technically, I don't have the same ability as Misty," she said. "Or any special abilities at all."

"I think Misty would beg to differ," Sawyer said with a smile after taking a long sip of his beer. "She'd be dead right now if it weren't for you. Hell, so would the rest of us."

Brielle picked up the slice of cheese pizza from her plate and took a bite, chewing slowly. It was loaded with mozzarella, and the tomato sauce had a touch of sweetness to it, just the way she liked it. "I didn't mean it that way. I meant that I don't have any special abilities of my own. I could only help Misty because my gift let me *borrow* her abilities. That's how my thing works. I can sense the abilities that a person possesses, and once I touch them, I absorb their knowledge and skills, and for a period of time, I can do what they do."

Beside her, Caleb seemed as surprised by that as everyone else.

"How close do you have to be to a person to sense their abilities?" Harley asked. "I mean, can you get a read on everyone in this pub?"

She nodded, letting out a long sigh. "Yes. I know it sounds crazy, but while all of you see a room full of people with blond or brown hair, blue eyes or hazel, leather jackets or wool, I see abilities."

Brielle gestured toward the people at the bar sitting with their backs to them. "That guy is good at darts, that one sings in the shower, the woman to their left can write with both hands at once, and the petite girl next to her can drink a gallon of milk and eat a loaf of bread in under a minute. And that guy all by himself down at the very end of the bar? He can breathe underwater."

As she expected, everyone stared at her until Hudson shook his head in shock.

"That is frigging amazing," he said.

She nibbled on her pizza. "It's exhausting is what it is. It's always there, and if I don't force myself to shut it all out, I'll be picking up on the abilities of every person within a thousand miles. Farther, sometimes." She glanced at Caleb. "That's how I tracked down supernaturals for Yegor, by the way."

He tilted his head sideways, regarding her with a curious expression. "That's how you were suddenly able to speak that obscure Indonesian language after you touched that man's hand in the restaurant, isn't it? And after you touched Forrest when we first entered the tunnels in Siberia, you could suddenly fight hand-to-hand and fire those automatic weapons, right?"

Brielle nodded. She'd thought he might have noticed her touching that one goon in the restaurant but figured Caleb had been too distracted to notice her brush his teammate's hand with hers down in the tunnels in Surinda. It had been rather chaotic.

"Wait a minute," Hudson said. "You're telling me that you can mimic the abilities of anyone you touch, human or not?"

That comment earned him low growls and a snarl from Caleb, Harley, and Sawyer.

"Just because we're werewolves, that doesn't mean we aren't human, you jackass," Harley said angrily.

Hudson dropped the crust of the piece of pizza he'd been working on and held up his hands in surrender, looking around the table. "Point taken. Poor choice of words. Hearing Brielle can borrow talents from anyone she touched caught me a little off guard. For some reason, I assumed Hudson it was limited to other supernaturals. You have to admit, it's kind of mind-blowing to think she can pick up things like languages or how to fire a weapon."

"Or run like an Olympic sprinter, do martial arts like a black belt, shoot sniper rifles like a combat veteran, cook a five-course meal like a Parisian chef, or eat more hot dogs than a competitive eater," Brielle added, just to make sure they got the full picture. "Not that I'd ever want to do that last one. I don't even like hot dogs."

Caleb looked like he was about to take exception to that comment, but Hudson interrupted before he could say anything. "I realize now why this wasn't something you wanted everyone to know about. With this ability, there's literally no limit to what you can do. Hell, you could take over the world if you wanted to."

Brielle couldn't help but laugh harder than she'd laughed in a long time. "You can have the world. I only want my brother back and a normal life. Besides, it turns out there are limitations when it comes to borrowing gifts that would interfere with me taking over the world."

"Such as?" Caleb prompted, biting off half the slice of pizza in his hand in one go.

"Well, for one thing, I'm forced to take the good with the bad when I'm borrowing someone's abilities. So if they can fight really well but can't run any faster than an angry tortoise, then I'm stuck being a slow-moving fighter."

Hudson frowned like he was actually disappointed by this facet of her gift. "That sucks."

"Tell me about it," she said. "I can also only borrow a specific person's abilities once, and then it's out of reach forever. I'm also limited on how long I get to keep that skill. The stronger the ability, the shorter the duration I get to use it. So while I was able to speak that Indonesian language in Zagreb for almost four hours, I could only mimic Forrest's fighting style for about an hour, maybe a bit longer if I pushed it. And Misty's abilities to slip inside a computer?" She shrugged. "I doubt I could have held on to that gift for more than thirty or forty minutes. The one-time use and the short time span I have to work with kind of limits my chances of taking over the world."

Around the table, Caleb and his teammates seemed to consider everything she'd said as they went back to eating. Brielle finished the slice on her plate, then reached for another, stunned to see that they'd almost polished off all five pizzas. Well, Caleb, Harley, and Sawyer had done most of the damage, but she and Hudson had helped.

"I have another question about your gift," Harley said, picking up her glass of wine.

Brielle was okay with that. She'd already told them so much

that it didn't make sense to hold anything back now. In for a penny and all that.

"You talked about there being a time limit for how long you can use another person's gift," Harley said curiously. "Does that mean you can't use someone else's abilities until the first one is gone?"

"I can jump from person to person if I want, but that's exhausting," Brielle said. "When I broke Julian out of that prison in Turkey, I had to borrow from about a dozen people, one after the other. I was so weak by the time we got free that I nearly passed out. If I'd pushed any harder, I likely would have killed myself."

Out of the corner of her eye, Brielle saw Caleb tense all over again. His eyes even flared with that blue glow for a second. She would have asked what that was about, but then the waitress came by with the check, telling them the takeout pizzas were ready whenever they were.

Harley, Sawyer, and Craig seemed more than ready to get back to the safe house, and considering it was almost midnight at the end of one hell of a long day, Brielle couldn't blame them. But with the nap she'd had on the plane, she wasn't ready to call it a night quite yet.

"I think I'm going to walk around and see some more of the city," she announced as they walked out of the pub. "I've never been to Odessa before and figure I might as well see some of the sights while we're here."

"I'll go with you," Caleb said, handing the pizza boxes he'd been carrying to Hudson. "Nobody should be out wandering the city alone, especially at night," he added when Brielle turned and raised a brow in his direction.

She decided not to berate him too much, since she would prefer to have some company if she was going to walk around a city she wasn't familiar with at this time of night. Harley warned them not to stay out too late since they had no idea when they'd need to leave for wherever the chase for the nukes led them next.

"And call if you get yourselves in trouble," Sawyer said as the three of them started walking away. "Or even if you get a sense you're being followed or anything like that."

Brielle couldn't imagine what sort of trouble she and Caleb might get into or who'd be following them but assured Sawyer they would all the same.

Caleb seemed content to let Brielle take the lead on their late-night stroll, falling into step beside her as she turned left on the main road outside the pub and headed that way, not familiar enough with the city to have any particular destination in mind. He didn't say anything as they wandered but simply walked along beside her as she took in the sights along the brightly lit streets.

She realized she'd picked a good part of the city to explore as she caught sight of the beautiful Odessa Opera and Ballet Theater. The ornate neobaroque architecture of the circular building made her wish it were open so they could go inside and explore, but since it wasn't, she contented herself with digging out her cell phone and taking photos of the exterior. From there, they wandered past Vorontsov Palace, where they stopped again so she could get more photos, once more wishing they were on this little sightseeing walk during the day, so she'd be able to see even more of the historical landmarks.

When they reached the top of the impressive Potemkin Stairs fifteen minutes later, they both stopped again, this time on the bridge, and gazed out at the shimmering expanse of the Black Sea beyond. Brielle was so caught up in the lights of the city sparkling off the water that she didn't realize Caleb had spoken.

"What?" she said, glancing at him.

"I asked how old were you when you first realized you could borrow other people's abilities by touching them," he said patiently, as if realizing she'd been lost in thought.

She turned to gaze out at the water, a smile curving her lips.

"Remember that family friend I told you about? The one who let me work in his grocery store?"

"Uh-huh."

"Well, one night he was doing the store's inventory when his wife called and told him she needed him at home. I knew he was stressed about getting the inventory done, but I couldn't offer to help because I didn't even know how to use the computer program. He was in such a hurry that he almost left without his coat, and when I handed it to him, my fingers brushed his, and all of a sudden, I *knew* how to do the inventory. I finished the whole thing in a few hours, which surprised the heck out of him. Especially since I could barely remember how to even start the program the next day."

"That must have freaked you out," he murmured as they started walking down the broad stairs.

"Not really." She stuck her hands in the pockets of her coat. "I wasn't even fifteen years old at the time and was so focused on everything going on in my life that this one weird moment barely registered on my radar. It wasn't until a year or so later, after the same scenario played over and over with different people, that I finally figured out what was happening. And yeah, at that point, it did freak me out."

"Did Julian ever figure out what you could do?" Caleb asked, pausing along with her on one of the steps to watch a big cruise ship sail into the harbor. "I mean, at some point before you helped him escape from that Turkish prison."

She nodded, standing close enough to Caleb that she could feel the heat his big body generated in the cold night air. "Julian can be a bit slow sometimes—and since I'm his sister, I'm allowed to say that—but he noticed after I slipped up and borrowed someone's martial arts skills to fend off a mugger as we were walking home. After that, he wanted me to use my ability all the time, while I went out of my way never to use it."

"Why don't you like to use your ability?" he asked curiously as they started walking again. Whereas before she'd been warm and toasty, the temperature must have dropped five degrees when he put a couple feet between them. "I would have thought they'd come in handy, considering how things were so difficult for you at that point in your life."

"You sound like my brother." She sighed. "He always wanted me to use my ability to take advantage of people. He saw it as nothing more than a way to make money and was jealous that I had this ability when he didn't. Whenever I refused to use it the way he wanted, we'd end up arguing." She swallowed hard at the memory. "I can't tell you how many times I thought my ability would be the thing that finally pushed us apart."

Caleb moved a little closer, his shoulder so near her arm that she could feel his warmth again. "Would using your ability to make your lives easier have been so bad?"

She shrugged as they continued down the steps. "It's hard to explain, but I never felt right about using my ability for something so cheap. It made me feel like I was misusing it."

Brielle expected Caleb to laugh at her and call her silly, like Julian had done so many times. But instead, he grinned.

"I'm impressed," he said. "It's definitely not the way I would have handled the situation had I been in your shoes. If I had gotten your gift at that age, I probably would have used it to rob a bank or something. The fact that you resisted the urge to go the supervillain route says a lot about you."

She laughed. She had to admit it was nice to hear Caleb say something like that. She'd certainly never gotten praise like that from Julian, that was for sure. "You should probably refrain from being too impressed. Because, while I didn't ever want to use my ability, that doesn't mean I never did. Mostly because my brother has his own unique ways of forcing my hand."

"What do you mean?" Caleb asked as they reached the wide

street at the base of the stairs and started across it. "Because I gotta tell you, that sounded a little ominous."

She couldn't help but laugh again. "Sorry, I didn't mean for it to come out like that. It's just that Julian has always been good at getting into trouble and usually left it up to me to find a way to get him out of it. Unfortunately, that usually meant I had to use my ability, whether it was for finding ways to get money to bail him out of jail or fighting to keep someone from killing him. Once I even had to break into a jewelry store to return the stuff he'd stolen before they realized it was missing. And yeah, there was other stuff, too. Sometimes it scares me to think about how many times I broke the law for my brother."

Brielle wasn't ashamed of what she'd had to do for Julian, but that didn't keep her from looking away into the darkness out on the water, wishing she hadn't been quite so honest with her criminal confession. Did Caleb honestly need to know about the jewelry store thing?

He stopped and put his hand on her sleeve, gently turning her to look at him. "Before you start worrying that I'm going to judge you for your wayward youth, I should probably let you know that I have more than a passing knowledge of what it's like to be on the wrong side of the law. And for reasons not nearly as noble as saving a sibling's ass."

She gazed up at him, wondering if he was making that up to make her feel better. Then she thought about the way she'd seen him fight, both on this mission and the previous one, and how he'd always seemed on the ragged edge of control or well beyond it.

"Yeah, I can see you having problems with the police." She smiled. "You definitely have that proverbial bad-boy vibe going on."

Most guys would have preened at least a little at that description. In her experience, men liked to think of themselves as being dangerous. Caleb didn't seem to notice the label. Probably because he really *was* dangerous.

"I'd like to be able to blame my inner omega for all the trouble I've gotten myself into over the years," he said casually, taking her hand and leading her out onto one of the concrete piers in the bay. "But since I've been getting into trouble since I was old enough to walk and the werewolf thing didn't happen until much later, I guess I can't use that as an excuse."

They stopped halfway down the pier to lean against the metal railing and look out over the dark water. Brielle wanted to ask Caleb about his formative years and where he'd grown up. She got the feeling he'd gotten into as much trouble as Julian. And yet, he had ended up completely different than her brother. Then again, Caleb was different from any man she'd ever met.

"If you got in so much trouble, how did you end up working for STAT?" she asked, moving closer to him, telling herself it was the heat rolling off him in waves that she was seeking. "I mean, I'm sure they wouldn't have recruited you if they thought you were that much of a troublemaker."

He snorted as he leaned in a little closer to her, still gazing down at the soft waves lapping the base of the pier. "I think you're giving them a little too much credit. STAT was so eager to get their hands on another werewolf that they simply ignored my background, figuring that was Jake's problem to deal with."

"Even if you're right about the people at the top seeing you as nothing more than a risk/reward calculation, what does any of that matter when it's obvious your teammates couldn't care less about your past?" she asked, looking over and capturing his eyes. "You guys are closer than Julian and I have ever been. Or ever will be. He might be my brother, but in all the ways that matter, I'm on my own. I can only dream of what it's like to be part of something bigger, knowing you've got someone on your side."

Caleb regarded her silently for a long moment, his face unreadable. "I meant what I said earlier when I told Hudson that you're part of the team. After what you did for Misty and all of us in Siberia, I know Forrest and the rest of my teammates think of you like that, too."

She let out a little laugh. "That's a nice thought, but somehow, I doubt it's that easy. They all know I only agreed to work with STAT to find my brother. Doing one thing right isn't going to outweigh that fact. People don't trust that quickly."

"I would normally be the first to agree with you since I'm not big on the whole trust thing myself," Caleb murmured. "But when it comes to my team—my *pack*—I think you'll find it's easier than you think. You risked your life for them. That's all they're going to care about. So give them a chance, okay? Like you said, they accepted me, even with all my baggage. If you let them, they'll be there for you, too."

Brielle didn't know what to say. Suddenly, she found herself blinking to keep tears from welling in her eyes. Where had these emotions come from? Was she so needy for acceptance that merely thinking about being part of the STAT team was enough to make her cry?

Sadly, the answer to that question seemed to be yes.

She and Caleb stood there at the metal railing, gazing out at the passing ships and chatting about some of that baggage he'd mentioned earlier. Unfortunately, beyond getting him to admit to having been in jail more than once, she couldn't get anything else out of him. If she didn't know better, she would think he didn't want to make himself look bad in her eyes, which was insanely hilarious. He was amazing. Nothing he could say would change that.

"Why hasn't there ever been anyone else?" he asked quietly. "I mean, you've mentioned several times that it's just been you and Julian. Why aren't you with a guy?"

The question was so blunt that all Brielle could do was stare at him with her mouth open.

Caleb held up his hands apologetically. "I didn't mean that the way it came out. I just meant that you're a beautiful woman. I find it hard to believe there haven't been men interested in spending time with you."

Brielle felt a burst of warmth and happiness swirling up inside her chest at his words, and suddenly, she wasn't upset by his choice of words anymore. The fact that she was reacting so strongly to him calling her beautiful struck her as both silly and juvenile. What was she, a sixteen-year-old going gaga over the latest boy band singer?

"I tried a few times," she said, brushing her hair back when the breeze coming in from the water tossed it playfully around her face and forcing herself to answer his question instead of thinking about the way his casual compliment made her feel. "I dated a few guys, but it never went anywhere. Having a brother around who was constantly getting into trouble certainly didn't help. What about you? Do you have anyone waiting for you back home when you return from saving the world?"

He let out a snort of amusement that quickly turned into a laugh. "I'm an omega. By definition, I'm a loner. Like you, I've dated, but it never seemed to work out. I've never had a connection with anyone."

Brielle gazed up at him. Why did it bother her so much that this amazing man hadn't found someone to share his life with? For some reason, it seemed like such a waste.

"Maybe you simply haven't found the right woman yet," she murmured, fighting the urge to reach up and caress his chiseled jaw. She wanted to do it so badly, she could almost feel his scruff under her fingers.

"Or maybe I have," Caleb said, bending his head to touch his lips to hers.

He kissed her slowly, tentatively, like he wanted to give her a chance to pull away if she wanted to. She didn't pull away—or want to. Instead, she reached up and buried her fingers in his shaggy hair, pulling him down and opening her mouth to invite him in, desperate to let him know how much she wanted this.

Her tongue tangled with his, and she moaned at how good he tasted. One of his strong arms wrapped around her, tugging her against him, lifting her up on her toes a little until her breasts were pressing firmly against his powerful chest as he slipped his free hand into her hair.

It felt amazing.

Heat poured through her, and she came damn close to wrapping her legs around him and climbing him like a tree. The need to be even closer to him was overwhelming.

They quickly went from kissing to making out with an intensity that kind of scared her. She'd never come close to getting swept away by a man's kiss before. She'd never even considered letting it happen. But with Caleb, it was almost too easy to lose herself in the moment. To let the fire fill her up inside and make her burst into flames right there in the middle of Odessa.

As Caleb's big hand tightened in her hair, tugging at the strands in the most delicious way she'd ever experienced, Brielle couldn't help but wonder what it was about him that made her respond this way. Then she felt his rumbling growls welling up through his chest, the vibrations slipping inside her to do crazy things to her soul, and she stopped caring about why or how. She simply enjoyed the sensation of being in his arms.

When something grazed her tongue, sharp enough to draw blood, it wasn't that hard to figure out it was his fangs. Why they had extended in the middle of them kissing was a mystery, but she decided she didn't mind them at all. In fact, the sensation of those fangs scraping across the surface of her sensitive tongue was kind of interesting.

Before Brielle had a chance to experiment a little with that, Caleb abruptly broke the kiss and pulled away. The move was so jarring she almost fell over.

Opening her eyes, she saw that Caleb looked dazed, his eyes glowing vivid blue as he gazed down at her. The tips of his fangs were peeking out over his lower lip, and he was growling softly with nearly every breath. She knew all of that put together meant that he was on the verge of losing control of himself and going omega, as he liked to call it. She'd be lying if she said it didn't worry her a little, but she refused to believe he would ever hurt her, no matter how much control he lost.

Unfortunately, from the expression slowly crossing his face, Brielle wasn't too sure if Caleb believed that as much as she did. She could tell he was fighting hard to regain his control, his eyes darting left and right like he was wondering if running away might be the best option. If it weren't for several other tourists walking along the pier, he might have done it.

"Caleb," she said softly, reaching out to place her hand on the sleeve of his leather jacket and wondering what she'd done to make his inner werewolf come out. "Just breathe and tell me what's wrong."

Caleb didn't say anything, but as she stood there watching, his breathing slowed, the blue glow fading from his eyes and his fangs retracting. But even then, Brielle noticed he still didn't move to close the distance between them. It was ridiculously stupid, but the separation hurt all the same. And for the life of her, she couldn't understand why.

"Caleb, are you okay?" she asked. "Why did you push me away? Did I do something wrong?"

"I'm fine. You didn't do anything wrong," he said, but the flat expression on his face made her doubt the sincerity of his words. "We should get back to the safe house. We don't know when we're leaving Odessa, and we should get some sleep while we can."

Brielle wasn't sure what hurt worse: the fact that he was lying to her or that he hated kissing her so much that he'd rather go back to the safe house and the company of his teammates than stay out here with her.

CHAPTER 10

Russia

"I WOULD NORMALLY TRUST MISTY WHEN IT COMES TO STUFF like this," Caleb said, looking through the window at the crowded Moscow street below and the collection of office buildings across the street. "But for some reason, I have a hard time believing a construction firm was responsible for setting off a nuclear warhead beneath that village in Siberia."

Caleb felt more than saw the movement beside him. Turning slightly, he saw Brielle move over to look out the window with him. He held his breath, wondering if she was actually going to say something. It had been over twenty-fours since that uncomfortable moment in Odessa when he'd pulled away from her. In all that time, she'd barely said two words to him. Hell, she'd barely allowed herself to be in the same room with him for more than ten seconds at a time. She probably wouldn't be here now if Jake hadn't put them on the same team, maintaining external surveillance of this side of their target.

Brielle didn't say anything. Instead, she gazed down at the crowd of people in their heavy winter coats leaving the well-appointed office spaces of Barclay Plaza, home to several of Russia's most well-known companies, including the multinational building and design firm known as Aldaran Construction.

"Misty thinks Aldaran was only brought in to do the rough work on the tower, elevators, and control room," Brielle murmured softly, never taking her eyes off the office across the street. "They probably ran all those power cables and lights thinking they were building some kind of military facility."

"Maybe." Caleb shrugged. "I only wish we had more to go on than a word Misty caught a glimpse of as you were dragging her out of that computer. At this point, it seems like we're wandering around Eurasia, hoping to get lucky. Are you sure you didn't see anything while you were in there with her?"

Brielle shook her head. "I was a little too busy trying to get the both of us out of there to be doing any sightseeing. Not that I would have noticed anything as generic as the name of a construction firm, even if I'd had the time to look."

Caleb couldn't argue with any of that. He remembered how freaked out he and the rest of the team had been as they'd stood around while the clock counted down, praying Brielle and Misty would find their way out of the computer. Considering how much worse it must have been for Brielle and Misty trapped inside a computer with no idea how much time was left on that damn clock, it was amazing Misty had found anything useful at all.

The name of the construction firm had led them to Moscow and Aldaran's corporate headquarters. They hoped there was something in those offices that would tell them who was behind all of this, but Caleb had his doubts. If Misty was right and Aldaran wasn't even aware of what they'd been building under all that Siberian snow, then what were the chances of them finding anything in there?

"Everybody sit tight," Jake said over the radio in Caleb's earpiece. "We can't go in until those offices clear out, so everyone might as well get comfortable."

He heard murmurs of agreement from the rest of the team, as they responded from their various hiding places in and around the Barclay building. Caleb tuned out as Jake went over the evening's game plan again. Not that there was much to talk about. Misty, Forrest, and Genevieve would go in and sniff around the company's hard files and computer servers while everyone else hung back and made sure there weren't any problems. None of them expected any. This was an office complex for a construction firm. It wasn't like the place was filled with military secrets.

Taking Jake's advice to heart, Caleb dragged one of the heavy office desks closer to the window, then took a seat atop it, making sure he had a good view of the Barclay building and most of the street below. Leaning over, he reached down for his backpack, dragging it up into his lap and unzipping the main compartment. He took out his beloved .45 Colt, which was sitting right on top, and set it down beside him. The large caliber weapon wasn't what he was most interested in at the moment.

"What's in the bag?" Brielle asked as she hopped onto the desk beside him and leaned in to take a peek into his backpack. This close, her scent hit him full in the face, and Caleb had to work hard to resist the temptation to shove his nose into her hair and take a deep, long sniff.

"Food," he said, pulling out the packages and boxes of snacks he'd picked up at the store earlier until there was a pile of them on the desk between them. "I thought we might get hungry while we wait."

She stared at him, stunned. "We ate dinner an hour ago. That steak you had must have weighed two pounds, and you had three baked potatoes with it. If I ate that much—and I never could—I wouldn't be hungry for weeks."

"I'm a werewolf. We eat a lot." Caleb took two bottles of soda out of the bag and held them up. "You want the cucumber-flavored Sprite or this Baikal stuff? The guy in the store said it tastes like a cross between Coke and Pepsi."

Brielle regarded the bottles for a moment before taking the cucumber Sprite. Caleb was silently thrilled. He wasn't a fan of cucumbers—in soda or otherwise.

There was a rustling sound beside him as he set his backpack on the floor, and he looked over to see her holding up two big bags of potato chips. While it had been nice to see a recognizable brand name like those sitting on a convenience store shelf in Russia, he wasn't so sure what he was getting himself into when it came to flavor. One bag had a big dill pickle on the front while the other had a bowl of soup on it filled with what looked like mushrooms. He obviously couldn't read the writing, since it was Russian, but something told him that neither of these bags was gonna be BBQ flavored.

Brielle opened the bag with the pickle on it and reached in to grab a chip, nibbling on it thoughtfully. Was it sad that he thought the way she ate was cute? Probably. But he couldn't help it. He was so used to inhaling his food that the sight of a beautiful woman taking dainty bites did something for him.

"These are definitely dill pickle," she said. "Emphasis on the dill."

He was so transfixed watching her eat that he didn't realized she'd opened the other bag of chips to taste them.

"I'm pretty sure this one is mushroom and sour cream," she said. "They're kind of good, actually."

He leaned over and grabbed a few chips from the pickle bag, shoving them in his mouth, then washed them down with the Baikal drink and tried the mushroom and sour cream. It didn't take long to figure out he wasn't a fan. They tasted sorta earthy but tangy at the same time. Definitely not his thing.

"That's going to be a no on the mushroom flavor," he said, shoving that bag toward Brielle.

She laughed, reaching over to help herself to some more dill pickle–flavored chips, agreeing they were better. "What else did you bring?"

They opened up the rest of the snacks, taste testing each and sharing their thoughts. He'd grabbed stuff at random from the little shop he'd stopped at outside their hotel, but he had to admit he'd done a pretty good job picking.

"This is good," he said, taking a big bite of a chocolate bar that looked similar to a Hershey bar from back home, right down to the little scored lines so you could break off smaller pieces. "It's not as sweet as the chocolate I'm used to, but it works. Not sure what I think of the design on the wrapper, though." He studied one and then the other. "I'm not sure what it's supposed to be, but it's kind of scary in a Stephen King kind of way."

Brielle laughed and took the bar from him, contemplating the wrapper while she nibbled on the chocolate. "I've never read his books. I'm guessing you have, though."

"I've seen the movies at least," he admitted. "Not a fan of horror movies?"

She shrugged.

As they sat there munching on other kinds of Russian snacks while talking about how different horror movies were in France compared to the U.S., he was surprised at how easy it was to talk to her. After the way things had been since that kiss, he thought any conversation between them would forever be tense and awkward. It was difficult to put into words how relieved he was to realize that wasn't the case.

"Caleb, can I ask you something?" Brielle said softly, pausing to take a nibble of something called a Halva, which reminded him of a small Milky Way bar and was just as delicious.

"Um...sure," he said, forcing himself to look away from the chocolate smeared across her lower lip, begging to be licked off. "Whatever you want."

"Why did your eyes turn blue like that when we kissed on that pier in Odessa?" Her voice was small, almost timid. "Was it because kissing me was that bad?"

At the question, Caleb was immediately transported back to that moment near the water, the feel of her lips on his, her body pressed so tightly to his chest that he could feel every scrumptious curve of her exquisite form. It had been like nothing he'd ever experienced. It was so exhilarating it had been damn near overwhelming—at first in a very good way but then in a scary way as he'd felt himself losing control. His body had started tingling, his heart racing, his fangs and claws extending. Even then, it had been perfect. The sensation of his fangs scraping gently along her tongue had made him feel like he was about to lose his mind. It had been beyond perfect. It had been heavenly.

Right up until he'd felt her heart beating against his chest like a drum when fear had consumed her. That realization had been like a knife through the chest, and he'd immediately pulled away, feeling like a fool for letting his omega side almost slip out with her.

And for thinking he could ever have something with her.

He'd done it to protect her and keep her safe. Caleb had thought that was blindingly obvious. But he'd never considered she might have taken it a different way, that she'd thought he was rejecting her. He bit his tongue to keep from laughing at the absurdity of such an idea. That Brielle would think someone like him wouldn't give half a dozen body parts for the mere privilege of tasting her lips for even a second.

A woman like her should have been the one to walk away from him.

Even better, she should have run.

Didn't she know that?

"No," he said, lifting his head to look at her when he was finally capable of stringing a few semi-intelligent words together. "It was nothing like that at all. My eyes turned blue because, when I was kissing you, I started to lose control. I'm an omega. Losing control is sometimes what I do."

She gazed at him, her expression caught somewhere between hurt and confusion. "So kissing me wasn't that bad?"

He shook his head, a slightly out-of-control laugh on the edge of escaping. "No. It was that *good*. I've kissed women before. Lots of them. But losing it like I did has never happened before."

That earned him another long look, this one more curious—and assessing—than before. "I suppose I should take that as a compliment, then. Is that why you pulled back on the pier? Because you hate losing control that much?"

He was still musing on the whole compliment thing and how it definitely wasn't what he'd been expecting her to say. Then the second part of what she'd said filtered through his fuzzy mind, and he realized she was waiting for an answer.

"Actually," he started softly, "when you were in my arms and my fangs came out, I felt your heart start to beat like crazy, and I knew I was terrifying you, so I pulled away."

Behind her bangs, Brielle lifted an elegantly arched brow. He decided she looked good when she did that. "We were making out and my heart started thumping, so you decided I was terrified? Tell me, how many women have you kissed before and were they actually in the room with you at the time?"

He snorted, ready to say something snarky, when he realized exactly what she was implying. Her heart hadn't been racing because she was scared. She'd been...

"Oh," he murmured.

"Yeah, oh."

She went back to nibbling on her Russian version of a Milky Way. He told himself to not look at her lips as she ate...and failed miserably.

"So losing control seems to be a recurring theme for you as an omega," she observed in between bites. "I'm guessing that sucks."

Okay, he supposed that was Brielle's way of making conversation.

And people say I'm socially awkward.

"Pretty much," he admitted, taking a sip of cola. "There are some things I like about being an omega werewolf and other things I could do without. But I deal with it. I mean, it's not like I have a choice."

Brielle took another bite of chocolate. "This is probably going to sound really stupid, but I've never had a chance to sit and talk with a werewolf before, so I'm just going to come right out and ask. Did you get bitten by another werewolf? Is that how you turned? Or were you born this way and have been losing control, wolfing out, and destroying stuff since you were a baby?"

Caleb took a second to imagine that scene, thinking she'd hit much closer to the truth than she probably realized. He genuinely *had* been making a mess of his life since he was little. Maybe not since he was a baby, but damn close. Of course, he couldn't blame it all on the werewolf gene.

"No, I didn't get bitten. And no, I haven't been this way my whole life, either. That isn't how it works for us."

"How does it work, then?"

He sipped his drink, trying to figure out how to explain it. "I'm not a doctor—or a science geek—so don't hammer me on the details, but basically, some people are born with a gene in their DNA that predisposes them to becoming a werewolf if they're exposed to the right stimuli."

"That sounds rather ominous," Brielle said. "When you say the *right stimuli*, I'm guessing you're not talking about a nice, friendly full moon or anything like that?"

Caleb snorted. "I wish it would have been something that simple. No, we have to go through a traumatic event that typically involves a lot of adrenaline and pain. The rush of chemicals in the body flips the gene, and we change. The specific details of the event decide what kind of werewolf we turn into when we come out the other side."

She considered that. "I have a basic understating of the difference between each type of werewolf, but I don't understand how the trauma affects what kind of werewolf you become."

He sighed, really not wanting to talk about this part. Normally, it never bothered him to tell people the nasty details of what had happened to him. But for some reason, he wanted to hide those aspects of his past from Brielle. He didn't want her knowing about the things he'd done to end up where he was now. But he didn't want to lie to her, either.

"It's not all that complicated," he said, reaching into the bag for some more dill pickle–flavored chips but not eating them yet. "If you go through all that pain and suffering with the best of intentions to save someone else's life, you come out an alpha. If the pain and suffering isn't due to any fault of your own and it was one of those wrong-place-wrong-time kind of situations, you come out a beta."

"And an omega?" she murmured when he didn't continue. "What has to happen for that outcome?"

He turned his head to look at her, his gaze coming to rest on those beautiful dark eyes, worried that his next words would destroy something that didn't even exist yet.

"Omegas are the result of going into that horrible, traumatic event with the worst of intentions," he said softly. "Alphas are created from acts of heroism, betas from morally neutral acts, and omegas from acts of revenge, greed, anger, or hatred. I acted out of revenge. I went into a situation intending to kill some people for what they had done to someone I cared about. It wasn't about saving anyone. It was about making them pay, pure and simple. And it ended up with me turning into the most out-of-control omega in the world."

Caleb held his breath, waiting for Brielle to slide off the desk in her desire to put space between the two of them. But instead, she simply nodded and ate a few more potato chips.

"Well? You going to tell me the story or what?" she asked after a few moments of silence, leaning over to nudge his shoulder with hers. "You can't leave me hanging, not after a confession like that. And, by the way, I doubt you're the most out-of-control omega werewolf in the world. I'm guessing you're not even the most out-of-control omega werewolf in Moscow."

Those were the exact words Caleb needed to hear right then. He had no idea why, especially since that latter part she'd said was almost certainly nonsense, but the fact that Brielle wasn't horrified made it seem like a weight was being lifted from his shoulders, and he couldn't help chuckling.

"What do you want to know?" he finally asked.

"Everything," she said simply, offering him the last of the dill pickle chips with a soft expression that nearly did him in.

"Toby Spencer was my best friend growing up," he said after finishing the last handful of chips. "Hell, to be honest, he was my only friend. I didn't have much of a family, so I spent more time at Toby's place than my own. We were a matching pair of idiots, always skipping classes together, getting into trouble and fights, getting arrested. I probably would have dropped out of school if not for him, but he talked me into going, even though I couldn't see the use for it."

Her lips curved in a small smile. "He sounds like a good friend."

Caleb sighed, lost in the memories. "He was the best. Unfortunately, that wasn't enough to keep me from being stupid. When we were in high school, we got involved with some bad people. At first, we just stole merchandise. You know, computers, stereos, car parts. Nothing too serious. All they wanted us to do was the grunt work at that point. We picked up stuff, delivered it, and handled the money. But over time, as we got involved in the drugs and gambling side of the organization, they began to want more from us. We started carrying guns, and the work started to get more violent. Toby wanted us to get out, but I wouldn't listen. I liked the money, and to a certain degree, I guess I liked that I'd found something I was good at."

"What happened?" Brielle asked quietly, her expression sympathetic, and he couldn't help but remember that she'd looked much the same when she'd talked about her brother. He guessed there were a lot of similarities between their lives.

Caleb took a deep breath. "The guy we worked for—I'm not even sure I ever knew his name—decided he didn't like Toby's attitude." This was the first time he'd ever told anyone about this part of the story. "The asshole stood up in the middle of a drug deal and shot him. Just like that. Like Toby's life didn't matter at all."

"What did you do?" Brielle whispered.

"I killed the son of a bitch." Caleb felt tears in his eyes and quickly blinked them away before she could see. "I didn't think. I didn't wait to consider if there was a better way to deal with the situation. I simply walked right up to him and put a bullet through his forehead. Then I turned and started shooting at everyone else who worked for him. I was so frigging angry; I wanted to kill them all. I didn't care what happened to me."

Brielle smiled again. "Don't take this the wrong way, but it seems like you haven't changed all that much since then. You're still shooting first and thinking later."

More weight slid off his shoulders at her teasing and he let out a soft laugh. "Yeah, I guess you're right. I nearly died that night and ended up doing five years in prison. But in a lot of ways, I suppose I'm still the same person I was back then. I just have fangs and claws now."

He picked up the package of Russian oatmeal cookies and opened it, then held it out to Brielle. He felt a lot more relaxed now, after unloading his history on her and realizing she wasn't totally disgusted.

"Okay, you got involved with bad people, shot a few of them, and went to jail." She took a cookie in her slender fingers and nibbled on it. "How did you get from there to STAT?"

Caleb laughed as he grabbed a few cookies. "It was a long and winding road, involving a series of increasingly poor life choices and a run-in with the Dallas SWAT team that just so happens to be made up entirely of alpha werewolves. I was looking at an extended stay in a fine Texas facility when McKay paid me a visit. The guy in charge of the SWAT team I mentioned sent him my way, thinking I might be the kind of person he was looking for to start up this new kind of STAT field team that was a mix of regular people and supernaturals, fighting the good fight and all that jazz."

"I don't really know you that well, but I have to say that doesn't really seem like the best way to recruit you," Brielle murmured.

"Actually, it would say you know me better than you realize." He popped a cookie into his mouth and chewed slowly. "The whole fighting the good fight approach was a waste of time, and for an omega, the team concept wasn't exactly a winner, either."

"So what ultimately closed the deal for you?" She reached over to nab another oatmeal cookie. "Was it the big gun they gave you?"

He snorted. "McKay promised to wipe away my criminal record in return for staying with the STAT team for three years. The fact that I get to carry a .45 is just extra."

She let out a soft laugh. "What has it been like being on the team?"

"Honestly?" Caleb grinned. "It's been way better than I imagined. In the beginning, I didn't think something like this would work. I mean, after Toby, there'd never been anyone on my side. Becoming an omega werewolf—aka the ultimate outsider—only made it worse. But with this team, sometimes I feel like I'm one of them. Like I'm really part of the pack. Or at least as close to being part of a pack as someone like me is ever going to get."

He expected her to nod and eat another cookie or maybe comment on how she was happy for him. Instead, he got a pair of arms thrown around his neck and a mouthful of hair as she tucked her face in his shoulder and squeezed the stuffing out of him. Being trapped in her embrace, buried under the overwhelming scent of honeysuckles, was heaven.

Admittedly, it was a little awkward with the way they were sitting there side by side on the desk, but Caleb's arms found their way around her anyway. Having her in his arms was as natural to him as breathing, and once he had her there, it was impossible to keep his mind from wandering back to what happened the last time he had Brielle there.

As if reading his mind, Brielle pulled back, gazing up at him with knowing eyes. "I'm not terrified of you, Caleb. You know that, right? And your glowing blue eyes, claws, and fangs don't bother me at all. In fact, I find the fangs, in particular, very intriguing."

"You had me at fangs," he murmured, bending his head to kiss her.

Caleb told himself not to go overboard, but the second their lips touched, he felt his inner werewolf start to wake up, his gums and fingertips beginning to tingle. He wanted to blame his inner omega for the way his hands found their way into Brielle's long, silky hair, fingers twisting and tugging as their kiss deepened, but that was a cop-out, and he knew it. He wanted her so badly it hurt and trying to deny it was only making it worse.

A rumbling growl started from deep in his chest when Brielle suddenly moved, one of her jean-clad legs coming up to gracefully swing across his legs, wiggling until she was settled on his lap, the heat of her body pressing against the growing hard-on in his jeans. Then she started grinding, and he felt his fangs erupt, the quick metallic tang of his own blood quickly disappearing as he was consumed by her taste. There was no way he was going to be able to stop now. They were going to make out on this desk in an abandoned office in the middle of Moscow.

And Brielle seemed completely cool with that.

"Okay," Jake's cock-blocking voice interrupted over the radio. "Looks like the coast is clear. Time to go. Misty, you and your team head inside. Everyone else, move to your backup and overwatch positions."

Brielle continued to kiss him as if she hadn't heard the same thing in her earpiece, and for a second, Caleb thought she might ignore the call. But finally, after several more exquisite moments of pleasure, she gently broke the kiss, pulling back to look down at him with desire in her eyes.

"We'll finish this later," she promised as she gracefully climbed off him. "That's a promise."

"Damn straight," he agreed, the words slurred ever so slightly by the fangs extending over his lower lip.

CHAPTER 11

"I'M GETTING A REALLY BAD FEELING ABOUT THIS," CALEB murmured.

He and Brielle were hiding in a janitor's closet a few hundred feet from the server room where Misty, Forrest, and Genevieve were busy snooping. Jake and the rest of the team were stationed throughout the building, positioned to intercept anyone approaching the top level of the building, where the server room was located.

Brielle looked away from the partially open door she'd been peeking through and frowned at him. "What do you mean? The building is nearly deserted, and Jes is watching the security camera video feeds. It's not like anyone can sneak up on us."

Caleb didn't answer her. Instead, he stood there in the middle of the cleaning supplies, mops, and various tools, staring off into space, tension radiating off him in waves. It was difficult to believe that, a little while ago, she'd been grinding on his lap, ready to rip both their clothes off and make love to him right there on a desk in the office building across the street. Now, here they were in a janitor's closet, and Caleb's fingers were twitching like his claws were going to make an appearance any second. She was tempted to blame his paranoia on the same hesitancy he had about sleeping with her—heaven knew she had to practically hit him over the head before he finally figured out that she wanted him as much as he wanted her—but she knew it wasn't that.

"What makes you think something is wrong?" Brielle asked when he didn't say anything. If he'd even heard what she'd said before.

At first, she thought he wasn't going to answer, but then he sighed and slowly shook his head. "I don't know." He closed his eyes and tilted his head to the side like he was trying to listen to something only he could hear. "But my instincts are telling me that something is about to happen."

She didn't bother to ask if it was something bad. It went without saying that Caleb's werewolf instincts wouldn't be acting up for anything good.

"Jake, this is Brielle," she murmured softly into the radio. "Caleb's instincts have suddenly started ringing like a bell. He has no idea why, but I think we need to be closer to Misty, Forrest, and Genevieve in case he's right."

"Copy that," Jake said. "Jes, are you seeing anything on the video feed? Harley, do you and Sawyer get the sensation that anything's wrong?"

"Negative" was the answer from all three members of the team.

A moment later, Jake was back on the radio. "Okay. Brielle, you and Caleb move closer, but be careful. Everyone else, get ready. There's a reason Caleb's inner wolf is talking to him, even if we don't know what it is yet."

Caleb was on the move the moment Jake finished speaking, his long strides carrying him down the dimly lit corridor of the office complex, leaving Brielle to hurry to catch up. He didn't have his weapon out yet, but she could tell from the set of his shoulders that he was ready to attack the first thing that stepped in his path. She reached inside the back of her jacket, checking to make sure the 9 mm auto was still secure in its holster. Jake had refused to let her come on this mission without a weapon. She hadn't bothered to mention that she barely knew how to use it. Yes, she understood the basics—take the weapon off safe, pull the trigger, gun goes off—but she seriously doubted she'd be able to hit anything. Not if she had to depend on her own ability alone.

Brielle's eyes darted toward every dark corner and hallway they passed, trying to uncover the threat that Caleb's instincts insisted was here somewhere. She couldn't see anything, but if he trusted his inner wolf, then she would, too.

Her biggest concern at the moment was how empty the place was, as strange at that might seem. But if they were attacked, this isolation meant she'd have no one to borrow any tactical abilities from...except Caleb. And she was more than a little worried about tapping into his particular skill set. If he could barely control the raw, aggressive omega inside him, what chance did she have?

"Forrest, we're heading your way," Brielle whispered into her mic as they approached the alcove containing the vault door leading into the Aldaran server room. "What's going on in there? Are you almost done?"

"Genevieve is digging through the company records the old-fashioned way, looking for something that will tell us who had that facility in Siberia constructed. Misty is doing it her way," Forrest said. "As for us being almost done, I have no idea. Hang on, and I'll open the door for you guys."

Caleb glanced over his shoulder as they waited for Forrest to let them in, and Brielle saw that his eyes were starting to glow a little as he darted his head back and forth to keep a visual on both ends of the corridor in front of the server room.

"How long has Misty been inside?" he asked the moment Forrest opened the door and they stepped inside.

"She went in the second we got here." Forrest's face was clouded with concern as he glanced at Misty, where she stood beside one of the server stacks, her hand buried inside the cabinet. "We're getting close to fifteen minutes. She was supposed to come out after ten."

Caleb cursed.

"Does this happen every time she does this?" Brielle asked Forrest. On the other side of the room, Genevieve was sitting at a desk clicking away at a keyboard. "You know I can't go in and get Misty this time, right? I've already told you that using her abilities was a one-time thing."

"I know," Forrest said with a single sharp nod of his head. "We'll have to wait for her to come out, no matter how long that takes."

If we have the time to wait, Brielle thought.

"Guys," Jes said over the radio, her voice full of anxiety. "Half the security cameras in the building just went blank. I think it goes without saying that trouble is on the way."

Before Brielle could even begin to digest that information, she heard a distinctive dinging sound coming from the end of the hall to the right of the server room. She didn't need a werewolf's hearing to know it was the elevator doors opening.

"Jake, they're here," Caleb growled into the radio even as the STAT team leader promised that help was on the way. "I can hear them getting off the elevator now. Sounds like they're all heavily armed."

Brielle closed her eyes, opening herself up and using her gift to figure out how many people were coming their way and whether they were supernaturals or not.

"Six people got off the elevator," she said, immediately sensing how dangerous they were. "There are two more coming up the stairwell at the other end of the hallway. They're all supernaturals."

"What kind?" Caleb and Forrest asked at the same time, the latter looking back over his shoulder at Misty, who still appeared to be stuck in the servers with no indication of coming out any time soon.

She closed her eyes again, trying to get a read on the people they were about to face. "They're all strong, fast, and comfortable using a lot of different weapons, like they've been training and fighting most of their lives. They also seem to be able to heal quickly from anything short of a fatal wound."

"They aren't frigging werewolves, are they?" Hudson asked over the radio.

"No, but they're still dangerous." She opened her eyes. "Oh yeah, and one of them appears to possess some kind of telekinetic abilities." When Caleb stared at her with a baffled expression on his face, she added, "He can move things with his mind."

He frowned. "I knew what it meant. I just didn't think that kind of stuff was real."

Was he serious?

"You're a werewolf," she pointed out. "And you still question the world you live in? If you've ever wondered if something exists, it probably does—the good and the bad."

Caleb opened his mouth to say something, but before he could, bullets ripped into the Sheetrock inches from his head, clouds of white dust exploding into the air.

Merde.

Brielle had foolishly hoped that the new arrivals might be building security or even Moscow city police responding to some kind of silent alarm she and the rest of the team had accidentally tripped. But that hope was dashed the moment the bullets began flying. Those people were here specifically to kill them, which meant they likely knew who they were. Of course, how they knew, Brielle didn't have a clue.

"Stay in here," Caleb growled over his shoulder as he opened the door and slipped into the alcove outside the server room to fire several shots down the corridor.

The booms from the big handgun made her ears ring, but Brielle ignored it, pulling her own weapon and slipping around him to deliver a few shots of her own. She didn't hit anything—and almost dropped the weapon from the unfamiliar recoil—but at least she got a clear look at the people shooting at them.

Five men and one woman, they were dressed in black tactical gear with no discernible markings on it. Regardless of their supernatural origins, they looked like any other humans, except for the fact that every one of them had pitch-black hair and skin that was way too pale. She could practically see the dark lines where their veins pulsed under the bare skin of their arms and neck. They advanced toward her and Caleb, moving so fast from corner to corner that it was impossible to get a clear shot at them.

"The tall one in the front is the leader," she shouted at Caleb, shooting a couple times in that guy's general direction for added emphasis. "He's the one with telekinetic abilities."

As if to prove her right, the tall guy—Uriel, according to the shouts of his friends—suddenly flicked out a hand and moved aside one of the bullets Caleb sent at him, making it hit the wall instead.

"That's just wrong," Caleb muttered as gunfire filled the hallway behind them. Brielle turned to see that the other two supernaturals she'd sensed coming up the stairs had arrived. They had her and Caleb in their cross fire.

She knew their only choice was to fall back into the server room so they could keep Misty safe until Jake and the other members of their team arrived like the cavalry. So of course, she shouldn't have been surprised when Caleb let loose a wall-shaking roar and turned to attack the two latecomers instead.

Brielle emptied the remainder of her magazine at Uriel and the other five killers coming at them from the elevators, hoping to keep them ducking long enough to give Caleb a chance to finish whatever he was planning. Forrest joined her, doing a better job of at least hitting the bad guys. But while the bullets definitely drew blood, the wounds didn't seem to slow the attackers down very much.

Brielle didn't have a chance to see what Caleb was doing, but she could definitely hear it. A lot of growling and snarls, the sound of claws rending flesh, and loud thuds of something heavy slamming into the walls.

When the shooting from behind them slowed, Brielle took that as a hopeful sign, until a body fell on her, slamming her to the floor so hard the air was knocked out of her lungs. She was just beginning to scramble to get out from under the heavy weight on top of her so she could breathe again when her hand came into contact with skin that was distinctly cold and clammy. She had a second to wonder what the hell was happening, then her body was absorbing abilities out of pure instinct and she was suddenly shoving the man's body aside like he was a toy at the same time her hands snatched the short assault weapon right out of his hands.

Jake was shouting into the radio that the rest of the team would be there in seconds, but Brielle wasn't sure if that was going to be fast enough. The bad guys were closing in from both sides, getting near enough to angle shots into the server room where Misty was standing right out in the open, completely defenseless.

Brielle had no idea why she was so sure, but something about how the attackers were coming at them convinced her that Misty was their primary target. She knew if the supernaturals got close enough, they wouldn't hesitate to kill the technopath. Brielle couldn't let that happen, so she followed Caleb's insane lead and charged into the fight.

A flick of Uriel's hand sent her flying sideways through the air, but her newfound abilities let her come down in a graceful roll, then she was up and moving even faster than before. Brielle didn't realize how fast she was running until she nearly ran into one of the pale-skinned men garbed in rugged tactical gear. Her sudden appearance must have surprised the guy because he hesitated for a fraction of a second before lifting his assault rifle.

His mistake gave Brielle time to get her weapon up first. She pulled the trigger and put a three-round burst straight into the man's chest and stomach, momentarily marveling at how much easier it was to shoot a weapon now compared to a few seconds ago. Then again, these new abilities also made it easy to shoot another human being at point-blank range without batting an eye, too. That was something she'd normally never even consider being able to do.

Her gift worked in strange ways sometimes.

Jake's voice in her ear announced that he and the others had arrived, but she ignored him and focused on moving before the bad guy she'd shot had a chance to hit the floor. She pulled back to intercept another attacker heading straight for the door of the server room, his weapon blasting away in Misty's direction. Brielle fired on the run, desperate to stop the man before it was too late. The first several rounds missed and slammed into the floor to ricochet down the corridor, but then one hit him in the upper leg, distracting him enough to stop shooting at Misty.

Brielle immediately regretted gaining his attention, though, as he ignored the leg wound and spun in a blur of motion to send a hail of bullets in her direction. She dived to the side, tucking and rolling, but still felt a slight pinch right above her hip bone. It took a second—and the sight of blood staining through the right side of her shirt and coat—to realize she'd been shot.

She froze, instinctively waiting for the pain to assault her. She knew lying there unmoving on the floor in the middle of a firefight wasn't the smartest thing to do, but she'd never been shot before. So she tried to cut herself a little slack. But when the pain came, it wasn't as horrible as she expected. Maybe increased tolerance to pain was another aspect of the abilities she'd absorbed.

She pushed to her feet and moved to put herself between Misty and the next attacker. There might not be a lot of pain, but it was obvious that the bullet wound she'd suffered was serious. Would her abilities hide the pain right up to the point that she bled out? Or would she heal like they could?

There wasn't much time to ponder that question as she found herself face-to-face with two more of the eerily pale-skinned, dark-haired men coming at her fast. Out the corner of her eye, Brielle saw Harley and Sawyer charge into the main corridor, weapons out and blazing, hitting multiple attackers.

There was no way they'd reach Brielle in time to help. And dealing with two of the supernaturals at once, while injured, was

likely more than she was ready for, even with her recently borrowed abilities. But she still took a step back to block the doorway
into the server room, ready to protect Misty as long as she could.

The two bad guys lifted their weapons in her direction and
began to fire, but before she could even consider diving to the side,
a bone-rattling howl shredded the air, and a blur rushed in front
of her. The second she saw the blazing blue eyes, fangs, and claws,
she knew it was Caleb—and that he'd completely lost control for
some reason. Worse than she'd ever seen.

He wasn't carrying the Colt handgun she was used to seeing
him with. Instead, he was holding one of the attacker's assault rifles
by the barrel, smashing it back and forth like a big club. Even when
Uriel ripped the weapon out of Caleb's grip with a single flick of
his hand, he kept going, picking up one of the black-garbed men
and physically tossing him at the telekinetic supernatural, putting
both of them right through a wall.

The next few minutes seemed to last a lifetime. Her teammates
were fighting all around her while Uriel smashed people into walls
and deflected bullets like he was swatting flies. If it hadn't been for
Caleb and his berserker strength and fury, they would have been
overwhelmed already.

Then, as soon as it started, it was all over. The supernaturals
in black were fighting one second, then pulled back in an all-out
run the next, leaving two of their own dead behind. Brielle started
to breathe a sigh of relief until Caleb let out another growl and
moved to take off after them.

Brielle stepped in front of him without a second thought, ignoring the snarls and the rage-filled eyes. Dropping the rifle she was
holding, she reached out to put her hands on his chest, pushing
against him a little. But even with the enhanced strength she'd borrowed, she didn't have the muscle to hold back an out-of-control
werewolf. Caleb tried to move around her, his hand coming down
to her hip to push her aside.

She grunted in pain when his fingers touched the bullet wound. That seemed to be the thing that finally stopped him.

Caleb looked down at his hand, where it rested against the blood that had soaked through her jacket, then brought his fingers up to sniff the red stain there. His growl changed to a tortured whine, then he let out a snarl, his fangs growing another half inch to jut out well below his lower lip.

He snapped his head up, staring down the hallway that Uriel and the attackers had fled, and Brielle knew, without a doubt, that he was going to go after them because they'd hurt her.

Brielle slid her hands up his chest, ignoring the evidence of his injuries as she got up on her tiptoes and weaved her fingers in his hair until she had a good grip. Then she dragged his head down until he was close enough to kiss.

"Calm down, Caleb. I'm okay," she murmured against his mouth, nipping at his lower lip to get his attention. "You don't have to go after them. I'm fine. Now, calm down."

He resisted for a moment, like she had caught him off guard, but then his hands were sliding around her, one along her lower back and the other cupping her butt, pulling her close. Then his mouth was on her, his kiss urgent, his tongue slipping out to tease hers, the growls turning into a rumble of pleasure.

It was different kissing Caleb when his fangs were out this far, but she definitely didn't mind. In fact, Brielle could see herself getting used to them.

"You're bleeding," he finally whispered against the tender skin of her neck, his warm breath making a shiver race from her core and up her spine even as his fangs remained almost fully extended. "How bad is it?"

Caleb slowly set her down, giving Brielle a chance to open her coat and yank the right side of her shirt up to get her first look at the wound there. While there was a lot of blood, she was relieved to see that the neat hole the size of her little finger as well as the slightly larger one right above her waist further around her side had already stopped bleeding and were healing. Thankfully, she had gotten the supernatural's healing ability, too.

The sight didn't seem to assure Caleb as much as it did Brielle. He immediately reached out to press his big, clawed hand gently against the wounds with a low growl. She rested her hand on top of his.

"Shh. It's okay," she murmured softly. "I still have the healing abilities I borrowed from that supernatural. I'll be completely healed in a few minutes. So relax. I'm going to be okay, all right?"

Relief shone in Caleb's eyes, and he bent his head, resting his forehead against hers, his hand remaining on the gunshot wound. As she watched, the blue glow faded from his eyes, and his fangs retracted. She couldn't see them at the moment, but she assumed his claws had disappeared as well.

She and Caleb stood there like that for a long time, the tension slowly draining from both their bodies as they relaxed against each other. Brielle would have happily stayed there for the rest of the night, Caleb's warmth surrounding her, but then someone cleared their throat nearby, and she looked over to see Jake standing there with an amused look on his face.

"What?" Caleb grunted. "We're having a moment here."

"Obviously," Jake said. "But unfortunately, we don't have time for this. We need to get the hell out of here."

That's when Brielle heard sirens. Lots of them.

"I've got dozens of cars coming from multiple directions," Hudson shouted from farther down the hallway. "This place is going to be crawling with Moscow police within minutes. We need to go. Now."

Brielle was all for that. But one look at Misty, who was still in the server room with her hand on top of the closest server rack, told her they weren't going to be so lucky.

"We really need to come up with a dog whistle or something that can get Misty's attention in a situation like this," she muttered.

Caleb chuckled at that, but before he could say anything, Misty abruptly stumbled back from the server rack, looking exhausted. She glanced around, taking in the two dead men on the floor and the bullet-riddled wall, her violet eyes filled with confusion.

"What did I miss?"

CHAPTER 12

"Who the hell is Xavier Harrington?" Brielle asked, looking at Caleb, then around at the rest of the team seated at the table, wondering if the name meant something to them. But with the exception of Misty, who'd revealed the name of the person she believed to be behind the stolen nuclear weapons, it seemed that everyone was as lost as she was.

Getting out of the Barclay building had been a nerve-racking experience, at least for Brielle. As the sound of police sirens had filled the air, they'd slipped down one of the back stairwells and then out through a loading dock area cluttered with bundles of compacted cardboard and half-filled dumpsters. With the aid of Caleb's and the other werewolves' keen senses, they'd just avoided the cops rushing into the building from the same direction, ultimately having to low crawl on their bellies across a few hundred meters of pitch-black parking lot before they could finally make a run for their vehicles several blocks away.

No one said anything until they'd gotten back to the safe house on the outskirts of Moscow, and even then, the first thing they'd all focused on was getting cleaned up and making something to eat. But while Brielle had been thrilled to get all that blood off— and watching Caleb inhale a mountain of peanut butter sandwiches had brought her more pleasure than she could properly describe—she couldn't deny what she was really interested in were some details on what Misty had found in those Aldaran computer servers.

"Right now, I don't have much more than his name," Misty said, picking up the cup in front of her and sipping her tea. "All I can say for sure at this point is that he's the head of some international corporation based out of New York called the Harrington Group. I also confirmed that the telekinetic supernatural you told me about, Uriel, is the head of Harrington's personal security. All it takes is ten seconds on Google to find pictures of the man guarding Harrington at major appearances all around the world. It's also obvious that Harrington has gone to extreme lengths to hide his involvement in the theft of the nukes out of Incirlik and building the facility in Siberia."

That generated a lot of conversation around the large table in the safe house's spacious dining room. Everyone seemed to have a theory except for Caleb. But that was because he was too busy devouring a bag of dill pickle potato chips he'd found in the kitchen along with the peanut butter. The only time he slowed down was when he glanced at Brielle sitting beside him every few minutes, like he was worried she was going to disappear on him or something.

"Maybe you should start from the beginning," Jake said to Misty. "Explain exactly how you stumbled across this Harrington guy's name and what convinced you that he's involved."

Misty reached across the table to snag a few chips from Caleb's bag, earning her a growl. She stuck out her tongue and sat back, nibbling on one of the chips while he dumped the few left in the bag into his mouth.

"When I slipped into Aldaran's servers, it took me only seconds to confirm they'd built the facility in Siberia," she said. "They didn't even try to hide the construction plans and approval paperwork. Now, figuring out who paid for the work was a little harder, but not nearly as difficult as it should have been."

"What do you mean?" Hudson asked from the other side of Brielle. "I thought you were a wiz at digging through these computer systems. Nobody can hide anything from you, right?"

Misty grinned. "True, but normally, people who are trying to hide things at least attempt to make it difficult. They bury the information in places you wouldn't normally look, pile a mountain of encryption on top of it, and separate key pieces so it's hard to connect them. But in this case, it was as easy as opening the folder filed under the letter *I* for incriminating evidence."

"So what'd you find?" Caleb asked around a mouthful of peanut butter he was now eating straight from the jar with a spoon. At one time, Brielle might have been shocked by something like that, but now she couldn't help but think of him as anything but a big, adorable goofball—with fangs.

Misty ate another chip from the pile in her cupped hand. "All the evidence clearly shows that Aldaran was working for a group of hard-liners within the Russian Federal Security Service...the old KGB. Anyone finding the same thing I did would assume this splinter cell is pursuing a new technology that would give Russia a military advantage years beyond the other major superpowers."

"But you don't believe that?" Sawyer asked curiously.

Misty shrugged. "Not really. Like I said, the evidence was too easy to find. And worse, if you look at the upload times, you'll notice that all the evidence was dumped onto the servers at nearly the same moment. That tells me that someone hacked in and staged the evidence, assuming everyone would immediately believe it without digging any deeper."

Beside Misty, Forrest chuckled. "Except you, because you're the suspicious type."

"I am." She smiled. "I ended up following the evidence trail along an endless assortment of communication cables and satellites, out of Europe, across the Atlantic, all the way to the computers in Harrington's office in New York City."

"Wait a minute," Jake interrupted, sitting up straighter in his chair, an alarmed look on his face. "You actually hacked your consciousness all the way around the world? Isn't that dangerous?"

Brielle could understand why Jake was so concerned. She'd been terrified of getting lost inside the relatively small computer network inside that facility in Siberia. The idea of leaving her body that far behind and surfing the internet infrastructure all the way from Moscow to New York made her knees shake.

"It wasn't as much dangerous as it was exhausting," Misty said as Harley got up to walk into the adjoining kitchen. "The best way I can describe it is sort of like running a marathon while breathing through a straw. I don't plan on ever doing it again, but it paid off; that's what matters. We might not know why Harrington is doing it and what his endgame might be, but at least we finally know who's behind this whole thing."

Harley came out of the kitchen with a few more bags of chips, tossing them on the table, then sitting down beside Sawyer again as they all discussed what to do next. Since Julian had fallen completely off the radar, Brielle couldn't add much to the conversation, so she sat there and listened as Misty and Genevieve talked about what they'd be doing the rest of the night, namely working with the analysts back in DC to build a file on Xavier Harrington and everyone associated with him.

"Speaking of which, is anyone else concerned that those supernaturals we fought tonight seemed to know exactly where we were and what we were doing?" Hudson asked. "They shut down the video feeds and hit the server room as if Misty was their target all along. They probably would have gotten to her, too, if it wasn't for Caleb losing his damn mind."

Brielle glanced at Caleb, wondering if he was offended by the remark, but he didn't even lift his head as he tried to get the last of the peanut butter out of the bottom of the jar with the spoon.

"What are you saying?" Jes asked. "That you think someone in STAT tipped off Xavier Harrington about Misty being a technopath and that he sent his goons to try to take her out?"

That started a whole new discussion—although maybe *argument* was a better word—until Jake finally shut it down.

"We don't have enough information to know if there's a

mole inside STAT, and arguing won't change that," he said. "Unfortunately, Misty and Genevieve will probably be up most of the night, but that doesn't mean the rest of us can't get some sleep. We're already booked on the first flight to New York City tomorrow and I, for one, am beat."

Within minutes, the dining room emptied out, everyone heading for the bedrooms they'd claimed when they'd first gotten there. Brielle followed more slowly, Caleb falling into step beside her as they made their way upstairs.

"Thanks for pulling me out of that downward spiral I was trapped in," he said softly as they reached the landing. Brielle wondered if he was keeping his voice low so his teammates wouldn't hear or because he was embarrassed about losing control and not being able to stop. "If you hadn't gotten through to me when you did, I'd probably still be running around Moscow like a psycho trying to find those guys."

Seeing Caleb standing there looking lost and almost a little hurt, Brielle had to fight the urge to wrap her arms around him and hug him tight. While he might like kissing, hug therapy didn't seem like his thing. Instead, she took his hand and led him over to the couch in the center of the common area off the stairs. With the bedroom doors closed, they shouldn't disturb anyone if they talked quietly enough.

"You don't have to thank me for that," she said.

"Yeah, I do." The corner of his mouth edged up. "Most people stay out of my way when I go all omega."

She returned his smile with a small one of her own. "I'm not most people."

He regarded her thoughtfully for a moment. "No, you aren't."

"If you don't mind me asking, what made you lose control like that?" she asked. "I've seen you do it before, but this seemed more extreme than the other times."

Caleb was silent for so long that she thought he wouldn't answer, but then: "It was. Or at least, it felt like that to me."

"But why?" She nudged gently when he didn't continue.

He let out a heavy sigh. "I was pretty far gone from the moment the bullets started flying because I knew it meant you were in danger. Then afterward, when I smelled your blood, it was like the human part of me was gone completely, leaving nothing but an enraged, scared omega werewolf behind."

Enraged seemed to be the default setting for Caleb's inner werewolf, so that wasn't surprising. It was the other part of his confession that had her a little confused.

She turned on the couch so she could look at him, tucking one knee under the other. "Why would smelling my blood terrify you?"

Caleb didn't say anything right away, and from his expression, it seemed like he was still wondering that same thing himself.

"Because you're special," he finally said, the words coming out slowly, carefully, as if he was worried he'd get them wrong. "In some ways, I think I've known that since the moment I met you all those months ago. But I didn't understand exactly how special you are to me until I smelled your blood and realized you'd been wounded. That's when it hit me that I could lose you before I even got a chance to get to know you."

As he spoke, Caleb's eyes began to glow blue at the edges, and before she knew what she was doing, Brielle was off the couch and climbing into his lap. His hands immediately found their way to her hips, but she caught one and slid it under her shirt to rest on top of the well-healed bullet wound.

"But you didn't lose me. That's what matters," she said urgently, enjoying the feel of his warm skin against hers, his firm thighs beneath her legs. "The wound is completely closed up and barely hurts at all. So that chance you wanted to get to know me? Well, there's nothing stopping you."

"Nothing right now," he murmured, his hands slowly pushing up her shirt, fingers grazing their way up the sensitive skin of her stomach. "But what happens the next time or the time after that? There aren't always going to be supernaturals with healing abilities hanging around that you can borrow from to save you when you get hurt."

"Maybe we should worry about tomorrow…tomorrow," she whispered, leaning forward until her lips were close to his. "Right now, I'm more interested in tonight and getting to know each other better."

He opened his mouth to say something, but she put an end to any further conversation by kissing him. She groaned at the taste of his tongue on hers. It was that unique favor she'd come to associate with Caleb's mouth mixed with the perfect hint of peanut butter. What could she say but yum?

Caleb's hands began to tease their way up her stomach as the kiss deepened. But as good as his fingers felt, Brielle caught his hands in hers, stopping their exploration. He immediately pulled away with a questioning look on his face.

She smiled down at him. "Not that I'm complaining, but before this goes any further, maybe we should find a room. I have no interest in putting on a show if one of your teammates decides to come out here."

That earned her a soft chuckle, his breath warm against her neck as he nuzzled there, teasing little kisses along her pulse point. "Do you want this to go any further?" he hummed in her ear, the low rumble of his voice sending slivers along her spine.

"It damn sure better," she warned, leaning in to kiss him again, harder this time, as if her intensity could clue him in on how much she wanted this. Because she did want him, more than she'd ever wanted any other man.

"Well, never let it be said I would ever disappoint a lady," he murmured against her mouth.

Caleb stood, his hands coming down to cup her butt as she instinctively wrapped her legs around him. He carried her across the common area in a few quick strides and into one of the rooms. In the dim light of the bedside lamp, Brielle made out a large backpack in the corner of the room—the one Caleb used to carry his clothes and stuff instead of a suitcase, because apparently, he hated suitcases. She got a funny quiver in her stomach when she realized he'd brought her to his room. It was absolutely silly, but she couldn't help feeling the choice meant something big.

He kicked the door closed behind them with a growl before moving over to the bed. Brielle expected him to place her down gently on the puffy comforter. Hell, knowing Caleb, a toss wouldn't have been out of the question. But instead, he turned and slowly sat down on the edge of the mattress, easing her legs from around his back until she was comfortably straddling his lap like she'd been earlier.

"Now, where were we?" he whispered as he pulled her head down for another kiss, his teeth nipping at her lower lip as his hands found their way under her shirt, his long fingers inching their way up the sides of her ribs until he was cupping her breasts. Brielle let out a soft moan as he began to tease her nipples through the silken material of her bra with his thumbs, the peaks stiffening immediately. The tingles his touch generated only added to the heat building between her legs—a heat that grew when she started grinding herself against the hard-on rapidly tightening the front of his jeans.

Before she was aware of what he was doing, Caleb gently pushed her shirt up. He moved slowly, though, like he wanted to give her a chance to change her mind.

Like that's going to happen.

Instead, she reached down to help, grabbing the hem of the top and pulling it over her head, then casually tossing it aside.

"If I remember correctly, I think this is where we were heading," she said with a soft laugh as his warm mouth started tracing kisses down her neck and along her collarbone, to the top of her breasts.

Reaching around behind her, she unclasped her bra, slowly taking it off and dropping it to the floor to join her shirt.

The heat in Caleb's eyes was a tangible thing as he gazed at her half-naked body, and Brielle silently reveled in the sensation of being visually consumed like she was the most beautiful woman in the world. It was an expression she could get used to.

Those big, wonderful, warm hands of his came up slowly to cup her bare breasts this time, fingers squeezing, almost driving the breath from her body as he massaged her in a way no other man ever had. His touch was aggressive, almost rough, and altogether intoxicating. It was obvious that someone like Caleb would have such a firm touch. Only Brielle hadn't realized how much she'd like it.

"Yes," she babbled. "Just like that."

She was more than ready to have him caress her breasts like that for the rest of the night, but when he dropped his head down and closed his mouth around one of her sensitive nipples, she decided that, actually, this was what she wanted to do for the rest of the night.

Brielle sat there in Caleb's lap, trying hard not to lose her mind. The way he nipped and teased, scraping his slightly extended fangs across the stiff peaks with the absolutely perfect amount of pressure was heavenly.

"Oh, mon Dieu," she moaned, slipping into French without even thinking about it, her back arching, hands coming up to wrap around the back of his head, fingers gripping his hair as she yanked him closer, silently begging him to keep going. "Don't you dare stop."

Caleb did stop, but only long enough to move his mouth over to her other nipple, dragging the edge of one of his fangs across the tip and drawing a yelp of pleasure from her. Brielle never thought she'd be so aroused by something like this, but he was driving her absolutely crazy. It had never been like this with any man she'd ever been with.

Like they had a mind of their own, Brielle's hips began making little circles, grinding her clit right against Caleb's hard-on. Even through all their clothing, it still felt amazing. After a minute or so, she felt that familiar tingling building deep inside, the one that always made an appearance right before she climaxed really hard.

Caleb urged her on, pulling back when the tremors began to crest, his eyes glowing blue as she ground herself against him, her breathing coming faster and faster until she couldn't stop herself from opening her mouth to scream.

His mouth covered hers as she came, muffling the keening sound that ripped its way out of her body as she shook and trembled against him. The pleasure was so intense she bit his lower lip a little, but he didn't seem to mind. Throughout her entire climax, his eyes never once left hers. Somehow, that only made the ride even better.

She felt limp and boneless by the time the orgasm was done with her and didn't complain a bit as Caleb shifted her to the side and gently urged her back onto the bed. She lay there contentedly as her big, hunky omega werewolf carefully worked her shoes and jeans off, her panties soon joining the pile of clothes on the floor.

"You're not going to eat me, are you?" she asked with a grin as Caleb gazed down at her with an expression that could only be called hungry—if not starving.

He moved closer, casually reaching down to slowly wrap his hand around her right ankle, gently lifting her leg. "I must admit, the thought has entered my mind," he said with a soft growl that did all kinds of crazy things to Brielle's pulse. After the orgasm she just had, she thought it would take a few minutes to get ready for another. It appeared she was wrong.

Caleb's mouth came down and pressed a kiss to the inside of her leg, his warm lips grazing her sensitive ankle bone, which was clearly an erogenous zone she never knew she had.

His glowing blue eyes never left hers as he worked his way up the inside of her leg, nibbling and kissing the entire way. Brielle was shivering by the time he reached her inner thigh, his long fangs scraping along the tender skin there. For a second, she wondered if Caleb would bite her. There was a part of her that wished he would. Just a little.

But then his mouth was on her pussy, and any thoughts of fangs and biting disappeared in the delirium of Caleb's tongue gliding up one side of her folds and down the other. He applied the perfect amount of pressure—studiously avoiding her clit for the moment—as if he could read her mind and knew exactly the way she liked it.

She spread her legs wide, making room for Caleb's broad shoulders even as she twisted her fingers tightly into his hair. It wasn't that she felt like she needed to control his movement or keep him in place. It was quite obvious he knew what he was doing when it came to making love to her. But still, she liked the idea of being able to encourage him to keep going if she wanted to. And in her mind, nothing screamed *don't stop* like a good hair yank.

Brielle barely noticed when one of Caleb's fingers began to tease the opening of her pussy. Mostly because the sensation of his tongue tracing little circles around her clit was too much of a distraction. But she definitely noticed when he slid one of those fingers deep inside. He had long fingers.

"Yes, just like that," she murmured in French when he made curling motions with his finger and began caressing.

As her body spasmed and writhed in rhythm with his movements, she kept up a constant stream of French. She knew he didn't understand what she was saying, but the intent must have been clear, because he started to move his finger faster. His mouth came down directly over her clit, rapid flicks of the tongue shoving her roughly over the edge into the second climax of the night, this one even stronger than the first.

Brielle cried out in pleasure. She knew full well that everyone in the safe house would hear and know exactly what she and Caleb were doing, but she didn't care. She didn't care about anything but how good Caleb was making her feel.

Her thighs clamped around his shoulders so hard that it probably would have hurt if he wasn't a werewolf. Instead, he barely seemed to care as she yanked his hair and rode her way through what had to be the longest orgasm of her life.

Her vision was dim, and the muscles of her thighs and stomach were wrung out to the point of exhaustion by the time the pleasurable tremors finally faded away. This man would be the death of her, she was sure.

She lay there on the bed doing a very good imitation of a puddle of goo, half-listening to Caleb moving around. The thuds of boots hitting the floor told her that Caleb was getting naked. That fact should have been enough to make her lift her head and watch the show—because she seriously wanted to see him naked—but she was too tired. So instead, she stayed where she was. There was no doubt she'd be seeing plenty of naked werewolf in a few seconds when he climbed into bed with her.

Her mind cataloged the clink of his belt buckle as it was undone, then the sound of heavy fabric joining the boots on the floor. She didn't hear the shirt follow but had no doubt that piece of clothing was gone now, too. She found her mind imagining what he looked like without clothes, using all her previous glimpses of his body as the starting point. He would be beautiful, she was sure of that.

It took him a bit longer to come back to bed than she'd expected, but then she heard him digging through his backpack and realized he was grabbing a condom. For some reason, she hated that he had those so readily at hand, but then decided that was stupid. Caleb was a lot of things, but a monk wasn't one of them. What he'd done for comfort before he'd met her was his business and no different than the men she'd slept with before meeting him.

But as reasonable as that internal dialogue might be, it didn't change the fact that she didn't like the idea of Caleb sleeping with anyone but her, or the insane thought that he wouldn't be doing it anymore, now that she had him.

Had him?

What the hell was he, a puppy she rescued from a shelter?

She was still lost in those thoughts when Caleb finally came back into view, his very large, very naked body appearing above her as he stopped by the side of the bed.

The breath left her body at the sight of him. Oh, damn, her earlier imaginings had missed the mark by a kilometer. Yes, he was beautiful. But that one word simply wasn't adequate to describe the man in front of her right then. Actually, now that she thought about it, she decided there wasn't a word for a man this perfect.

Caleb's shoulders were broad and thick with muscles, and his arms and pecs had her thinking he could likely bench-press a truck. As her gaze traveled downward, she felt her fingers twitching at the sight of his well-defined abs, suddenly having a crazy urge to trace every single line of them with her nails so she could see them flex and ripple.

Slightly lower, nestled between his powerful thighs, stood the most scrumptious cock she'd seen. Just imagining him inside her made her moan in delight.

As he tugged at the foil wrapper in his hands, she was up in a flash, reaching for it. "Let me do that."

She wanted—needed—to get her hands on him.

She sat on the edge of the bed, dropping the package on the sheet so she could wrap both hands around him and slowly caress up and down. He was warm under her grip, hard and throbbing. She leaned over to kiss him, but he only let her have a quick lick or two before pulling her up and handing her the condom packet.

"You need to put that on—now," he growled. "If you want to revisit that particular activity later, I definitely won't complain, but right now, I need to be inside you."

Smiling up at him, she tore open the foil packet and quickly rolled the condom down his rock-hard shaft.

Caleb moved so fast he was almost a blur, and a second later, she found herself lying back on the bed. He quickly settled himself between her legs, his huge, naked body hovering over her, heat pouring off his bare skin.

"You need to tell me now if you want to slow down," he said softly, that faint blue glow ringing the outsides of his irises again. "I don't want to lose control and scare you again."

Brielle grasped his shoulders and pulled him down on top of her so his arms were on either side of her head, the head of his cock finding her wetness easily, like he was made to be inside her.

"You don't scare me, Caleb," she whispered. "I want to be with you—all of you. Let yourself go. I know you'll never hurt me."

Caleb took Brielle at her word, sliding in deep with one long plunge. The feel of him inside her made her gasp in the best possible way. She'd always read about women being touched in places no one had ever touched and had to admit that it had always struck her as prose reserved for romance books. But it turned out that those novels were right. It really *was* a thing, and Caleb had let her experience it. The feel of him buried fully in her core had her panting for breath, ready to beg if he didn't start moving soon.

Her legs came up and wrapped around his hips of their own accord, even as he pulled out halfway, then slid back in with a slow, steady glide that rocked her whole body and almost knocked the air out of her lungs.

Caleb started slow, but as soon as Brielle began to rock her hips in time with his, he changed the pace, until he was pounding into her like nothing she'd ever experienced before. At the same time, his mouth came down on hers, stealing what little breath she had left before his lips moved down to her neck and shoulder. As his fangs scraped lightly against her skin, she once again found herself wanting him to bite her.

Which had to be totally insane.

Right?

She was certain there was no way she'd be able to come again, not three times in one night, but as Caleb continued to thrust into her at the same wild pace, she couldn't mistake that familiar tingle beginning to build again deep inside her. Slipping a hand down between their bodies, she made little circles on her clit with the tips of her fingers.

"Harder," she moaned, the words barely making it past her clenched teeth. "I'm going to come again."

Caleb must have understood her because the next several thrusts were hard enough to slide her up the bed a few inches. That was all it took to tip her completely over the edge, and she came so hard she had to bite her knuckles to keep from screaming out loud.

A few seconds later, Caleb was coming, too, growls rumbling up through his broad chest. This time, he *did* sink his fangs in her shoulder, hard enough to leave marks, she was sure. But rather than being painful, the sensation was so pleasurable that it nudged her orgasm to the next level.

She barely realized what was happening when Caleb suddenly flipped them both over, letting her ride out the last of her orgasm from on top, his hands gripping her hips as she collapsed on his chest, gasping for air and trembling like a kitten.

It was only afterward, when she was draped happily across his body, his warmth seeping into her like a drug, that Brielle realized exactly how much trouble she was in. She'd only slept with Caleb once and already couldn't imagine ever being with anyone else.

CHAPTER 13

New York City

CALEB TUGGED AT THE ROUGH COLLAR OF HIS OFF-THE-RACK dress shirt as he looked around the expansive but crowded lobby area outside the United Nations General Assembly Hall, biting his tongue to hold in the growl of discomfort.

"I don't understand why you get to be the debonair diplomat while I have to play the part of the hulking security goon," he muttered.

Forrest let out a snort as he casually adjusted the jacket of his much nicer, much more expensive suit and took a sip from the crystal flute of champagne he'd been carrying around as he toured the hall. Champagne that Caleb couldn't drink because he was *working*.

"Maybe it's because I look like a debonair diplomat," Forrest said without looking in his direction, "while you look like a hulking security goon."

Caleb would have punched his teammate if it wasn't for the fact that Forrest was completely right. Caleb probably could have pulled off Forrest's role right up until he opened his mouth. Smooth talking wasn't his thing. Especially at a huge international humanitarian conference like this one, where everyone would expect him to be knowledgeable on all the latest environmental and social issues going on around the world. Now was one of those times he missed not reading those newspapers.

McKay was fully aware of Caleb's shortcomings, which explained why the boss had sent him undercover as one of the extra security guards brought in to supplement the UN staff for the big event. Then again, McKay had also slipped Harley in as a member of the security force, and she certainly couldn't be described as big and hulking. So maybe, it was merely a coincidence.

Forrest moved away, leaving Caleb standing there alone against the wall. Well, not really alone, since he was surrounded by at least five or six hundred well-dressed snobs of both the foreign and domestic variety. With so many people around, he couldn't help but feel a little worried. Jake, Jestina, Sawyer, Misty, Hudson, and Genevieve were all down in the Financial District sneaking into the Harrington Group's business offices, leaving Caleb, Brielle, Forrest, and Harley here in Midtown on their own to keep an eye on Xavier Harrington and let Jake know if the billionaire left the UN. Jake also wanted Brielle or Harley to get close enough to Harrington to figure out if the guy was human or supernatural, but only if they could do it without risking themselves or causing a scene.

"We don't want a confrontation in the middle of the frigging United Nations General Assembly," Jake had warned, looking directly at Caleb the entire time.

Still, as low risk as this part of the mission might seem, Caleb knew that if something went wrong, the four of them would be on their own, because there was no way Jake and the rest of the team could provide backup.

Caleb glanced around the huge atrium, keeping his face as expressionless as every other security guard in the place. From the corner of his eye, he could see Harrington standing maybe a hundred feet away, holding court with a group of fawning dignitaries. It wasn't hard to understand why. Fifteen minutes earlier, the man had stood at the podium in front of the entire United Nations and committed the Harrington Group to donating a billion dollars for water treatment, sustainable food, and renewable energy throughout Africa, the Middle East, and Indonesia. Other business leaders had practically fallen over themselves in an effort to try and match his offer.

Harrington was tall—six foot two at least—with dark hair that had the slightest touch of gray at the temples and the quintessential aristocratic features that gave him a distinguished look. While not overly muscular, he seemed fit in a wiry kind of way. His most defining characteristic had to be his eyes. Pale green, they reminded Caleb of jade. They made you either want to stare at him or look away as fast as you could, Caleb still wasn't sure which.

What he did know for sure was that Xavier Harrington was rich beyond belief. It was hard to say exactly how wealthy, since most of his money was tied up in the Harrington Group, which almost seemed more like a family business than a major corporation. But it was safe to assume the man was probably among the top five richest people in the world. That billion dollars he'd just donated was probably a proverbial drop in the bucket to him.

Harrington and his group had an extremely diverse portfolio. They were involved in banking and finances, real estate, energy, construction, communications, and food production. Surprisingly, the one area the group was not into was arms and weaponry. Between his generosity and violent opposition to the defense industry, it was difficult to believe that the man could be behind a scheme to steal twenty nuclear weapons and apparently use them to power a laser strong enough to destroy half the world. No matter how hard Caleb tried, he couldn't make sense of the dichotomy.

Not that he thought there was a snowball's chance in hell the man wasn't involved. Misty and Genevieve had found enough evidence to confirm it several times over.

First, there were pictures of people from one of Harrington Group's advanced research teams arriving and departing from a small airport only a few hours away from the underground facility in Siberia. Next, ownership of one of the ships leaving the port near Incirlik had been connected to Harrington through a complicated series of shell companies. That ship had sailed straight to New

York City, where it had been met by people from the Harrington Group, who had unloaded crates that looked perfect for holding the stolen nukes. And if those two pieces of evidence weren't good enough, just this morning, STAT had confirmed that the satellites used to redirect those laser beams had belonged to a communication company that essentially answered to Harrington.

Once Misty and Genevieve laid it all out, Caleb had a hard time believing it had taken so long to get to this point. Shouldn't the combined resources of three intelligence agencies have been able to figure this out faster?

Unfortunately, while they might know for sure that Xavier Harrington and his international conglomeration were involved in the theft of the nukes, that didn't mean they had any idea where the man might be keeping them or what he intended to do with them next. Hence Jake's scheme to sneak into the Harrington Group offices so Misty could surf her way through their secure computer servers while Xavier was at the UN conference.

Caleb moved a little closer to Harrington and his entourage, hoping to pick up the man's scent…and failing. Unfortunately, he didn't know if that was because Harrington wasn't a supernatural or simply because his nose was so worthless.

"Uriel Cerano and about a half dozen members of his security team just arrived," Harley announced softly over the radio in Caleb's ear. "But right now, they seem content to wait in the parking garage with Harrington's limo. I'll stay out of sight and keep an eye on them so I can let you know if they head your way."

Caleb breathed a sigh of relief at that announcement. If they wanted to avoid that confrontation Jake had been worried about, staying out of sight of the supernaturals they'd fought in Moscow was obviously necessary.

While they were still digging when it came to learning the identity of most of Harrington's bodyguards, Misty and Genevieve had come up with quite a bit on the telekinetic supernatural who ran the security team. Uriel Cerano had been born and raised in Palermo, Italy, where he'd lived until he was in his late teens, when he'd gotten into some kind of trouble and had abruptly fled his hometown to join the French Foreign Legion.

Caleb skirted the perimeter of the atrium, the well-dressed and the well-to-do ignoring him for the most part but still subconsciously making room nonetheless. Caleb almost laughed out loud when he thought about Uriel being in the Foreign Legion. Honestly, he'd thought the legion wasn't even a thing anymore, but as it turned out, he was wrong. Uriel had fought in a few dozen battles in Africa as part of the global war on terrorism, even earning himself French citizenship when he'd been seriously wounded during one of those battles. That was another thing that had surprised Caleb. It didn't matter where a person was from. If you bled for France, you became a citizen. He had to admit that was kind of cool.

But then something happened four years ago that got Uriel dismissed from the Legion. Misty and Genevieve were convinced it had something to do with him coming into his telekinetic abilities. There was no way of knowing for sure, but regardless, a few months later, the man had begun working for Harrington.

Caleb stopped when he reached an alcove along the wall where the UN staff had set up a temporary bar. With the crowd of people waiting for their orders, he wasn't too worried about Harrington noticing him standing there staring.

Harrington was talking with a stocky, blond-haired man in a language Caleb didn't recognize. A few moments later, he turned and addressed a dark-skinned woman in yet another language, all three of them laughing at whatever had been said. The people standing with them joined in. Apparently, Harrington was an expert at working a crowd. Maybe that was his supernatural gift, Caleb thought. He supposed that was possible, assuming the guy actually was a supernatural and not simply a smooth talker.

"Xavier Harrington is definitely a supernatural," Brielle

announced softly over the radio, as if reading Caleb's mind. "Though I'm not exactly sure what his abilities are yet. He gets visions. In fact, he's getting them right now. But they're only a blur of random images coming so fast I can't tell what they mean."

Caleb looked across the atrium to see Brielle watching Harrington out the corner of her eye. McKay had gotten Brielle assigned as an interpreter for the French delegation, which had to be the most perfect cover ever. She was even wearing a glamorous black cocktail dress that let her blend right in with the other fancy people. Except she didn't really blend in at all. On the contrary, she stood out like a rose among weeds. Hands down, she was the most exquisite woman here.

It took Caleb a few minutes to realize he was staring. It wasn't his fault. Brielle was so damn beautiful. It was hard being close enough to see her but not able to touch her. Actually, hard was an understatement. A better word for it would be painful.

It had been like that since they'd made love in the safe house outside of Moscow. While his nose was as crappy as ever, for some reason, he still found himself able to pick up her honeysuckle perfume. Even now, he could smell it across a room this large. But while touching her was pure heaven, being separated from her when they were in the same room was agony. It seemed he couldn't go five seconds without thinking about what it had been like sleeping with her.

He clenched his jaw as a member of the French delegation leaned close and whispered something in Brielle's ear, then laughed at his own joke. It was impossible to miss the slimy bastard's interest in her, and it was all Caleb could do to stop himself from striding across the atrium and ripping the guy's face off.

"Dude, you might want to chill out a bit," Forrest said from beside him. Crap, he hadn't even realized his teammate was there. "Your eyes are starting to glow. That might be a bit hard to explain if someone sees."

Caleb dragged his gaze away from Brielle, taking a deep breath and forcing himself to focus on Forrest and the small plate of hors d'oeuvres his teammate held, hoping it would calm his omega side.

"What was that all about?" Forrest asked after it seemed like the impending bout of berserker werewolf had been forestalled. "Not that I really need to ask, considering all the noise the two of you were making the other night."

Caleb grimaced. "You heard?"

Brielle would be mortified if she knew Forrest had overheard them having sex.

"You kidding me?" Forrest let out a soft snort and turned slightly away from him so it wouldn't be obvious that a diplomat was talking with a security guard. "Dude, half the neighborhood probably heard you growling and her screaming. Hell, Genevieve almost pounded on your bedroom door more than once, worried you'd gone all werewolf and were devouring poor Brielle."

Caleb almost chuckled. Yeah, Genevieve seemed like the shy type. She probably would have blushed so hard she passed out if she knew what he and Brielle were doing in his room. "I'm surprised nobody said anything the next morning when we came down for breakfast."

"We wanted to," Forrest admitted. "But we decided as a group that Brielle wasn't ready for teasing like that, so we agreed to bite our tongues for now."

"Thanks," Caleb muttered, not sure what else to say.

He and his teammates ribbed each other about pretty much anything and everything. The fact that they'd decided Brielle and her night of loud, wild sex with him was off-limits was definitely surprising.

"Don't mention it," Forrest murmured. "Besides, when the time is right, you better believe we're going to remind you and her of that night. It would be irresponsible of us not to."

Forrest walked away to help himself to more hors d'oeuvres

from the bar area. Caleb would have loved to eat a few dozen of those pigs in a blanket right then, but security guards weren't supposed to eat on duty. So he couldn't.

Instead, he turned and glanced at Brielle again, a growl slipping out when he saw another Frenchman talking to her.

"So, you and Brielle, huh?" Forrest said, coming back over to him, casually eating a tiny pastry-wrapped hot dog. "Gotta say, while I didn't see it coming, you're good together."

Caleb started to say that, yeah, he thought so, too, but he stopped, the words getting mixed up somewhere between his head and his mouth.

"I'm not sure we're going to keep seeing each other after this whole thing is over."

The thought of never seeing Brielle again hurt so much he could barely breathe, and he actually swayed a little on his feet.

Forrest looked his way, surprise on his face. "Why would you say something like that?"

Caleb suddenly felt stupid for even opening his mouth. When the hell had he suddenly become the *sharing* kind? But it was too late to backtrack now. Forrest would never let this go. Besides, if he didn't talk to someone about it, he'd go frigging insane.

"We're too different," he said, finally putting words to the doubts filling his head. "She's a beautiful woman who could have any man on the planet. I'm a soup sandwich with anger management issues, a criminal record, and one screwup in STAT standing between me and a ten-year prison term. I mean, seriously, why the hell would someone like Brielle ever want to have anything to do with me?"

"Don't ask me," Forrest said with a chuckle. "You're right about her being way too good for you. But considering the fact that you two are sleeping together, it's obvious she sees something worthwhile in you."

Caleb shifted from one foot to the other, rolling his suddenly tight shoulders. "That was just sex," he mumbled even as a part of him hated to think that was the case.

Forrest frowned. "You honestly don't believe that, do you?"

Caleb didn't say anything, mainly because he wasn't sure what he believed. He wanted to be wrong about this but...

"Look," Forrest said. "Even if you are right about it not meaning anything to Brielle—which I don't think you are, by the way—I can tell that sleeping with her obviously means something to you or we wouldn't be having this conversation. Am I right?"

"Yeah," Caleb admitted quietly. "Which only makes this situation more difficult. I find myself hoping that the other night meant as much to her, but I have no way of knowing. So now, I'm left to wonder, thinking the worst and driving myself crazy."

Forrest regarded him thoughtfully for a long moment. "Okay, I know this is probably going to sound a little out there, but have you ever thought about simply talking to Brielle and asking her what that night was about for her?"

Caleb stared at Forrest like he was a pig wearing a Rolex. Hell, for all he knew, the watch STAT had given his teammate to wear might *actually* be one. "Talk to her. Just like that. Are you on drugs? I can't talk to Brielle about something like this."

"Why not?" Forrest asked. "Don't tell me you're scared of talking to her. I've seen you charge into a tunnel full of cannibalistic humanoid underground dwellers without thinking twice. Having a serious conversation with Brielle can't be any more terrifying than that."

"I wouldn't be so sure," Caleb muttered. "The worst thing those creatures down in the tunnels could do was eat me. Brielle could hurt me a lot worse than they ever could."

Forrest didn't say anything for a moment, and Caleb wasn't sure if the guy's expression was one of happiness...or pity.

"Wow," Forrest finally said. "You really got it bad for her, don't you?"

Ingrained instinct demanded that he deny that accusation, but Caleb knew it was too late for that. Forrest already knew the truth.

"How the hell did you get so smart about women, anyway?" he demanded, deciding that a good way to avoid answering a truly painful question was by asking one of his own.

Forrest shrugged, eating the last of his hors d'oeuvres before setting the small plate on the tall cocktail table beside him. "The same way every man learns about women…from a woman. In this case, Misty. She made me work for it before letting me get close to her. That meant lots of talking, which is how I learned that women like to know what a guy thinks. That's why I suggested you and Brielle spend some time talking—preferably before sleeping together again—so you can figure out where you stand with each other."

Caleb considered that. "How did you and Misty meet?"

He knew he was simply grasping for any topic that would allow him to avoid talking—or even thinking—about his own problems, but since he didn't know their story, it seemed as good a time as any to ask.

The look Forrest gave him said he knew exactly what Caleb was doing. But Forrest let it go, for the moment at least.

"I was her backup on her very first mission," Forrest said. "STAT was just starting to put supernaturals on the teams back then and was having problems finding people willing to work with them. I didn't see what the big deal was, so I volunteered. I ended up saving her butt that first trip out, so STAT started putting us together more often. We hit it off right from the beginning but kept it professional for months. We talked for a long time before deciding to sleep together. You know, that adult-conversation thing I mentioned? Even then, we were limited to those occasions when we were on a mission together and were able to slip away and be alone. It wasn't easy."

"How did you two end up together on this team?"

"We talked about what we were both looking for, what kind of future we wanted, and what we were willing to risk to have that future." He pinned Caleb with a look. "You know, that serious conversation stuff I keep mentioning? Anyway, long story short, Misty hacked STAT's human resources computers and got us put on this new team together. The rest is history."

"Wow," Caleb muttered, a little stunned they'd done something like that. "Weren't you worried that it wouldn't work out between you and you'd end up stuck being teammates?"

Forrest didn't even have to think about it before he shook his head. "Not at all. Because we talked about it and realized that being together was what we both wanted. We were both willing to risk anything—including our jobs—to do it."

Caleb wasn't sure he could ever be that bold and put himself out there like that.

"Okay, now that we've wasted enough time talking about Misty and me, why don't you tell me why you're having doubts about you and Brielle?" Forrest murmured as he pretended to sip his champagne. "And don't try that crap about her being too good for you. I know there's something else going on."

Caleb glanced over at Brielle, his gaze lingering on her for a moment before turning back to Forrest. "I'm an omega," he said, the words so soft he wasn't sure if his teammate would even be able to hear them. "That means I don't get to have what you and Misty have. Or what Jake and Jes or Harley and Sawyer have. Being an omega means being alone. Forever."

Caleb knew that sounded rather dramatic, but Forrest seemed to take it in stride. "Even if Brielle is *The One* for you?"

He wasn't surprised his teammate had jumped straight to that conclusion. After seeing it happen firsthand with Jake and Jes, then Harley and Sawyer, Forrest probably knew as much about the legend of *The One*—that one person each werewolf was supposed to spend their lives with—than anyone on the planet.

"She's not *The One* for me," Caleb said firmly.

Forrest lifted a brow. "You sure of that?"

His teammate wasn't going to let this go, was he?

Caleb bit back a growl. "Look, omegas don't get soul mates, okay?"

Finally putting into words the one thing that terrified him more than anything else in the world was one of the hardest things he'd ever done, but there it was. The thought of getting shot, stabbed, or even blown up had never worried him. Hell, he wasn't even scared of dying. But the thought of being alone forever ate away at him from the very darkest corners of his mind like it was a living thing.

"Says who?" Forrest asked quietly, the look on his face suggesting he thought Caleb was full of it.

"Says every omega I've ever met," Caleb ground out. "Trust me, it's all omegas talk about when they stumble across each other. It's the one thing we all have in common. Besides a complete lack of control, I mean. We don't get to have soul mates."

Forrest sighed. "This may be completely off base, but I'm going to say it anyway, because I think you need to hear it. I think all this crap you keep spouting about omegas not getting to have soul mates is merely cover for the fact that you're scared that this thing with Brielle could be real and that you're going to mess it up like you have with so many other things in your life. So you figure, if it's all going to blow up at some point, just do it now and get it over with. Less pain for you that way, right?"

Caleb wished he could deny it, but truthfully, Forrest had hit the nail on the head. He'd known Brielle was *The One* for him since the first time he' smelled her honeysuckle perfume. No, not her *perfume*. Her honeysuckle *scent*. But he'd spent every second since then trying to ignore the obvious, listing one reason after another for why it couldn't be true because he couldn't imagine the world letting him have something so perfect. Not when his life had been nothing but one big disappointment piled on top of an effing train wreck.

"Assuming you're right," Caleb muttered, scanning the room so he would have an excuse for not looking at his teammate, "what the hell am I supposed to do, then?"

"I've already told you what to do," Forrest said with a shake of his head. "Sit down and talk to her. Honestly tell her how you feel and find out if she feels the same."

Caleb blew out a breath. "You make it sound so easy. But I'm not sure I'd even know where to start. I'll probably open my mouth, nothing will come out, and I'll look like an idiot."

He was hoping Forrest might give him a few suggestions—maybe even tell him the exact words he should use—but before his friend could say anything, a burst of static over the radio interrupted them.

"Harrington's driver just started the limo, and two members of his security team are heading into the atrium," Harley said. "I'm going to move closer so I can pick up Harrington's scent when he comes out and figure out what kind of supernatural he is."

"I'm moving closer, too," Brielle added, slipping away from her French contingent before Caleb had a chance to tell her to stay where she was. "Sometimes I can get a better feel for a supernatural's abilities when I'm closer to them."

Caleb growled under his breath and started moving to intercept Brielle, Forrest at his heels. They had no idea how dangerous Harrington might be, and Caleb sure as hell wasn't going to let her be the test dummy to find out.

Even though he and Forrest were still half an atrium away, Caleb could hear the billionaire announcing to his avid audience that he had to leave to deal with another crisis. With that, Harrington turned and headed toward one of the side corridors—and Brielle.

Caleb's heart thumped faster.

"Fall back," Caleb growled softly into the mic hidden in the cuff of his suit jacket. "Do not follow Harrington out of the main lobby, Brielle. I repeat. Do. Not Follow. He could be setting us up for an ambush."

Caleb felt his fangs trying to shove their way out as he realized that Brielle wasn't listening to him. Instead, she moved closer to Harrington and the two bodyguards waiting to escort him to the garage with every step she took.

Caleb picked up his pace, Forrest right there with him. But with all the people in the atrium, there was no way they'd get there in time to stop her.

"Dammit, Brielle, stop," he said.

But it was no use.

Caleb watched in a near panic as she followed Harrington and his guards around the corner that led to the parking garage and the limo waiting there for them. At this time of the evening, with the social event still in full swing, the hallway would be nearly empty.

And the perfect place for an ambush.

Caleb lifted his arm, bringing the mic in his sleeve close to his mouth. "Harley, move in now."

Saying the hell with his cover, he picked up speed. As he ran for the corner Brielle had disappeared around, he realized he wasn't even sure where Harley was at the moment. She'd been keeping an eye on his limo in the garage from wherever she'd been hiding. He only hoped she was closer to Brielle than he was.

Caleb reached inside his jacket and grasped the small automatic secured in the holster under his left arm. He didn't want to cause a panic, so he didn't draw it. But he had his hand around the grip, thumb moving to release the safety.

The moment he rounded the corner into the long hallway that led to the garage, he froze, his fangs and claws extending. The laughs and murmurs of polite conversation in the atrium behind him faded away to nothing at the sight of Brielle standing in the middle of the wide corridor, her weapon out of the holster hidden under her dress, Harrington's bodyguards pointing their weapons straight at her head.

Harley was a little farther down the hallway, closer to the garage, four more men holding weapons on her as she stood with one clawed hand wrapped around the throat of another bodyguard and the other pointing a small-frame Glock straight at Xavier Harrington. Uriel was at his boss's side, ready to put his body in front of Harley's weapon, his large-caliber automatic already pointing in Caleb and Forrest's direction. Harrington didn't seem surprised by their appearance. It was almost as if he'd known they were coming around the corner at just that moment.

Caleb's instincts shouted at him to either pull his weapon and start shooting or tearing his way through everyone standing between him and Brielle. Caleb wasn't sure which one he was going to opt for even as he stepped forward.

Harrington folded his arms over his chest, jade-green eyes locked on Caleb. He was the only unarmed person in the corridor and yet he didn't seem the least bit concerned about that.

"My, my, my," Harrington said, his New York accent slight but easy to pick up. "You are a hard one to get a read on." He glanced at Brielle, then back at Caleb. "But your protective instincts when it comes to her are quite obvious."

Weapons abruptly skewed around all over the place, some coming to rest on Caleb and Forrest, others coming around to threaten Brielle, as if the bad guys decided she was the key to this situation. Uriel especially had a glint in his eye as he aimed his gun at her heart. The thought of someone so important to him being in so much danger pushed Caleb even closer to the edge. He knew, without a doubt, that he was seconds from losing all control, and he didn't give a damn. From the way Harrington and Uriel were looking at him, Caleb could only guess that his eyes were glowing like a blue neon sign.

Caleb glanced at Brielle and saw the fear clear in her gaze. For a moment, he wasn't sure if she was more scared of the men with the guns or of what he was about to do. But then he decided it didn't matter. He'd kill them all to save her. He didn't even care about who'd go down first.

Hating to take his eyes off Brielle but knowing he needed to, he dragged his gaze away from her to look at Harrington. The man regarded him curiously, like Caleb was some sort of puzzle he was trying to figure out.

"I expected something would happen here but definitely not this," Harrington murmured. "Which, if I'm being honest, is extremely concerning. Almost as concerning as those friends of yours currently searching the offices of the Harrington Group. Then again, I have been distracted lately. Now that I know what you're looking for, I realize I need to do something about it."

Fingers started to tighten on triggers, and Caleb knew the shooting was about to start. Less than twenty feet from an atrium full of UN dignitaries. As werewolves, he and Hayley would likely survive a shootout with Harrington's bodyguards, even at this range. But Brielle and Forrest almost certainly wouldn't. He had to get to Brielle and protect her. He only hoped Harley was aware enough to know she had to do the same for Forrest. Misty would be devastated if anything happened to him.

Caleb extended his fangs and claws further. He was gonna kill as many people as he could on his way to Brielle.

Starting with Harrington.

"Father, what's going on?" a soft, feminine voice interrupted just as Caleb was about to launch himself forward.

A moment later, a slender woman with long, blond hair wearing a dress so expensive it probably cost more than the last four or five cars that Caleb had stolen walked into the middle of the crowd of armed people, an irritated expression on her face. Like she was dealing with a room full of first graders arguing over a video game controller.

"You were going to start shooting people in the hallway at a United Nations humanitarian conference?" she demanded, disgust dripping off her words as she stepped in front of Harrington, pushing Uriel's weapon aside without even looking at him. "What the hell is wrong with you?"

"Kiara, you need to leave. Now," Harrington said, his voice a mix of exasperation and anger as he stepped forward and took her arm.

She yanked her arm free of her father's grasp. "Don't even try it. I don't know what you think you're doing, but I refuse to be part of it. Nor will I walk away and act like I didn't see anything."

Caleb was still grappling with the idea that someone like Harrington could have a daughter when the young woman suddenly stepped away from her father and looked around at his bodyguards.

"Put your weapons away, you idiots, before someone comes around the corner and sees you," she ordered.

Caleb wasn't sure that the woman's angry tirade would work, but with a gesture from Harrington, the men slowly holstered their guns. Brielle was immediately at Caleb's side. At the far end of the hallway, Harley finally dropped the man she'd been choking, blood from where her claws had dug into his skin running down his neck. Harley and Forrest took their places to either side of Caleb and Brielle, weapons still out.

Harrington obviously wasn't happy with his daughter's interruption, but after another gesture at his men, they began to peel off and head for the garage one by one.

"I'd like to think we won't be seeing each other again, but we all know that's unlikely," he said, eyes on Caleb. "So instead, I'll admit to looking forward to our next meeting."

Turning on his heel, he strode down the hallway toward the garage. Caleb expected his daughter to follow, but she stayed where she was.

"I don't know who you people are, but if you're smart, you'll stay away from my father," she said to them. "He's more dangerous than you can possibly comprehend."

With that, she hurried to catch up to Harrington, her high heels echoing in the hallway.

"What the hell just happened?" Forrest asked as Kiara disappeared from sight. "I thought we were seconds away from starting the UN version of the O.K. Corral."

"I don't know," Caleb murmured, fighting the urge to wrap his arms around Brielle and hold her close. "But we need to get the hell out of here and warn Jake and the others that Harrington knows they're searching his offices. They could be facing an ambush there, too."

They headed for the garage where they'd parked their SUV. Harrington's limo was nowhere in sight. It was only after they were in the SUV and on their way back to the safe house that Caleb was finally able to breathe freely again. Brielle was safe at the moment, but he had no delusions about how close she'd come to dying. And that thought nearly crushed his soul.

CHAPTER 14

"I CAN'T COME UP WITH ANYTHING ELSE TO EXPLAIN HOW HE knew what we were planning," Jake said, running his hand through his hair in exasperation as he sat down wearily on the big, comfortable-looking couch. "Harrington must have someone inside our organization feeding him information. There's no other way he could have known we were both at the UN and his group offices at the same time."

From where she was perched on the stool at the granite island dividing the living room from the kitchen in the Englewood, New Jersey, home they were using as a safe house, Brielle waited for someone to tell Jake that he was wrong, that there was no way anyone in STAT—or the CIA or NSA for that matter—had ratted them out. But nobody did.

"I'm less concerned about how Harrington knew we were in his building than how his security people seemed to know which way we were going to run during our escape," Sawyer murmured. He was sitting beside Harley on the couch, his face grim. "Even after Misty shut down the building's security cameras, those guards were ahead of us every step of the way. It was like they knew where we were going before we did. We're lucky to have made it out of there alive."

"I've been wondering the same thing." Jake frowned. "Especially since it might mean we don't just have a spy in our organization but somewhere on our team."

As one, everyone—including Brielle—looked at Hudson, who was leaning against the island. He promptly gave them all the finger.

"You've got to be kidding me," he muttered. "I was nearly killed three times trying to get us out of Harrington's offices. And it sure as hell wasn't like I had a chance to communicate with anyone while we were running our asses off."

Sawyer regarded him coolly. "Maybe you have a tracking device on you."

Hudson stepped away from the island, spreading his arms. "Feel free to search me. Right here in front of everyone."

"The tracking device could be one of those high-tech thingies that slip under your skin," Caleb said with a low growl from the kitchen where he was searching through the mostly empty cabinets for something to eat. "I'd have to slice you apart to make sure I don't miss it, though." He glanced over his shoulder, eyes flashing blue for a split second. "I don't think anyone would have a problem with that."

Brielle was surprised by how angry Caleb was. Now that she thought about it, he'd been like that since they'd left the UN building in Midtown.

She was about to ask him what was bothering him—as quietly as she could, of course—but before she could, Hudson circled around the island and strode toward Caleb, a pissed-off, determined look on his face.

"I don't know what the hell your problem is," Hudson said. "But if you have something to say to me, why don't you try it when I'm right in front of you?"

Caleb's eyes turned blue again—and stayed that way this time. Brielle tensed.

Oh crap.

She'd been around her stupid brother enough to recognize a testosterone-laden display of masculinity when she saw it. If Caleb and Hudson got within arm's reach of each other, all hell was going to break loose. The fact that Caleb was not only a werewolf but an omega at that only made it worse. There was a good possibility of someone dying.

Well…there was a good possibility of Hudson dying, anyway.

Before she knew what she was doing, Brielle was off the barstool and hurrying around the island to get between the two of them. She put one hand on Caleb's chest and the other on Hudson's, shoving to keep them apart.

"Stop it right now," she said as firmly as she could, hoping to get through their thick male skulls.

Jake and Sawyer were already on their feet and moving in to help, but she backed them off with a warning look, figuring this whole thing was less likely to turn into a fight with her in the middle of them instead of another werewolf. Jake and Sawyer must have realized that, too, because they stopped where they were.

"Caleb," she said quietly but firmly. "Hudson almost died helping your teammates get out of Harrington's offices. I don't know how Harrington is always a step ahead of us. Maybe he does have someone on the inside. Or maybe he has a supernatural working for him who can read minds. One thing I do know is that Hudson isn't carrying a tracking device under his skin. He's as much a part of the team as I am, and you aren't going to claw him up just because you're in a grouchy mood. Got it?"

She hadn't really meant to call him grouchy, but the words stopped everyone cold, including Caleb, who stood there, mouthing the word to himself, a confused look on his face.

A moment later, the kitchen was filled with laughter as everyone started teasing Caleb for being grouchy. Forrest even went so far as to call him *Oscar*. Brielle held her breath, hoping that wouldn't upset his inner wolf even more, but to her relief, it seemed like the tense situation had been defused. Caleb didn't look like he was ready to punch anyone anymore. He even chuckled a little.

The conversation slowly turned back to what had happened with both teams today—without the finger-pointing this time. Not that it helped them come up with anything useful. As far as Harrington and the debacle at the UN building, all Brielle could say for sure was that he was a supernatural whose abilities seemed to revolve around seeing random images in his head on a nearly constant basis. His daughter, Kiara, seemed to have the same talent, though the visions weren't as chaotic or overwhelming.

The search of Harrington's offices had been the same dismal failure. Misty had gotten inside the firewalls of the corporate servers only to discover that they'd been wiped completely clean of anything dealing with Aldaran or the facility in Surinda. Even the data she'd discovered in Moscow had disappeared.

The worst part was that, even though they knew Xavier Harrington was involved in the theft of the nukes—and that he'd almost certainly brought them to New York—they still had no idea where to turn next.

They'd gone from Incirlik to Zagreb, then Surinda to Odessa, and finally Moscow to New York, yet they were no closer to finding the stolen nuclear weapons than they'd been at the beginning. On top of that, Brielle was no closer to finding her brother, either. She didn't want to let her mind go there, but it was getting harder and harder to believe Julian was still alive.

"We could check out Harrington's other facilities," Genevieve said, distracting Brielle a little with her hopeful expression. "He has at least a dozen different office complexes spread throughout New Jersey and New York. We might get lucky."

Jake shrugged. "It won't hurt to try, but I find it difficult to believe Harrington would have cleaned up his tracks so well at his corporate headquarters but left evidence behind in other places. He doesn't strike me as a careless person."

Everyone agreed with that, including Brielle.

A little while after that, the conversation turned to the one topic she noticed always seemed foremost in the STAT team's mind—food. Not that Brielle could blame them. She could definitely go for something to eat. While Sawyer and Hudson wanted to simply order pizza, everyone else wanted to get out of the house for a while.

"I'm tired of takeout," Harley added. "Let's go to a restaurant for a change."

"And then do some grocery shopping afterward," Misty suggested. "We have no idea how long we'll be staying at this safe house, and there isn't much in the way of food here."

Brielle thought Caleb would be the first one heading for the door, so she was surprised when he wandered back into the kitchen. She walked over to him.

"Aren't you coming out with the rest of us?" she asked.

He shook his head without looking her way, eyes trained on the cabinet he'd just opened. "Nah. I don't feel like going out. I'll find something to eat here."

Brielle threw a quick look at Misty, who nodded and urged a curious Forrest out the front door, saying she'd grab takeout from the restaurant.

"You should have gone with them. The food options are limited here," Caleb said, taking a box of graham crackers and a jar of peanut butter out of the cabinet.

How did she know he'd find peanut butter? He was like a peanut-butter-sniffing bloodhound. Or peanut-butter-sniffing werewolf, she guessed.

"I'm fine with peanut butter and crackers if you are."

She frowned when he turned his back to her, focused on opening the box of graham crackers and ignoring her completely. For some reason, the idea that he didn't even want to look at her hurt more than it should.

Sighing, she walked over to the fridge to grab two bottles of water. It didn't exactly go with peanut butter, but the other option was some generic-looking beer in a can, which she flat-out refused to drink.

After the night they'd spent together in Moscow, Brielle had been so sure there was something between them. Something she hadn't allowed herself to even consider as a possibility. She'd tried to talk to him about it the next morning when they'd woken up in each other's arms, but before she'd had the chance, Jake was knocking on the bedroom door saying they had to move fast to make the flight to America. Between the long flight and then the mission at the UN conference, they hadn't been able to talk since.

Considering that Caleb was acting like he wished she had gone out to dinner with everyone else instead of staying with him, maybe she'd been wrong about there being anything between them. Hell, maybe he was regretting getting involved with her at all.

They stood at the kitchen island in silence, taking turns using the same butter knife to spread peanut butter on the crackers, the loud sound of their crunching as they ate becoming more uncomfortable by the second. Finally, Brielle couldn't take it anymore. Shoving the knife into the jar of peanut butter, she picked up her bottle of water and turned to leave the kitchen.

"Why didn't you stop when I told you to?" he suddenly asked from behind her, the soft, almost tentative tone of the question making her stop and turn back around to look at him.

"What?" she said, more to give herself time to think about what his question meant than anything else. It wasn't like she hadn't heard him clearly.

"When you started following Harrington and I told you to fall back," he said, the words a soft growl as he paid an inordinate amount of attention to the peanut butter sandwich he was busy making out of two crackers. "I told you not to follow him out of the main lobby. That it could have been an ambush. But it was like you weren't listening to me at all. Even when I practically shouted at you to stop. You just kept going. And it *was* an ambush."

All Brielle could do was stare and pray her jaw didn't fall open to leave her standing there looking ridiculous.

"What?" she asked again, not proud of her total lack of

loquaciousness. But truthfully, she was baffled right now. She honestly had no idea why he was going on about something that had happened hours ago.

"Brielle," he whispered, her name slipping out in an anguished tone as he finally lifted his head to look at her. "You could have gotten yourself killed. You nearly did."

It hit her then what was going on, and she was almost embarrassed that she hadn't figured it out before. This was why Caleb had been so grouchy since they'd come back to the safe house. It had nothing to do with Hudson betraying them and the possibility there was a tracking device underneath the CIA agent's skin.

Caleb had been worried about her.

It was childish, but Brielle couldn't stop the surge of happiness that spiraled through her at the knowledge that men didn't get worried about another person's actions like this unless they really cared.

Caleb *cared* about her.

Brielle almost laughed she was so giddy. Until she saw the utter devastation on his face. Her heart plummeted into her stomach, and she stepped closer to him, only keeping herself from throwing her arms around him by the strongest force of will.

"I'm so sorry," she whispered, reaching out and placing her hand gently on his chest. His skin was warm through his shirt, his heartbeat steady. "I didn't mean to scare you. I freely admit that following Harrington was the dumbest idea ever, But I haven't heard from Julian in almost two weeks, and the idea of letting the only man who might know where he is get away without learning anything..." She shook her head. "I simply couldn't do it. I had to take the chance for my brother."

Tears welled in her eyes, but she knew Caleb wouldn't understand. Not after all the stories she'd told him about Julian and his colossal number of screwups. Hell, sometimes *she* wondered why she kept risking everything for her brother when it was his own fault for getting into these situations in the first place.

Brielle was more than a little surprised when the tension drained from Caleb's features and he stepped forward to close the last bit of distance between them, wrapping her in a hug. She hugged him back, not sure what to say.

"I'm sorry," he murmured, resting his chin on the top of her head. "It was wrong of me to unload on you like that. But when I came around that corner and saw Harrington's guards holding you at gunpoint, I can't put into words how hard that was on me. I nearly lost it."

Brielle closed her eyes, breathing in his scent, once again amazed at how being in his arms calmed her down. "And I'm sorry I ran off like that. I know it isn't much of an excuse, but part of the reason I did was because I knew you would be there if I got into trouble. It probably doesn't make you feel any better, but knowing you're there for me makes me a whole lot braver than I normally would be."

Caleb pulled back, gazing down at her with an unreadable expression. "I don't know about all of that. You seem like a pretty brave woman all on your own. But if it helps, just know that I'll always be there for you. For as long as you want."

Brielle couldn't help but wonder if Caleb realized the significance of that promise. Regardless, the words had meant more to her than she could bring herself to admit.

Wanting him to know, without saying it out loud, she did the one thing she knew he'd understand—without the need for any words at all. She kissed him.

It started rather tame, as a gentle touch of her lips to his. But Caleb *was* Caleb, so it definitely didn't stay that way for long. One second it was all chaste; the next second there were graham crackers and peanut butter on the floor, and her butt was on the kitchen counter.

Not that she was complaining.

She pulled the cocktail dress she still had on from the party up so she could spread her legs and welcome Caleb between them, reveling in the low growl that erupted from his throat as she wrapped herself around him.

"Damn, you taste so good," he murmured, his tongue capturing hers.

With a sexy, animalistic growl, he moved his hands down to her butt, pulling her so tightly to his body that she could feel every flex and chiseled plane of all those delicious muscles. Felt his hard-on grinding against her core through her barely there panties. It thrilled her beyond words to know he was a turned on as she was.

Her hands worked with a mind of their own, unbuttoning his dress shirt and shoving it off his shoulders. Only then did she break their kiss, leaning back to take him all in. As she admired the way his shirt now hung from his muscular arms, she couldn't help thinking there was nothing in the world sexier than a half-dressed man.

She took her time tracing her fingers back and forth across his chest, lightly scraping her nails across her skin. The sensation of muscles tensing and rippling under her touch was mesmerizing… as were the sounds of pleasure he was making.

Brielle leaned forward, kissing his neck before moving her mouth downward, trailing soft kisses across his chest muscles. Caleb's skin was so warm—almost hot—that she couldn't help moaning.

"Damn, woman," Caleb growled, his fingers coming up to tighten into her hair. "Do you have any idea what that sound does to me?"

She lifted her head to smile at him. "Why don't you tell me? Or better yet, maybe you could show me."

Brielle barely felt the tug when Caleb reached down and ripped her panties off. The remnants of them disappeared into one of his pockets, and then his fingers were on her, tracing slowly up and down her folds, making her fully aware of exactly how wet she was.

"Should we move this upstairs?" he asked, his eyes smoldering as he gazed down at her. "Or I could run up and grab a condom if you're comfortable right here."

Her first instinct was to say, *get me upstairs now*. But truthfully, she liked where they were right then and hated to interrupt the moment with a mad dash for a condom.

She cupped his jaw. "I'm on long-term birth control, get myself checked every six months, and have never had unprotected sex with anyone. If you're clean, I'm okay without the condom."

His eyes blazed vivid blue for a moment before the color disappeared again. "STAT has us checked between every mission, even though werewolves are immune to all disease. Still, I haven't had unprotected sex in years. It's just not something I do. But if you're okay with it, I wouldn't mind changing that rule for you."

She gazed at him, sliding her hand around to run her nails along the back of his neck and up into his disheveled hair. "I want to be with you that way. To really feel you inside me. All of you."

Those eyes of his flared even brighter, and this time, they didn't fade, even as he reached down to unbuckle his belt and slacks, shoving everything down in one quick move. She guessed that answered the question of whether he wanted her like this.

Brielle watched in fascination as he wrapped a hand around his thick shaft and stepped closer, teasing her folds with the head and coating himself with her wetness. When he slid across her clit, it was like someone had touched her body with a live wire, and she caught her breath. Something told her that, if he kept doing what he was doing, she might come just from that.

But he only teased her for a few more seconds before slowly sliding into her. The feeling as he buried himself deep was as amazing as she remembered, yet it was even more glorious having him bare like this.

More real.

More intimate.

She wrapped her legs around his bare hips, so happy that she hadn't taken her dress off. Being dressed and half-naked at the same time was a heady aphrodisiac.

Caleb started slow, his hands on her hips keeping her steady. But his pace soon picked up, the height of the granite island ensuring the tip of his cock nudged her G-spot with every thrust. She pulled him in for a kiss, even though it was damn hard to focus on his lips when she was bouncing on the counter and gasping for breath. But still, it was the feel of his fangs against her tongue that helped pushed her over the edge. Then again, she supposed the fingers she slipped down to tease her clit didn't hurt. The fact that she could scream without worrying about scaring the rest of his teammates was a definite plus, too.

She was mid-orgasm when Caleb buried his face in the crook of her neck and let loose a long, low growl. Then he was coming inside her, his fangs almost breaking skin in the most perfect way she'd ever imagined. The sensations of his heat pouring into her at the same time he claimed her with his mouth was enough to push her climax back up to a second peak, and she would have fallen off the counter if he hadn't been holding her so tightly.

It took a long time for the tremors of her orgasm to fade away. It was hard to describe how amazing it felt to be able to stay like this, Caleb still deep inside, her legs wrapped around him.

"That was beyond perfect," he whispered in her ear as his mouth moved slowly along her shoulder and neck. "But you might need to wear a turtleneck or something tomorrow. I think I've left a few marks."

Her fingers came up to trace along her skin, finding the sensitive spots at the junction of her neck and shoulder. "It was so very worth it."

He chuckled softly. "If that's the case, how about we take this upstairs now? There are a few other places I'd like to nibble on."

Brielle laughed. She couldn't remember ever being so happy. "I definitely like the sound of that."

Caleb slid her off the counter and swung her up into his arms. "Grab the jar of peanut butter and knife, would you? I have plans for them—and you."

She looked around, quickly finding the requested items on the island. Picking them up with one hand, she looked at him. "Should I get the crackers, too?"

"No way," he said. "Have you ever tried to sleep in a bed full of crumbs?"

Brielle couldn't argue with that logic. Though something told her that they wouldn't be doing a lot of sleeping.

CHAPTER 15

BRIELLE WALKED SLOWLY DOWN THE STAIRS, MOVING carefully so she wouldn't make too much noise. It was barely four o'clock in the morning, and she didn't want to wake anyone up. It was bad enough that everyone had stayed out until almost midnight to give her and Caleb some alone time. That was probably for the best, since the two of them had just settled down fifteen minutes before everyone came home.

She did her best spy-in-training tiptoe routine as she crossed the living room and headed into the dimly lit kitchen wearing nothing but Caleb's shirt, which hung down almost to her knees. She'd burned through those peanut butter and crackers she and Caleb had earlier after the second round of sex, and while Caleb was upstairs in their bed sleeping like a rock, her stomach was growling too much to let her even close her eyes.

But while the need for a post-lovemaking snack might have played some part in Brielle's inability to sleep, it wasn't the only thing keeping her awake. Truthfully, she'd been lying in bed staring at the ceiling for a while, her head spinning over the things Caleb had said to her—before making love, during, and after.

No, he hadn't dropped the L-word on her or anything. But he'd said enough for her to recognize that the *something* she'd thought might be developing between them was now a lot more than *something*. A reasonable person might even say it was *serious*. And while that idea had thrilled her initially and turned her insides all warm and gooey, once the sex hormones had worn off, she'd started to *think*.

That was never a good idea.

Not for her.

And definitely not on an empty stomach.

Heading straight for the refrigerator, she prayed Misty had remembered to grab some takeout for her and Caleb from wherever they went for dinner.

"I thought you'd be out like a light until morning."

Brielle spun around so fast she nearly fell over. Misty was sitting at the kitchen table, the small glow from the lighting under the cabinets illuminating the piece of chocolate cake she was nibbling.

"There's more cake in the fridge if you're interested. Second shelf," Misty said. "It tastes so decadent you'll feel like apologizing to yourself for eating it."

Brielle opened the fridge to find the aforementioned cake looking back at her. Unable to resist, she cut a slice, then put the piece on a plate. Chocolate cake with loads of coconut buttercream frosting, it looked delicious. And while it was probably insane to be eating this much sugar at four o'clock in the morning, she was going to do it anyway.

Grabbing a glass of milk and a fork, she sat down across from Misty.

"You're up early," Brielle said. "Or really late."

Misty grinned. "I woke up thinking about this cake and knew I wouldn't be able to get back to sleep until I satisfied my craving and had a piece." She licked some frosting off her fork. "What about you. Couldn't sleep? Or does Caleb snore? He seems like the kind of man who would snore. Or growl. I can see him doing that, too."

"No, he doesn't snore," she said with a soft laugh. "He doesn't growl in his sleep, either. Though if he did, I don't think I'd mind."

Misty lifted a brow but didn't say anything.

Brielle loaded her fork with an equal ratio of cake to frosting. It tasted as good as it looked. The chocolate cake was moist and rich, and the coconut frosting was delightfully sweet. As she eagerly took another bite, she realized she'd never fully answered Misty's question.

"I think I'm falling for Caleb," she announced, stunned she'd said the words even as they popped out of her mouth. That hadn't been what she'd intended to say. Or was it?

Misty took another bite of cake, chasing it down with some milk. "I'm not trying to be a smart-ass here, but I'm pretty sure I heard the thud of you falling for Caleb back in that safe house in Moscow. So I would have to say that the past tense form of the verb would probably be called for."

Brielle took a second to think about what Misty had said, even if her first instinct was to deny all. But she owed Misty at least a moment of serious introspection because, regardless of the way it had come out, she was being serious.

"Part of me wants to tell you that my night in Moscow with Caleb wasn't about anything more than great sex," she murmured, focusing on the cake in front of her instead of looking at the woman who was fast becoming her friend. "But that would be a lie. We'd barely finished making love, and I already knew I was in trouble. By the next morning, I realized there was something more there. That I was *looking* for there to be something more."

"Sounds promising so far. Did something happen tonight to change that?" Misty asked, getting up and walking over to the fridge. A moment later, she was sliding another piece of cake onto her plate, then one onto Brielle's, even though she'd barely started on the first piece.

Brielle opened her mouth to point that out, but Misty interrupted her.

"Don't worry about the calories," she said as she put the box back in the fridge. "Anything eaten after midnight and before six a.m. only counts half. Something to do with the food getting confused and not knowing if it's really today, yesterday, or tomorrow." She grinned. "Trust me, I would never lie about something as sacred as chocolate cake and calories."

Brielle was still trying to find the flaw in that logic when Misty sat down again.

"So, you were about to tell me what happened tonight with you and Caleb. It had to be something significant, or you wouldn't be sitting down here eating cake with me instead of upstairs spooning with your warm, cuddly werewolf."

Brielle laughed. "I can't see Caleb appreciating being described as warm and cuddly."

She'd worked with other women before and hung out with a few in a way that could almost meet the definition of friendship. But she'd never really had a girlfriend she could talk about guys with and stuff like that. The things going on in her life never gave her the opportunity. But if she'd had a close friend, she liked to think that it would be something like this.

Misty smiled and shook her head, nibbling at another bite of cake and then licking the icing off the fork. "No, probably not, but I won't tell if you don't. So, what happened? Did he say something stupid?"

Brielle thought about that for a second, wondering if that was the right way to put it. "The opposite actually. He said something really amazing. He said he'd always be there for me for as long as I wanted."

Misty nodded but didn't say anything right away. She just kept eating until several more bites of cake had disappeared.

"I guess that was too much too fast, huh?" she finally murmured, still not looking up.

"I don't know. Maybe?" Brielle admitted. "Don't get me wrong. I like the idea of being in a relationship with Caleb, but honestly, I don't know how."

Misty looked across the table at her curiously. "What do you mean, you don't know how? Surely, you've been in relationships with other guys. Just because those situations might not have worked out, doesn't mean you didn't learn from the experience, right?"

Brielle shook her head. "Actually, no. For as long as I can

remember, my life has revolved around taking care of either my alcoholic dad or my twit of a brother. There's never been time to even consider getting in a relationship. I mean, I've dated guys and slept with some, but I never had anything I would consider a relationship. Whenever I tried it, Julian would end up ruining it." She shrugged. "After a while, I gave up thinking it would ever happen."

"It goes without saying, but that completely sucks," Misty said with a frown. "I can't wait to meet your brother just so I can punch him for being such a jackass. At least now, with Caleb, it's happening."

"Yeah, it's happening," Brielle said quietly. "And I'm a little scared. I mean, this thing with Caleb, it came on kind of suddenly, you know? One second, I'm tumbling into bed with him, and the next, I'm thinking about having a future with the guy. That's the definition of crazy, right?"

"Yeah. Crazy." Misty regarded her thoughtfully. "Especially the part where you can't go five minutes with thinking about him. Or the way you can smell his scent even when he's not in the room. Oh, and that scary twisting sensation you get in your stomach when you think about not being with him after this mission is over. That's really crazy, right?"

Brielle started to laugh, sure Misty was teasing her. Until she realized the other woman had pretty much nailed it when it came to what she'd been going through lately. Right down to the funny feelings in her tummy and being able to smell Caleb's yummy, masculine scent even when he wasn't in the room.

"Wait a minute," she said, abruptly realizing that it seemed like Misty was fighting to hold in a smile. "How could you possibly know about that stuff? It's not exactly normal."

Misty gave her a disarming smile and ate another bite of cake. "Actually, in this case, it *is* normal."

Brielle sat there, forkful of cake poised halfway to her mouth, waiting for Misty to keep going. Just when it seemed like her friend was going to be stubborn and refuse to continue, Misty let out a long sigh.

"Look, this is something you should be hearing directly from Caleb, but since he hasn't—and probably won't—I'm simply going to tell you and deal with the fallout later. Just don't shoot the messenger, okay?"

Hearing all that made Brielle think maybe she didn't want to know what Misty was talking about after all. But before she could consider saying that, Misty set down her fork and leaned forward to start, and Brielle knew it was too late to stop her.

"Werewolves have this...legend...for lack of a better word," Misty said slowly, like she wanted to make sure she got it right. "It says that each werewolf has a true love out there who accepts them for what they are. It's called *The One* for them...aka their soul mate."

Brielle set down her fork on the plate with a clatter. "Soul mate?" she echoed, the words slipping out in a barely comprehensible stutter. "That's impossible. I mean, soul mates are make-believe. Right?"

"Make-believe?" Misty asked with a smile. "You mean like werewolves, technopaths, and people like you who can borrow another person's abilities just by touching them?"

"Okay, when you put it that way, I guess I can see your point," Brielle muttered, having a hard time arguing with that kind of logic. "But still, how can you be sure I'm Caleb's soul mate when he doesn't even seem to know?"

Misty laughed and picked up her fork to dig into her cake again. "Trust me—Caleb knows. Everything you're feeling, he's feeling times ten. He's just in denial. Based on my extensive experience with the phenomenon, it seems that refusing to believe your soul mate is right in front of you is a required part of the process."

"*Experience with the phenomenon?*" Brielle said, shocked. "You've seen this soul-mate thing happen before?"

Misty nodded. "Oh yeah. We were told that werewolf soul mates are supposed to be rare, like a one-in-a-million kind of thing, you know? But Jake and Jes fell for each other within days of meeting, even though she hated him at first sight. Then it happened again when Harley and Sawyer met. With you and Caleb, that makes three matches in a few months. So I'm thinking this soul-mate thing isn't nearly as rare as werewolves seem to think."

Huh.

"And what about you being sure I'm *The One* for Caleb?" Brielle murmured, trying to wrap her head around everything.

"I'm definitely sure," Misty said, sipping her milk. "You probably don't even see it, but the rest of us do. When you two are together in a room, there's a spark between you that makes me wonder if you'll burst into flames at some point. The way you can calm him out of his omega rage with simply a kiss is something I never thought I'd see. I mean, the rest of us usually have to smack him to snap him out of it and pray he doesn't eat our faces off. Literally."

Brielle considered all that and decided it felt right. There was no denying the connection between her and Caleb. The attraction she'd felt for him the first time they'd met, the way the tension had disappeared when she saw him again in that hotel in Ankara, how light her heart felt when she sat beside him watching him eat peanut butter.

But while she was ready to accept there was something real going on—something magical even—she still found herself wanting to fight the idea of predestined soul mates. There was something about that part that made her feel uncomfortable.

"This soul-mate thing," she said slowly. "If Caleb and I are meant to be together and if it's fated, is it real? Do we even have a say? Does love come into this at all, or are we sort of magically stuck with each other like those people who get tattoos when they're drunk?"

"That sounds like something you need to sit down and talk to Jes or Harley about." Misty reached across the table and squeezed her hand. "But I can say that neither of them has ever complained about who they ended up with, so I can't imagine you will, either. You and Caleb are perfect for each other, and you know it."

"Know what?" a low, rumbling voice asked from somewhere beyond the living room, the question immediately followed by the sound of footsteps. A few seconds later, a barefoot and bare-chested Caleb wandered into the kitchen wearing nothing but a pair of jeans and a curious expression.

Her first thought was that he'd overheard her and Misty talking about soul mates, but before Brielle could ask him how much of the conversation he'd heard, she noticed he had her cell phone in his hand.

"It's your brother," he growled, apparently deciding to drop his question now that she'd seen the phone. "He wants to talk to you. He's in trouble—again."

Brielle scrambled from the chair, almost knocking it down in her haste to get to her phone and hold it to her ear. "Julian, is that really you? It's Brielle. Talk to me!"

"Brielle…it's…can…hear me?" Her brother's voice came through the phone broken and barely recognizable, but it was Julian. She knew that for sure. "Need…help."

They yelled back and forth at each other, trying to figure out what the other one was saying over the crappy connection. Misty was on her own phone, motioning for Brielle to keep talking. She prayed that meant Misty was trying to track the call.

"Julian, I'm having a hard time understanding you," she said. "Can you move to someplace with better reception?"

"Can't…underground," he replied, the words getting harder to hear by the second. "We escaped through…tunnels…got lost down…here. Need…dark. Phone's dying."

Brielle's head spun with all the questions she wanted to ask.

Like where the hell her brother had been all this time, how he'd ended up in a dark tunnel with a nearly dead cell phone, and who else was with him to have him saying *we* when he'd never cared about anyone but himself.

Then she felt Caleb take her hand, his gentle and reassuring as he tried to calm her down. She looked over at Misty, who shook her head.

Brielle took a deep breath, focusing on the most important issues. "Julian, you have to give me some idea where you are. Anything you got."

"New…City." Julian said, the words barely above a whisper now. "Old tunnel…subway…abandoned…sign…fourth street." There might have been more, but her brother's voice was really fading now. "Hurry. Something…down…here…us."

The phone abruptly went dead, and when she tried to call the number back, the message said the line had no service. Brielle glanced at Misty, but her friend shook her head. Brielle's heart dropped into her stomach.

Caleb gently turned her around to face him, his hands on her shoulders. "Hey, stop spinning, okay? I know we didn't get a lock on where he is, but I could hear everything that Julian said while he was talking to you, and I know he was able to give you some clues. We'll find him. I promise."

Brielle knew there was no way Caleb could make that promise, but he had, and she started thinking that maybe everything really would be all right.

CHAPTER 16

"Why can't we ever have a mission in a well-lit shopping mall?" Misty asked from somewhere behind Caleb as he led them down the long decrepit staircase, the light from his flashlight barely illuminating the darkness that was closing in around them. "Just once, I'd like to walk into a situation able to see what we're dealing with."

"Where's the fun in that?" Forrest questioned, his voice coming from somewhere very close to Misty. As usual.

Forrest, Misty, Genevieve, and Hudson had come with him and Brielle to find her brother while Jake and the rest of their teammates were busy chasing down a lead on Xavier Harrington and the nukes that had come in a few minutes after Julian had called. Jake had hated splitting up the team, but the chance to find the nukes had been too good to pass up.

Having been in the middle of a rather erotic dream involving Brielle and a jar of peanut butter, Caleb had nearly missed the call from Julian. Things in dreamland had just gotten interesting when someone started playing the piano. Really hoping it would go away, he'd tried to ignore the music, but it hadn't worked. He'd popped up in bed and realized that Brielle wasn't in it with him and that it was her cell phone ringing. And that her ringtone was piano music.

Caleb still wasn't sure why he'd answered other than the fact that if someone was calling her at that god-awful time of night, it must be important. When he'd heard a man's voice coming through the horrible connection wanting to talk to Brielle and demanding to know why Caleb had her phone, he'd come damn close to hanging up. Because whoever the hell the d-bag might be, Caleb had no use for him.

But when the caller let slip that his name was Julian, Caleb figured he should probably find Brielle and bring her the phone even if he had already decided he didn't like her brother.

Even though the jackass hadn't given them much to go on, Misty had still come up with a possible location—the South Fourth Street Subway Station, located about thirty feet underneath the intersection of Broadway and Union Avenue in Brooklyn. Misty was supersmart and amazingly good at digging up stuff on the internet, but it still seemed like a long shot. Brielle was desperate to find her brother, though, and if she thought there was a chance he was down here, Caleb would help her.

"I'm guessing the street-level entrance to this station isn't around anymore?" Hudson asked, his steps on the crumbling stairs amazingly soft for someone who wasn't a werewolf. Caleb hadn't liked the CIA agent when he'd first joined the team—and there were definitely moments when he would have gladly smashed his face in—but he had to admit, the guy was beginning to grow on him.

"Unfortunately, no. It was closed up and paved over decades ago," Misty answered, reciting the information without even having to pause and think about it. "The station itself was abandoned before World War II and never reopened. Almost all of the other entrances have been sealed up. I found this service entrance in the basement of this old apartment by pure luck. If I hadn't, we would have been wandering around the subway tunnels beneath Brooklyn for hours looking for a way in."

"Which makes me wonder how Brielle's brother ended up here," Genevieve said. "We didn't even have a clue he was in New York, and now he's lost in the subway tunnels below the city, forcing us to split up the team to find him."

Caleb couldn't miss the accusation in Genevieve's voice. She'd been openly against the plan to rescue Brielle's brother. In fact, she'd been pretty adamant that Julian was nothing more than bait for a trap. The worst part? Caleb couldn't say he disagreed. Using Brielle's weakness for her brother to lure them down into these abandoned tunnels seemed exactly like something Harrington would do.

Behind him, Brielle sighed. "I know you think the only reason my brother called is to lead us into an ambush, but he'd never do anything to put me at risk. For all his faults, Julian loves me and would never let me get hurt."

That announcement seemed to ease the tension a little bit, making the darkness around them seem at least a little less suffocating.

"It's not that hard to believe Julian has been trapped inside Harrington's organization since arriving in New York on the ship carrying those nukes, unable to get a message out," Forrest said. "Maybe slipping into the subway tunnels was the only option he had to get away from Harrington, and without knowing where he was going, he got lost. Misty showed me the drawings of the NYC underground system. It's a rat's maze down here."

Genevieve snorted, but Caleb appreciated Forrest sticking up for Brielle. It almost sounded like his teammate believed all of that stuff he'd just spouted. Almost.

"Where's this service entrance supposed to be anyway?" Genevieve asked when they finally reached the lowest level of the building's basement. "I can't see anything down here."

Caleb didn't need the flashlight in his hand to see, but he swung the beam around mostly for everyone else's benefit. The basement was jammed with what looked to be fifty years' worth of dust, trash, furniture, and old packing crates. There was nothing that even suggested a door or passageway out of the place, and for a moment, he feared the entire trip had been a waste of time.

"Over here," Hudson called out, shoving aside a huge armoire to reveal a chained and padlocked section of grating. The age of the lock and the amount of dust collected along the chain suggested that the gate hadn't been opened in years. Decades, maybe.

Caleb moved over to give the padlock a sharp yank. It snapped easily under his grasp, as did the chain. A moment later, he was leading the way through a dark corridor that led to a rusted metal door that nearly collapsed when he pushed it open. The area it led to must have been huge because the beams from their flashlights didn't even reveal any of the walls. Instead, all Caleb could make out were a low ceiling, cracked tile flooring, and a random support column.

It was sort of creepy.

"Tunnels," Misty murmured. "It had to be tunnels. I never really had a position on the subject, but after this mission, it's official. I absolutely hate tunnels."

Caleb figured out soon enough that they'd come out right in the middle of the subway station. The unfinished rail beds to either side of the platform were a dead giveaway. In both directions, he could see the gaping holes in the walls where the rails would have been installed if the whole place hadn't been abandoned. Flicking his flashlight toward the far side of the station, he could see more tunnel openings in that direction. It seemed like the openings had originally been blockaded with wooden planks and steel bars, but most of that had given way over time. Now, there was nothing keeping someone from crawling into any of those passages.

"I don't suppose you can smell whether Julian is down here, can you?" Brielle asked, moving closer to Caleb. He could hear her heart thumping a mile a minute, and he wasn't sure if it was the thought of finally finding her brother or simply being down here in the dark.

"Nothing but dirt and dust at this point," he said after taking another long sniff. "Maybe a bit of grease and electrical discharge, too, but that's fainter. You know my nose isn't the greatest, so if Julian's down here, we'll have to track him by some other method than scent."

Brielle nodded, leaning her head to the side and resting it

against him. He wrapped his arm around her shoulders, hugging her close. When she was distraught or in pain, he couldn't stop himself from trying to help her.

After making love last night, Caleb had planned it all out. First thing this morning, as soon as Brielle woke up in his arms, he was going to have that talk with her that Forrest suggested. He was going to honestly tell her how he felt about her and hope she felt the same. If that conversation went well, he would then try and tiptoe his way into the soul-mate thing.

Maybe.

Then stupid Julian had called, and that whole plan had gone to shit. Just another reason to hate the man, as far as Caleb was concerned.

"I've got some fresh scuff marks in the dust," Hudson suddenly called out.

Caleb looked across the platform to see the CIA agent standing all the way over by the far end, pointing his flashlight toward the floor. Glancing at Brielle, he took her hand and led her over there, everyone else at their heels.

There were two sets of marks on the floor near where Hudson stood. From the looks of them, it was like whoever had made them had been running at the time. One set of prints was definitely smaller than the others, too.

"Take a look at this," Hudson said, using his light to illuminate a rusted platform sign above their heads. The only word that could be seen clearly was *Fourth*. "It looks like Julian and whoever is with him were coming from the direction of the tunnel behind us when they called Brielle, then came up on the platform and saw the sign. But then they jumped back down to the rail bed for some reason and kept running that way."

Caleb followed the direction of Hudson's flashlight, seeing the tunnel entrance at that end of the platform.

"Julian said there was something down here with them," Brielle murmured, falling into step beside Caleb as they all headed in that direction. "Do you think there was someone chasing them?"

Before Caleb could answer, a loud clanking sound erupted from the tunnel ahead of them. The noise was immediately followed by grunting and gunshots.

Caleb took off running in that direction, knowing he needed to move before Brielle did, because he had no doubt she would assume her brother was in the middle of whatever was going on up ahead. He tore through the few boards blocking the entrance to the tunnel, then tossed his flashlight aside. Drawing his weapon, he raced through the passage at full speed, trusting his werewolf instincts to warn him before he ran into trouble.

The sounds of fighting grew louder as he ran down the tunnel, the metallic clanking of a steel pipe smashing into something solid interspersed with random gunfire. He could hear the occasional grunt as someone got hit. Though whether they were getting hit with a bullet or the pipe, he didn't know.

Then the smell assaulted him. It was a combination of old dirt and that distinctive oily musk that he'd smelled before, back in those tunnels in Turkey.

Caleb opened his mouth to warn Brielle and his teammates as he sprinted around a curve in the tunnel, but the sight in front of him stopped him cold.

Harrington's daughter, Kiara, was on the ground, her back wedged against a wall. Blood soaked her blond hair from a wound along the left side of her head, and she looked a bit woozy. There was a rusted steel pipe on the ground beside her, but from the dazed look in her eyes, he doubted she'd be able to defend herself with it.

A dark-haired man stood in front of her, his body positioned protectively, another one of those rusted steel pipes in his hands. His light dress shirt and dark slacks were heavily smudged with dirt in some places, ripped and tattered in others. It only took a fraction of a second for Caleb to realize that some of the stains weren't dirt. The guy was bleeding. Badly enough to soak through his clothes.

Yet no matter how badly the man might have been injured, he was still standing strong, facing off against an armed man wearing dark tactical gear and night-vision goggles as well as two of the baboon-sized creatures—aka "diggers"—they'd run up against under Incirlik. The man with the gun wasn't supernatural, but the two creatures more than made up for anything the goon might lack.

Caleb got the sensation that the bad guy and both creatures were trying to get past the man with the pipe in order to reach the girl on the ground, but shockingly, they seemed leery about getting too close. Maybe because there was a dead man in matching tactical gear lying on the ground a little farther down the tunnel right beside a dead digger.

The first thought that hit Caleb was that this guy had apparently killed a digger with nothing but a steel pipe. The second was that this guy was probably Julian Fontaine. Caleb wondered if he should be impressed, but then decided he'd rather keep hating the man.

The matter became irrelevant when the sound of boots on gravel and the flickering glow of five moving flashlights alerted the bad guys that they weren't alone anymore. The man in the tactical gear took a step to the side and lifted his weapon in Caleb's general direction. Caleb wasn't too concerned about getting shot, but the bullets from the guy's assault rifle would hurt Brielle and his teammates a hell of a lot more than they would hurt him.

Caleb threw himself forward, closing the distance between him and the guy with the weapon, doing his best to keep his inner omega in check. He hated the idea of losing control with Brielle and his friends crushed into the tight confines of the tunnel. But containing his werewolf half was even harder to do than normal with Brielle in danger.

As soon as Caleb took down the man with the assault rifle, the two diggers retreated, crawling into holes that looked way too small for them to fit into. A second later, Brielle was at his side, her eyes catching his in the darkness. The gentle touch of her hand on his jaw calmed the omega immediately. Then, just that fast, Brielle was moving away, crossing the tunnel at a run to throw her arms around the guy with the steel pipe.

Caleb now had confirmation the guy was Julian—the fact that Brielle was calling out his name and asking him over and over if he was okay was kind of a dead giveaway.

"You're bleeding!" Brielle said, tugging at her brother's shirt. "Were you shot?"

Caleb stepped closer as Julian quickly hugged his sister, then started extricating himself from her grasp. "No, I wasn't shot. It was those damn ghouls. They clawed the hell out of me."

"Ghouls?" Forrest asked curiously, dropping down beside Kiara to check on her. She still seemed out of it but was reaching for Julian all the same.

"Yeah. That's what we call those things," Julian said, pointing to the dead baboon-shaped digger a few feet away.

Julian moved across the tunnel and knelt beside Kiara, murmuring softly to her that it was going to be okay. Even as unobservant as Caleb normally was, he could tell that Julian had a thing for Kiara Harrington.

"Careful," Forrest warned. "She probably has a concussion, maybe a neck injury, too. We should wait to move her until the support team can get a medic down here to look at her."

Julian stared first at his sister, then at Caleb. Then he slowly scanned the rest of the team. Caleb had built an image of Brielle's brother in his head based on what she'd told him. He had to admit, the reality wasn't matching up to the preconceived notion. Caleb had pegged him as juvenile and selfish, but given how hard he'd fought to protect Kiara and how attentive he was being to her right now, he guessed those assumptions might not apply to the man in front of him.

"I'm assuming you people are all from STAT," Julian finally said. "And any other time, I'd be more than willing to defer to your expertise in a situation like this, especially since you saved our lives. But after being herded for the last few hours, I don't think staying here would be a very good idea. We need to get out of these tunnels, the faster the better."

Caleb frowned. "What do you mean, herded?" He scanned the part of the tunnel that was drenched in darkness, just out of reach of the flashlights. "The ghouls we saw weren't the only ones after you?"

"Oui," Julian said. "There are more of them out there, cutting us off every time we got close to escaping. I swear it was like they knew exactly where we were going. If it wasn't for them closing in around us, we never would have come into this abandoned part of the subway system. But we didn't have a choice. I assume they steered us this way so they could attack without anyone hearing anything. I doubt they're going to give up simply because you arrived. Harrington isn't the kind to let anything important out of his grasp. And Kiara is very important to him."

While Caleb didn't know much about Xavier Harrington, something told him Julian was right. About everything.

"We're getting out of here," he announced.

Julian didn't need to be told twice. Ignoring his own injuries, he immediately bent down to tenderly scoop Kiara up in his arms, cradling her like she was the most precious thing in the world to him.

They'd barely gone twenty feet before Caleb's ears and nose let him know that a handful of bad guys and as many ghouls were closing in around them. *Shit.* It looked like Julian had been right about being herded into an ambush. The few attackers he'd been trying to hold off were probably intended to slow him and Kiara down and stop them from getting away while everyone else moved into position.

"We're being surrounded," Caleb said. "Move!"

The next few minutes were insane as they ran back to the Fourth Street Station as fast as they could. He thought they just might make it all the way to the platform and the basement stairs that led to the surface when three ghouls stepped out of the darkness, teeth bared and claws at the ready as they blocked their escape. At the same time, two of Harrington's goons closed in on them from the rear. Only they weren't regular humans. They were the pale-skinned supernaturals they'd gone up against in Russia.

Caleb didn't pause to think. He simply holstered his .45 automatic, let himself shift as far as he could, and then slammed his body into the ghouls, driving them away from the exit and the way out. He punched, clawed, and snapped his jaws, picking up one of the ghouls by the leg and using it like a club to bludgeon the other two, then turning his attention on the pair of supernaturals. He must have moved them back twenty or thirty feet when he heard Brielle yelling at him to follow. Normally he would have ignored anyone trying to call him away from a fight like this, but the sound of her voice broke through the fog of rage around him, and within seconds, he turned and headed after his team.

He raced up the stairs, hearing the sounds of claws and boots behind him. A few gunshots smashed into bricks around him, but none found their targets. Seconds later, he was through the front door of the apartment building. Sliding to a stop on the curb outside, he drew his weapon and turned to point it back at the door he'd just come out of. All around him, his teammates had their guns out as well, ready to shoot whoever and whatever came out of the building as early-morning sunlight flooded the street.

But no one and nothing came after them.

Holstering his weapon, Caleb finally turned and glanced at Brielle, needing to make sure she was okay. She was standing beside Julian, unharmed. His gaze shifted to her brother and the woman passed out cold in his arms.

"I'm worried about that head wound," Caleb said. "She's going to need medical attention."

Julian frowned down at Kiara, his face filled with concern. "I know, but I doubt there's any emergency room Harrington can't get into. Is there somewhere safer to take her?"

Caleb threw a look at Misty, who was already on the radio with the support people.

"They have a complete med team ready and waiting at the safe house for us," she said. "They can take care of her there."

"All right. That's the plan, then," Caleb said. "Let's get off the street."

He looked at Brielle's brother again, thinking once more about how the guy wasn't anything like Caleb thought he'd be. And if the expression on her face was any indication, it seemed that Brielle had been caught a little off guard as well.

CHAPTER 17

"I KNOW THIS PROBABLY ISN'T THE BEST TIME, BUT MAYBE you could explain how you ended up in an abandoned New York City subway tunnel with Kiara Harrington?"

Brielle folded her arms and leaned her shoulder against the wall of the second-floor hallway, half her attention focused on her brother, who was sitting on the carpeted floor near her, and the other half on the pretty blond woman in the bedroom directly across from them. Nathan McKay had arrived at the safe house a few minutes ago, and through the open door, Brielle could see him and Jake trying to interrogate Kiara at the same time that the STAT medical team was checking her out. Kiara seemed to be doing her best to answer their questions.

Brielle turned her gaze on Julian again. "Considering you were the one who helped her father steal twenty nuclear weapons from the United States military, I mean," she added in case her idiot brother had forgotten what put them all in this situation.

At first, Brielle wasn't sure Julian had even heard her. His dark eyes were locked on Kiara, a half-eaten ham and cheese sandwich held forgotten in his hand. Brielle had made him a whole stack of them, sure he must be starving after spending hours running through the New York City subway system. She'd made her brother a lot of sandwiches over the years, and putting these together a little while ago in the kitchen downstairs brought back a lot of memories. It felt like only yesterday when she was cutting the crusts off for him. He was high-maintenance, even when he was a little kid.

But since getting to the safe house, he'd barely eaten more than a few bites of the first sandwich. That wasn't surprising. It didn't take a genius to figure out he was worried about Kiara. When he finally glanced Brielle's way, she noticed for the first time how exhausted he looked. She was pretty sure he'd lost weight since she'd last seen him, and there were lines on his forehead and around his mouth that hadn't been there a month ago. But the most noticeable difference was in his eyes—always twinkling like he was up to something, they seemed flatter than she'd ever seen them. Like he'd been through hell. Or seen it at least.

"I ran into her a few days after I arrived in New York," he said slowly. "I was trying to get away. She was snooping around Xavier Harrington's place. I had no idea she was his daughter when we first met. I just knew she sucked at the whole sneaking around thing, so I decided to stay and help her look for whatever she was searching for. After she found it, I finally got her out of there, but Harrington's people chased us into the tunnels. She tried to get me to run, saying her father only wanted her, but I couldn't leave her. That's when I called you."

Jaw dropping, Brielle stared, trying to comprehend what she was seeing. Julian had always been selfish. It was the defining characteristic of his whole life. Her brother had never done anything for anyone but himself. Not even for his own sister. Now, Brielle was faced with the reality that he'd given up a chance to escape from people who would kill him without a second thought over a woman he'd only just met.

She turned her head and studied the woman in the bedroom again. There must be something extremely special about Kiara Harrington. Because, truthfully, Brielle barely recognized this version of her brother. That said, she had to admit she liked what she was seeing from him right now.

"When I got that call from one of my friends saying someone with a lot of money was putting together a crew in Turkey for a big job, I knew I should just hang up," Julian said, looking down at the floor as he took another bite of the sandwich in his hand.

Brielle frowned. "If you knew you should hang up, why didn't you? I mean, crap, Julian…nukes? Seriously?"

Julian winced. "In my defense, I didn't know about the nukes at first." Finishing the sandwich he'd been playing with, he drew up both legs and rested his arms on his knees, his gaze going to Kiara again. "But even if I had, I doubt it would have changed anything. We both know I have a long history of making stupid decisions when it comes to stuff like this. But this time, I'd like to think I redeemed myself. At least I got Kiara out."

There was a time when Brielle would have been tempted to point out that getting one thing right by accident didn't make up for the things he'd done wrong on purpose. But then she saw the unmistakable expression on her brother's face—one she'd never expected to see there—and it was difficult to stay mad at him.

Julian was in love.

"Were those people after you tonight genuinely trying to kill Kiara?" she asked quietly.

He nodded, not taking his eyes off Kiara as she talked to Jake and McKay. "Yeah. At first it seemed like they were only trying to capture her—even the ghouls—which makes sense, considering Harrington is her father. But after I was able to get cell reception and got through to you, things changed. Harrington's men became much more aggressive, like he'd told them that Kiara was expendable or something. Right after that, one of those jackasses hit Kiara in the head." He swallowed hard. "I thought they were going to kill her."

The fear in Julian's voice was so real and so powerful that Brielle crouched down beside him and put her arms around him. She was prouder of her brother in that moment than she'd ever been in her life. "But you stopped them."

Julian nodded. He opened his mouth to say something, but the thud of heavy boots on the stairs interrupted him. Brielle knew it was Caleb before he even reached the landing.

"How is she?" Caleb asked, bending down to snag one of the

ham and cheese sandwiches as he walked over to stand beside Brielle. They both got to their feet. Caleb didn't even look the least bit apologetic as he shoved half the sandwich in his mouth.

"I think she's doing okay," Brielle said. In the bedroom, the doctor seemed to have finished his examination of Kiara and was busy writing notes in a folder while Jake and McKay continued to talk to her. "We'll probably be able to talk to her soon."

She glanced over at her brother to see what he thought of her assessment, only to realize that he wasn't listening to her at all. He wasn't even paying attention to Kiara now. Instead, he was glaring at Caleb as he finished the rest of the sandwich he'd helped himself to. Crap. If looks could kill…

For reasons that defied explanation, Caleb didn't seem to like her brother, and Julian didn't like him, either. The two of them had been circling each other like a couple of tomcats since coming out of those subway tunnels. They looked like they were going to start fighting at any second.

Now that she thought about it, Brielle supposed Caleb disliked Julian because of all the negative things she'd told him about her brother and how difficult he'd made her life. As far as where Julian's animosity was coming from, she had no idea. Unless Julian had somehow figured out that she and Caleb were sleeping together and decided Caleb wasn't good enough for her. That was insane, though. Her brother had never once cared about what she did with her life. Hell, he probably assumed she didn't have one.

She would have told both of them to grow up and stop acting like children, but she'd be wasting her breath. They were men, which meant they pretty much *were* children.

"I'm surprised you're not in there getting checked out by the doc," Caleb said, looking at Julian. "I know firsthand that those ghouls can be hard to handle. It isn't your fault if they roughed you up some."

Brielle rolled her eyes at the thinly veiled insult. There hadn't been much conversation between Caleb and Julian since they'd gotten to the safe house, but what little there had been was exactly like this, all snarky hidden jabs and petty taunts.

Julian didn't rise to the bait. Instead, he gave Caleb the most fake smile she'd ever seen him bestow on anyone. Which was saying a lot, since her brother was full of crap nearly every minute of his life.

"Thanks for your concern," Julian said. "But I got through the fight with those ghouls with nothing more than a few scratches. They aren't all that hard to deal with."

"Really?" Caleb lifted a brow, clearly curious despite himself. "I was wondering how you managed to kill one of them. Like I said, I've fought them before and found them damn near impossible to even damage."

"Impossible to damage?" Julian snorted. "Maybe you didn't hit them hard enough. It's not your fault, of course. You don't look that strong."

Beside her, Caleb stiffened. Brielle immediately put herself between him and Julian even as Caleb's eyes began to shimmer with a blue glow and a low growl erupted from deep in his chest. Oh, crap. The guy she was falling in love with was going to kill her brother.

Fortunately, Jake and McKay chose that moment to step out of the bedroom, forcing Julian and Caleb to step back from each other whether they wanted to or not.

"Good, you're here already," McKay said as he glanced at Caleb, completely ignoring the fact that his eyes were still glowing blue. "Get everyone together in the living room. Jake and I talked to Kiara Harrington enough to know that her father's plan is worse than we even imagined. I want everyone to hear the details ASAP."

Caleb threw one more glare at Julian before heading down the steps with another growl, giving Brielle a chance to let out a sigh of relief. They might be facing whatever nightmare Xavier

Harrington had planned, but at least her brother and soul mate weren't at each other's throats—yet.

"In a nutshell, my father has completely lost his ever-loving mind," Kiara said from where she sat beside Julian on the couch. The wound on her forehead directly above her left eyebrow hadn't needed stitches, but the doctor had put a small bandage on it. While she still seemed a little worn-out, Caleb noticed she wasn't as pale as she'd been earlier. Then again, that might have something to do with the fact that she was near Julian. The moment he'd draped his arm around her shoulder, the tension had visibly drained from her body. "He wants to destroy the world to save it."

That announcement was met with the requisite stunned silence, but Caleb still found himself focusing more on Julian than the words Kiara had just spoken. He couldn't help it. Something about the guy irritated the hell out of him.

Based on everything Brielle had told Caleb about her brother, it was hard to think of him as anything other than a self-centered, selfish douche canoe. Kiara Harrington either didn't know that or didn't care. Either way, it seemed clear she was enamored with the man. Caleb knew it was none of his business. Kiara was an adult and could do whatever the hell she wanted—with whomever she wanted to do it with—but Julian was trouble. Caleb could recognize that better than anyone. The man had used his sister like a Get Out of Jail Free card for most of his life without any thought to the danger it put her in. And now, he was already trying to work his way back into Brielle's good graces, probably wanting to make sure she'd be ready to come save his ass when things went bad again. There was no way in hell Caleb was going to stand by and let her brother use her again. Not now that he'd finally realized how important she was to him.

"Maybe you should back up a little bit and start at the beginning," McKay said. He was leaning back against the mantel in front of the unlit fireplace, arms folded and a grim look on his face. "Tell them why your father and the Harrington Group stole the nukes."

Kiara took a deep breath, nodding as Julian hugged her closer. "Before I do that, I should probably mention that my father isn't like any of you. Actually, I'm not, either. No one in my family is. We're videns. You would call us seers."

"You mean like fortune-tellers?" Forrest asked, and Caleb could tell from his teammate's expression that the man thought Kiara was messing with them.

"Actually, you're closer than you think," Kiara admitted. "There have been times in the past when my people have posed as fortune-tellers, clairvoyants, oracles, and psychics in order to earn money. But we haven't done that in recent times, mostly because it simply isn't necessary now."

"Because your family—aka the Harrington Group—is rich, right?" Misty asked curiously. "I imagine being able to see the future would make financial investments easier."

Caleb had to admit he hadn't thought of that, but Misty was right. Knowing what the next big tech trend would be, what city would see a housing boom, or where the next war might happen would make it easy to get rich.

"All videns can see the see the future to a certain degree," Kiara said. "Though it would be more correct to say that we see the different possible futures. We call them different pathways. Some of us are better than others at reading these pathways and winnowing down the thousands and thousands of event paths, separating the more likely from the merely possible. My father is the best who has ever lived at this and it has made the family rich beyond belief. It's why he has been the head of the family and the CEO of the group for so long. Unfortunately, it has also driven him a little insane."

Beside Caleb on the love seat, Brielle's brow furrowed in

confusion. "I don't understand," she said, echoing the exact same thing he was thinking. "How did walking these pathways do that to your father?"

Kiara reached up to tuck her long hair behind her ear. "For many years, my father walked the pathways that would lead to money and power for the family. But over time, his focus shifted from gaining wealth to protecting us from those he thought might harm us."

"Such as?" Caleb prompted, leaning forward to rest his forearms on his knees.

"At first, it was SEC regulators planning to investigate the group," she said. "Then it was other supernaturals scheming to steal from us. Soon, he was looking for individual criminals intent on kidnapping or stealing from members of our family. That's when he hired Uriel and those other Vandals to be his security goons."

"Wait a minute," Caleb said, holding up a hand. "Vandals? You mean like the people on the History Channel?"

Kiara's lips curved. "Actually, yes. A number of the Germanic warriors that ravaged a good part of southern Europe and northern Africa were supernaturals like the ones you've been fighting. Once they were defeated by the Roman army, they scattered and disappeared for a time. They've recently started showing up again, hiring themselves out as mercenaries all over the world. Many of them have flocked to Uriel because of his powers, which none of the other Vandals possess, as far as I know. The moment my father heard of them, he hired as many as he could. He sees them as the foundation for his future army."

From where he stood by the overstuffed chair Misty was sitting on, Forrest frowned. "Hiring these Vandals is bad enough, but spending so much time looking for enemies under every rock and tree sounds a little bit obsessive. It must have consumed a lot of his time and energy to do that."

"Obsessive is a good word for it," Kiara replied. "My father would spend hours—sometimes days—walking the pathways, looking for information and links between one unlikely possibility and the next. Spending that much time on the paths can be addictive for all but the strongest videns. No one else would even consider trying to do what he did on an almost-daily basis."

"Am I the only one who feels like I'm missing something here?" Caleb asked, looking around at his teammates before turning his attention to Kiara again. "How does a man—even one who's obsessed and addicted like your father—go from using his supernatural talents to make billions of dollars to stealing nuclear weapons?"

Kiara sighed. "Because it's the nature of the pathways to show the viden walking them exactly what he or she wishes to see. If you're looking for paths to fortune, that's what you'll see to the near exclusion of anything else. If you seek power, the paths will skew you in that direction. And if you look long enough and hard enough for death and destruction, very soon, that is all you will see."

Caleb nodded. He completely understood that. It was the main reason he'd stopped reading the news. Almost everything in it was depressing as hell.

"That's what really drove my father mad," Kiara continued. "Spending so many years walking through one horrible event path after the next and trying to see how they might come to pass has essentially twisted his view on everything. All he can see now is the evil in the world. He can't see the good, even when it's all around him."

"Regardless of his twisted view of good and evil, I'm assuming there's some particular future event that has your father worried?" Misty said. "Something that scared him enough to think that stealing all those nuclear weapons is the better alternative."

Kiara nodded, her expression turning desolate. "He's become obsessed with the threat of worldwide nuclear war. He's convinced that in the very near future, some rogue nation will launch a weapon that will trigger an immediate retaliation from the target nation, which will be followed by a launch from an allied nation. On and on like dominoes, until every nuclear power has committed themselves completely."

"You're talking about the end of the world," Brielle murmured while everyone else in the room was stunned to silence, including Caleb. "Is this truly what he's seen? Isn't launching the nukes he stole going to start the chain in the first place, like some sort of self-fulfilling prophecy?"

Kiara shrugged. "My father doesn't care about the world. He only cares about the group. As far as whether he's seen it, the short answer is yes. The longer answer is that his perspective has become so twisted that it's unlikely we can trust in anything that he sees related to this subject. By stealing those nukes, he's practically willed the whole thing into existence. As for why he stole them, he isn't planning to use them in a preemptive strike. At least not like you think."

Caleb exchanged looks with Brielle, then the rest of the team. The trepidation he felt was mirrored on everyone's faces.

"My father has decided that the best way to deal with the possibility of full-scale nuclear war is to destroy all of the world's nuclear weapons—or at least as many as he can reasonably reach," Kiara added. "That's what the nineteen remaining weapons are for. He's going to use them to power an enormous laser strike that will annihilate every weapon they can reach."

No one said a word for a long time. Even Jake and McKay, who had already heard most of what Kiara had just told them, seemed shocked.

"What you're saying is impossible," Hudson finally said. "I mean, I don't know exactly how many nuclear weapons are in the world, but I know it's a lot. We're talking thousands of them. And they're going to be inside bunkers, missile silos, and submerged submarines, aboard ships, and hidden in the middle of nowhere. Your father will never even be able to find them all, much less destroy them. I'll be the first to admit that laser thing we saw in Siberia was amazing, but it can't take out that many nukes."

Kiara regarded them sadly. "My father and the Harrington Group have more money and influence than a lot of countries in the world. He's currently sitting on the precise locations of more than 3,700 active nuclear warheads scattered around the world, and another few thousand partially dismantled and decommissioned weapons held in long-term storage. And as for that event in Siberia, that was a small-scale test to prove that the system works. When my father fires the real one at full power, it will level mountains and penetrate to the depths of the ocean to reach its targets. But you're right. He won't be able to destroy all of them, but I guess he thinks taking out five thousand of them is a good start."

"That small-scale test, as you call it, killed hundreds and scattered nuclear waste for miles," Jake said, shaking his head. "Destroying thousands of nukes on the level you're talking about—along with ships, submarines, and probably aircrafts, as well—will kill hundreds of thousands of people. And the deaths from the contamination will be even worse. Would your father honestly do something like that?"

Her mouth tightened. "I asked my father that same question after I finally figured out what he was planning. When I told him that he needed to stop all of this before it was too late, he had the nerve to tell me he was doing all of this for me and for our people. When I kept trying to talk him out of it, he locked me up, saying he wouldn't let me interfere with his plans. I barely got away." She glanced at Brielle's brother, her eyes softening as she gazed at him.

"That's when I ran into Julian. Without his help, I never would have escaped."

Julian pressed a kiss to her forehead before looking around at them. "Harrington was ready to murder his own daughter, so if you want to know whether he'll go through with his plan, the answer is yes."

Kiara reached up to cover the hand Julian still had resting on her shoulder with her own. "Julian is right. My father won't hesitate to kill hundreds of thousands of people if he thinks it's the only way to stop World War III."

Silence filled the safe house once again.

Caleb had dealt with more than a few homicidal psychos before working for STAT and a lot more after coming on board. But in all that time, he'd never dealt with a maniac so willing to destroy the world under the assumption that he was saving it. It seemed like Xavier Harrington was his very own flavor of fruitcake.

"Do you know where your father is planning to fire the laser from?" Brielle asked softly. "Julian said the ship carrying the nukes came into the New York Harbor, so I assume it's somewhere close."

Kiara nodded. "I was able to sneak in and get a look at the plans for the underground facility my father built for his crazy scheme. It's directly below the Harrington Group Headquarters in Lower Manhattan and spreads outward in an enormous collection of tunnels that cover all five boroughs and even goes as far as Newark to the west and Hempstead to the east."

Caleb's jaw dropped. Brielle and his teammates looked just as floored as he was.

"If the ground heave effects are the same as we saw in Siberia, we'll likely see the total destruction of the entire city and much of the surrounding area," McKay said. "Unless we figure out how to stop Harrington, we're talking about the deaths of over eight million people."

Shit.

"When is all this supposed to go down?" Caleb asked.

He only prayed they had enough time to come up with some kind of plan, because running into those tunnels like they had in Siberia wasn't going to work any better than it had there.

"I don't know for sure," Kiara said. "Based on the way my father was talking, it sounds like it'll be soon."

"Shit," Jake muttered.

"Exactly." Kiara frowned. "While I'm worried about that, I'm even more concerned that my father is almost certainly aware of where I am and everything I'm telling you right now. When we go after him, he's going to see us coming and will already have a plan to stop us. We need to come up with a way to distract him and muddy the waters if we have any hope of making it more difficult for him to see what we're going to do."

Well, crap. Caleb hadn't thought of that. How the hell were they supposed to sneak up on a guy who could see them coming before they even got there?

"I know what you're all thinking," McKay said, stepping away from the fireplace to look at each of them in turn. "That we don't have a chance of stopping this guy. And while you might be right, for the next few hours at least, I want you to stop thinking about that. Grab something to eat, get some sleep, and give me some time to make some calls. Because no matter what we do, we can't do it alone. Not with a crew this small, anyway. There are nineteen nuclear weapons buried underneath New York City, hidden in what might be twenty or thirty miles' worth of tunnels. We're going to need help—and one hell of a plan."

Caleb hated the idea of letting outsiders in on this operation. He might be a big, strong werewolf, but the thought of more people knowing that he and his teammates were supernaturals still scared him sometimes. And while he liked to believe he and his team could handle anything the bad guys threw at them, he knew McKay was right. This one was too big for them to take on alone. And the stakes were too high to risk failing.

CHAPTER 18

"I APOLOGIZE FOR KEEPING EVERYONE IN THE DARK ABOUT this operation and how you're involved in it," McKay announced from where he stood in front of the group of people he'd assembled in the small New Jersey warehouse. "But as you'll understand in a minute, it was necessary."

Brielle glanced at the thirty or so people seated in rows of folding chairs set up around either side of her and Caleb. Other than Julian, Kiara, and the STAT team, she didn't recognize anyone. From the dark suits and tactical gear the newcomers wore, it was obvious the men and women came from some type of law enforcement or military organization.

To say that Caleb and his teammates hadn't been thrilled at the idea of bringing in outsiders to help take down Harrington was putting it mildly. But in the end, they'd realized there simply wasn't any way around it. Based on what Kiara had told them about the drawings she'd seen, there could be as many as ten or fifteen miles of interconnected tunnels under the city—a rat's maze beyond comparison. There were entrances scattered from east Jersey to Long Island. There was no way STAT could do this on their own even if they pulled in every field agent they had around the world.

Hence, the backup McKay had brought in.

"Before we start, I ask that you take a moment to look around the room at the people here with you," McKay added quietly. "Seated in this warehouse are members of the CIA, NSA, FBI, and NYPD, as well as the organization that I represent. Few of you have ever met before, but I can promise you that if you're still alive come morning, it will be because of the person sitting next to you."

Beside her, Caleb let out a soft snort as the room began to fill with the murmur of quiet consternation. Brielle couldn't blame him. McKay was laying it on kind of thick. But then again, she supposed he needed to. Once the people he'd recruited got an idea of what they were walking into, how many of them would want to bail on the mission before it even got started?

"Maybe it's time you told us who you are and what we're doing here," some guy in the back of the room said, pitching his voice to be heard above the background noise. "If you could fill us in on why the hell we had to sign a nondisclosure agreement that promised us five years in a federal supermax prison if we ever reveal any details of this mission, that'd be great, too."

"While you're at it," a woman said from directly behind Brielle, "can you also explain why you brought us here in vehicles with blacked-out windows and why the driver wouldn't tell us where we were going?"

Brielle had to admit that last part had unsettled her a little bit, too. About an hour ago, five vans with blacked out windows had shown up at the safe house. McKay hadn't given them any information about who was driving them or where they were going. He'd simply told them all to pair up and get into a vehicle. Twenty minutes later, Brielle and Caleb's driver had dropped them off at the warehouse where they'd found the rest of the STAT team and Julian and Kiara waiting. Brielle knew she was dealing with covert types, but really?

"My name is McKay," Caleb's boss said, his voice calm, clearly not flustered by the group's rapid-fire questions. "The agency I work for is unimportant. And as far as why you're here, to put it bluntly, you're here to help save the world."

That answer prompted the results Brielle expected. While most of the federal agents and cops grumbled about why he was being so mysterious, a few actually stood up, like they were going to head for the exit.

"As we speak, there are nineteen nuclear warheads set to detonate under New York City," McKay said, his firm voice cutting through the chatter and stopping everyone in their tracks. "Conservative estimates put the death toll from the underground blast and the subsequent collapse of the city at somewhere around four million people."

A guy in tactical gear who'd gotten to his feet a moment ago dropped heavily into his chair, his face pale. "You're joking."

McKay pinned him with a look. "I assure you I'm not. Unfortunately, it gets worse."

Everyone else still standing took their seats again, the warehouse falling silent.

"The nukes are being used to power a series of lasers positioned around the city," McKay continued. "Those laser beams will bounce off a network of satellites that will direct them back down to earth, taking out the majority of the nuclear weapons in the world, along with the ships, planes, submarines, and missile platforms carrying them. We're looking at as many as three million deaths from the initial attack and another ten million from the long-term effects of the radiation scatter. It will take years—decades even—to clean it all up. On top of that, you can add in the likelihood of multiple countries launching preemptive large-scale conventional attacks against their neighbors in order to take advantage of the suddenly crippled superpowers. We're looking at generations of war with countless deaths."

Around Brielle, the federal agents and cops alike looked stunned. She didn't realize she'd reached out and taken Caleb's hand until she felt him give hers a reassuring squeeze. A few seats down from them, Julian stared at their joined hands for a moment before meeting her gaze, a surprised expression on his face.

"Can we evacuate the city?" a worried-looking guy with gray seasoning his otherwise dark hair asked quietly. "Get the rest of the NYPD, fire department, and mayor's office involved? Try to get as many people off the island and out of harm's way as we can? That will save some lives, right?"

McKay sighed. "As much as I'd like to, we can't do that. Even if we could come up with a way to evacuate the island without causing widespread panic, we can't do it without tipping off the people we're trying to stop. We don't know when they plan on setting off the nukes, but we can't risk them doing it sooner if they see us coming. Bottom line, it's on us to save the city and everyone else."

"Who the hell are we up against, anyway?" the same older man with the salt-and-pepper hair demanded. "More importantly, how do we stop them?"

When McKay didn't say anything right away, Brielle glanced at Caleb before doing the same to Kiara and the rest of the STAT team farther down the row. As soon as it became clear they'd have to bring in outsiders, the issue of protecting the team's supernatural secrets had come up.

Some of them—well, mostly Caleb—thought they should simply let the backup personnel figure things out on their own. Sort of a survival-of-the-fittest kind of thing. But the idea of letting good people get slaughtered when they ran into Uriel Cerano and his nearly indestructible security force—or, even worse, those terrifying ghouls—was more than the rest of the team were willing to accept. So they decided as a group to tell the federal agents and cops as much as feasible, leaving McKay to decide exactly what and how much to reveal.

"The answer to your first question is more complicated than you could possibly imagine, and it's the reason all of you had to sign those extremely restrictive NDAs," McKay said, "which is why the answer to your second question is going to end up being less straightforward than I'd like."

No one complained this time, even though McKay had said a lot without actually saying anything at all.

"The people you'll be facing today possess supernatural abilities," McKay said in a flat, no-nonsense tone. "Xavier Harrington, the man behind this nuclear nightmare, can essentially see the future…or at least different possible futures. His personal security force is filled with men and women who will be faster, stronger, and harder to kill than any of you because they cannot only heal from almost any wound but also survive damage that would kill a regular human. On top of that, the head of that security force—a man named Uriel Cerano—possesses telekinetic abilities."

Everyone stared at McKay, disbelief on their faces.

"You're telling us this guy can move objects with his mind?" a man said incredulously.

McKay gave him a nod. "Including bullets and anything else you throw at him."

"That's impossible," another man said. "People don't have supernatural powers."

McKay let out another sigh. "Jake, could you please give them a demonstration?"

Brielle thought Jake would shift, showing off his fangs, claws, and glowing eyes, but when he stood and walked to the front of the room to join McKay, he took a folding pocketknife from his cargo pocket and flicked it open, then rested his other hand on the table and plunged the blade into it.

There was a mix of gasps and curses from everyone in the room who wasn't part of STAT. Brielle couldn't help wincing a little herself. Even for a werewolf, that had to be painful as hell. But Jake merely wiped off the blood with the cloth that was on the table, then held up his hand to show off the wound as it healed, becoming nothing more than a scar right before their very eyes.

All around, people were staring, their jaws hanging open.

"How is that even possible?" a blond woman asked.

"It's possible because Jake is a supernatural," McKay said simply. "And in a few hours, you'll be going up against people who aren't like Jake at all but have those same healing abilities. They're going to be damn near impossible to kill, but you're going to have to go up against them anyway."

Silence filled the warehouse for a long time.

"What's the plan?" a woman a few seats away from Brielle finally asked.

McKay's brows drew together in a frown. "Actually, I don't know the plan. Xavier Harrington's gift makes having one almost impossible. At the advice of Harrington's daughter, we're going to abandon the traditional approach and go with something that will hopefully muddy the waters enough so he won't see us coming. Harrington doesn't necessarily see the future. Instead, he sees the decisions people make—or might make—and how those decisions affect what happens next. One chess move affects another, affects another, and another, one after the other until the game is over. His gift allows him to see the most likely outcome of the game well before it's played."

At McKay's nod, two people from the STAT support team moved along the rows of chairs, handing out thick manila envelopes to everyone, including Brielle. It had her name on it along with a string of numbers.

"Which is why we had to turn over this entire operation to an AI computer," McKay continued. "It came up with the plan with no outside assistance from anyone, using its knowledge of the threat we face as well as each of your particular skills and personality traits. When you walk out of here, someone will direct you to a vehicle, which will drop you off at an undisclosed location somewhere in the city. When you get there, open your envelopes. Inside, you'll find instructions that will tell you where to go and what to do. Many of you have multiple envelopes inside the one you're holding that will give you the information you need at the proper time. We're hoping that, if we're vague enough, Harrington will have a hard time figuring out what we're up to until it's too late to stop us."

Brielle saw doubt—and panic—in the eyes of everyone around her. She didn't blame them. Her own heart had started to bang like a drum as the implication of what McKay said started to hit home. The thing she was most afraid of about this plan that wasn't a plan was that she and Caleb would be separated. She simply couldn't imagine that.

She was still trying to wrap her head around that when McKay announced there were food and weapons in the back of the warehouse and that they should help themselves to both before heading out.

"I'm gonna grab something to eat," Caleb said. "You hungry?"

Brielle wasn't but nodded anyway. Hopefully, they could find some privacy where she could confide her concerns about the possibility of them getting split up.

Unfortunately, everyone seemed to be as hungry as Caleb, because there was a crowd around the tables where the food had been set up. She nibbled on a chocolate chip cookie that tasted like dirt in her mouth instead of delicious, like her head kept telling her it was, because she was so worried, while Caleb helped himself to several cheeseburgers. As they moved away from the table, Julian and Kiara walked over to them. He had two manila envelopes in his hand.

Julian glanced at Caleb before looking at her. "I was too worried about Kiara last night to ask what McKay threatened you with this time in return for helping me."

"He only asked me to help STAT find the stolen nukes," Brielle said.

Her brother seemed genuinely surprised. But also relieved. "So you're free to leave anytime you want?"

Brielle felt more than saw Caleb tense beside her. "Yes."

"Good." Julian nodded. "Because Kiara and I are leaving, and I want you to come with us."

Kiara's eyes went wide. "Leaving? What are you talking about? I'm not leaving."

"Neither am I," Brielle said.

Julian cursed under his breath in French. Folding the envelopes in half, he shoved them in his back pocket, then took Kiara's hands in his. "While I really hope STAT is able to stop your father, I'm not willing to risk either of us being anywhere near New York City in the event that they can't. If we have any hope of finding a safe place to take cover before it's too late, we need to leave now."

Kiara slowly shook her head, a small, sad smile curving her lips. "Even though we just met, I've come to care about you, Julian. More than I've ever cared about anyone. I know you want to keep me safe, but I can't leave. My father is the one responsible for all of this. His bizarre plot to save the world by destroying it is certifiably insane, but if I leave instead of staying here to help stop him, then I'm no better than he is."

Genuine panic filled Julian's eyes. "What are you talking about? You don't know the first thing about fighting or even how to shoot a gun. You'll only end up getting yourself killed."

"Maybe. But I hope not." She sighed. "Julian, I promised McKay that I'd walk the pathways and try to give his team an advantage. I may not be as strong as my father when it comes to walking the pathways, but I can do enough to confuse him a little bit and make him doubt what he sees."

Julian didn't say anything, and Brielle could see the dilemma going on in his head. His desire to leave was warring with the need to stay with the woman who obviously meant so much to him. After a moment, he turned to Brielle, giving her an imploring look.

"Help me talk some sense into her, Brielle. Tell her that we all need to leave," he begged. "Please."

Brielle opened her mouth to say she couldn't do that because she wasn't leaving either, but Caleb interrupted.

"Your brother is right, Brielle," he said. "You and Kiara should both go with him. There's no need for you—or her—to go on this mission."

All the air left Brielle's lungs, making speech impossible, even if she knew what to say. So instead, she stared at him in disbelief as he stood there stone-faced. Caleb was doing this to keep her safe, she knew that. But the thought of him going into whatever danger awaited him without her had her heart suddenly beating out of control.

"I know what you're doing, Caleb, but it's not going to work," she said. "Did you really think I'd be okay with you facing heaven knows what kind of danger while I'm safe and sound somewhere far away from here, going out of my mind worrying about you? And don't even suggest that you'll leave me behind because I'll only follow you."

Caleb let out a soft growl. "Dammit, I'm trying to keep you safe. Why can't you understand that?"

"I do understand," she said softly, reaching up to rest her hand against his scruffy jaw, not caring that they were going to have this conversation with her brother and Kiara standing right there. "But part of getting close to someone is accepting that the worry goes both ways. You don't want me to get hurt, but I don't want you to get hurt, either. So I'm going with you to watch out for you, because you never watch out for yourself."

She couldn't tell if Caleb was ready to capitulate or not, but before he could say anything one way or another, Julian spoke.

"Wait a minute," her brother said, glaring first at Caleb, then at her. "You *like* this guy? I mean, I saw you holding hands before, but are you two *sleeping* together?"

Brielle returned his glare, furious that her brother had the nerve to say something about her choice in men when she'd been forced to deal with his questionable taste in girlfriends for years—up until now, of course. Kiara seemed like a really sweet girl.

"And what makes you think that the answer to either of those questions is any of your business?" she demanded.

"Because I'm your brother," Julian replied. "I worry about you, and I don't want to see you get hurt."

Brielle's anger immediately faded. Her brother would never have any say when it came to her and Caleb, but hearing him admit that he cared enough to be worried about her was nice. She only wished it weren't the first time he'd said it out loud.

"I appreciate the concern," she said, giving him a small smile. "But you don't have to worry about me. Caleb is the man I'm supposed to be with."

Caleb did a double take at that, regarding her with the most adorable stunned expression on his face. Julian seemed equally amazed, and for a moment, Brielle thought he was going to argue, but then he sighed.

"It looks like we're all staying then," he said, looking from Kiara to her. "For what it's worth, I think you're both making a big mistake, but I won't let you make it alone."

Kiara wrapped her arms around Julian, hugging him tightly. "Since we're staying, maybe we should get a gun for you to carry."

Julian nodded, letting Kiara take his hand and lead him away. But after a step or two, he stopped and turned back to pin Caleb with a look. "Just so you know, I don't think you're good enough for my sister, but she seems to like you anyway. You better not hurt her, or I'll kill you."

It was Brielle's turn to be stunned. Speechless, she watched her brother and Kiara head toward the tables loaded down with more weapons than she could even identify, where Julian picked one up and handled it with way too much familiarity.

"I would never hurt you," Caleb murmured. "Never."

Brielle turned to smile at him. "I know."

"That part you said…about me being the man you're supposed to be with," he said, the words as unexpected as they were soft. "Did you mean it? You truly think you're supposed to be with me?"

She nodded. "Yes."

Caleb seemed to consider that for a moment. "Brielle, there's something important I need to tell you. About these feelings you have for me, I mean. There's a folk tale that says werewolves…"

Brielle had no doubt that Caleb was about to tell her about *The One*—and she was more than ready to listen—but before he could get the words out, McKay was shouting for everyone's attention from the front of the warehouse.

"Okay, people, time to go!" he called. "There's a number on the upper left corner of your envelope that corresponds to a vehicle outside. Grab weapons, ammo, explosives, and whatever food you need and get moving. And good luck."

Caleb cursed, but Brielle put a finger to his lips. She didn't want something as important as this conversation to be rushed.

"You can tell me later," she promised. "Right now, why don't you help me find a weapon? Until I touch someone who knows what the hell they're doing with a gun, I'm clueless."

Caleb hesitated but nodded. "Okay. But we do need to talk— and soon."

CHAPTER 19

"ACCORDING TO THE MAP, THERE'S SUPPOSED TO BE SOME KIND of electrical room about half a dozen turns up ahead," Brielle whispered, looking intently back and forth between the paper that detailed where they were supposed to be heading and a rough map that Kiara had drawn from memory, which McKay had copied for everyone. "I have no idea if there are people guarding the place, but according to the AI computer, if we blow up the room, it will cut power to most of the complex and hopefully end this whole crazy scheme before it starts."

"Why do I have a hard time believing that ending this will be as simple as setting an explosive charge and running away?" Caleb murmured, his ears straining to pick up any sound that might suggest there were bad guys up ahead.

"Because you're a naturally cynical person," Hudson said.

Genevieve let out a soft snort of amusement at that.

"I'm only cynical because of how many times I've been right about crap like this," Caleb quipped.

He focused his attention on the dimly lit tunnel ahead of them, occasionally glancing over his shoulder back the way they'd come. The idea that Xavier Harrington might already know they were here and that he had his goons sneaking up on them even now had crossed Caleb's mind more than once. And from the tense expressions on everyone else's faces, it was obvious they were worried about the same thing.

Caleb wondered again why McKay's AI computer put Brielle, Hudson, and Genevieve together on their own. Because that was the way it was supposed to have played out—if he had been better at following directions.

He hadn't bothered to open his envelope or even read the numbers written on the outside of it. When Brielle had headed for one of the vans near the front of the line of vehicles outside the warehouse, he'd followed as if it was the most natural thing in the world. When the vehicle's GPS had led the driver to the building off Union Turnpike and Brielle, Craig, and Genevieve had gotten out, he'd climbed out with them.

Truthfully, he didn't really care what some stupid computer thought he should do. Hell, he rarely did what people he respected told him to do, so why would he follow a computer's instructions? Besides, there was no way in hell he was leaving his soul mate on her own. Or in this case, leaving her with Hudson and Genevieve as backup, which was almost as bad as leaving her alone.

As they moved along a dimly lit corridor, Caleb caught sight of Hudson dropping a small black box on the floor and nudging it into a corner, trying to make the thing as inconspicuous as possible. The box—a radio repeater pack—was designed to boost the strength of any radio signal it picked up. All the teams moving into the complex were dropping them at random locations, hoping it would allow everyone to stay in contact with each other as they moved deeper into the tunnels. Of course, no one had ever used the system underground like this, so no one was sure whether it would work.

The tunnels Caleb's team was in were bigger than the ones in Siberia. Maybe a bit smoother, too. If it wasn't for the fact that their driver had dropped him, Brielle, Hudson and Genevieve outside a small Harrington facility in Queens, Caleb could have easily believed he was right back in the frozen tundra of Russia.

Getting into the building and down into the subbasement, into the tunnels below, had been easy. Maybe *too* easy. Brielle had borrowed Hudson's weapon-handling abilities and helped take out the two guards they'd run into. The fact that those men had barely put up a fight had Caleb more worried than ever that they were walking into a trap. It would have been nice to check in with the other teams to see what they thought. But McKay's plan had them operating under radio silence until someone ran into trouble. The fact that the radio had been quiet so far could be taken as a good sign—or that everyone had been wiped out without having a chance to even touch their radios.

As they moved through the tunnels, Caleb tried to stay focused on what was ahead of them, knowing they could walk into an ambush at any second, but he found his mind wandering. Walking this close to Brielle, listening to her rapidly beating heart and breathing in her intoxicating honeysuckle scent, made it difficult not to think about everything that had been said back at the warehouse barely an hour ago.

Brielle had said she was willing to follow him because she thought they belonged together. He hadn't been able to say anything—not with so many people around—but those words had meant more to him than she would probably ever know. For the first time in his life, he had someone who was there for him... really there. He only wished he'd had the chance to tell her how he felt—and about the soul-mate bond—before this insane mission.

Now he only prayed he got the chance.

"The electrical room should be around this corner," Brielle said softly when they reached a sharp left-hand turn in the tunnel they'd been following.

"Wait here," Caleb said, motioning for her, Craig, and Genevieve to hang back while he edged up to the corner and stood there for a second, listening for any sounds of movement. "We're clear," he added moments later when he figured out that the tunnel ahead was as empty as the rest of the tunnels they'd been in so far.

Caleb led the way around the corner, Brielle and the others right behind him. He immediately caught sight of what had to be the electrical room a little farther down the tunnel, directly across from a branch in the passage. As they moved closer, he realized the room resembled a closet. Hell, there was barely enough space for more than a few people to fit. Not that it mattered, because it would only take one of them to go in and set the explosive charges.

They were still a couple strides from the open door of the room when Caleb heard heavy footsteps coming their way. He only had a heartbeat to react, grabbing Brielle and dragging her into the electrical room with him just as the shooting started and alarms echoed throughout the tunnels, warning lights flashing.

"So much for the element of surprise," he muttered, pushing Brielle as far into the little room as he could, putting himself between her and the doorway, and using his body to shield her from the half dozen or so men shooting in their direction. "If we ever had it to begin with."

From the corner of his eye, he saw Hudson and Genevieve duck back down the tunnel they'd been in, barely making it to cover before a hail of gunfire exploded all around them. Hudson and Genevieve immediately returned fire, making the men coming their way slow down at least.

Caleb's radio earpiece popped to life, voices stomping all over each other as everyone on the various teams attempted to provide situation reports, the words barely audible over the sound of gunfire from right outside the door as well as throughout the rest of the complex. Several teams reported that they couldn't get near the tunnels where the nukes were supposed to be while others freaked out when they came face-to-face with Uriel and the Vandals.

"McKay's plan obviously didn't work," Brielle said, wedging herself between two electrical junction boxes mounted on the back wall even as she peeked out the door at the people trying to kill them. "Harrington knew exactly when we were coming and where we'd be. One of those men out there is a supernatural like the ones we went up against in Moscow. I can't believe Harrington left his own private security force down here in these tunnels."

Caleb had to admit, he was kinda surprised, too. "I'm hoping that means he won't pull the trigger on those nukes anytime soon." He flinched a little as bullets bounced off the rough stone of the doorjamb, peppering his face with rock fragments. "He might be psycho enough to sacrifice himself for the cause, but he wouldn't kill his own people, too, would he?"

"I'm not sure I'm willing to bet our lives on that," Brielle said, leaning out to fire her handgun into the passageway. "We need to blow these electrical panels now and take the option out of Harrington's hand."

Caleb fired a few .45-caliber rounds toward the bad guys. "Um…not that I have a problem with that idea, but since we seem to be trapped in this closet right now, I'm a little worried about how we're going to set off a dozen or so pounds of C-4 explosives in here."

"Me, too." Brielle reached into the cargo pockets of her tactical pants, coming out with several blocks of explosives. "We're just going to have to come up with a way to get out of here in time."

Peeling the sticky tape off the back of the explosives, she slapped them against the side of the nearest electrical junction box. Twenty seconds later, she had the charges set and the delay timer attached.

Caleb's hand hovered over the red start button, his eyes locked on Brielle's. "The moment I hit this button, we'll have ten seconds to get clear. Not one second more."

She nodded.

"Hudson…Genevieve…cover us," she murmured into her radio. "We're coming out, and we're going to be moving fast."

Caleb didn't even wait for confirmation they'd heard. He simply slapped the button, watching the red number ten appear and change to nine way too fast, then he was scooping Brielle up in his arms and running as fast as his werewolf legs would carry him. He turned left, curling his arms and shoulders protectively around her as he sprinted for the corner in the tunnel that Hudson and

Genevieve were using as cover even as they fired their weapons nonstop at the bad guys in the other corridor.

He didn't have to look to know that the men who'd ambushed them were running straight at them now, weapons blazing away on full auto, trying to kill him and Brielle before they were around the corner. A few bullets clipped him—one in the shoulder, another in the right calf, and a third at his hip. He ignored the minor stabs of pain and threw himself forward toward safety.

The explosion caught him by surprise, his head telling him that there was no way ten seconds could have elapsed already. Then the blast wave was nudging him in the back, giving him a little shove. He rolled when he hit the floor, tucking Brielle into his body and protecting her from the impact as much as he could.

Caleb was still on the floor, staring up at the ceiling of the tunnel, Brielle lying across his chest, when all the lights went out.

Crap. This might just work.

But before he could take a breath, dim red lights popped back on, illuminating the tunnels all over again. Of course, Harrington had thought of emergency power.

So much for the idea of stopping the nukes the easy way.

"Just me being cynical, huh?" Caleb muttered.

Gently sliding Brielle to the side, he quickly checked her over for injuries. Thankfully, she didn't have any. Helping her to her feet, he moved to help Hudson and Genevieve deal with the last of the bad guys. Not that there were many to worry about. The blast they'd set off had taken care of the majority of them. Even the lone Vandal from Uriel's crew was done for.

Caleb gazed down at the supernatural, then looked at Brielle. "Okay, this is going to sound morbid, but can you borrow this guy's abilities? I'd feel a lot better about you running around in these tunnels if I knew you had their healing skills."

Brielle came over to stand beside him, her face twisting in revulsion. "Hard no to that. I can't borrow from dead people. If you want me to pick up their healing and fighting skills, we'll need to find one who's breathing."

Before he could say anything, Jake's voice came over the radio with new instructions. With the AI computer's scheme a complete train wreck, the new plan was much simpler. Everyone would head toward the center of the complex and find the nukes, then disarm as many as they could—however they could—before Harrington set them off.

A few moments later, they were running through tunnels now barely illuminated by the red glow of the facility's emergency lights, Caleb praying they were able to find the nukes before Harrington hit that trigger.

The sound of their boots thumping against the floor of the tunnel might have been hypnotizing if Brielle wasn't so worried about the occasional bad guy darting out of the shadowy tunnels to either side of them to take potshots at her, Caleb, Hudson, and Genevieve before disappearing again. It was like something out of a nightmare.

They'd probably only been running for five minutes or so, but it like felt much longer. That was probably because she expected a blinding flash of white light to fill the tunnels at any second. The anticipation made time creep by. Brielle clutched her 9 mm tighter in her hand as she glanced down at the map she held in the other. She was doing her best to keep track of where they were. It might be something nice to know if they had to get out of the tunnels quickly. But with the darkness, the constant twists and turns of the underground network, the eerie red lights, and the random bad guys popping out at them, reading the map was a little difficult.

"Okay." McKay's voice suddenly crackled through her earpiece, his tone telling her that whatever he was going to say was bad before he uttered a single word. "Misty was able to access

Harrington's security network but only long enough to figure out that he's started the countdown timers on all nineteen nukes. We're already under thirty minutes, and before you ask, Misty can't get back in the computer system because Harrington took it completely offline. Unfortunately, there's no way to shut down the nukes easily. There's a chance he has a remote control with him, wherever the hell he might be. But short of that, you'll have to get to each warhead and disarm it manually."

Other than the random burst of gunfire audible over the radio, silence met McKay's words, followed by a lot of cursing. Brielle silently echoed their sentiments. Everyone who'd come down into these tunnels had essentially volunteered knowing this would be a difficult task to accomplish. Now it seemed damn near impossible.

"Shit, he's really going to do it," Hudson whispered, his words barely loud enough to hear. "Harrington's going to set these things off with his own people down here. Do you think they know?"

McKay's sigh was audible. "It's possible he hasn't told them the countdown has started. The alternative is to accept that all of his people are willing to die to help him accomplish his insane plan, and I have to believe that can't be true."

Brielle wanted to think that there couldn't be *that* many crazy people in the world, but unfortunately, she knew that wasn't true. All it took was a psycho with a dream, and people would follow him right off a ledge.

"My team has found one of the nukes," Harley announced a minute later, her words barely understandable over the near-constant barrage of gunfire from her location. "But we can't get close to it. They have a lot of bad guys down here, and they're toting some serious weaponry. Even Sawyer and I don't stand a chance against machine guns."

McKay immediately rerouted teams to get backup to Harley and Sawyer's part of the complex. "We need to hurry up or things are going to get ugly," he added. "The CIA has alerted the military.

They're calling up a squadron of F-22 fighters from Langley right now. If we can't take out the nukes, they plan on bombing every single Harrington Group building in the New York area to destroy the laser towers. It won't stop the nukes from collapsing the city, but it will prevent the destruction of the world's nuclear weapons and all the fallout from that. We have to disarm those nukes, or the U.S. will be forced to bomb one of its own cities."

Merde.

Brielle ran faster, keeping pace with Caleb. A second later, she let out a gasp as he scooped her off her feet and threw himself sideways into a small opening on the right side of the tunnel, shouting a warning to Hudson and Genevieve as bullets slammed into the floor and walls all around them.

They hit the floor hard, the air getting knocked from her lungs even with Caleb's body protecting her from the worst of the impact. She twisted her head around to see down the narrow passageway across from them, trying to see how many people were shooting as Caleb dragged her to the side and wedged both of them behind a section of wall that jutted out enough to give them a place to hide.

Brielle peeked around the corner of their hiding place to see two men with machine guns and another three with assault rifles, all of them doing their best to kill her and Caleb. She panicked for a second when she realized she couldn't see Hudson and Genevieve anywhere. Then she remembered that they'd been far enough behind her and Caleb to retreat when the shooting had started. On the upside, that had probably kept them from getting shot, but on the downside, that meant the four of them were split up again.

A single glance at Caleb out the corner of her eye let her know that he was seconds away from charging at their attackers, guns be damned. But then he looked at her, and Brielle swore she knew he was thinking about what would happen to her if he went down under the first hail of bullets and how she'd be left on her own. In that moment, she saw something that looked like realization flash in his eyes. A moment later, the tension left his body as he pulled back fully behind the small outcropping of rock keeping the both of them alive.

"We're pinned down," he shouted into the radio. "If we even pop our heads out, they're going to whack us like a couple of moles."

"We're coming to help," Genevieve called out. "Just hold on."

"Don't," Caleb answered. "If you take a single step into this corridor, you'll be dead before you can get a shot. You two need to go back the way we came and work your way around behind these guys. I need you to either take them out or at least make them duck for a few seconds."

Neither Hudson nor Genevieve was very thrilled with that plan, but after a moment, they agreed to it.

"We're on the way," Hudson said. "But you two have to hold on for us, okay?"

Caleb didn't bother to answer. Instead, he stuck his arm around the rocky outcropping they were hiding behind and fired half a magazine's worth of ammo at the men across the tunnel from them. The number of bullets that came right back at them was terrifying, and Brielle pressed herself against Caleb as tightly as she could.

"Hudson and Genevieve are going to come back as fast as they can," he said soothingly. "We just have to keep these guys off us until they do."

As another burst of gunfire tore into the wall near them, Brielle resisted the urge to tell him that might be easier said than done. Instead, she pressed her face against Caleb's muscular chest and hoped for the best.

"Um…I know this probably isn't the best time to have a serious conversation, but there's something I need to tell you," Caleb said, something in his tone making her lift her head. "And please don't think I'm telling you now because I don't think we're getting out of here. It's just that getting pinned down like this has made me realize I should have told you way before this."

She flinched as another bullet bounced off the wall so close to her head that she swore she could feel her hair flutter from its speed. Caleb gazed at her in concern, which only worried her more than she already was. That was saying a lot, considering they were currently hiding behind a piece of rock barely big enough to conceal a bunny—or at least it felt that way—waiting for an army of nuclear weapons to go off.

"What's wrong?" she asked, for the first time praying this wasn't going to be one of those bizarre "it's not you it's me" kind of conversations.

"Nothing's wrong," he said quickly, as if he'd read her mind. "It's just that there was something I wanted to tell you after the briefing at the warehouse, but I didn't get the chance, and I need to tell you before I go out of my mind. Even if it freaks you out."

Hearing that made Brielle more uncomfortable than she'd been before, but she bit her tongue, telling herself she needed to wait and see where this was going.

"This is going to sound insane," he said, pausing to fire several more rounds down the tunnel toward the bad guys to keep them from moving any closer. Then she had to wait impatiently as he awkwardly reloaded in the tight space available to them before looking at her again. "But I'm asking for you to listen with an open mind until I get it all out there, okay?"

All Brielle could do was nod, even if she was on the verge of screaming at him to spit it out already. People shooting at them was bad, but this was worse.

"I was drawn to you from the first moment we met," he said, and even though she knew it was a trick of the mind, the sounds of gunshots and wailing alarms somehow faded away until it was simply the two of them having a quiet, private moment together. "I'll admit that I tried hard to ignore it. Mostly because I'm stupid, but also because I was scared. I didn't think someone like me would ever have anything good in my life. Definitely not anything as good as you."

She gazed at him intently, part of her wanting to think she knew where this was going, especially since her recent conversation with Misty was still fresh in her mind. But she forced herself to wait as patiently as she could for him to continue.

"Based on what you said at the warehouse about me being the man you're supposed to be with, I want to believe you're feeling this connection between us, too." When she nodded, he continued. "So I don't want you to freak out when I tell you that...well... we're soul mates."

Brielle had been sure she was ready to hear this—until Caleb said the actual words. Then the air left her lungs so rapidly she didn't see it coming. *Soul mates.* Misty hadn't been kidding. This was real. She'd met the man that destiny had decided she was supposed to be with for the rest of her life.

Caleb must have taken the expression on her face as one of panic because he took her hand in his free one, pausing a second to shoot at someone trying to sneak up on them.

"I know what you're probably thinking," he said urgently, like he was worried she'd jump up and try to run off right in the middle of the firefight. "That being soul mates means we don't have any say in this and that what we feel for each other isn't real, that it isn't love. But you know what I think about all that?"

"What?" Brielle murmured breathlessly, barely able to get the word out.

"I think, who cares?" he said. "All I know is that I love you, and I don't care how I got here. You're the best thing that has ever happened to me—an omega werewolf who has spent his entire life alone. You're *The One* for me, and I hope that, in time, you can come to accept that I'm *The One* for you. And before you ask, I want you to know that I'm willing to give you all the time you need to figure that out. I won't push you or anything."

It took a second for the words to finally filter in. But in the end, there was no denying what she'd heard.

He loves me.

The words created a warmth inside her that she'd never experienced—or expected. It was almost as surprising as the fact that Caleb, a big omega with anger management issues, could be so romantic. She'd certainly never expected that, either.

When she didn't say anything, alarm clouded Caleb's handsome features. He opened his mouth—almost certainly to apologize—but Brielle couldn't have that. Wrapping her hand behind his head, she dragged his mouth to hers. And as bullets ricocheted off the walls and floor around them, she kissed him so hard that he'd never doubt she loved him as much as he loved her.

She pulled back, ready to tell him she loved him, too—as crazy as it was to fall in love with a man this fast, she was still going to tell him—but then the radio chirped, interrupting their perfect moment.

"We're in position to take out the enemy," Hudson announced. "Please tell me you two are ready to move or this is going to be the shortest rescue in history. Because if any of them get their weapons turned our way, Genevieve and I are screwed. We'll have absolutely no cover once we step out into the corridor."

Caleb's gaze never left hers. "You get the heat off us for a couple seconds, and we'll be there when you need us."

Brielle almost screamed in disappointment at not getting out the words she so desperately wanted to say, but then they heard shooting from the far end of the corridor. Caleb gave her a nod, then he was up and running, shouting at her to stay behind him.

She jumped to her feet and followed right on his heels, refusing to let him run into danger without her, even if this was the most insane thing she'd ever done in her life.

CHAPTER 20

"WE NEED BACKUP, AND WE NEED IT NOW!" JAKE SHOUTED over the radio as a deep rumble shook the tunnel around Caleb, dropping dirt and chunks of rock all over him, Brielle, Hudson, and Genevieve. "We've gotten to three of the nukes and disarmed them, but Uriel and his people have started blowing the tunnels that lead to the others. If we don't reach the rest of them in the next fifteen minutes, we aren't getting there at all."

Caleb growled and dropped the bad guy he'd just taken out. The distraction Hudson and Genevieve had created worked well, allowing him and Brielle to get close enough to finish the rest of the bad guys. But Caleb had still been hit with bullets three times during the fight, and Brielle now had a ragged crease across the left side of her tactical vest. He didn't want to think about how bad it would have been if the bullet had hit her a few more inches to the right. Without her having any access to supernatural abilities at the moment, he knew it would have been bad.

"We need to move. Before it's too late to matter," Hudson said, looking down at the bodies on the floor, then at Caleb. "Are you okay to keep going? You're bleeding a lot."

Caleb looked down to see blood soaking through the dark material of his tactical uniform on the right side of his stomach as well as on his right hip and right above his knee. As scary as the wounds looked—and yeah, Brielle's eyes were so wide he could make out the white all the way around her irises—it was actually the one in the leg that hurt the most. The other two rounds had punched right through him, and the wounds were already closing up. The bullet that hit his leg had bounced off the bone and was still in there. Saying it hurt like shit was an understatement. If he had time, he'd dig it out with a pocketknife and a pair of pliers.

But he didn't have the time. None of them did.

"I'm fine," he growled, at the same time giving Brielle a look he hoped was reassuring. Then he turned and started moving down the tunnel in the direction they'd been heading before this last ambush, his stride picking up until he was jogging at a pace that would cover a lot of ground quickly while still allowing everyone else to keep up.

As he ran, Caleb replayed the conversation he'd had with Brielle a few minutes earlier. There was a huge part of him freaking out that he had so openly confessed his love for her, dumping the whole soul-mate thing on her out of the blue like that. He never would have imagined putting himself out there. Then again, he never imagined feeling this way about a woman.

On the downside, she hadn't said she loved him in return. But she *had* kissed him. A real kiss. That counted for something, right? He only hoped that once she had a second, she'd tell him she loved him back. Unless she didn't feel the same. His stomach twisted at the realization. That was a possibility, too, he guessed.

Caleb heard shooting long before they reached the action. He had to run down a long stretch of tunnel and around two corners before sliding to a stop at what he found. Four of Harrington's Vandal security guards blocked the far end of the passageway. A man and a woman Caleb recognized from the briefing at the warehouse were lying on the floor of the tunnel bleeding badly. Kiara and Julian probably would have been in the same condition, but they'd found some protection behind a stack of equipment crates left to one side of the tunnel. But those crates were quickly being shredded by the onslaught of bullets coming their way, and Julian was already bleeding from a hit he'd taken while trying to shield Kiara with his body.

Caleb didn't have time to think. He simply charged, hoping

Brielle and the others were smart enough to not do anything stupid. Well, at least not as stupid as him. No such luck. Brielle followed right behind him, Hudson and Genevieve on their heels.

When the Vandals caught sight of him, they didn't step forward to meet him like he'd expected they would. Instead, they stayed where they were and poured all their fire in his direction, obviously recognizing him as the biggest threat.

Caleb closed on the first one, emptying an entire magazine into the man. Then he holstered his weapon, extended his claws, and started slashing. He grabbed one of the remaining three Vandals and punched him so hard in the face that he heard something break. Then he tossed him in Brielle's general direction.

"This one's alive this time," he shouted without looking back.

A few seconds later, Brielle was at his side, smashing and shooting, ignoring the damage done to her own body by the last two Vandals. Caleb knew she could handle the injuries, but damn, it hurt to see anyway.

Under the cover he and Brielle provided, Craig and Genevieve peeled off, dragging the two injured federal agents from the warehouse back down the tunnel toward safety. With all the gunfire, it was impossible to make out individual heartbeats, and Caleb could only hope those two were still alive. He didn't imagine Hudson would bother with them if they weren't.

Two of the Vandals were down—maybe dead—while a third was bleeding badly. Julian and Kiara slipped out from behind the crates to help, and Caleb thought the fight was just about wrapped up. Then one of the Vandals pulled something from his belt—a black key fob thing with a couple buttons on it. He and his Vandal buddy backpedaled quickly, the one with the fob glancing up toward the roof of the tunnel.

Shit.

"They're about to blow the tunnel!" Caleb shouted just as the man pushed the button and the whole world came apart.

He went down, barely getting his body over Brielle's to shield her. He saw Julian do the same for Kiara, vaguely thinking that, even if he thought the guy was a complete jackass, at least he wasn't a coward.

By the time the world—and the roof of the tunnel—stopped collapsing, the passage behind them was completely blocked. Caleb stared at the car-sized pieces of rock lying a few feet away. They would have all been crushed if they'd been only a little farther back that way.

Shaking his head to clear the cobwebs, he looked around, seeing that Brielle was okay and quickly figuring out that the two Vandals who'd still been fighting were now long gone. Kiara and Julian seemed okay, but it looked like the other two Vandals who'd been lying on the floor behind them were buried under all the rubble.

Caleb started to panic when he didn't see Hudson and Genevieve, only then remembering that they'd been much farther back along the tunnel, trying to save the two federal agents from McKay's backup force.

His radio had fallen off his tactical vest during the explosion, and he fumbled around on the ground for it.

"Hudson…Genevieve…come in," he called, trying to stay calm as he realized he'd started liking the two newest members of the STAT team way more than he'd thought he would. "Are you guys okay? Where are you?"

There was no answer for an agonizingly long time. Brielle, Julian, and Kiara all moved closer, their faces full of worry. Then a burst of static came through his earpiece, followed by Hudson's rough voice.

"We're okay. But there's no way we can get through that debris," he said, the words difficult to make out even with Caleb's keen hearing. "The best we can do is try to backtrack and find another way to reach you. But that's going to take time and means we'll have to leave the two injured agents behind. They probably won't make it if we do that. They're in really bad shape."

Caleb glanced at Brielle, who was already shaking her head.

"Forget it then," he told Hudson. "Get the hell out of these tunnels and find some help for them first, then come for us. This whole thing will probably be over by then, though. One way or another."

Hudson and Genevieve didn't even try to argue this time. They simply wished Caleb and Brielle good luck, and then they were off.

Caleb checked over Brielle one more time to make sure she was unharmed, reloaded his weapon, and gave Julian and Kiara a nod, then they were all moving again, with him taking point. Catching sight of the blood droplets on the floor from the Vandal who'd been injured, he followed the red trail, hoping it led somewhere good.

"We've taken out two more nukes," Jake announced over the radio a few moments later, his voice nearly drowned out by the shouts and gunfire on that end. "But it's taking us too long. There are still fourteen left, and Harrington's people have already collapsed too many of the tunnels. If any of you are already blocked off by the debris from going any farther, head for the exits—now. There's nothing you can do anyway, and it's stupid for all of us to die down here for nothing."

Caleb glanced over his shoulder at Brielle as he ran, desperately wanting to tell her to leave as well. But he knew she wouldn't listen. She wouldn't leave him any more than he would ever leave her. That knowledge filled a hole in his soul he hadn't known was there. For the first time in his life, he had someone who would stay with him through it all. And the worst part was that he was going to lose her anyway. That thought hurt so effing much he wanted to scream.

He hadn't realized how fast he and Brielle were running until he saw that Julian and Kiara were far behind and losing ground quickly. Borrowing the Vandal's abilities had nearly made Brielle a match for his werewolf speed.

"Keep going," Kiara yelled, waving them on. "We'll catch up when we can."

If it wasn't for the nukes waiting somewhere ahead of them, Caleb would never have left the couple, but there was no time to slow down. So he simply ran faster, Brielle staying right there with him.

Time started to blur, but they were both running at full speed when they came into a large open area, the first they'd found in the entire complex. The room was more brightly lit than the rest of the tunnels they'd been in, with dozens of lights attached to the walls and ceiling overpowering even the red glow of the flashing alarms and emergency lighting.

Looking around, he decided it was almost like being in the middle of a wagon wheel, with the central atrium they were standing in acting as the hub of the wheel, and the spokes heading off in at least twenty-five or thirty different directions. Thick, heavy cables ran along the walls and ceilings of many of those tunnels, weaving back and forth across each other in a mad pattern as they converged in the middle of the open area where he and Brielle stood. Here and there, cables ran in and out of large metal boxes. They must have something to do with setting the nukes off. Or maybe harnessing their power for the lasers.

But while all the cables and control boxes were interesting, it was the rather harmless-looking metal cylinder positioned in the exact center of the room that grabbed Caleb's attention. About four feet long, a little more than a foot in diameter, and practically buried under the mess of wires and cables running in and around it, the stainless tube didn't look like much. Definitely not anywhere as dangerous as the warhead from a nuclear weapon should. But that was what it was.

Glancing at the branching tunnels leading off the central hub of the wagon wheel, Caleb realized it wouldn't be very difficult to figure out where the nukes were. All they had to do was follow the cables. And that was what they'd do—as soon as they disarmed this one.

"Brielle and I found one of the nukes," Caleb said into the radio. "And I'm pretty sure the others are nearby."

"Roger that. But hurry," Jake said, his voice almost lost in the static filling the connection and the alarms still ringing throughout the tunnels. "Misty figures we barely have more than seven minutes left."

Shit.

He and Brielle had just started across the rough rock floor when eight people came into the room from one of the tunnels directly across from them. For half a second, Caleb saw the black tactical gear they wore and thought it was his teammates. Hell, he would have even been happy if it had been some of the agents and cops from McKay's backup team.

But then Caleb saw Xavier Harrington and Uriel Cerano and his whole body tightened, his inner wolf letting out a snarl. He drew his weapon, his claws and fangs extending at the same time. While he'd been stunned Uriel and his fellow Vandals were down here with the nukes, he'd never dreamed Harrington would be as well. Caleb guessed the psychopath was more committed to this new world he wanted to create than anyone had realized.

Or maybe he was simply a frigging whack job.

"What is it about you that makes it so difficult to know where you're going to show up?" Harrington asked, eyeing Caleb curiously as Uriel and the other members of his supernatural security force drew weapons and began to spread out to surround him and Brielle. "Sometimes I can read you clear as day, but other times, it's like you don't have a clue what you're going to do until you've already done it."

Caleb snorted. Unknowingly or not, Harrington had described Caleb's muddled journey through life. He had never known what path he would walk down until he was already on it, for better or for worse. Mostly worse, he supposed. Not that he was going to throw any praise the man's way for his exceptional guess.

"Maybe you're simply not as good at this seeing the future crap as you think." Caleb goaded. "In fact, you suck so bad at it that I'd drop this whole insane scheme if I were you."

"But you aren't me," Harrington said. "You haven't seen what I've seen. You've never been burdened with the knowledge of where humanity's ignorance will lead us and watched as the world burned in endless nuclear fires as every living soul on the planet is snuffed out in an instant."

"No, I can't say I've seen any of that," Caleb answered, fighting the urge to say something snarky instead. "But even if I did, I wouldn't destroy a good portion of the world to save the rest. I'd find another way."

"That's because you're naive and foolish," Harrington ground out, glancing at Uriel as his right-hand man continued to move closer to Caleb and Brielle. "Don't you think I looked for a better way to do this? There isn't one. It's this. Or the end of the world."

Out of the corner of his eye, Caleb saw Brielle moving to a position so she could cover him while keeping an eye on all the bad guys at the same time. But that was getting harder to do by the second as the Vandals continued to spread out. He'd hoped Julian and Kiara would show up at some point to even the odds a little, but they hadn't yet. And they might not show up at all. At least, not until it was too late to matter.

Caleb turned back to lock eyes with Harrington. "You can't honestly believe we're going to let you do this, can you? We've already taken out five of the nukes. You can't stop us from reaching the rest."

Harrington barely reacted to that announcement. "The five

you've disarmed don't matter. The ones that are left are more than enough to do what I want. They *will* go off. You will all die. And then the lasers will fire. Just as I planned. Exactly as I've already seen it."

Caleb might have considered arguing, but Uriel and the other Vandals were lifting their weapons. And his first instinct was to protect Brielle.

But Brielle was already moving, and damn, she was fast. She charged across the room, smashing one of Uriel's guards in the face, ripping the assault weapon out of his hand, and then firing half a dozen rounds into his chest at point-blank range. She was moving on to the next man before the first one hit the floor, her hand reaching out to borrow the next person's abilities even as she took him down.

Caleb had watched Brielle fight before, but this seemed to be the first time she'd gone all in with her gift like this, absorbing one fighting style after the next, dropping one empty weapon only to strip another loaded weapon off the next bad guy. Even as Caleb launched himself at Harrington, knowing he had to get through him to go after the nukes, he found himself staring a little at his soul mate. Because seriously, she was frigging awesome.

Then Uriel flicked a finger in her direction and Brielle went flying across the room, smashing into a wall so hard that Caleb felt the impact. A second later, Caleb's .45 was ripped out of his hand and sent flying down one of the tunnels.

Caleb's instincts warred over the desire to both run to Brielle's side to see if she was okay and kill the man who'd hurt her. In the end, he retained enough logic to realize that if he didn't stop Uriel, the asshole would hurt Brielle again and again. So he swerved to the right, closing the distance between him and the lead Vandal in the span of a single heartbeat. Caleb brought his hand up in a slashing sweep, his claws raking across the man's chest. But even as he drew blood, Uriel was reacting, shoving Caleb across the room without barely lifting a hand.

Caleb flew through the air, watching as Uriel turned to focus on Brielle again. Then he lost sight of everything as he crashed into something extremely hard. There was a cracking sound, and the obstruction broke under the force of his impact, the entire structure clattering to the ground with him on top of it. When a sharp pain lanced up his back, suggesting he'd broken something, he looked down to see that he'd landed on the nuke.

Seeing Uriel heading for Brielle, Caleb panicked. He picked up the nearest thing at hand that he could use as a weapon. It was only after he'd beaten one of the supernatural security guards with it, then tossed the weapon across the room toward Uriel that he realized he'd picked up the nuke. But Uriel batted it away it with another wave of his hand, smashing the weapon so violently against the far wall that it knocked out a chunk of rock.

A small part of Caleb's mind pointed out that bouncing a nuke around like that probably wasn't a good idea, but then Uriel turned to Brielle, and Caleb stopped worrying about the damn nuke.

Caleb ran toward Brielle, but Harrington of all people stopped him, picking up an MP5 submachine gun from one of his dead security guards and using it with more proficiency than Caleb would have ever given him credit for. No matter which direction Caleb leaped, the older man seemed to know exactly where he was going. That was likely true, considering Harrington could see the future. Caleb had no idea how many times he was hit, but he was pretty sure there wasn't a part of his body left unharmed.

For a second, he wondered why Harrington was able to read him so well right now when earlier he'd said he couldn't always get a read on him. But then he saw that Uriel had reached Brielle, standing right over her, about to shoot.

Caleb lost it then, his thoughts going hazy as his omega took over and reacted. He sprinted toward Brielle, his bullet-riddled body hurting like hell, slowing only long enough to pick up the nuclear warhead and sling it in Harrington's direction.

Then he was on Uriel, only to get smashed to the ground like a rag doll. He slid across the rough floor, coming to rest against Brielle's side. The look in her eyes when she saw how badly he was bleeding was heart-wrenching. Then she reached out and touched his face.

Brielle's dark eyes glowed vivid blue, then pearly white fangs extended and claws appeared at the tips of her slender fingers.

Uriel smiled at Caleb as he aimed his weapon at Brielle's back and pulled the trigger. She barely flinched as she jumped to her feet and leaped through the air at Uriel, her claws tearing into him while her savage snarls had him stumbling backward as fast as he could.

Harrington and the last of his security guards turned their weapons on Brielle and pulled the triggers.

With a snarl, Caleb was up and charging across the room, his omega werewolf taking complete control, slashing through one person after another, ready to kill anyone and everyone who'd ever considered harming his soul mate.

Caleb was fully aware of his tendency to lose control. It was so commonplace that his STAT teammates had almost come to expect it. But in truth, no matter how bad it had ever gotten, he'd always fought tooth and nail to retain at least some small piece of himself, terrified that if the werewolf inside him took over completely, he'd never find his way back. But this time, seeing Brielle being hurt, there was no thought of holding anything back. He let go, freely watching as his omega consumed every last shred of that which he thought of as Caleb Lynch.

He felt his body twist and spasm, claws and fangs extending even further than before, muscles bulking and flexing along his back shoulders and legs, rage filling his chest, urging him to tear anyone between him and Brielle to pieces.

Harrington was the one who ended up getting in his path.

The seer moved his weapon rapidly left and right but hesitated to pull the trigger as if he wasn't sure which direction Caleb's attack would come from. But if the man was waiting until he got a read on what Caleb was going to do next, he'd be waiting a long damn time. Because Caleb wasn't in the driver's seat any longer. Hell, he wasn't even in the car.

Jake's voice was in his ear, shouting that they couldn't reach anymore of the nukes, that there was only a minute left. "It's up to you and Brielle to stop this now."

His inner omega simply reached up and pulled out the earpiece and tossed it aside.

A feint to the side, a jump in the other direction, followed by a long leap, and Caleb found himself landing on top of Harrington. The man collapsed under him, bones crunching and flesh tearing under savage claws.

Harrington lay stretched out on the floor, bleeding, his weapon knocked far across the room. From the corner of his eye, Caleb saw Brielle deal with the last of the security guards.

"It doesn't matter what you do to me," Harrington hissed, lips stained red with blood as Caleb stepped forward to finish him. "You've gotten some of the weapons but not enough to matter. And it's too late for you to stop the rest from going off."

"But it isn't too late for you to stop it," a woman's soft voice said from the far side of the room.

Caleb spun to see Kiara standing there, Julian hovering protectively close by.

Harrington gasped, and Caleb turned back around to see the man staring at his daughter like he'd seen a ghost. As the seconds passed, the man's face grew paler and paler. Before, he'd looked satisfied with the outcome of the battle; now, he looked terrified.

"You aren't supposed to be here," he said brokenly. "I saw that you'd left, that you'd gotten away with the rest of our people."

"I may not be as strong as you, but I am still your daughter."

Kiara moved closer to her father, gazing down at him with an unreadable expression. "I hid myself along the pathways, kept you from seeing that I would be here. Because I knew that my presence here was the only thing that could make the difference."

Harrington swallowed hard, panic filling his eyes. "I never meant for you to get hurt. I did all of this for you. You have to get out of here. Now. Before the nukes go off."

Kiara shook her head, taking another step closer. Caleb felt the urge to stop her, his omega wanting to finish what it had started with Harrington, even if the nukes were going to do it anyway in just a few seconds. But then Brielle was at his side, her claw-tipped hand on his arm, calming him instantly. And just that fast, the omega retreated, leaving Caleb back in control.

"You know it's too late for me to get to safety," Kiara murmured, kneeling down beside her father. "And I wouldn't leave even if I had the time. You didn't do this for me. You did it for yourself, and I came to stop you. But I see now that there's no one who can stop this but you. You were okay with killing yourself and all the innocent people in this city. All the innocent people in the world. But are you okay with killing your own daughter?"

Harrington shook his head slowly, tears welling up in his eyes, slipping down his cheeks. "No, never. But I can't stop this. I can't. I've seen the future. I can't."

"You can. Because by making a choice, you change the future," Kiara insisted. "And that is what *I* saw. But you have to be the one to decide."

Caleb stood there, Brielle at his side, holding her breath. A few feet away, Julian gazed down at Kiara, the expression on his face suggesting he thought he was about to lose the most important thing in the world to him. Caleb completely understood the sentiment. All of them were waiting for the end, for that bright flash of light and then nothing. It couldn't be more than a few breaths away. His hand blindly reached out for Brielle's.

Harrington reached for something on his belt and came up with one of those key fobs, making Caleb tense all over again. His gaze never leaving his daughter, Harrington pushed the button.

Nothing happened.

Caleb had no idea how long they all stood there, waiting for something to happen. It never did. Then Kiara was reaching out to take the fob out of her father's hand and place it gently on the floor beside her before wrapping her arms around him, crying as she hugged him.

Caleb vaguely heard Brielle murmuring into her radio that it was all over, that the nukes had been disabled. He heard the sounds of excited shouts coming from her earpiece, and for a moment, he couldn't remember what he'd done with his. Then Brielle wrapped her arms around his neck, kissing him, and he didn't care about anything else. He didn't even care when Julian caught his eye and gave him an approving nod. Like he needed that stupid jackass's approval anyway.

"Do you have to be so rough?" Brielle asked as Jake removed bullet fragments from a wound in her shoulder.

The ones Jake had already taken out were seriously impressive. Caleb couldn't help but be ridiculously proud of her for some reason. Silly, but what the hell, it was a werewolf thing.

"I need to get all the bullets out before the healing abilities you borrowed from Caleb fade," Jake said, working as urgently as he'd been all along. "Based on what you told me, it's been almost an hour since you touched him, and none of us know how much longer you'll retain his werewolf skills."

Brielle couldn't argue with that logic. Neither could Caleb. But it was still hard watching his soul mate grimace in pain as another bullet fragment came out and was added to the pile. He'd considered doing it, but truthfully, the thought of hurting her as he took them out was more than he could deal with, so instead, he sat there beside her, holding her hand and letting Jake do what he had to do, hoping this would be over soon.

He saw Brielle trying to distract herself from what Jake was doing by focusing on everything going on around them. He doubted that would work well, since Harrington, Uriel, and a surprising number of surviving Vandals had already been hauled away a while ago, along with the last of the disarmed nukes. About the only thing still being done was a thorough scrub of the tunnel complex for any more explosive charges left buried in the ceiling, and there was the occasional science nerd wandering around admiring Harrington's laser rig, trying to figure out how it worked.

Harley and Sawyer were also busy sniffing around to see if there were any ghouls to be found, but so far, they hadn't discovered any. From what Harrington told them, the ghouls had left right after digging the complex. Caleb wasn't complaining. Dealing with Uriel and his Vandals had been bad enough. He shuddered to think how much worse the outcome of this mission would have been if they'd had to fight a bunch of those freaking monsters.

"How's everything going?" McKay asked, walking into the large open space from one of the tunnels, immediately coming over to see how Brielle was doing.

Caleb was a little surprised the boss cared enough to come down here to check on her, considering all the other stuff he obviously had going on. But still, Caleb appreciated it.

"She's not enjoying Jake's makeshift surgery skills," Caleb said. "But the last of the bullet frags should be out soon, which is the important part."

"Speak for yourself," Brielle grumbled, throwing him a perturbed look. "I would have preferred anesthesia, given the option."

"I can't say I blame you," McKay agreed, then gave Caleb an appraising look. "Speaking of Jake, he mentioned that we have you and Brielle to thank for stopping the whole mess. He said that your team was the only one that managed to get inside this part of the complex in time to stop Harrington. I'm impressed. Job well done."

Caleb snorted. "I doubt you'll be as quick to congratulate me if you knew I completely blew off the instructions your fancy AI computer came up with."

He expected McKay to be pissed, but the man laughed. "Am I right in assuming you never even bothered to open your envelope?"

Caleb shrugged, giving Brielle's hand a squeeze. "I figured there was no reason to bother. I was going to stay with Brielle no matter what your computer said."

That answer earned him a hearty laugh, which confused the hell out of him. "Well, if you *had* bothered to open the envelope, you would have found nothing but a single piece of paper that instructed you to *Do Whatever You Want*."

"What?" Caleb, Brielle, and even Jake all said at the same time.

"Our AI planning system is very sophisticated," McKay said with a smile. "It predicted that you would never follow any directions or orders that it gave you, so it left you as a wild card, trusting in your instincts for being in the right place at the right time. Turns out it was correct. Which means you did exactly as the computer wanted."

Brielle and Jake laughed. Caleb, on the other hand, thought McKay shouldn't give up his day job to be a comedian.

"Okay, I think we're all done," Jake announced. "Looks like you're going to heal up fine, but let Caleb or one of us know if anything continues to hurt. There's always a chance I missed a small piece in there somewhere."

Brielle definitely didn't look thrilled at that idea.

Jake and McKay left soon after that, the boss once again thanking Caleb and Brielle for doing such a great job. "The two of you really do work well together. You should consider staying on the team, Ms. Fontaine."

Caleb thought that was an excellent idea, but he couldn't really see that happening. While they were soul mates, she had a brother to keep an eye on. A stupid brother who got into more trouble than even Caleb did.

"While I love the idea of you staying with STAT," he said as he helped her up off the floor. "I understand that's not really feasible. Not with your responsibility to Julian. So I'm completely ready to bail on McKay and STAT and live in Quebec with you."

Brielle gazed at him, and for a moment, he was terrified she was going to tell him she didn't ever want to have a damn thing to do with him again. Then she went up on her toes at the same time she threw her arms around his neck and dragged his head down for a kiss.

"First, I'd like to pick up on our earlier interrupted conversation and tell you that I love you like mad," she said with a grin, then added, "or like a soul mate, I guess. And the fact that you're willing to walk away from STAT because you think that's what I want makes me love you even more. But," she continued, preempting his complaint with a warm finger against his lips, "you know as well as I do that if you walk away from STAT before your three-year agreement is completed, they'll revoke your parole and send you back to prison."

He snorted. "They'd have to catch me first. I have no doubt I could find some place in Quebec to hide that they'd overlook. They'd give up after a while."

Brielle shook her head. "Even if I were willing to let you take that risk, which I'm not, I'd never ask you to walk away from your teammates. You told me once that they're the closest thing you have to a family. I won't take that away from you."

He reached up to brush back a stray piece of silky hair that had come loose from her ponytail. "You're right. They are like a family to me. But as important to me as they are, you're more important. You're my soul mate, and I'll do anything to be with you. Even if that means walking away from STAT and my pack."

"And I appreciate that. I also have to admit I find it incredibly romantic," she said, kissing him again. He definitely couldn't complain about the kiss, even if those soft, warm lips were making it difficult to think clearly. "But you don't need to do anything that drastic—or stupid. My brother can take care of himself, and if he can't, then Kiara can take care of him. Regardless, I'm staying with you and STAT. When your three-year deal with them is up, we can decide where we go from there. Together. Though something tells me that we won't want to ever leave the pack. Deal?"

Caleb was the one to drag her close for a kiss this time, his mouth demanding as he nibbled hard on those scrumptious lips and held her tightly to his chest. "You know," he murmured against her lips, "I'm not complaining, but you took this whole soul-mate thing much better than I expected. Even considering that I did drop it on you in the middle of a firefight."

She kissed him again, this time with more urgency, and if he wasn't dreaming it, it seemed she was digging into his back with two sets of very sharp claws.

"I didn't get a chance to tell you at the time," she said softly, breath warm on his skin, honeysuckle scent beginning to overwhelm him. "But Misty already clued me in to the whole soul-mate thing a couple days ago. So me being *The One* for you didn't really catch me by surprise. At least not completely. Though I have to admit, I expected you to bring it up before people started shooting at us."

"Sorry about that part. Not about anything else, just that I should have found a better time to tell you about us," he agreed, kissing her again. Then he felt sharp fangs against his tongue and figured out that Brielle must still be dealing with some of his more aggressive omega tendencies, including his habit of wolfing out when making out.

"I can't believe I'm saying this, but maybe we should back off on the kissing stuff for a little while," he said. "I get the feeling you're still feeling your inner omega, and if we keep going, it might get a little rough."

Brielle pulled back and looked up at him, her eyes glowing vivid blue now. "We can stop if you want, but the way I look at it, this is the only time I'll ever get to be an omega werewolf. Are you seriously saying you want to waste this opportunity?"

He gazed down at her, overwhelmed that he'd ever stumbled across someone this perfect. Someone he could have never dreamed of finding. Then he bent his head and kissed her, his words rumbling up through his chest as he started to let himself go just a little. "I guess we need to go find someplace a bit more private, then, because this might get loud."

Scooping her up in his arms, he strode across the room and headed down one of the smaller tunnels, eagerly looking for someplace he could be alone with his soul mate who just happened to be the most perfect woman in the world for him.

CHAPTER 21

"I KNEW WE DIDN'T HAVE TIME TO STOP BY OUR PLACE BEFORE coming to the party," Brielle grumbled as she and Caleb walked quickly down the hallway toward Jake and Jes's apartment. "I told you we should have driven straight here when we got back into town instead."

"Then we would have been early," Caleb pointed out casually as he walked beside her with the bags of chips and sodas they'd brought with them. "And we wouldn't have gotten a chance to unload all your stuff."

"Unpacking the back of your SUV." Brielle snorted and knocked on the heavy wood door. "Yeah, I'm sure that's honestly why you insisted we go back to our apartment at the last minute."

"Well, the sex on the kitchen counter was nice, too," he said as the door in front of them opened.

Jes's gaze went back and forth between her and Caleb, brow arching as an amused smile tipped up the corners of her lips.

"Should I close the door and let you two finish this conversation before you come in?" Jes asked, obviously having heard that last part Caleb had said. "I'll tell everyone it was a neighbor wanting us to keep the noise down."

Brielle threw a quick look at her soul mate to see that Caleb wasn't even trying to hide the smirk on his face. He'd known Jes had been about to open the door when he'd said that stuff about them having sex on their kitchen counter.

"That's okay," Brielle said, stepping forward to give Jes a hug. "Ignore Caleb. He was only messing around. Sorry we're late."

Jes waved her hand. "Don't worry about it. Hudson just got here a few minutes ago, too. Besides, Jake hasn't even finished grilling the burgers yet, so I would say you're right on time."

Brielle took in the crowded apartment as Jes closed the door behind them, waving at everyone who shouted out greetings. She couldn't help but smile at how fast she'd been accepted into their group—*pack*. But she supposed that came with the territory of almost dying together.

Forrest and Misty went into the kitchen to help Caleb unload the snacks and drinks they'd brought for the party while Hudson and Genevieve sat in the living room with Harley and Sawyer, chatting about something bizarre going on with the name of the local football team. Brielle didn't understand American football, so truthfully, she wasn't too interested in their conversation. Hudson had transferred from the CIA to STAT at some point over the past few weeks, and Genevieve had been permanently assigned to Jake's team.

A flash of color caught her attention, and Brielle turned her head to look through the open doors at the two young girls hanging out on the balcony with Jake and two cute lab-mix puppies as he grilled the burgers. The tall, slender teens had platinum-blond hair, long and straight and so bright that it almost glowed in the late afternoon sunlight.

"That's Zoe and Chloe, and the adorable puppies are Sam and Dean," Jes said softly. "The girls' parents passed away a little while ago, and Jake became their guardian. Though, I have to admit, I've come to think of them as our kids. They're amazing."

Both of the girls turned to look at them, the movement of heads perfectly synchronized, as were the smiles that crossed their faces. That's when Brielle realized the girls were twins and that they were werewolves. It was impossible to feel their abilities and not know that. But there were also some supernatural skills there that had nothing to do with the fact that the two of them were beta werewolves.

"They've just started school at the University of DC," Jes added, interrupting Brielle's silent assessment of everything the two young women could do. "But they're living here with us versus in the dorms."

"How'd everything go with your trip?" Genevieve asked from where she sat on the couch in the living room, motioning for Brielle to come over and join them. "Jake mentioned that you had to go up to Quebec and then stop by NYC on the way back."

Brielle decided to drop any questions she had about the twins, joining her teammate on the couch. Caleb came over to hand her a glass of soda, then sat on the floor in front of her, tipping up his beer bottle to take a drink as he leaned back against the couch.

"It was good but exhausting," she said. "We've been going non-stop since the mission. McKay brought Caleb and me straight back here after we stepped out of those tunnels so I could formally join STAT. I thought I'd sign a few forms and be done with it, but he had me doing paperwork for hours."

She'd come to the conclusion that Americans—or at least their government—were obsessed with paperwork. The form for her security clearance was twenty-four pages long. Then there had been forms for getting health and dental coverage, straightening out her long-term visa, and even signing for all of her tactical gear. They even had a form to sign for her weapons. Yes, she was now the proud owner of a handgun and a small submachine gun. She had no idea how to shoot them yet, but she had them.

"Then the next day, we went out looking for a new place to live," she added. "Even though I would have been happy living in Caleb's one-bedroom apartment."

"You say that now," Jake said, stepping in from the balcony with a platter loaded with delicious-smelling grilled burgers. "But wait until you both have to get ready in a hurry for a mission. Then you'll be thrilled to have two sinks in the bathroom."

Jake had made a ridiculous number of burgers, but it quickly seemed there was a reason for it, as the werewolves on the team began to pile their plates high with food.

"Did you have any problems getting out of your apartment lease in Quebec?" Jes asked as they all moved back to the living room to sit down.

"Not really," she admitted. "I lost my security deposit and the last month's rent that I'd already paid, but it was worth it to be able to get all my stuff out of there before they tossed it out on the curb. There wasn't much, but I had a few photo albums and some important documentation like my birth certificate and stuff like that. It all fit in the back of Caleb's SUV."

"You stopped in New York to see Julian on the way back, right?" Harley asked, loading her fork with potato salad.

Brielle opened her mouth to answer, but Caleb beat her to it.

"Uh-huh," he said. "Kiara has taken over the Harrington Group while her father is being held at STAT's supernatural supermax prison and asked us to stay for a few days at her mansion outside the city so she could tell us a little more about him."

"How's she handling the fact that her father is going to be locked up for the foreseeable future?" Jake asked, doing his best to knock a respectable dent in the four burgers on his plate.

"Extremely well, considering that the alternative is him being dead," Brielle said, picking up her cheeseburger. "But she's gotten a chance to Skype with him a few times. She's pinning a lot on the agreement he made with STAT to use his gift to try and prevent this nuclear holocaust he's so worried about. If things go well and the leads he provides to STAT pan out, he could be set free at some point."

"How's Kiara's relationship with your brother?" Misty asked. "He's not on the verge of bailing and leaving her wondering where he's disappeared off to, is he?"

Everyone groaned at that. Brielle couldn't blame them. While she'd been fairly sure the feelings Julian had for Kiara were real, it still hadn't kept her from expecting him to ditch her at some point. It was what he did. He might be in love, but that didn't buy him much benefit of the doubt. That had to be earned.

"You may not believe this, but he's living with Kiara," Caleb said. "In addition to being her boyfriend, he's her full-time personal bodyguard now."

More than one of Brielle's new teammates seemed stunned at that, and, once again, she couldn't blame them. Brielle hoped for the best, praying Kiara hadn't made a decision she'd come to regret.

As they continued to eat, the topic of conversation slowly drifted away from Kiara and Julian to revolve mostly around the unexpected outcome from the New York mission.

"McKay told me that almost half of the people he'd brought in as backup for the mission have requested a transfer to STAT," Jake said. "Since seeing everything that happened down in those tunnels, they all want to work with a supernatural—or more precisely Caleb, for some reason. McKay's been interviewing each of them and says there are a handful with some real promise that he could easily put together on another three or four teams. Of course, the problem is that he doesn't have enough supernaturals to go around."

"I guess you don't find a lot of supernatural résumés on LinkedIn, huh?" Hudson said with a chuckle. "I'm guessing it might take him a long time to find those willing to sign up with STAT."

"Probably," Jake replied. "Until then, let's assume we're going to be really damn busy. We're the only supernatural team McKay has."

After that, Jes called a moratorium on shop talk for the rest of the night. Instead, they talked about personal stuff, laughing about family and their various romantic exploits. Brielle relaxed on the couch, her fingers casually playing with Caleb's shaggy hair as he sat on the floor, one shoulder resting against her leg. She took great pleasure in the fact that he was practically purring at her touch— did wolves purr?—and in the fact that this was the first time in her life she was surrounded by people she truly thought of as friends.

After all the excitement of the past few days, combined with all the driving they'd done, Brielle soon found herself zoning out, minutes away from falling asleep. That was probably why she completely missed the sound of a phone ringing until Jake dug his cell out of his pocket.

"McKay, what's up?" he said as he walked into the kitchen to take the call.

As everyone in the room fell silent to listen to the one-sided conversation their pack leader was having, Brielle forced herself back to full awareness and sat up straighter.

"Is it another mission?" Jes asked when Jake walked back into the living room.

"Actually, we have two of them this time, which means McKay is going to need us to be in two places at once," Jake said.

Brielle was trying to figure out what he meant by that when Jake continued.

"Caleb, McKay has you Brielle, Hudson, Genevieve, Forrest, and Misty booked on a plane for Oslo, Norway, tonight. There's a radical group in the area that has all the makings of a developing terrorist organization with supernatural indicators. We have no idea what their target might be, but the intel analysts feel sure they're moving soon."

Brielle wanted to ask if all their missions started out this vague, but before she could, Caleb spoke.

"Okay," he said. "So where are you and everyone else going?"

"Jes, Harley, Sawyer, and I are heading to Manaus, Brazil. It seems they have some kind of reptilian shifter near the Amazon River that drags people off to sacrifice them—when it doesn't simply eat them. Since he doesn't know a lot about what's going on in Oslo, McKay wanted to give you more resources to deal with that situation, figuring the four of us can handle the mission in Brazil."

No one said anything, and Brielle could only guess that they were all thinking about what it was going to be like without having the whole team together. But soon enough, the ribbing started, as everyone tried to convince each other that they'd gotten the better mission.

"Any mission that takes me to a major European city instead of the Amazonian rainforest is a big win for me," Genevieve said. "Nothing against rainforests, but my hair and humidity don't get along."

From where she sat on the floor on the other side of the coffee table, Misty nodded her head in complete agreement.

"Well, you can keep your wannabe terrorists," Jes said, popping a potato chip in her mouth. "I'd much rather tangle with man-eating reptile shifters any day."

The teasing continued, but Brielle ignored it as Caleb took her hand and urged her off the couch and onto his lap. "You ready for this?" he asked softly.

Brielle draped an arm around his shoulders and kissed him, then shrugged. "It would have been nice to get in a little practice with those shiny new weapons McKay issued me, especially since I've already borrowed abilities from you, Forrest, Misty, and Hudson."

He chuckled and kissed her back. "I wouldn't worry too much about that. I'm sure I can find a supernatural terrorist or two to toss your way. Until then, Genevieve will do just fine. Besides, the most important part is that we're doing this together."

She smiled. "Then in that case, I'm definitely ready for this."

Caleb gazed at her, his sensuous mouth curving into a grin she was becoming familiar with. "Think we have time to go back to the apartment before we head to the airport?"

"To pack some clothes?" she teased. "I hope so."

"Oh, yeah," he murmured, kissing her again. "We should probably do that, too."

Read on for a sneak peek at the next book in Paige Tyler's SWAT series, Kat and Connor's story.

Coming soon from Sourcebooks Casablanca.

"THEIR VEHICLES ARE STILL HERE," LANDRY SAID AS HE STEPPED out of the SWAT SUV in which the four of them had driven down to San Antonio, glancing around the abandoned and overgrown condominium complex with a worried expression. "Maybe Kat was on to something when she said the guys are in trouble."

Kat had to bite her tongue to keep from saying something rude as she, Rachel, and Becker joined Landry in front of the main entrance to the dilapidated building. *Of course* she'd been on to something when she said Landry and his pack mates were in trouble. She didn't simply make up crap to get attention. And she certainly didn't need to manufacture drama. Unfortunately, it seemed to naturally follow her everywhere she went. Put her in the middle of a pack of werewolves and chaos was a given.

She only wished they'd taken her warning seriously enough to bring extra backup with them. She hoped they didn't end up regretting that decision.

"Connor! Hale! Where are you?" Becker called out, wandering around to the left side of the building.

Assuming he was following their scent, Kat went with him. But it wasn't long before Becker stopped in his tracks. She thought it was because the high brush in front of them was too thick for anyone to get through, but then she realized he was studying the ground.

"They turned around and started running," he said, motioning for her to go back the way they'd come.

"Like someone was chasing them?" she asked, hurrying to catch up to him as he strode past her.

Before he could answer, Landry interrupted, his deep voice echoing through the air. "Kat! Becker! Get over here! We found something."

Becker looked her way for a second, then they were both hurrying around to the front of the building. There was no one there, so they kept going around to the right side. It was only a couple hundred feet, but even that short distance had Kat breathing hard. The change from feline to human form had sucked a lot more out of her this time than usual. Not even the two-hour nap she'd taken on the way to San Antonio had seemed to help. Of course, there was also the matter of her being a little behind on her cardio. For reasons that didn't seem to make a lot of sense, she'd never wanted to exercise when she'd been in her cat form. It seemed so undignified, at least to her cat sensibilities.

They found Landry and Rachel standing near an open stairwell along the side of the building, gazing at something on the wall to the right of the stairs. Curious, Kat stepped closer to see what they were looking at so intently. A little shiver of fear rippled down her spine when she saw the runic symbol painted there. There was no doubt this was a trap.

"They took these steps," Rachel said, eyeing the dirt- and leaf-strewn entryway. "I guess the bloody graffiti on the wall was enough to make them suspicious."

Landry and Becker immediately started to follow Rachel down the steps without realizing how dangerous it was. Kat supposed it wasn't their fault. They didn't know what that kind of magic could do.

"Stop!" she called out quickly. "Don't go down there yet or you'll be trapped like Connor and the rest of them. I need to break the rune first."

The three alpha werewolves stared at her like she was speaking a foreign language. Which, from their perspective, she probably was. Instead of trying to explain it, Kat reached out with her senses and searched for the flow of magic through the rune on the wall.

She grimaced the moment she came into contact with the energy powering the twisted protection spell. In its raw form, magic was clean and pure, kind of like crystal-clear water running down a mountain stream. But the stuff she was touching now felt oily, leaving a bitter tingle in her mouth. Like she was chewing on aluminum foil.

Not that the magic itself was actually repugnant, of course. That couldn't happen. Magic simply existed. It wasn't good or evil. But the people who used magic could sure as hell be good or evil. And their intent for the magic could be good or evil, too. That's what Kat felt in the rune spell. It was put there with the intent of trapping and killing people. That kind of act could taint the magic around it for a long time the same way that dumping a barrel of toxic waste in a clean, pure stream could contaminate it for decades.

She closed her eyes, letting herself see the tainted magic with her senses. It ran all over the building like greasy spiderwebs but was concentrated most heavily over the doors at the bottom of the stairs. If she wasn't mistaken, quite a lot of the magic currently powering the spell was coming from inside the building. That meant it was slowly draining the life from Connor and everyone else in there.

The thought suddenly made it hard to breathe and she had to force herself to focus. To disable the spell, she had to disrupt it. Now, she had to find the least taxing way to accomplish that. Because she definitely wasn't in any shape to channel a butt load of magic at the moment. Not unless she wanted to face plant right there in the overgrown weeds surrounding the building.

In the end, it wasn't as difficult as she'd feared. Magic could be twisted to do all kinds of unsavory things, but that didn't mean it liked it. Water could be forced uphill, but it would always try to find its way back down. All Kat had to do was reach out a hand toward the bloody rune and channel a line of clean magic into it, willing it back to its intended protection purpose. The magic helped her a bit since that was what it was supposed to be doing in the first place.

She still got a little weak-kneed from the effort, but the results were exactly what she'd been going for, if a bit more dramatic than she'd expected. The pulsing, tainted spider web began to ripple, visible sparks and embers cascading down the walls and doors at the bottom of the stairs. When the spell finally collapsed completely, it was with an extremely loud snap that sounded like a gunshot.

"What the...?" Landry started to say before being interrupted by the cacophony of real gunfire from inside the building, along with shouts and more than a few fierce growls. For a moment Kat wanted to say *I told you so*, until she remembered Connor was down there amongst all that insanity.

"Go! The spell is broken," Kat yelled even as Landry, Rachel, and Becker raced down the steps.

She'd seen how fast werewolves could run, but they were a blur as they slammed through the double doors at the base of the stairs.

A little voice in the back of her head suggested waiting until the werewolves could check out the situation and get a handle on things. But then her heart pointed out that those could have been shouts of pain she'd heard from beyond those doors. What if one of those shouts had come from Connor?

Kat ran down the steps into the darkness, weaving around piles of trash and stacks of boxes as she moved deeper into the basement, following the sounds of gunfire, shouts, and growls. She liked to believe she could recognize Connor's growls from among all the others, but maybe that was simply wishful, romantic thinking.

In the darkness her feet hit something that made a metallic

clatter as it bounced across the floor. She was no expert, but she thought the things she'd almost stumbled over were bullet casings. A lot of them.

Her heart pounded like a drum as she tried to move faster. After she'd run through a dozen rooms, each one dirtier and more cluttered than the last, Kat finally stumbled into a large open area where Connor and his pack mates were, along with…well, hell…at first, she wasn't sure what it was. It looked like a pile of moving debris. But then she made out the vaguely human form and realized she was looking at some kind of simulacrum—a collection of random debris shoved together to look like a person and then magically imbued with movement and behaviors meant to imitate true life.

She'd never had a reason to try and make a sim like this herself, but what else would be made out of wood and trash, running around trying to kill a pack of werewolves?

It took several seconds for the reality of that last part to sink in—along with the image of Connor standing over the unconscious bodies of Zane and Alyssa with blood soaking his uniform—before she started running forward to help.

One of the sims was trodding ponderously toward Connor and the two injured people he was trying to protect. As she watched, her favorite belly scratcher put a bullet through the thing's head. As expected, it didn't do much. Then again, shooting something in the head when it didn't have a brain was a waste. Why did people want to treat every supernatural thing they met like a zombie? It was almost offensive.

Then she realized that Connor seemed to be out of bullets and had dropped his weapon to extend his extremely long claws. While she had to admit that they looked good on him, Kat felt the urge to point out that if putting a bullet through the creature's head didn't do anything, a set of claws probably wouldn't be any more effective.

Wiggling her fingers, Kat solidified the air around the sim and sent it flying toward the nearest wall as fast as she could. Channeling that much magic in her exhausted state damn near knocked her off her feet, but it was still nice seeing the thing explode into chunks of kindling as it hit the concrete wall. Unfortunately, as soon as the wood, metal, and cardboard stopped drifting to the ground, the sim began to reform. That positively sucked. But seeing the bits of cardboard fluttering around abruptly reminded her that there was a way to end this before anyone got hurt.

Or at least, more hurt than they already were.

"There's a stone token in the center of its chest!" she shouted, taking another wobbly step forwards on legs that were suggesting she sit down right where she was. "You need to rip it apart and find the token. Once I destroy it, they can't reform."

Connor and the rest of his trapped pack mates all turned and stared at her. In between fighting the sims, of course. Kat could see the doubt on their faces and had no idea how to resolve the situation in the short amount of time they had available.

"Do what she says! She knows what the hell she's talking about!" Landry yelled before turning on the creature closest to him and unloading an entire magazine of bullets straight into the thing's chest.

While painfully loud to Kat, the hail of bullets was effective, bits flying as the creature's upper torso turned into Swiss cheese. The sim was close to completely breaking in half and stumbling backward when Landry surged forward and shoved his clawed hand into its chest and started rooting around. A few seconds later, he came out with a round flat piece of stone, two or three inches in diameter, dozens of blood-red runic symbols carved into both sides. Landry studied it for less than a second before turning and tossing it in Kat's direction.

Kat didn't pause to think about the possibility of being too weak to do it, but simply reached for the magic around her, then pushed it out toward the token.

"Perdere," she murmured softly.

With the simple destruction spell, the air between her and the fast-approaching piece of stone began to ripple and swirl with darkness. The stone slowed and then stopped, hanging there in midair. It began to vibrate as Kat poured more magic into the stone even as her vision started to dim.

A moment later, the token shattered into a hundred pieces, the remains drifting to the ground leaving little more than dust on the floor. Half a second later, the sim who'd been trying to re-form collapsed into pieces, chunks of metal inside it making a loud clanking sound as they struck the concrete.

The rest of the werewolves went after the three remaining sims, the violence they displayed almost terrifying. But then stone tokens came flying at her all at once and she stopped worrying about how dangerous werewolves could be.

Kat channeled as much magic as her exhausted body would allow, and destroyed the three spell-worked pieces of stone before they reached her.

Her legs turned to jelly from manipulating so much magic in her condition, and her insides weren't far behind. She would have dropped to the floor, but the thought of needing to use more energy she didn't have to get back up was too much to think about.

The three remaining sims disintegrated, wood flying everywhere, but she was too tired to care. At least until Connor appeared in front of her, concern clear on his face. There was confusion there, too, but she ignored that. The same way she ignored all the other werewolves who were gathering around the two of them. They weren't important right then.

Connor was so damn gorgeous, it was sinful. Regulation-cut dark blond hair, hazel eyes, a strong jaw with the perfect amount of scruff and the sexiest dimples any man could possess. Yes, he looked tired, and more than a little bloody. But she knew he was okay, and oh-so-scrumptious.

Taking a few careful steps forward, Kat threw herself into his arms, dragged his head down and captured his lips with hers. Connor seemed a bit surprised at first, but he figured out the plan soon enough and started kissing her back. And like she'd always imagined, damn, could the man kiss. And the way he tasted should have been illegal.

Kat wasn't sure how long they made out, but she was vaguely aware that she was getting a little dizzy. Purely from all the magic she'd been using, of course. Nothing to do with forgetting to breathe.

When she finally pulled back from Connor's magically perfect mouth, she couldn't hide the smile crossing her lips, even though she was definitely starting to swoon now. "I've been waiting to do that for nine months and it was just as good as I imagined."

"Um, don't take this the wrong way," he said slowly, his arms still wrapped around her. "But do I know you?"

A part of Kat was disappointed he didn't recognize her. Then again, she had looked a little different the last time he'd seen her. Taller...hair definitely different.

"I would certainly think so," she said with a lazy smile. "It's not like I let just anyone rub my belly, you know."

When Connor looked even more confused, she decided to cut him a break.

"I'm Kat."

Her big guy didn't have a chance to answer as Trevor chose that moment to appear at their side, leaning in close and messing up the mood.

"Sorry to interrupt," Trevor said, an expression halfway between amused and pissed. "But what the hell were those things, what the hell did you do to them, and how the hell did you know how to do it?"

Kat opened her mouth to answer, but then closed it again as everything around her started to get fuzzy. Wow, she really was out of it. Taking a breath, she tried to settle herself, only partially succeeding. Her vision cleared a bit but stayed dim at the edges.

"Those were simulacrum—or sims for short," she said softly, looking from Trevor to the rest of his pack mates. "Magical constructs that follow simple instructions imbued into them with an empowered token. When I destroyed the stones, I removed the intent and purpose that powered them. As for how I knew how to do that, or how I knew how to break through the bind rune outside, it's simple. I'm a witch."

She would have said more—a lot more—about how she'd gotten to this point in her life, how she'd ended up at the SWAT compound, and why she'd felt the irresistible need to come save Connor's life, but unfortunately, at that particular moment, the dizziness reappeared with a vengeance. She swayed, and slumped into Connor's arms, her eyes fluttering closed.

Any more answers would have to wait until she'd had a nap.

PROLOGUE

Titnore Woods, 1668

THIS WOULD BE ÆLFRIDA'S FOURTH AND LAST ATTEMPT. THE
Pack at Essex had refused, as had Anglia. Even the tiny remnants of
the Pack at Gyrwe had sent her away empty-handed. Now staring
at the strong and plentiful wolves of Wessex, her heart sank. She'd
even caught sight of a pup staring at her from under a dead oak,
the first she'd seen in England in over a decade.

Her own Mercia Pack hadn't had a pup since Halwende, and he
was almost an adult. As she waited to be announced, subordinate
wolves circled Mercia's Alpha, sniffing her curiously and gathering her scent to take back to the dominants. Others, still in skin,
watched from a distance.

"*Ælfrida, Alpha of Mercia. Wessex þu wilcumaþ swa beódgæst.*"

Ælfrida, Alpha of Mercia. Wessex welcomes you as table guest.

She'd made sure her wolves had learned the English of humans
years ago. It was ridiculous to pretend that the Packs were still the
top predators. That title belonged to humans now, and Ælfrida
studied them as carefully as deer studied her.

"Greetings, Wulfric, Alpha of Wessex, and many thanks for
your hospitality."

"*Sprecest þu ne Englisc?*" the huge man growled, though that was
one of the ambiguities of the Old Tongue: it sounded growled,
whether one meant it to or not.

"This *is* English, Wessex." She brushed her hand against her breeches, feeling scaly bits of fur there. "Is Seolfer here?"

"*Seolfer? Min nidling?*"

"Yes, *your nidling.*" She was distracted momentarily by the scabrous clumps in her hands. Sniffing her palms to be sure, she wiped them against a tree trunk. These wolves might look well fed, but some, at least, had mange. Maybe all was not well in Wessex. Maybe Wulfric would listen to her.

For now, though, the old Alpha scowled.

"*Ic þearf wealhstod,*" she said, even though she actually didn't need a translator. Ælfrida was an Alpha who issued commands and was obeyed. This bluntness had not served her well when dealing with the other Alphas, and Ælfrida hoped that Seolfer would know how to translate that bluntness into something the conceited oaf Wulfric might find more acceptable. Besides, she liked the young woman and had looked forward to seeing her again.

"*Seolfer!*" Wulfric yelled without bothering to look.

The woman who emerged from behind Wulfric's lodge had dark-blond hair, typical of silvers when they were in skin. A runt, she was destined to life as a *nidling*, a bond servant to her Alpha pair.

Many moons ago, looking for something more than a life of endless submission, Seolfer had made a desperate run all the way to Pack Caledonia. Unfortunately, wolves tolerate neither weakness nor strangers, especially not with resources so strained. Caledonia, Essex, Northumbria, Strathclyde: all of them had sent her away with nothing but a bite to her pastern.

Then she arrived at the Forest of Dean and planted her short legs and shook her shredded hide and challenged the famously fierce and powerful Alpha of Mercia for a place in the Pack. Ælfrida took one look at the runt and laughed. Then took her in. Not because she had any room for weakness, but because she saw in Seolfer a kind of strength that Packs almost never had: the courage to face the unknown.

The runt was, as wolves say, strong of marrow.

Unfortunately, the great Forest of Dean was falling fast to the humans' rapacious desires for lumber and grazing and iron, and with her Pack on the edge of starvation, Ælfrida had sent Seolfer back to Wulfric. She knew what waited for the girl, but submission was better than death—at least that's what Ælfrida told herself.

Seolfer said nothing; her head was bowed low.

"How are you, Seolfer?"

"As you see, Alpha."

"Hmm. I don't need you to translate. I need you to make what I say palatable to the old fart. *Gea*?"

The Seolfer that Ælfrida had known would have laughed, but not this one. She just nodded and bent her head lower, trying to avoid Ælfrida's attempt to catch her eye. She didn't have much time, so Ælfrida coughed a little and started her set speech. "The time of the wolves in this country is over. It is now the time of the humans."

She waited for the girl to translate. Wolves, both wild and in skin, came close to listen to the rugged cadences of the Old Tongue. Ælfrida wrinkled her nose and sniffed; even human, she could smell the sick sweetness of rot. Something was definitely wrong in Wessex.

"The land in Mercia is dying, and with it, our Pack. It is the same everywhere: Anglia and Sussex and Gyrwe."

"*It is not the same here*," interrupted Wulfric, looking at Seolfer to translate, but Ælfrida waved her off.

"How can you say that? When I was last here, just fifty years ago." Seolfer stumbled over the word *year*, and Ælfrida waited for her to translate it into six hundred moons, a span Wulfric would understand. "The last time I was here," she started again, "I ran into a tree to avoid a deer. Now there are neither. The same is true of Mercia, which is why I have arranged for a boat to take my Pack to the Colonies. I am asking you to join your bloodlines with ours. Make a truly great Pack in the New World."

"*Landbuenda*?" Wulfric repeated, missing the larger point in his fretting about the whereabouts of these "colonies."

"America," Ælfrida said irritably.

"Omeriga?" Wulfric echoed, still confused.

"Oh, by the Moon, Wessex. *Vinland*." Recognition dawned on Wessex's face, then he laughed, and Ælfrida knew that for Wulfric, Vinland was still nothing but a rumor west of Iceland. "It is real," she snapped. "I have talked to humans who have been there. It is a great land, a wild land. There are vast forests that we could buy and have legal title to and—"

Before Seolfer had even finished translating *we could buy*, Wulfric interrupted.

"*Why should I travel across the water to* buy *land, when I have* land here. Land that has been ours for centuries."

"You have *lived* here for centuries, but it *belongs* to Worthing, and the humans will have it."

"*And since when does a wolf care what humans think?*"

"Since they have become stronger than we are, you sodding ass." Seolfer glided without comment over the last bit. Ælfrida'd had a long and depressing fortnight, and her patience for Pack obstinacy was nearly exhausted. "Since they have armed themselves with weapons that will kill us from afar. Since they tear down our woods to build their ships and graze their sheep. Since they rip up the very ground to find rocks to melt into those guns and bullets. It is time for you to face the truth and do the hard thing. Do the right thing. Be an Alpha, and bring Wessex to America with us. Let us start something great and new."

As soon as Seolfer had finished translating. Wulfric signaled impatiently for Ælfrida to follow him toward a stone shed with a sod roof. The tall Alpha of Mercia had to fold herself nearly in half to get inside.

Wulfric looked at her smugly. "*You see, Mercia. I have faced the truth.*"

It took time for the weak eyes of her human form to adjust to the dim light, to see the neat rows of muskets lining the walls. To make out the shelves below loaded with flint and powder and cartridge.

"But…how did he get these?" she asked, turning to Seolfer. "Tell me you didn't help him do this." The girl shook her head firmly. "Then who negotiated with the humans? How—?"

Ælfrida froze as she sensed another presence enter the shed, someone with a new and terrifying stench. She turned to the man who was only slightly taller than Seolfer and then bent down, sniffing him. Just to be sure. Just to be sure she wasn't mistaken in that lethal combination of steel and carrion. That she wasn't mistaken in that fugitive but equally deadly hint of wild. The man smiled at her, and Ælfrida knew that Wessex had bet the survival of his Pack on a deal with the devil.

"It was my pleasure to help the Great Wessex Pack," said the man with the thinning blond hair who was the size of a large human and human in disposition, but was not human.

He was *Hwerflic*. Changeable and inconstant. A Shifter. More than anything, Packs feared Shifters. Because they could be wolves if they wanted, but they never *had* to be. Unlike Packs, which were ruled by the Iron Moon. For three days out of thirty, when the moon was pregnant and full and her law was Iron, the Packs must be wild.

Shifters mostly lived as humans, but they had much stronger senses and could sniff out Packs. And because all Shifters believed that Packs, like dragons, sat on vast hoards of treasure, they slaughtered them with terrifying regularity.

"The moon is nearly full," Ælfrida said to Wulfric. "The Iron

Moon is coming. How will you protect yourself when you have no hands to load the powder and ball? When you have no fingers to pull the trigger?"

"If I may, Alpha," said the Shifter in his polished voice. "I have been able to arrange for a human guard who protect the Pack during those days. Times being what they are, they are glad of the employment and will ask no questions."

Wulfric smiled smugly at Ælfrida.

"Leave us, Shifter," she said. The man hesitated until Wessex nodded. As soon as she was sure he was out of earshot, Ælfrida whipped around to Wulfric. "What are you doing, you old fool? Once they know how vulnerable you are during the change, the Shifter and his humans will kill you. Then they can take as much time as they want to find your gold."

Wulfric didn't wait for Seolfer to finish translating.

"*Wessex does not fear prey!*" he snarled, his lips curling back from dark-yellow teeth set in pale gums. He belched loudly and stalked out of the shed, followed by his Pack and his Shifter, leaving only his *nidling* and a sour fug behind.

"*What do you mean by 'prey,' Wessex?*" Ælfrida yelled from the doorway.

The big male did not stop and did not answer.

"*Wulfric, betelle þu. Tell me.* What have you done?"

Seolfer plucked hard at Ælfrida's loose sleeve. She'd been a tough little thing, outspoken and smart, but now she looked haunted. She shook her head, her finger raised to her lips. Peering around until it was clear that the Pack had followed its Alpha, she moved quietly, her bare heel eliding to bare toe, clearly used to gliding noiseless and unnoticed around the Pack.

The two of them climbed an incline alongside a fast-moving stream. Wessex hadn't offered her anything to eat, a terrible breach of Pack laws of hospitality; still, Ælfrida needed something to drink, at least. But before she could kneel at the water's edge,

Seolfer grabbed her arm and pulled her roughly away. For such a tiny thing, she was remarkably strong. Then the *nidling* pointed her toward a springhouse a short distance away. She pulled a rag from her waistband. "Cover your mouth, Alpha."

Ælfrida ran as fast and hard as she could. She had left her clothes with the young woman, as well as the details of her Pack's departure from Portsmouth on the day after the Iron Moon. Had she said they'd be sailing on the *Assurance*? She couldn't remember anymore, because all she could remember were the partly eaten humans cooling in the springhouse. Everything made sense now: the guns, the fat, the mange, the yellow teeth, and the stench. The smell of carrion and man-eaters.

The wolves of England were already dead. Running at night and through streams and in the cover of whatever trees she could find, Ælfrida headed fast for her own Mercia Pack, praying that they were where she'd left them, hiding in tight dirt dens in Sussex.

When the Iron Moon passed, Ælfrida led her scraggly group to Portsmouth. She could barely stand to look back over the thirty thin adults who were all that remained of the one-time greatness of Mercia. Breeding had always been difficult for Pack, without adding in starvation and ferocious hostility to lone wolves and fresh bloodlines. She had used too much of the treasure her Pack had accumulated over the centuries for a ship that was larger than she needed, hoping and praying that some Alpha had the sense to join her.

What a waste.

A murmur roiled the Pack, alerting Ælfrida to the faint scent of wolf. Even with her poor human nose, she recognized it instantly, running it down until she came to the end of the dock where the *Assurance*'s captain stood yelling at a small woman seated with her legs over the side of the dock, her arms clenched around the harness of a dog cart, piled with three large chests.

Seolfer was weaving slightly, staring at the blood falling from her leg into the water in rapidly dissipating gusts. The little *nidling* looked up with difficulty, her eyes barely focused in her pale face. "The guards shot them during the change. Clubbed them. Cut off their heads and stove them onto the branches of our trees. Bleeding into our earth. They are right now tearing up our land, looking for money. But I have them all, Alpha. I have them all."

Ælfrida breathed in deep and said a silent prayer of thanks to the pale remnants of the daylit waning moon. She yelled for her Delta, the one she'd sent to Glasgow to study medicine.

"This is Seolfer," she said. "Heal her."

Untying the rag around the woman's calf, the doctor frowned. "Alpha, the ball is lodged in her tibia, and she has lost a great deal of blood. It is doubtful she will survive and sure that she will lose her leg." He shook his head sadly.

"Do *not* wag your head at me." Ælfrida bent down, one strong hand clenched around his jaw. "You *will* do what I tell you, and she will live."

"Then what?" Ælfrida's Beta yelled from the back where he'd been serving as rear guard. "Are we to embark on this foolishness saddled by a crippled runt who is not even of Mercia?"

It is not in the nature of a Pack to accept change quietly. Mercia's wolves had not seen what she had. While she had visited the Packs, they had dug holes in the dirt and eaten rats, which had done little to improve their disposition.

Ælfrida bolted through the Pack, straight for the enormous male. She hadn't eaten enough for months, but there was a reason she was Alpha, and every muscle tightened in explosive anticipation. Her lungs expanded as she plowed her struggling Beta to the edge of the dock and then threw him into the disgusting murky water lapping against the quay.

She glared at the rest of her Pack, every tendon and bone wanting to shift. Her shoulders curved high behind her lowered head. Her teeth needed to tear into muzzles; her fingers ached to claw at flanks.

"Your Alpha," she growled, her body heaving, "says that *this* woman and *these* chests are Mercia now."

She might have been weakened by the long, slow hunger, but one by one, her Pack dropped their eyes and submitted.

"You," she barked at the goggle-eyed captain of the *Assurance*, who was staring at her huge Beta flailing in the water. "Fish him out."

She left two wolves to help the captain and two more to help the doctor. Then she commanded the rest of the Pack to carry the chests to the hold. "Gently, gently. Don't jostle them." She sent Halwende, the Pack's single juvenile, for as much water as he could carry.

"Hurry," she whispered as soon as they were in the hold, away from the humans. She couldn't keep the anticipation and dread from her voice. Fastened only with sticks, the chests opened easily, and her heart clenched in her throat. The Pack gathered around the boxes smelling of piss and terror, and one by one they picked up the silent, cringing pups, cradling them against the warmth of their bodies. They gave them water from their cupped hands and stroked their fur and rubbed faces against muzzles to mark them.

And for the first time in many years, Ælfrida, the last Alpha of the Great Pack of Mercia, allowed herself to feel hope.

"Be sure to wash them well," she said, more softly now. She would not have the pups coming to the New World smelling of the corruption and death of the old.

Unfortunately, Ælfrida had one last thing to do to make sure her Pack could leave safely. It was a shitty job, but that's what it meant to be Alpha.

She'd seen the Shifter lingering near the dock and walked until she found his scent and tracked him to a nearby tavern. He seemed no more surprised to see Ælfrida than she was to see him. He was, he said, devastated that the human guards had betrayed Wulfric. Humans, he said, had no sense of honor, of a promise made and kept. But he could not bear life as a lone wolf, he said, and would serve her in whatever way she needed in return for a place in the Pack.

He never mentioned Seolfer or the three great chests that he had tracked to Portsmouth. Nor did he mention the pistol he carried, though the scent of gunpowder was tart in Ælfrida's nose.

Ælfrida watched a young human woman, barely out of girlhood, smile at a customer and saw the customer's body relax. When the girl touched his arm, he leaned forward, his scent becoming suddenly receptive. Ælfrida turned to the Shifter and gave him the same barmaid smile and the same barmaid touch, and his scent became musky. The blandishments that Ælfrida presumed he had used on poor Wulfric he now used on her, along with his fingers and palm. Finally, they went to one of the back rooms. "To formalize things," he said archly.

"If you're going to puke, puke leeward," the captain of the *Assurance* had said, muttering something impertinent.

Ælfrida was beyond caring about impertinence. She leaned over the rail he had pointed to, and as she started to vomit once more, she called upon the moon to witness that as long as she lived, she would never eat Shifter again.

CHAPTER 1

Upstate New York, 2018

WOLVES WHO DRINK SMELL LIKE BAILEYS AND KIBBLE.

It doesn't matter that Ronan's poison is a 7 and 7 and chimichangas at the casino over at Hogansburg, there's something about our livers that still makes him smell like Baileys and kibble.

He lies slumped partly on his stomach, partly on his side at the edge of the Clearing, the broad expanse of spongy grass and drowned trees that is what remains of an old beaver pond that fell into disrepair when the Pack ate the beavers one lean year. New beavers have established a new pond nearby. Eventually we will eat those too.

And so it goes.

The Clearing is used for ceremonies and rituals because it is open and accommodates larger numbers. Usually the Pack prefers the cool, muffled, fragrant darkness of the forest, treating the Clearing like an anxious Catholic treats the church. We shuffle in on major celebrations and otherwise give it a wide berth.

The *Dæling*, which I suppose translates most conveniently as "Dealing," is one of those celebrations. It marks the transition of our age group, our echelon, from juvenile to adult. Here, we are paired off, not as mates yet, but in practice couplings. We will also have our own Alpha who answers only to the Pack Alpha and is responsible for keeping our echelon in line. The whole hierarchy will be set up. Not that it's permanent or anything, more like the start times assigned before the lengthy competition that is Pack life.

Basically, the *Dæling* is one enormous squabble. There are

challenges for the right to pair with a stronger wolf and challenges for a more elevated place in the hierarchy. Our whole youth has been taken up with tussling and posturing, but now it really counts. A wolf who is pinned to the ground in front of the Pack Alpha is the loser. Period. This sorting out of rankings and couples takes a long time, and the others watch it with endless fascination.

Me? Not so much. Born crippled and a runt, I've had to struggle long and hard for my position at the dead bottom of the hierarchy. I've never fought anyone, because there is no honor in making me submit, no rank to be won by beating the runt.

Ronan, on the other hand, is big and was once strong enough to be the presumptive Alpha. But he is, as they say, weak of marrow. With no determination or perseverance, he has become filled with fat and drink and resentful dreams of life as it is lived on Netflix. His nose is cold and wet when he's human and hot and dry when he's not.

"He's not much, our Ronan." That's what Gran Drava said to me. "But he's a male and…"

She gave me one more sniff before leaning back on the sofa in the Meeting House, where the 14th Echelon was gathered for her inspection. Her eyes and back are failing, but her sense of smell and her knowledge of Pack bloodlines are not. "And he isn't within the prohibited degrees of consanguinity."

So because he is weak of marrow and I am weak of body, we find ourselves together at the bottom of the 14th.

When the Pack Alpha eventually turns our way, I nudge Ronan, who doesn't stand until I bite him. Finally, he hobbles up, looking at me mournfully with his greasy eyes. Nobody much pays attention as we approach the Alpha. They're all too busy debriding each other's wounds and sniffing new companions' bodies.

John's paw hangs lazily over the edge of a granite outcropping shot through with mica that shimmers slightly in the moonlight.

It seems like a nervous eternity, waiting for John's pro forma nod of approval.

It doesn't come. Instead, he pulls himself up, one leg at a time, until he reaches his full height. The paler fur of his belly shimmers as he shakes himself and jumps down to the damp sod.

His nose flares as he approaches us. Anxiously, I push myself closer to Ronan's flank. John presses his muzzle between us, shoving me away. He sniffs the air around Ronan and starts to slap at Ronan, each hit of his head getting harder until Ronan stumbles backward.

John bares his teeth, snarling.

Ronan blinks a few times as though he is just waking. He wavers unsteadily, trying to comprehend the simple gesture that was all it took to exile him from the protection of our law, our land, our Pack. The sentence that forces him into a life wandering from Pack to Pack searching for a place until he dies in a puddle of blood and/or vomit, like most exiles do.

I scuttle to John, my head and stomach scraping the grass, my tail tucked between my legs, submitting into the earth not because I care about Ronan, but because if he leaves, then I am a lone wolf. There's an old saying that lone wolves are the only ones who always breed, their children being Frustration and Dissent. That's why they are given over to their echelon's Alphas to be their servants, their *nidlings*. A *nidling* has nothing, is nothing. Even at the bottom rank, you're paired with someone who is just as shit a wolf as you are, so at least at home, you don't have to submit. But the *nidling's* life is one of endless submission.

John snaps at me, then at Ronan. I roll on my back, my eyes averted, whimpering. But since he's made up his mind, no amount of groveling is going to make any difference. John wants Ronan gone. He stands erect, leaning over Ronan's now-shivering body, and a low growl emerges from deep in his chest. Any second now, he will attack.

Ronan backs away, shell-shocked. He stops for a moment, still looking hopefully at John, until the Alpha lunges forward. The exile trips over his own feet as he turns to go.

He doesn't even bother to look at me.

John stays alert, watching until Ronan lurches into the dark forest. He listens a moment more to be sure the exile is truly gone before he howls and signals an end to the *Dæling*. The newly reordered 14th finds their pairs and their places behind John. I'm all the way at the end, where I'm used to being, until our Alpha, Solveig, runs back and, with a growl, reminds me that I am to follow her and her companion, Eudemos, the pairing who now control my life. I take up my place behind them, my tail dragging between my legs.

Stopping suddenly with one paw raised, John focuses on a sharp bark in the night. It is a warning from a perimeter wolf. Probably signaling that a hunter has trespassed on our land. Wolves will be gathering around the interloper now, following the hunter at a silent distance. As there's nothing like an honor guard of seething wolves to scare off prey. hunters usually give up pretty quickly.

John lifts his head, his nose working hard as he looks toward the north woods. I can smell it too. Over the fragrance of fecund grass and swollen water and bog and sphagnum come the subtle scent of a half-dozen Pack and the overwhelming stench of salt and steel and blood and decay.

With a quick snap of his jaws, our Alpha sends our echelon's fastest wolf back to Home Pond for older reinforcements. John runs around to the north flank, closely followed by Solveig and Eudemos and the other newly minted leaders of the 14th. His forefeet are light on the damp grass, his hind legs ready to jump. Hunters don't come this far in. *This* is past the high gates and barbed fences and threatening signs and the trackless tangle of ancient, upended spruce and their young that are the reminders of a violent blowdown ten years ago.

The footsteps are soft and definitely human. Heel, the controlled curve along the outer rim of the foot. The toe barely grazing the grass. It is the footfall of someone used to stealth. I wouldn't have heard it at all, except for the occasional stumble.

Solveig's haunches tighten in front of me.

Finally, a man appears. He blends in with the night, so it is only when he walks into the moonlit clearing that we can see him. Sometimes we say someone has a heart or an ego or an appetite "as big as night."

But this tall, broad-shouldered human is really as big as night.

He pauses for a moment before threading his way through the wolves and lowering his body into the center of the Clearing. He crosses his jeans-clad legs. His feet are bare. Aside from a dark jacket, he has only two things:

A gun and a gaping hole in his stomach.

CHAPTER 2

"I KNOW WHO YOU ARE, AND I WON'T HURT YOU," THE STRANGER says in a voice that is cool and hard and perfectly calibrated to reach even to the outer ring of the wolves who were following him. "This." His hand caresses the gun. "This is just for protection."

As soon as John gives a nod, I start forward. When I am wild, I am a strong tracker. More importantly, I am expendable. If the man shoots me, then we will know what he's up to. He is armed and will kill many of us. And though he will eventually die, the careful ordering of our Pack will be undone.

His eyes lock on mine, and he slowly moves his hand to his knee so I can see that he's not touching the gun.

I creep close, starting with the wound. He has been clawed and not by one wolf; I can make out at least three different scents. They circled him and came at him from different directions.

For us, only the most heinous crimes warrant a disemboweling. But the *Slitung*, flesh-tearing, is a solemn ritual, not butchery. Every muzzle must be bloodied, so the tragedy of a life that we have failed is borne by all.

This man may not look it, but he is extraordinarily lucky. There is damage to the fascia and muscles, and while there is blood—and a lot of it—there is not the distinctive smell of a gut wound. Those things are hard to repair and go septic quickly.

Lifting my nose to the spot behind his ear, I almost gag at the overwhelming human smell of steel and death. But before I recoil, I catch the scent of something else. Snorting out air to get a clear hit, I try again. It's faint but it's here—crushed bone and evergreen—and it's wild.

There's only one creature in the world that smells both human and wild, and it is the creature we fear most.

Shifters are like us, but not. We can all of us change. But *we* cannot always change back. We are the children of the Iron Moon, and for three days out of thirty, we must be as we are now. It doesn't matter what you're doing—putting coolant in the backup generator, coming back late on the Grand Isle ferry (retrieving the car required some explaining)—Death and the Iron Moon wait for no wolf.

It is our great strength and our great weakness. We depend on one another. We support one another. Without the Pack, we are feral strays, trapped in a human world without words or opposable thumbs.

Shifters can always shift. They are opportunists. They used to change back and forth as it suited them, but now that humans are top predator, it suits them to be human. Like humans, they are narcissistic, self-delusional, and greedy. But they can scent things that humans can't, and they are dangerous hunters.

They know what we are, and in these past centuries, our numbers have been decimated by Shifters coming upon a Pack during the Iron Moon and slaughtering us with their human weapons.

There is something else, though, about this Shifter's deeply buried wild. Something more familiar than simply wolf. Moving close to where the scent is most concentrated, I suck in a deep breath.

"Found something you like?"

Snarling, I back awkwardly away from his crotch, but moving backward at a crouch makes my bad leg turn under, and the pain tears through my hip. Bone grinds against bone, and I stumble.

"A runt *and* a cripple?"

I flash my fangs at him. I may be a runt *and* a cripple, but I am still a wolf, damn it. John and Solveig and Demos sniff at my muzzle and immediately know what I know. Ears flatten, fur bristles, forefeet are planted, haunches bend under, and a menacing rumble spreads through powerful chests.

"Yes, my father is Shifter, but my mother is...was...Pack-born. Mala Imanisdottir."

I knew it. I knew he smelled familiar. John sniffs my muzzle again, scenting for proof of his ancestry.

"I challenged our leader, and I lost. I escaped his first attempt to kill me, but I won't escape another." His mind seems to wander, and then, with a real effort, he focuses again. "My father told me to escape. Find you. You are my last chance."

John looks out across his Pack, now bolstered with the older echelons. He snaps at the air over one shoulder and orders the Pack home. Mala or no Mala, this is the Great North Pack, not a sanctuary. The enormous Shifter will bleed out, eaten by the coyotes who even now are signaling to each other that there is something big and dying. They won't come near us, but as soon as we are gone, they will move in.

Solveig growls softly, calling me to heel. I hadn't realized how far ahead they had gotten. I stumble after her with my tail between my legs.

"The runt," the man calls between panted breaths. "She's not mated?"

Without turning, John stops.

"My mother said that the Pack would accept a lone wolf if there was another willing lone wolf." A short cough tightens his face in pain. "She told my father," he says. His skin is graying, and the circles beneath his eyes are so dark. "Before she died. She told my father."

There is some truth in what the Shifter says. *Some.* Unfortunately, none of us has the paper, the pencil, the voices, or the hands to sit him down and explain the complexities.

John motions me toward him and rests his head on my shoulders. He's so huge and comforting. His smell is the smell of home, and I can't imagine not being surrounded by him. He represents protection from the outside and order at home.

He butts me lightly with his nose. The stranger doesn't know the complexities, but I certainly do. The choice is mine. If I return with my Pack, the stranger will die and I will be a *nidling*. As low as it is, I will have my place within the Pack.

But if I stay...

Then I am gambling that this Shifter and I are strong enough to fight for—and win—a *full* place in the Pack. It is a gamble, though, because if we can't, both of us are exiled. He will be no worse off, but I will career from bad decision to bad decision, ending up in the same damn puddle of blood and/or vomit as Ronan.

The enormous Shifter weaves in our midst. I run back and sniff at him. He's lost a lot of blood, but he looks really strong, and with a little help, he should make it. He lifts his head, and for the first time, I see his face. He's darker than John's mate, Evie, but where her eyes are pure black, his are black shot through with shards of gold.

He whispers something that even my sensitive ears must strain to catch.

"Runt?" he murmurs. "I don't want to die." Then he collapses into the grass.

The Pack is already filtering out of the Clearing. Demos gives a curious sniff of the prone body and snarls. He swings his fat head, hitting my backside, telling me to get a move on.

Maybe if he hadn't done that, I'd have crouched down and followed. This is my world, and the Pack is my life, but I haven't put this much work into surviving only to spend the rest of my life obeying every snarky whim of a thuggish half-wit like Eudemos.

I nip at his ear, the universally understood signal—at least among Pack, it's universally understood—to go fuck yourself. I shake out my back and straighten my tail and walk as tall as I can back to the Shifter. I lay my head across his shoulder.

John takes one look along his flank and starts to run. The Pack follows quickly until they are nothing but the occasional flicker of fur among the spruce.

Except for the low, slow plaintive cry of the loon on Clear Pond, it is silent. Then comes the reverberating howl signaling that John is home. The wolves stationed at the perimeter take up the howl.

"We are," they say.

I'd cry if I could, but I can't. I'd howl if I could, just to say *Me too*, but I can't.

All I can do is nudge the huge mound collapsed in a damp hollow of the Clearing. Early fall nights in the Adirondacks are too cold for humans, especially lightly clothed, partially eviscerated ones. It takes a few nips to find a good purchase on his jacket, then I lock it between my jaws. I don't like the plastic taste, but I pull anyway. In fits and starts, I move his inert bulk to a slight rise where it's not so damp, but there's no way that either the jacket or I are going to be able to make it much farther.

After pulling on the jacket to cover as much of his body as possible, I curl around him, giving him the warmth of my body.

The moon shines down on the Clearing. This is a place for a Pack, not for a single wolf on her own, and it feels exposed and huge and empty. Not to mention damp.

A coyote creeps closer, picked out by the moon. I jump up, straddling the body with my shoulders hunched and my fur bristling so I look larger. I growl in the way John would—or Tara or Evie or Solveig or any of dominant wolves would—and hope.

The coyote hesitates and then retreats. I settle back, covering more of this man's big body with my smaller one. As I drop my head to his broad chest, a warm sigh ripples through my fur.

I wish the loon would shut up.

CHAPTER 3

THE DULL, STEADY PRESSURE AGAINST MY CHEEKS WAKES ME at the same time as the yellowthroat's high, insistent call. *Widdiddy, widdiddy, widdiddy, wid.* That pressure is the first sign that the Iron Moon is finished with me. My upper arm stretches and the muscles at my shoulder blades tighten, broadening my chest. As I shake out my hands, the metacarpals shrink and the forearm lengthens and the fur disappears, sucked back in, until nothing is left but a pale, almost-invisible dusting. A few loose silver hairs dance away in the breeze.

The hip with the tendon that is too short pops back into place. It hurts at first, but as I walk the Clearing, the last remnants of pain and numbness subside, and my leg moves freely again.

Despite the pain and the bum leg, no one loves being changed more than I do. I love the freedom and the crush of sounds and smells. I love the close and quiet connection to my Pack. I love the stillness of the cold Adirondack night constrained by nothing but my own fur.

I'd change back to wolf right now, if I wasn't in such desperate need of fingers and a voice. I feel the heat emanating from the Shifter and poke around the wound. Too much of the gash is clotted by the material of his jacket, and peeling it off will reopen the wound. But still, I can't feel new bleeding.

I need saline. And bandages and suture and antibiotic. Probably lidocaine, because humans are cowards, and Tristan says the bigger they are, the louder they scream when they see a needle. I need blankets and clothes.

"Hey. You," I whisper.

A short breath.

"Hey! Wake up."

One eye opens slightly, then the other.

"Runt?" he croaks and then, "Water."

Of course he would need water. I pat at my naked hips like I might magically find a pocket with water in it. It'll take me at least an hour to make the run to Home Pond and back, and that's too long.

His jacket tasted like plastic and is probably waterproof. I start to pull at a sleeve; since much of the front is shredded, I just need to tear hard at the back. Holding the neck still, I continue the rip along the sleeve.

"Whatyoudoon?" he slurs, trying to move my hand.

"Getting you some water."

He protests weakly.

"I'll be back in a second."

Clear Pond is big and smooth and fed by innumerable springs. Stretching out on the overhanging rock, I fill the sleeve with the clear water away from the weedy edges. It won't hold much, but it's the best I can do. As soon as I siphon the few ounces left into the Shifter's cracked lips, he passes out again.

I know I have to move fast, and moving fast requires reversing the whole process I went through earlier. Taking back the pain that will shoot through my hip and leg, because even a three-legged wolf is faster than a human.

Heading from Clear Pond toward the mountains, away from the low-lying damp, I take the shortcut up through the tangled forests of young spruce and fir and paper birch. The early autumn sun is swept before dark clouds, and one of the frequent short rains starts in with its thick drops that make the bald hardpan slippery. I skitter down until I reach the mix of maple and beech behind Home Pond.

Long time ago, before the Pack was lulled into a false sense of security, an earlier generation dug a long tunnel that led from the basement of the Great Hall into the forest. In case of emergency. Gran Sigeburg told me about it, as she rambled on about a long-ago party thrown by her echelon and how all the juveniles escaped from the Alpha's fury through the tunnel. I think the moral of her story was supposed to be that you can never escape a furious Alpha, but the tunnel was the part that stuck.

I'd found the end of the tunnel in the root cellar, but the other end was blocked. I scratched through the ferns and duff until I found it and came back with hands and an ax and hacked away the spruce root that had grown over it. Like all children, I liked the idea of sneaking and used the tunnel from time to time to get in and out of the Great Hall. Then I got older and more persnickety about spiders, and since nobody really cared where I was or when, I figured I might as well just use the damn door.

There were two spruces: one big one and a small one. If you crouch down low like I am now, the tip of Whiteface is centered between them. I scratch around in the forest litter until I feel the hollow scrape of wood.

I didn't remember the space was so narrow, but I was smaller then and perhaps the taproots that broke through the tunnel roof were a little smaller as well. As soon as I get to the cellar, I squeeze through the light trapdoor and lay myself down, rolling my shoulders and letting the change twist through my body once more.

The doors to the storerooms in the basement are close together in the narrow hallway. As soon as I open the broad wooden door of dry storage, I hear the hum of the dehumidifiers. The open metal shelves are filled with carefully marked bins of clothes. Popping open one of the smallest ones, I find a pair of athletic pants, a Henley, and a hoodie for myself. The Shifter is huge, but so are my people. In one of the several boxes marked *XXXL* (and *Tall*), I find a pair of sweatpants, a Big & Tall flannel shirt, a bright-red sweatshirt, and a bulky anorak. Not stylish and not much, but it'll have to do because the clothes already take up more than half of the big backpack.

Dried apples, ground corn, matches, miso, protein bars, lentils, hazelnuts. Then cooking equipment, a collapsible water carrier, a tarp. I also nab the single bedroll, a sleeping bag, and the pop-up tent the pups use when they play Human.

How do they do it? The humans, I mean. I lasted about five minutes inside the nylon sleeping bag, surrounded by that shell of polyester and silicone, before I bolted out, falling to the grass, my feet already lengthening.

Before I leave the basement, I pull the hoodie tight around my head to hide my telltale hair. I am a silver. Silvers aren't common, but we aren't rare either. It just means a wolf with light underfur and pale gray fur on top. In skin, their hair tends to be dark blond or light brown.

When I'm wild, one tendon stays too tight and cripples me. When I take on skin, my hair stays silver. Just so I never forget who and what I really am.

Gran Tito is up early as usual. His nose has started to fail, but I still steer clear of him as I make my way to the med station behind John's office. Two hospital beds with bedside monitors, ventilators, a freestanding anesthesia system, ultrasound. Mobile storage units are loaded with drugs and first aid necessities. We're strong and resistant to illness and heal quickly, but if we get injured, we can't go to the hospital. Everything about us—our lung function, blood composition, urinalysis, resting heart rate, *everything*— screams alien.

Two big bottles of saline wash, gauze, erythromycin, absorbable suture, lidocaine. Electrolytes.

Someone has started the coffeemaker, which means the Pack will be up soon. Moving carefully out the front door of the Great Hall, I sling the backpack on and make a headlong rush deeper into the trees.

By the time the door closes, Home Pond is behind me.

I've never walked this far in my skin. I'm slow on the path and even slower when I leave it, and at least one of my two feet snags on every bush and root and rock and fallen tree. At Clear Pond, I heave myself into the water, panting like a hunted elk before filling up the water carrier.

The Shifter doesn't wake up easily, even when the saline sluices over his torso and his jacket. I give him water and wait until I'm sure he's awake to give him a tablet the size of a water bug. I add electrolytes to the rest of the water because if he gets the heaves, he'll vomit up the antibiotic.

I cut away at the gore-glued jacket, pouring on more saline and letting it soak, while I wash my hands with chemical cleanser and pull on the gloves.

"You the bitch from last night?" he croaks.

The jacket is still sticking, so I drench it with more saline.

"I said, you the—"

What he says next silences the birds for miles. He curls into a fetal position, his teeth grinding audibly.

The torn and bloody remnants of the jacket hang slack in my hand. *Wow. What happened to you?* Because ripping away the remains of the jacket has exposed not only the explosion of claw marks underneath, but also the vestiges of a whole lot of other savaging. He's got neat slices, like knife cuts, on one forearm. Three small craters at his left shoulder. I'm guessing a "hunting accident" like Sofia's "hunting accident" from twenty moons ago, when a hunter shot her twice. It was no accident, but we continue with the fiction because the pups already have so many nightmares about humans.

But the scariest marks? They're claw-made. Most Pack have scars of some sort, though John has asked that we avoid muzzles during fights, because gouged eyes and clawed cheeks make potential Offland employers nervous.

Still, our scars are not like this. They're not like this tattered collar at the base of his throat. One of the tears stretches all the way through his nipple.

The worst thing is I can tell they are old and he isn't.

"What…what wolf would do that to a child?" It's no more than a voiceless whisper to myself. He shouldn't have heard, but I think he may have.

"Do me the favor of losing the tragic face, runt." His voice isn't angry, just brusque and cold and quiet.

"Turn over," I say and start to pour chemical cleanser into his wound. "I will not answer to 'runt' or 'cur' or 'dog' or 'bitch.' Now, if you feel like playing nice, I can give you a local. If you don't, that's fine too, and I'll stitch you up raw. I'll warn you, though: I've helped doctors do this, but it'll be my first time doing it myself."

He licks his cracked, dry lips and with one hand gestures toward the wrapped lidocaine syringe I hold in my hand. I inject it in a circle around the wound.

"You were really lucky."

"This is lucky?"

"Well, what I mean is, something like this? There's always gut damage. But not here. There was some hemorrhaging, but that's already stopped."

"I heal quickly," he says, craning his neck to watch me cut the flat plastic container holding the suture and the needle. Starting with the muscle, I set the clamp. He lies back down and stares at me. I'm not used to being noticed, and it makes me uncomfortable. It's one of the perks of being a subordinate wolf. As long as you do your work and don't get in the way, nobody pays attention. Not like the dominant ranks, where someone's always watching to see if you're getting sloppy or slack or stupid and it might be the right time to take you down.

Hard to tell what he's thinking. Leonora, who teaches human behavior, says humans rely on words more than "nonverbal cues," but that we should still be careful because what humans say isn't always what they mean. Humans convey disapproval in many ways, she says. Unfortunately, none of them are as clear and expressive as carnassials slicing through your calf.

"Can we start over?" he finally says. "What's your name?"

"Sil," I say, holding the skin up with the clamp for a new anchor knot. "You can call me Sil."

"Sill? Like windowsill?"

"No, Sil like Silver."

His hand moves up to a silver strand that worked its way loose from the messy knot at the back of my head. He has long, strong fingers, smooth dark skin, and kempt nails. Not like my own rough, pale hands crisscrossed with scars from downed hawthorn branches and weasels that didn't want to be eaten.

"It's short for Quicksilver. It was meant as a joke. Irony."

"Well, *Quicksilver*, you can call me Ti."

"Tie? Like tie-dye?"

"No, like Tiberius."

"Pffft. No irony there."

"Nope. None at all," he says, his voice tight and fading. "Are we almost done?"

"Two down. Only four more to go."

"You know, if it's all the same t'you," he slurs, "I was thinking I mi' pass out."

And just like that, he does.

Fever, blood loss, shock, and cold all conspire to keep him passed out through the last stitch and the bandaging. I tape the edges of the dressing. This is going to leave a big scar. Another big scar.

When I smooth out the tape, my fingers stray beyond the edge of the tape. I pull back quickly at the warmth of his skin against mine. Sitting with my arms wrapped around my legs, I prop my cheek on my knees and watch the slow up and down of his chest.

When we first became *schildere*, I'd asked Ronan if I could touch him when he was in skin, because lots of *schildere* already had and I'd been prey to so many longings. Not for Ronan, but longings nonetheless.

"Remember what Leonora said when we asked her if humans had *schildere*?" he asked when he'd finished laughing.

I did remember. Still do. Leonora had thought for a moment and then told us that the closest thing humans had to *schildere* is buddies. "Buddies," she said, "will hold the bathroom door closed for you if the lock is broken."

That's what we are, Ronan had said, still chortling. *Buddies.*

I didn't like the word. Sounded silly and childish. I like the Old Tongue better. *Schildere*, a shielder.

But supposing the Shifter feels that the only thing a crippled runt is good for is holding the bathroom door closed when the lock is broken? Then what? I will have passed up my chance to touch him.

So, I do. I touch the scarred ring at the base of his neck. Those lines are thick and rough. No one cared for them, and they healed badly.

I touch the sweep of high cheekbones and soft, dark cheek that blends into what was probably once a neatly cropped beard and mustache but is now a little wild. I touch his full lips, leaning down until I catch his warm breath against my own mouth.

This man's body is tough and sinewy, packed hard into his taut skin. My fingers tease across, down to the contours of his chest, crisscrossed with veins that give way under the gentle pressure of my fingers and muscles that don't.

I stop at his waistband. We are always told not to smell or touch humans here, because that is considered bestial. I touch him, feeling him warm and solid and thickening through his jeans, because what am I if not a beast?

I hold tighter until a growl, like a dreaming wolf, rattles in his chest.

Covering him with the open sleeping bag, I go about shaking the pup fur out of the tent. With a good-size stone, I pound in the stakes, set up the tent, then stretch the bed pad across the top so that it can air out.

Between all the fur and the partly gnawed cheese chew, it smells like childhood.

CHAPTER 4

IT'S DARK WHEN TIBERIUS WAKES UP. I HAND HIM A BOTTLE OF icy spring water laced with more electrolytes and poke the embers of the fire I built close by. I add cornmeal and dried cranberries and ghee and maple sugar to the water in the pot hanging from the green aspen branch I angled into the ground.

He holds the sleeping bag tightly around himself and shivers.

"I brought you some clothes." I toss him the four enormous things that were taking up so much space in my backpack.

He pulls on the flannel shirt and the hoodie, then puts his hand to his blood-crusted jeans and looks at me.

I cock my head.

"Well?" he says.

"Well, what?"

"A little privacy?"

"For what?"

"I was in kind of a hurry when I left."

"Yes?"

"I'm not wearing underwear."

"Yes?"

"I will be naked."

"So? We are all naked when we change."

He stares at the sweatpants in his hands, pulling at the loose ends of the waistband ties.

"Phase? Turn? Shift?" I continue. "What do you call it?"

"*We* call it going to the dogs. It's something we avoid at all costs."

"*What?*"

"*We* are not like you. We don't run around sniffing each other's asses and pissing on trees. We drive and talk and shoot and make money. *We* are human. *I*," he repeats firmly, "*am human.*"

Dumbstruck, I turn away, giving him his stupid human privacy. "But...but...you *can* change, right?"

"Hmm? Can I? Yeah. Probably."

Probably? It never occurred to me that someone who could change wouldn't. Every minute I'm in skin, I can't wait to get out of it. When we are in skin, we are *anfeald*. Single fold: one and singular. Alone. But when we are wild, we exist beyond the limitations of our poor bodies and weak senses. We are ourselves, but we are also part of the land and the Pack. We are *manigfeald*, manifold and complex.

"You really have no idea what you got yourself into, do you?" I say to the fire, listening while his jeans come off in a cloud of dried blood. I can hear him hop from foot to foot.

"My mother died when I was born." He regains his balance quickly, and cotton swishes over skin. "But she'd tried to convince my father to join the Pack. She'd told him that all you needed was to mate a lone wolf and—"

"*Ohmigod.* You have no idea. None. I hardly know where to start."

I really *don't* know where to start. So I start at the beginning with our first Alpha. She knew that the natural Packish resistance to outsiders would eventually breed weakness. Strength, she said, could only come from fresh bloodlines, which meant taking new wolves from disintegrated packs. Some other Packs do now, but we were the first. And we are still the strongest.

We don't make it easy. A lone wolf can easily disrupt our carefully constructed order, so one of our wolves has to be willing to tie their fate to that of the stranger. To be the stranger's *schildere* during the three months when they are considered table guests. Three Iron Moons. That's how long they—*we*—have to prove ourselves worthy of the Pack.

"What's *schildere*?"

"It's… You don't speak the Old Tongue?"

"Unless by Old Tongue you mean French, no."

"It means…" I start, but I can't spit out the word *buddy*. "'Shielder,'" I say. "It means 'shielder.' But here's the thing… The Pack isn't going to bother even taking you as a table guest unless they're sure you can fight. They won't waste time on the weak or cowardly. And our fights are always wild. Fang and claw. Never in skin. Here."

Ti stabs his spoon into his bowl. "What is this?"

"Cornmeal."

He pokes his spoon into the cornmeal. "Any meat?"

"Are you listening? If we lose that fight, we're out, immediately. No three months, no nothing."

"I am listening. It's just that I figure if I have to dress up like a wolf, I should get some meat."

"Fine. Tomorrow. I'll get you some tomorrow. For now, there's cornmeal."

"Why did you agree to do it, then?" he says after he's taken a few bites. "If you have so much to lose?"

"Because I was going to be a *nidling*. Lone wolves are given to the Alphas as servants. Keeps us busy and out of trouble, but it's as close to being nothing as you can be without actually being dead. There aren't many. Mala was one. That's why she ran away. Do you want this?" I offer my untouched bowl. "I'm not really hungry."

He scrapes the bottom of his own bowl before taking mine.

"I guess I figured that one chance at living was better than a lifetime of being alive."

I think I am going to be sick.

Late into the night, the Shifter struggles with a tent and a sleeping bag that aren't really meant for his big body. His bangs and curses are accompanied by the slithery scraping of nylon against nylon that sets my teeth on edge. No good wolf likes to sleep in a clearing anyway, so I limp off to the edge of the woods and find a nice spot behind the bleached-out cedar stumps. I turn round and round among the dry, fragrant pine needles. Curling my muzzle on my front paws, I fluff my tail across my nose and close my eyes.

Doesn't matter that it's still black as night. It's not the light that tells me to wake up. Honestly, I don't know what does. A bird, maybe. When the temperature reaches dew point. Pull of the moon, whatever. I wake up when I'm supposed to give the Shifter his medication.

I feel the *sproing* in my neck, the pleasant pressure as my shoulders widen, the pain in my hips, and the ticklish rearranging of pastern and forepaw. I need fingers, because the clindamycin comes in a wolf-proof bottle that's in the backpack on John's rock. The same backpack that is currently being rifled through by the biggest mutant coyote I've ever seen.

ACKNOWLEDGMENTS

I hope you had as much fun reading Caleb and Brielle's story as we had writing it! The moment they met in *Undercover Wolf* (STAT #2) we knew they were perfect for each other. If you're a fan of our SWAT: Special Wolf Alpha Team series, then you'll remember Caleb first made an appearance as a background character in the book *In the Company of Wolves* (SWAT #3). But he was so dynamic that we knew he needed to be the hero of his own story. In fact, we'd go so far as to say that Caleb is the inspiration behind the whole STAT series!

This whole series wouldn't be possible without some very incredible people. In addition to another big thank-you to my hubby for all his help with the action scenes and military and tactical jargon, thanks to everyone at Sourcebooks (who are always a phone call, text, or email away whenever we need something). A big shout-out to their crazy-talented art department. The covers they make for us are seriously drool-worthy!

Because I could never leave out my readers, a huge thank-you to everyone who reads my books and Snoopy Dances right along with me with every new release. That includes the fantastic people on my amazing Review Team, as well as my assistant, Janet. You rock!

And a very special shout-out to our favorite restaurant, P. F. Chang's, where hubby and I bat story lines back and forth and come up with all of our best ideas, as well as a thank-you to our fantastic waiter-turned-manager, Andrew, who makes sure our order is ready the moment we walk in the door!

Be sure to look for the next book in the SWAT: Special Wolf Alpha Team series coming soon from Sourcebooks. Hope you look forward to reading the rest of the series as much as we look forward to sharing it with you.

If you love a man in uniform as much as I do, make sure you check out X-Ops, our other action-packed paranormal/romantic-suspense series from Sourcebooks.

Happy reading!

ABOUT THE AUTHOR

Paige Tyler is a *New York Times* and *USA Today* bestselling author of action-packed romantic suspense, romantic thrillers, and paranormal romance. Paige writes books about hunky alpha males and the kick-butt heroines they fall in love with. She lives with her very own military hero (also known as her husband) and their adorable dog on the beautiful Florida coast. Visit her at paigetylertheauthor.com.

Also by Paige Tyler

STAT: Special Threat Assessment Team
Wolf Under Fire
Undercover Wolf

SWAT: Special Wolf Alpha Team
Hungry Like the Wolf
Wolf Trouble
In the Company of Wolves
To Love a Wolf
Wolf Unleashed
Wolf Hunt
Wolf Hunger
Wolf Rising
Wolf Instinct
Wolf Rebel
Wolf Untamed
Rogue Wolf

X-Ops
Her Perfect Mate
Her Lone Wolf
Her Secret Agent (novella)
Her Wild Hero
Her Fierce Warrior
Her Rogue Alpha
Her True Match
Her Dark Half
X-Ops Exposed